PRAISE FOR PAT MURPHY'S PREVIOUS WORKS

The City, Not Long After

"An indisputable heir to a long and honorable tradition in Northern California literature. Ambrose Bierce, Jack London, Richard Henry Dana, John Steinbeck, Henry Miller, Jack Kerouac, to mention but a few, lived and worked here . . . strongly inspired by a sense of the place, produced a notable body of work celebrating its special beauty and its Bohemian way of thought and life. . . . Pat Murphy's fog-blessed city occupies the same territory in the geography of the imagination."—*Locus*

"An engaging tale . . . subtle and interesting."
—*Los Angeles Times*

The Falling Woman

"Murphy's sharp behavioral observation, her rich Mayan background, and the revolving door of fantasy and reality honorably recall the novels of Margaret Atwood."—*Publishers Weekly*

"A literate and absorbing tale."
—*Chicago Sun-Times*

Ask your bookseller for the Bantam Spectra Special Editions that you have missed:

POINTS OF DEPARTURE

Pat Murphy

SPECTRA

BANTAM BOOKS
NEW YORK · TORONTO · LONDON · SYDNEY · AUCKLAND

For Dad, with love,
and
as always,
For Richard.

✒

POINTS OF DEPARTURE

A Bantam Spectra Book / July 1990

ISBN 0-553-28615-3

Published simultaneously in the United States and Canada

Bantam Books are published by Bantam Books, a division of
Bantam Doubleday Dell Publishing Group, Inc. Its trademark,
consisting of the words "Bantam Books" and the portrayal of a
rooster, is Registered in U.S. Patent and Trademark Office and
in other countries. Marca Registrada. Bantam Books, 666 Fifth
Avenue, New York, New York 10103.

PRINTED IN THE UNITED STATES OF AMERICA

RAD   0 9 8 7 6 5 4 3 2 1

"Dead Men on TV," published in *Full Spectrum*, edited by Lou Aronica and Shawna McCarthy, New York, Bantam Books, 1988.

"Don't Look Back," published in *Fantasy Annual IV*, edited by Terry Carr, New York, Pocketbooks, 1981 and *Other Worlds 2*, edited by Roy Torgeson, New York, Zebra Books, 1979.

"Orange Blossom Time," published in *Chrysalis 9*, edited by Roy Torgeson, New York, Zebra Books, 1981.

"In the Islands," published in *Amazing SF*, March 1983.

"Touch of the Bear," published in *Isaac Asimov's Science Fiction Magazine*, October 1980.

"On a Hot Summer Night in a Place Far Away," published in *Isaac Asimov's Science Fiction Magazine*, May 1985.

"Sweetly the Waves Call to Me," published in *Elsewhere*, edited by Jonathan Strong, New York, Ace Books, 1981.

"His Vegetable Wife," published in *Interzone*, Summer 1986.

"Good-Bye, Cynthia," published in *Isaac Asimov's Science Fiction Magazine*, April 1988.

"Prescience," published in *Isaac Asimov's Science Fiction Magazine*, January 1989.

"Clay Devils," published in *Twilight Zone Magazine*, April 1987.

"A Falling Star Is a Rock from Outer Space," published in *Isaac Asimov's Science Fiction Magazine*, March 1986.

"With Four Lean Hounds," published in *Sword and Sorceress*, edited by Marion Zimmer Bradley, New York, DAW Books, 1984.

"On the Dark Side of the Station Where the Train Never Stops," published in *Elsewhere III*, edited by Terri Windling and Mack Arnold, New York, Ace Books, 1984.

"In the Abode of the Snows," published in *Isaac Asimov's Science Fiction Magazine*, Mid-December 1986.

"Rachel in Love," published in *Isaac Asimov's Science Fiction Magazine*, April 1987.

"Recycling Strategies for the Inner City" appeared in substantially different form (as "Scavengers") in *Omni*, April 1989.

"Bones," published in *Isaac Asimov's Science Fiction Magazine*, May 1990.

ACKNOWLEDGMENTS

Over the years, many people have read and critiqued my work. In particular, I would like to acknowledge the patience and assistance of Richard Kadrey, Michael Blumein, Ruth Brown, Lisa Goldstein, Richard Kearns, Mark Laidlaw, Avon Swofford, Mikey Roessner-Herman, Richard Russo, Mark Van Name, Cherie Wilkerson, and Pam Winfrey. I would also like to thank the participants in the Sycamore Hill Workshops in 1987, 1988, and 1989, the participants in the two Silver Lake Workshops, and the students and teachers at the 1976 Clarion Workshop for their comments on stories included in this collection. Finally, I would like to thank Kate Wilhelm, both for her teaching at Clarion and for the introduction to this collection.

Contents:

Introduction

BY KATE WILHELM

Students often ask, how can I develop a good style, and the answer is simple: Honor thy mother and father, eat your carrots, don't step on the cracks in the sidewalk, and as surely as your hair grows and your fingernails lengthen, your style will develop. The companion question is: What should I write about? And another simple answer comes to mind: Don't fret; your themes will find you.

If the novel is a doorway opening to another universe, then the short story is a window through which we can glimpse a contained piece of another world. In her novel *The Falling Woman* Pat Murphy opened wide the door into modern Mexico, as well as ancient Mayan times, and invited us in to walk and talk with compelling characters. In the stories in this collection we get glimpses of other strange and wondrous places and people. But a window works both ways: Not only can we see through to the other side, but from there we can look back and perceive the emerging writer. And this writer has eaten her carrots and done honor to her parents. Her style is emerging strongly, lucid, often lyrical, and uniquely hers. Her themes and concerns have discovered her and are demanding a voice.

From the earliest story in this collection, one recurring theme is undeniable: the meaning of personal power and talent. In "Touch of the Bear" power is denied, then accepted. It is shown to have a Shadow side that is both exhilarating and threatening. To carry the Jungian examination just one step further, we can see the strong line of continuity from past to present most clearly in this early story: The power is derived from sources so ancient they are the very basis for the collective unconscious, pure archetypes. The idea of the past as a dynamic force in the present surfaces again and again. This early story states the theme of creative power blatantly; the subtlety of the later stories is not yet developed, but the meaning is clear from the start. Again and again Pat comes back to the quandary that the possession of talent, of power, presents.

In "Don't Look Back" the question arises: Isn't talent enough to free one from a deterministic universe? In "Clay Devils" the creative power is recognized and dealt with in quite a different manner as a simple peasant artist comes to understand the high price creativity may exact. "Prescience" is a lovely story with a marvelous sustained tone that is a pleasure to read, and it deals with the question: If you knew what the future holds, couldn't you arrange your life better? This is a late story, with a subtle treatment of the same theme, with yet another approach and without despair. In it Katherine of the story is accepting of her strange talent; she uses it honestly and openly and takes whatever consequences that follow with good humor. Not so in "Bones" where the power is manifest in a giant among humans, but a giant who must suffer torment because he cannot find the outlet his gift demands. To have such power denied through any means can be dangerous; instead of liberation there may be destruction of the self.

Another of Pat Murphy's recurrent themes is the encounter with the stranger, the other who does not fit in, who is alien either literally or metaphorically. The stories in this group mature from the earliest, a simple wish fulfillment, through the alien as phantom lover, to a more complex treatment as in "In the Islands," where the alien is web fingered and ocean-bound, and the human is very human indeed. Nick in this story, and Michael in "Orange Blossom Time" react to the other with suspicion, awe, envy, resentment, all the human emotions that such an encounter must excite.

In "A Falling Star Is a Rock from Outer Space," a middle-aged, lonesome woman encounters an alien in a story that could have turned into just another horror story. Pat chose compassion instead of special effects to make the story rise above such easy categorization. And compassion is the key word for the very fine story "On a Hot Summer Night," in which a lusting Mexican hammock vendor meets a strange woman who cannot get warm. The usual xenophobic treatment of the alien, the other, is missing in both of these stories; instead, compassion and acceptance bring about peace, the filling of a void, or even redemption.

The final story in this series is the highly acclaimed, award-winning "Rachel in Love," which needs no further introduction here, of course.

One of the thematic threads interwoven throughout Pat's novel *The Falling Woman* was the relationships within the triangle of mother/father/daughter. The complexity of parent/child relationships, of male/female relationships surfaces again and again in her work, not stridently as in the most radical feminist mode, but thoughtfully and even painfully. The man searching for his father and the Yeti, the girl whose sister ran way to space to escape domestic battling, the woman whose clever fingers created devils that turned her husband into a devil, these are all very human problems, not necessarily feminist concerns, except that feminism embraces all humanity, all its relationships. What makes a man sacrifice his daughter to achieve a material success? Her revenge is to keep him imprisoned in the box, one of the "Dead Men on TV." What makes a man eschew a real woman for a vegetable wife? Her revenge is to teach him that even turnips have teeth. Explanations are not necessary; it is enough to have seen this situation unravel, or that one. We are given the vision; we can ponder the reasons.

And the "Women in the Trees," a frightening, haunting story, doesn't try to answer the questions either, but only poses them. The live oaks were old when the landlord's grandmother was young. They have always been there, have always held a community of women who escaped, have always sheltered them; the continuity is intact. This collection is like a house of many windows, and this is one of the encapsulated worlds visible from within, ugly, forbidding, mysterious, real. Our world, after all.

These stories span a ten-year period, hardly a beginning to what will surely be a long career. Pat is flexing her muscles; her grasp is growing ever surer, her reach more ambitious, her vision sharper. She is still staking out a territory, and she has found a voice. Read and enjoy these stories, and anticipate, as I do, the new vistas to be revealed as she opens more windows, opens the door wide, and invites us in.

October 1989

Dead Men on TV

I stay up late each night, watching my dead father on TV. Tonight, he's in *Angels of the Deep,* a World War II movie about the crew of a submarine. My father plays Vinny, a tough New York kid with a chip on his shoulder. He was about twenty when the movie was made; he's darkly handsome, and an air of danger and desperation surrounds him.

I've seen the movie half-a-dozen times before, but I turn on the TV and curl up in my favorite easy chair with a glass of bourbon and a cigarette. The cream-colored velvet that covers the easy chair's broad arm is marked with cigarette burns and dark rings from other glasses of bourbon on other late nights. The maid told me that the stains won't come out, and I told her that I don't care. I don't mind the stains. The rings and burns give me a record of many late nights by the TV. They give me a feeling of continuity, a sense of history: I belong here. The television light flickers in the darkened room, warming me like a fire. My father's voice speaks to me from the set.

"Can't you feel it?" my father says to another sailor. His voice is hoarse; his shoulders are hunched forward, as if he were trying to make himself smaller. "It's all around us—dark water pushing down. Trying to get in." He shivers, wrapping his arms around his body, and for a moment his eyes meet mine. He speaks to me. "I've got to get out, Laura. I've got to."

On the TV screen, a man named Al shakes Vinny, telling him to snap out of it. Al dies later in the movie, but I know that the man who played Al is still alive. I saw his picture in the newspaper the other day: he was playing in

1

a celebrity golf tournament. In the movie, he dies and my father lives. But out here, my father is dead and Al is alive. It seems strange to be watching Al shaking my dead father, knowing that Al is alive and my father is dead.

"I've got to get out," my father moans.

He can't get out. For the next hour and a half, he'll be stuck in the submarine with the water pressing in. I watch without sympathy as my father cowers in his bunk.

Late at night, I watch the movies, knowing that most of the men and women who move across the TV screen are dead. In my living room, they tell jokes and laugh, dance to big-band tunes played by dead musicians, lie and cheat and betray one another, argue and make love. And despite all that, they are dead. It seems strange to watch dead people on TV. Are they all being punished? What did the others do, who did they hurt, who must forgive them?

I never believed in heaven or hell or life after death until the day after my father's funeral. I was sitting alone in my father's house, and I turned on the television. My father's face stared out at me. He was surrounded by stone walls and darkness. It took me a moment to recognize the scene from *The Pharaoh's Tomb*. My father plays an archaeologist who is trapped in the tomb by a gang of criminals who want to steal the ancient artifacts.

"We're trapped in here," said a woman's voice. She was on the edge of hysteria.

"There's got to be an escape route," he said. "We'll find it. There's got to be a way out."

My father was right there on my TV screen, even though I knew he was dead. He spoke to me from the TV screen.

I figure it this way. The movie camera steals a person's soul. Just a little bit of the soul with each picture it takes. But if a person is in a great many movies—well, then, his whole soul is sucked up into the camera and caught in the movies.

The way I figure it, I have my father's soul in a box.

The Grocery-on-Wheels truck delivers my supplies: *TV Guide*, bourbon, eggs for breakfast, cold cuts for lunch, steak to grill for dinner, a few canned soups, fresh vegetables for variety. I cook for myself these days. I don't eat much. The last cook disapproved of my drinking and pestered me to eat more, go out more. So I fired her and now I cook for myself, eating only when my body demands fuel.

As a child, I was overweight: a round-faced little girl who, in all the photos, wears a sullen expression. Now I am thin. My wristbones are enormous. I can count my ribs. My face is angular, and I can see the bones beneath the skin. I order my clothes from mail-order catalogs, and they are always too large for me, but I don't mind. I wear them anyway, belting the pants tightly to keep them from falling.

After I put away the groceries, I don my bikini and lie by the pool, leafing through the *TV Guide*. My father left me this ranch house and the trust fund that supports me. The gardener tends the yard and the pool. The maid cleans the house. I keep my father's soul alive by watching his old movies. He's all I have left.

I was five years old when my mother died. I remember she had soft hands and dark curly hair. I have pictures of her: a soft-bodied woman tending to fat, with a round face and dark eyes.

She came to California from Georgia, a soft-spoken country girl with a slight southern drawl. She was working as a secretary at MGM, and she met my father there. At the time, my father was still taking bit parts in cut-rate monster movies and westerns.

The year I was born, my father landed his first big role—Vinny in *Angels of the Deep*. That movie was a hit, and he went on from there with a few more war movies. Then he played a hard-boiled detective in a series of movies and made a name for himself.

My mother started drinking heavily. Every afternoon she would sit by the pool, a glass of bourbon by her side. Some nights, my father wouldn't come home. The next day, my mother would start drinking early in the morning, lying in a lounge chair in her black one-piece swimsuit, dark circles beneath her dark eyes. I remember sticky kisses that stank of bourbon. I remember her telling me, "Your father's a no-good louse."

Bourbon and sleeping pills killed her. The coroner called it accidental death: She left no suicide note. But I know better: She killed herself; my father drove her to it. After that, my father was home even less. And when he was home, he seemed to look through me, as if I weren't real. I hated that.

I don't hate my father for the things he did to me. He didn't do anything much to me. I hate him for the things he didn't do. He didn't love me, he didn't want me, he didn't care about me—and that's what I can't forgive.

He sent me to private boarding schools, where I waited desperately for summer break. Then, during summer break, he sent me to camp. I lived in dormitories and cabins, cared for by teachers and counselors and housemothers. And I saw more of my father on the movie screen than I ever did in life.

He married again—three more times. Each marriage ended in divorce. But he had no more children. One was enough. One was too much. I don't think he ever wanted a daughter.

It's one in the morning, and I'm watching a videotape of *The Darkness Underground*. My father plays an impoverished coal miner, working the mine in a company town.

The living room is illuminated by the light from the TV screen. I love the light the TV casts—it makes everything seem unreal, fantastic, as if the living room had no substance. The couch and end table are dim outlines, barely visible. In this light, I'm not real. Only the world on the TV set is real.

The videotape is old: colored snow flickers on the screen. I watch the videotapes only when I have no choice; I'd much rather watch a broadcast and know that many people are watching my father. But the tapes have some advantages.

"I hate this life," my father says. He slams his fist down on the rough wooden table. "I hate it. I know why the fox gnaws off its leg to escape a trap."

"Don't," says the woman who plays his wife. I think her name is Mary. She dries her hands on her apron and hurries to his side.

I stop the tape, run it back, then play it again. "I hate this life," he says. Then he catches sight of me and stares at me from the television. "Laura, listen to me. Please." His face fills the screen. His skin is mottled with red and yellow snow that dances across his cheeks like flames. He slams his fist into the table. This time, I stop the tape before the woman can rush to comfort him.

I play the scene over and over, watching him strike the table and cry out in anger and frustration, unable to escape. "I can't stand this life," he says. "Laura . . ." His eyes watch me from the screen.

At last I let the movie run to the end. My father leads the miners in a strike. They triumph against the company, but my father dies. It's a good movie, especially the cave-in that kills my father. I play that over a few times.

At my mother's funeral, I walked beside my father, holding his hand. I've seen pictures of us standing at the grave. My father looks handsome in a black suit; I'm wearing a black dress, black gloves, and a broad-brimmed black hat. The only spot of white is my face: round, pale, and mournful, with black smudges for eyes. I remember that the dew from the grass in the graveyard beaded up on my new patent leather shoes. The droplets caught the sun and sparkled like diamonds. Newspaper reporters took pictures of us, but I would not look at the photographers; I was watching my shoes. When we left the photographers behind, my father stopped holding my hand.

We rode back home in a big black car that stank of dying flowers. I sat on one side of the big backseat, and he sat on the other. His eyes were rimmed with red and his breath smelled of whiskey.

I can't watch my mother on TV; she was never in the movies. I wonder what happened to her soul when she died. Is there a heaven for people who were never in the movies?

* * *

On Sunday afternoon, the two o'clock movie is *Summer Heat*. I've seen it before: my father plays a prisoner in San Quentin who was framed for a crime he did not commit.

At about one-thirty, I pull the drapes so that the room is dark and I switch on the TV. Instead of a picture, I get jagged lines, like lightning across the screen. I thump the side of the TV and the lightning jerks, but the picture does not return. The sound is a hash of white noise.

It's the maid's day off. I'm alone in the house and panic sets in quickly. I have to see the movie. I always watch my father's movies. I smack the set again and again, bruising my hand. I switch desperately from channel to channel. Nothing.

I look under "Television Repair" in the telephone book. In shop after shop, the phone rings unanswered. Sunday afternoon and no one is at work.

Finally, at a place called Pete's Repair-It, a man answers the phone. "Pete's Repair-It. Pete speaking."

"Thank God you're there," I say quickly. "My television's broken and I have to have it fixed."

"Sure," says the man. "Drop it by on Monday and I'll have a look."

"You don't understand," I say shakily. "It has to be fixed this afternoon. My father will be on at two and"—I glance at the clock—"it's quarter to two now. I'll pay extra."

"Sorry, ma'am," he says politely. "The shop's closed today. I just stopped by to—"

Then I break down. "You have to help me," I plead. "You just have to. My father's going to be on TV at two and I have to see him." I start crying and I can barely speak.

"Hang on," he mutters. "Just calm down. What's the matter with the set?"

Between sniffles, I describe the TV's behavior. He gets my address and promises that he will come right away. I pace, watching the clock. At five to two, I hear a van in the driveway. I meet the man halfway down the walk. He's a broadly built man, middle-aged, with glasses and curly brown hair. Over the pocket of his red shirt, his name is embroidered: PETE. He carries a toolbox.

"Please hurry," I beg him.

I watch him work: removing the back of the TV and

inspecting the tangle of wires inside. "Would you like something to drink?" I ask awkwardly.

"Sure. Have you got a beer?"

I shake my head. "How about bourbon and lemonade? That's what I'm drinking."

"All right," he says. "I'll try it."

He is whistling softly as I come out of the kitchen. "You could probably just get yourself a new TV for the price of this house call," he says.

I nod. "Maybe I'd better get another. So I'll have one as a spare."

He chats as he works, talking about what's wrong with the set, about how much a new set might cost me, but I pay little attention. I am watching the clock, waiting for the moment I can watch the movie. Finally, at two-thirty, he plugs in the set and the picture snaps into focus. "Thank you," I say. "Oh, thank you."

I curl up happily on the couch. On the TV screen, my father paces to and fro in his little cell. "I don't belong here," he says.

His cellmate, a wiry man with a thin face and cold eyes, lies back on his bunk and laughs. "You and every other con in the joint."

"You don't understand." The screen shows a close-up of my father's face, his tortured eyes, his square chin rough with stubble. "I'm innocent."

"This is a great movie," I say to Pete.

"You've seen this before?" He picks up his drink and sits beside me on the couch.

"Of course," I say. "Five times before."

"Sure, you're innocent," my father's cellmate is saying. "You and everyone else. We're all innocent." The wiry man takes a drag on his cigarette then blows the smoke at the ceiling. "But we're all stuck here together."

"If you've seen it before, then what was the big hurry to get the set fixed?" Pete growls. He is staring at me with puzzlement and frank curiosity. "You got me out here on a Sunday with a sob story about your father being on TV, and—"

"That's my father," I say quickly, pointing to the TV, where my father is lighting a cigarette.

"He's your dad?" Pete stares at the set. "I grew up watching his movies."

"So did I," I say. "I watch all his movies. All of them."

For a moment, Pete glances from the screen to my face and back again. "Yeah, I can see it," he says. "You look like his daughter."

I'm startled. "You think so?"

"Of course," he says. "Especially the eyes. You got the same eyes. I should have recognized you."

I notice that his glass is empty and I offer him another bourbon and lemonade. He accepts. I feel strangely comfortable watching the movie with him.

"He died about a year ago," I say. "But I watch all his movies. That keeps him with me."

"What a great guy he must have been." Pete hesitates a moment, then says soberly, "You must miss him a lot." He puts one arm around my shoulders as if to comfort me. I lean against his shoulder.

"Not really," I say. "These days, I've got him right where I want him. He can't get away."

Pete frowns. "What do you mean?"

"He's right here," I say. "I watch him every night." I laugh and Pete smiles uncertainly. But he stays for another drink. And another. We both get a little drunk.

I seduce the TV repairman by the light of the television, that flickering uncertain light where nothing is quite real. My father watches from the screen.

The late movie is a musical. My father plays a gambler who falls in love with a society lady. Dead men and women sing songs about love, and Pete's snores blend with the music, a rumbling bass voice. A vigorous chorus startles Pete; he wakes and blinks at me myopically.

"You okay?" he mumbles. He scratches his head sleepily, waiting for my reply.

"I just can't sleep," I say. "It's okay."

He struggles to a sitting position on the couch. "It's my snoring," he mutters gloomily. "I'm keeping you awake."

"No," I say. "Not at all. I just don't sleep much."

He sighs and pushes a hand through his hair. Half the curls stand on end. The curly hair on his chest matches the hair on his head. "My ex-wife always complained that I snored like a freight train."

I study him with new interest. Knowing that he has an ex-wife who complained about his snoring somehow makes him more real. He is naked and that suits him better than the shirt embroidered with PETE'S REPAIR-IT.

On the TV, three dead women in tight, sequined dresses sing about summer nights, moonlight, and love.

"What happened to your ex-wife?" I ask.

"She found someone who didn't snore and moved to Phoenix, Arizona."

"Do you hate her?"

"Naw. I figure living in Phoenix is punishment enough." He shrugs. "She's got what she wanted, but she still isn't happy. Some people just don't know how to be happy." He yawns and lumbers to his feet. "Want some hot milk to make you sleep?" Without waiting for my answer, he heads for the kitchen; I trail behind him. I watch him pour milk into a saucepan and rummage in the cupboards, a naked hairy man taking charge of my kitchen. "You got any brown sugar? It's better with brown, but I guess white'll do." He heats the milk to near boiling, sweetens it with sugar, and sprinkles cinnamon on top. Then he fills two mugs and leads me back to the living room. "My mom used to make this when I couldn't sleep," he says, giving me a mug.

The milk is sweet and soothing. I have never tasted anything so good. On the television, my father is dancing with the leading lady. Her head is resting on his shoulder and they look very good together.

"I hate my father," I tell Pete.

"Yeah?" He stares at the couple on TV and shrugs. "Why bother? He's dead."

I shrug, watching my father's face on the TV.

"Come on," Pete says. "Lie down and sleep." I lie beside him on the couch and he wraps his arms around me.

I dream myself into my father's movie. My father's arm encircles my waist and we waltz together beneath crystal chandeliers.

The ballroom's French doors open onto a clear summer night, but the room is cold and damp. The air stinks of decay, a charnel-house stench of rotting flesh and dying flowers.

My father and I spin together, and I catch a glimpse of the band. The bandleader is freshly dead; his body is bloated, the skin puffy and discolored. The dead musicians are in various stages of decay: a trumpet player presses the trumpet's mouthpiece to bare teeth; his head is a skull, precariously balanced on the column of vertebrae that rises from the collar of his tuxedo. The bass player plucks the strings with skeletal hands.

"Relax," my father says to me. He has held up better than the band, but his corneas have turned milky white, and the hand that holds mine feels suspiciously soft, as if it has begun rotting from the inside. "Isn't this where you've always wanted to be?"

At small tables around the dance floor, well-dressed men and women talk and laugh, but the laughter sounds like chattering teeth and rattling bones. A blond woman has lost clumps of hair and her sequined evening dress hangs limply on her shoulders, no flesh to fill it out.

"You can stay here with me," my father says. His eyes are sunken; his smile is the expressionless grimace of a skull. "I was never a good father. I can make it up to you now."

I try to pull away, but he clings to me, clutching at me with soft decaying hands, staring with cloudy sightless eyes. I tear myself free and run from him, toward the open doors.

On the TV screen, a woman in an evening gown is running away across the dance floor. My father, handsome and whole, stares after her. A lock of dark hair has fallen into his eyes. He looks handsome and charming. The dance floor is filled with beautiful men and women.

I slip from Pete's arms and unplug the TV before I can change my mind. The old television is too heavy to lift, so I drag it across the living room. The wooden legs make a horrible scraping sound on the Italian tiles in the entry-way, and Pete wakes up.

"What are you doing?" he mumbles.

"Give me a hand," I say.

Half-asleep, he helps me push the set down the hall and out the back door into the yard. He stops in the doorway, watching sleepily as I drag the set down the concrete walk toward the pool. Near the pool, I tip it off the path. It lies on its back in the damp grass, the screen reflecting the patio lights and the moon.

The VCR is light by comparison. I heap the videotapes on top of the TV. Then I clear the upstairs closets of my father's clothing: white suits, tuxedos, a trench coat, a drawerful of blue jeans. A tweedy jacket carries his smell even now: a hint of tobacco, a whiff of aftershave, a touch of whiskey. I stand in the wet grass for a moment, holding the jacket and fingering the rough fabric. Then I drape it over my shoulders to keep off the wind. Pete watches, shaking his head.

In the garage, I find the can of gasoline that the gardener keeps there for the power mower. I am generous, dousing the clothes repeatedly.

A single match, and the heap of clothing erupts with flames. It is like the Fourth of July, like orgasm, like the moment when the monster dies, like the happy ending when the credits roll. Pete is pulling me away from the fire, shouting something. I struggle away from him for long enough to strip the jacket from my shoulders and hurl it into the flames.

I stand in the circle of Pete's arms, leaning against his shoulder. The air smells of gasoline, flames, and wet grass. I watch the flames and listen to the distant sound of sirens. It's good to be free.

Women in the Trees

"This is our new place," your husband says. "We'll be happy here."

A white farmhouse with peeling paint, far from the nearest neighbor. Behind it, golden hills roll away into the distance. Trees crowd closely around it, sprawling oaks that grow outward as much as they grow upward. Their leaves are small and brittle; their thick branches are gnarled and twisted with age.

Your husband takes your hand and you stand very still, like a deer frozen in the headlights of an oncoming car. He kisses your cheek and squeezes your hand gently. "We'll be happy," he says again, as if repeating the words will make them come true. You hope that he's right this time.

That afternoon, after the movers have come and gone, you are unpacking clothes in the bedroom. You are putting your husband's shirts in the drawers of the dresser. You place each shirt with its collar toward the back of the drawer, the buttons facing up. His shirts must be right or you don't know what will happen.

You look up from the drawer and for a moment you forget about your husband's shirts. The leaves of the oak tree that grows outside the window filter the sunlight; the bare mattress of the bed is dappled with bright spots that shift and move with the breezes. You look out the window into the leaves of the tree. In the shifting patterns of light and dark, you see faces. Women's faces, looking back at you. When the leaves flutter in the breeze, the women laugh to see you in the bedroom, worrying about your husband's shirts.

Your husband didn't mention the women in the trees

when he told you about the house, but then it makes sense that he would miss them. You are accustomed to watching for tiny signals that others might not see: the tightening of a muscle in your husband's jaw, a sudden straightening of his shoulders, an involuntary movement as his hand begins to clench to form a fist. When you can see the beginnings of a frown from across the room, spotting women who live in the trees is simplicity itself.

You hear your husband's footsteps and look away from the window. He stands in the doorway, with one hand hidden behind his back. "Daydreaming again?" he asks in a playful tone. "What were you watching out there?"

You lie automatically. "A blue jay in the tree," you say. "It flew away."

"I brought you something," he says. From behind his back he produces an enormous bouquet of scraggly wildflowers, an assortment of California poppies, yellow mustard flowers, and dandelions. As he holds them out, yellow petals fall to the carpet, each one as bright as the spots of sunlight on the bed.

When you take the bouquet, he puts his arms around you and kisses you on the neck. You are glad that this is a day for kisses. He sweeps you up in his arms: he is not such a big man, but you are a small woman, a frail woman, barely twenty years old and light enough for him to carry. He lays you on the bare mattress and kisses you again, so gently, so sweetly. You know just now that he loves you; you are sure of it.

Your body responds to him, responds to his hand on your thigh, to his lips on your breast. His hand strokes between your legs and you moan and press yourself to him. Your body is fickle; it forgets the other times so quickly. He pulls you to him, and you cry out with each thrust, the pleasure coming in waves. Then he relaxes on top of you, and it feels good to have him near.

You look up at his face. His expression is distant, as if he is remembering something. He is looking down at your arm. On the pale skin of the upper arm there are bruise marks, left by four fingers and a thumb. Gently he touches the injury, matching his thumb and fingers to the marks. A perfect fit.

You push the thought away and look into the trees to see the women laughing. If he were to ask what you were thinking, you would lie.

You have acquired the habit of lying, the habit of covering up. To do otherwise would be admitting to failure. You have failed as a wife; you have failed as a woman. Your man is not happy and his discontent is your fault. On some level, deep down where your mother's voice is stronger than your own, you know this.

Your husband beat you for the first time just a month after your wedding. He was angry because one of his shirts had lost a button in the laundry, and you had forgotten to sew another on in its place. He yanked the shirt from the drawer, threw it at your face, and then came at you with his fists, punching you in the ribs, in the breasts, in the belly.

After it was all over, you lay on the bedroom floor, gasping for breath. You heard him weeping in the living room and you went to him. His face was wet with tears. He begged for your forgiveness. He said that he would kill himself if you left him. It would never happen again, he said. Never. You rocked him in your arms and the two of you wept together. He loved you and you loved him. How could it happen again?

A week after the beating, you still felt a stabbing pain with each breath. Solicitous and concerned, your husband drove you to the doctor's office.

In the examination room, the doctor asked you what had happened. How had you hurt yourself so badly? You looked at the doctor, an older man with a stern face. "I fell," you said. "I was getting a bowl down from a high cupboard and the chair slipped. I fell."

He studied your bruises. The purple marks had turned to a sickly yellow-green. Both arms were mottled where fingers had grabbed you, where fists had struck you.

"I see," he said. In his report he wrote, "Accident." And then he told you that you had two broken ribs.

Yes, you thought, it was an accident. Surely your husband would never have broken your ribs intentionally. He loved you. He said that over and over. He brought you flowers and gifts. He promised you it would never happen again.

And then, after a while, he said, "If only you wouldn't do these things that upset me."

If only you wouldn't flirt with other men. So you stopped smiling when you walked down the street, because a smile could be flirting if your husband was watching. If only you wouldn't neglect his needs. So you told your sister not to call in the evening when your husband was home. If only you wouldn't talk back. So you stopped stating your opinion, and he called you stupid because you had nothing to say.

He doesn't hit you often. And when he does, he strikes where the bruises will not show. Oh, sometimes he slaps you, but more often he uses fists. He doesn't use his fists on your face, because that would leave marks that you could not easily hide. He punches you in the ribs, in the breasts, in the belly. If you try to block his punches, he strikes the arms. He knows that you will wear long sleeves rather than reveal your failure, your shame, the bruises that are marks of dishonor.

At night, that first night in the new house, you hear the oak trees scratching against the roof. The branches of the one nearest the house rattle against the windowpane, tapping like fingernails on the glass, trying to get your attention. "Over here. We're over here." It's a comforting sound.

In the morning, your husband says that the damn branches scraping against the window kept him up all night. You know that isn't true: he was snoring while you lay awake. But you say nothing. The women in the trees will understand. You can't speak out.

After your husband leaves for work, you go outside and wander among the trees. Though the morning is hot, the shade is cool. Insects trill in the grasses, a soothing sound. Squirrels scold you from the branches, then fall silent, recognizing that you belong here. When you squint up at a squirrel, you see a woman's face staring back at you. Her eyes are blue, like the gaps between the leaves where the sky shows through. The wind blows and the woman vanishes.

She is shy, easily frightened—you understand that. No doubt she has reasons for hiding. You catch a glimpse of another woman, or perhaps the same one. You move suddenly, and she disappears.

The women in the trees are like those puzzles in children's magazines: "Find all the things that are hidden in this picture." When you searched diligently, you discovered a cocker spaniel in the patterns of the wallpaper, a hammer and saw among the flowers in the flowerpot, a high-heeled shoe in the window curtains. You know you must observe carefully; if you are quiet and attentive, you will see things that other people miss.

Though you walk quietly, you don't see the women again. But on your way back to the house you find a bright blue feather, and you know that they have left it for you as a sign. They are watching. They will take care of you.

Just as you get back to the house, the landlord drives up in his pickup truck. He has come to see that everything is okay. You are wearing a sleeveless shirt. He notices the bruises on your arms and asks about them. You shake your head, looking away so that he can't see the lie in your eyes. "I'm so clumsy," you say. "Always banging into cupboard doors and counters." The cupboard doors are too high to bruise your arms and the counters are too low, but the landlord says nothing more. People believe what they want to believe; people see what they want to see.

You give him coffee to drink. Your husband would not like having this other man sit in his kitchen, even though the landlord is an older man, potbellied and unattractive. Your husband would not like it, but it seems harmless enough and you are lonely. You ask him about the oak trees. He tells you that they are California live oaks, tough trees that flourish under difficult conditions.

"How long have they been there, so close to the house?" you ask him.

"A long time," he says, "a very long time." They were old when his grandmother was growing up. His grandmother had lived in the house alone for many years, after his grandfather had died.

You nod. You like the thought of a woman living alone in this house, happy among the trees.

"I offered to cut back the oaks for her," the landlord says. "They need trimming, sure enough. But she didn't want me to. Had a thing about them, she did."

You smile, understanding his grandmother across the years. She knew about the women in the oaks. You think you would have liked his grandmother.

You have lived in the farmhouse for two weeks when your husband decides that you must celebrate the two-week anniversary of the move. He calls you from work and tells you not to make dinner. He brings home a pepperoni pizza, turns the lights low, and puts an old Elvis Presley album on the stereo. Together, you eat pizza from paper plates, and he talks and jokes. He tells you about his boss, imitating the way the man puffs out his cheeks when he talks and making you laugh.

When Elvis sings "Love Me Tender," your husband takes your hand and pulls you up off the couch. He holds you close. As you dance, he sings along with Elvis, his voice deep and loving. When the song ends, he kisses you.

In the sudden silence, you hear the wind rattling in the branches outside. You ignore the sound. Your bruises have faded and you are happy. You think right now that you will always be happy.

When you were a child, your family moved a lot. Your father worked as a mechanic in a garage, and he could get work anywhere. When he didn't like his boss or the house or a town, he moved. Sometimes you stayed in one place for six months; sometimes, for three; sometimes, only for two. You and your sister were jerked from school; you packed your things in the cardboard boxes that your mother never bothered to throw away, and you drove to a new town, a new house, a new school. You had no choice.

Sometimes, you would cry about leaving your friends. Once, you ran away and tried to stay at a friend's house, reasoning that your parents might leave without you, they just might. But they didn't. Your father found you, and you moved again.

After that, your parents never warned you before a

move. You would notice an odd tension around the house, a peculiar feeling of activity even when everything was still. Then one morning, you would wake up and your mother would be wrapping the dishes in newspaper and packing them away in boxes.

After a while, you stopped making friends. What was the use when you knew you would be moving in a month, in two months, in half a year? No use. No use at all.

You swore that when you were grown-up you would live in one house. You would stay there with your husband who would take good care of you. You would live in the house all your life and never move. That's why you like thinking about the landlord's grandmother—an old woman living in the house that was hers, making friends with the trees. You like that.

You have been in the house for a month when your husband brings home a hammock made of colored twine. "Perfect for this place," he says. "It will look great hanging between the trees."

He takes a beer from the refrigerator. He's been drinking more and more beer lately. He says that he needs it to relax after the long commute. He has been late to work a few times, and his boss is on his back. He doesn't like his job. You try to be sympathetic and understanding.

When he goes out to hang the hammock, you go with him. He wanders from tree to tree, looking for two that are the right distance apart. The hammock came with some rope, but not much. None of the trees seem to be positioned right. This pair is too widely separated; this one, too close together.

As he searches for the right tree, your husband is getting angry. He carries his beer in one hand and the hammock in the other. He does not like the oaks—you know that. They have deep roots. He does not like things that are stronger than he is.

"What about these two?" you say. "They look about right."

"Too far apart," he says impatiently.

You look up into the leaves where the women live. You

can't see them, but you know they are there. You can feel them all around you. They will help you if they can.

"I think it might fit here," you say. He glares at you and throws the hammock at you in exasperation. You catch it, smiling as if he were doing this in fun. You pretend. You lie—to yourself and to him and to the women in the oaks. You don't fool anyone, but you do it anyway. It's automatic now.

The distance between the trees is perfect. The rope just reaches. You think gratefully of the women in the oaks as you tie the rope around the tree, stringing the hammock a few feet off the ground. Your husband is watching, angry that you succeeded where he failed. You speak to him softly, trying to placate him. You tell him that this will be a wonderful place for him to rest on weekends; you tell him that this is a fine house, that you are so happy, that he is so wise. He turns away as you are tying the rope and goes to the kitchen for another beer.

You test the hammock, lying down under the trees. The sun is gone and the first stars are out. You don't want to go back to the house, but you know that the longer you put it off, the worse it will be.

The sun is setting. In the leaves above you, the women are dancing. You can only catch glimpses of them, but you make up the rest. They are beautiful—slim and young, about your age really. You hear them calling to you; they know your name. Perhaps they overheard it when your husband was yelling at you. Your name sounds different when they say it—softer, gentler, like wind caressing leaves, like summer rain on the grass.

Your husband calls to you from the porch. Reluctantly, you leave the hammock and go toward the house. "Where's dinner?" he grumbles, and you smile as if he is just joking. As you go toward him, you see that he is holding a beer in one hand and a saw in the other. He's on his third beer; you see two empty bottles on the counter.

"It'll be on the table in just a minute," and you hear echoes of your mother's voice saying "Yes, dear. Of course, dear," while your father shouts about something or other.

"I'm going to take care of that damn branch that's been keeping me awake," he says, stepping off the porch and

heading toward the oak nearest the house. You stand by
the porch and watch as he climbs the tree. The branch
that scrapes against the bedroom window grows off a
sprawling trunk that is as thick around as your waist. He
straddles the trunk and saws at the branch awkwardly. He
is clumsy with the saw, a little drunk, you think. The tree
in which he is sitting trembles each time he jerks the saw.
You can hear the leaves rattling, the oak women talking
excitedly among themselves.

"Be careful," you say. You are not sure what you are
warning him against: the sharp saw, the oak women, the
danger of falling. Or perhaps you are warning the women.
You are not sure, but you know there is danger somewhere nearby.

He drags the saw toward him and the branch creaks, a
high cry of alarm. It dips lower to rest against the ground.
Only a thin strip of bark and wood holds the branch to the
tree. He pushes the saw forward and the bark gives way
suddenly. The branch falls and the saw slips through the
gap, striking his leg. He cries out. The crash of the branch
hitting the ground is like a burst of sudden laughter.

You bandage his cut, a ragged gash. The blood and pain
have calmed him, and he submits to your attention willingly.
At times like this, he is a small boy, grateful to be taken
care of. You baby him and bring him his dinner, happy
that the earlier tension has somehow dissipated.

That night, when he is asleep, you slip out of the house
and lie in the hammock. From the woods, you can hear
the creaking of insects, the rustle of small animals in the
underbrush, the low hooting of an owl. When you were a
little girl, a teacher read the class a story about an
enchanted forest. Dryads lived in the trees, coming out to
dance and sing in the moonlight. One day, a little girl
went to the forest and met the dryads.

You don't know what happened next. Your family moved
the next day and you never heard the end of the story. In
your mind, the little girl is still living in the enchanted
woods, never leaving, growing up among the dryads and
learning their ways.

You lie in the hammock and wait to see if the women

will sing, but you do not hear them. After a time, the moon comes up, and you go back to bed.

You have a red notebook, like the one that you carried to classes during the one year that you went to community college. Sometimes you write in your notebook, trying to tell the truth. You write, "I love my husband." You consider the words, remembering your broken ribs. You cross the sentence out, then write again. "I hate my husband." You cross that out too. The truth is a slippery thing, as elusive as the women in the trees.

The summer goes along. You try to take care of your husband. Small things anger him: He sees a letter from your sister and he says that she never liked him. You smile at the checkout boy at the grocery store and your husband says you are a slut. You ask him to take you to town so you can go to the library, and he insinuates that you think you are better than he is, you think you are so smart. But these are all minor complaints. You soothe him, you comfort him, you make him dinner.

Your mother writes you letters, telling you the family's latest address and asking how you are doing. You write back cheerful notes that say nothing. You have nothing to say. The first time your husband hit you, right after you were married, you asked your mother if you could come home. She was packing the dishes for another move and she said that you must stay with your husband. Make your husband happy, she said. In your letters, you tell her that your husband is happy.

When your husband is at work, you walk in the woods. You feel strong when you are among the trees. On a warm day, you kick off your shoes and climb a tree. High in the foliage, you find a place where two branches come together to make a natural seat, as comfortable as a rocking chair. When you look down, all you can see are leaves. You are alone at the top of the tree, hidden from view.

For a while, you sit and listen to the jays squawk and the squirrels chatter. The leaves rustle, fluttering in the breeze. When you squint your eyes, the flickering light looks like sunlight on water.

You fall asleep and the oak women gather around you. In your dream, you smile at them. "This is a beautiful place," you say.

They murmur to you, their voices no louder than the whispering of the leaves. "Stay. Stay with us." They stretch their hands out to you.

You look around. "I can't live in a tree."

They mutter reassuringly. "You can do anything."

You shake your head, knowing they are wrong.

Their eyes are shaped like almonds; their hair is the color of new grass; their fingers are slender and graceful. The smallest one, a young girl with a sweet smile, whispers, "You are beautiful."

You look down at your hands. You have been biting your fingernails again. Your wrists are so thin you can see the bones. Your hair is thin and stringy. You are ugly.

"You are not seeing clearly," she whispers. "Truly, you are beautiful."

The rumble of an engine drowns out her voice. A car is coming up the driveway—your husband is home. Startled, you clamber out of the tree and hurry home to greet him.

You call to your husband as you walk in the door. "Dinner will be ready in just a minute." You can hear him in the bedroom, changing out of his work clothes. You hear his footsteps crossing the living room. From the sound, you try to judge how angry he is that you weren't home when he got there.

He stands in the kitchen doorway for a moment, watching you slice tomatoes for salad. He gets a beer from the refrigerator, throws the bottle cap in the general direction of the wastepaper basket. He misses. The cap rolls across the floor, but he doesn't pick it up. "This place is a sty," he says. "Sometimes I don't know why I even bother to come home." He turns away and you hear the television go on in the living room. By the time the lamb chops are done, he is drinking his third beer. He eats half the chop and leaves the rest. As you wash the dishes, you can hear gunfire from a cop show on the television.

That night, you wake from a bad dream. You dreamed of a time past that you would rather forget. Your husband had his hands on your throat and he was choking you, shaking you, cursing you for something you had done. What was it? Smiling at the postman, maybe, or folding one of his shirts incorrectly. It doesn't matter. All that mattered was the air and the pain. He released the pressure just before you fainted. You gasped, "I'm sorry. I'm sorry." You didn't even know what you were sorry for, but whatever it was it must have been bad, very bad to make him so angry. You had to wear a scarf around your throat for two weeks until the bruises went away.

You wake and your husband is asleep, lying on his back with his hands at his sides. A fold of blanket is pressing lightly against your neck and you push it away. You can't go back to sleep and you are afraid that you will wake your husband with your tossing and turning. As quietly as you can, you slip from the bed and go outside. In the moonlight, the trees are beautiful.

You are on the porch when you hear footsteps. The door creaks open. Your husband sits beside you on the steps and for a moment you let yourself think that everything will be all right. You listen to him breathing beside you.

"I couldn't sleep," you say. "I came outside so I wouldn't wake you up."

"You woke me up by getting up," he says. He isn't looking at you; he is gazing out toward the oaks.

"I'm sorry," you say automatically.

"If I'm late again, that bastard will have my ass," he says, and somehow it is your fault. You are responsible for the long commute, for the unreasonable boss, for your husband's state of mind. He will be late to work and you will be to blame.

"Let's go back to bed," you say. "You need your sleep." Moving carefully, you reach out and take his hand. You lead him back to bed.

He falls asleep quickly, but you lie awake beside him, listening to him breathe.

You do your best. You have dinner ready on time. You serve his favorite foods. You keep the house very clean. But even so, there are small signs—you watch for them and you notice them. He stops complaining about the traffic and his commute to the city, although you know neither one has improved. He stops complaining about the boss who is picking on him, always on his back. You watch and wait, knowing that something is coming.

You try to make sure that everything is perfect. Everything must be perfect. If it isn't perfect—but you don't want to think about that. This time, you will follow all the rules. You will put all the shirts in the drawer just so. You will not say anything that makes it sound as if you think you're smart. You will not smile at anyone. And you will watch him, noticing the slightest signal.

Even though you are very good, sometimes you slip away to your place in the trees when he is at work. Once, when he has had too much to drink and falls asleep, you risk sneaking out at night, finding your way in the darkness. You are lucky. You don't get caught.

He is silent much of the time. When he gets home at night, he watches cop shows on TV. He drinks steadily, watching you over the rim of the glass. Sometimes, you catch him watching you. Something is coming, but if you can keep everything perfect, it will not come.

Your husband is at work when the landlord and his wife stop by. The Lions Club is having a pancake breakfast at the local high school and they want to sell you tickets. They want you and your husband to come; they say you will have a good time; they say you should get out more. Your landlord's wife says you need some meat on your bones.

You buy two tickets. You know, even as you buy them, that your husband will not go. But you smile and buy them to be polite. And you think about what it would be like if he decided to go and be charming. He could be charming. He could be sweet. You picture yourself in a sundress. You have no bruises on your arms and your husband is smiling at you the way he used to before you married.

You tell the landlord and his wife that you can't talk long. You must get dinner started. Your husband will be home soon. But they keep talking until the shadows stretch across the valley. When they finally leave, you make a pot of stew, a big green salad. Your husband is late and you're glad. Dinner will be ready when he gets home. Everything will be perfect.

It's dark. You see his headlights first, sweeping across the trees and spotlighting the house. You stand on the porch, ready to greet him. "Dinner is ready," you call to him.

He has been drinking. You can smell whiskey and cigarette smoke on his clothes. He pushes past you into the kitchen and you follow him, still trying to smile. He glares around the kitchen. The stew bubbles on the stove and it smells good. Surely he will be happy now: good food, a nice clean home.

"What's wrong?" you ask. You know as soon as you speak you have said the wrong thing. There was no right thing to say.

"That son of a bitch I work for fired me," he says. "Are you happy now?"

You can think of nothing to say. Are you happy? No, you're not happy.

He sees the tickets to the pancake breakfast. Carelessly, you left them on the table. He snatches them up and reads what they have to say.

"You spent money on this shit?" he says. He throws them down on the floor. Before you can speak, he grabs your hair and tries to slap you—once, twice, three times. You block his hand once, twice, but the third blow knocks your arm aside. You try to pull away, but he strikes again with the back of his hand, rocking your head to one side.

"I'll teach you a lesson," he says, and you remember other lessons that your husband taught with his fists. You bring your arms up to protect your face and he swings his fist low and buries it in your stomach. Lesson one: whatever you do, it's wrong. You double over, wrapping yourself around the pain, and he slams a fist into your head. Lesson two: the same as lesson one.

You fall to the floor and try to crawl away. He grabs your ankle and you turn on him, slapping at his hand. He grabs your wrist. Desperately you bite him, tasting blood and sweat and cigarettes. You have never fought him so hard before. You have grown stronger during your time among the trees.

When you bite him, he lets you go, and in that instant you are running—out the door, off the porch, into the protective darkness beneath the trees. You know your way. You can hear him behind you, clumsy in his drunkenness, shouting that he will kill you, you bitch, you stupid bitch. He is cursing you, screaming that you are useless and stupid, a burden to him, a drag on his life.

The wind is up and the oaks are alive. You run among them, ducking beneath the low branches. The women are calling to you in high thin voices like leaves in the wind. Behind you, you hear your husband trying to follow. The branches slap at him, clawing at his eyes. The roots trip him. You can hear him grunt as he falls.

You are far ahead of him when you reach your secret place and you climb quickly, knowing your way by touch. The oak women help you, their cool hands clutching your wrists, soothing your pain, urging you on. You find your place and you sit there, very still.

You hear your husband searching for you. He shouts your name, curses you, slams his fist into trees as he passes. He tells you that you must come out.

You sit very still, listening to your own heart pounding. For a moment, you think, "I'd better go back. It will only be worse later." But you remain still. After a time, you think, "I didn't do anything wrong."

A flashlight beam darts across the tree trunks. You can see it flickering through the leaves, but he can't see you. You are as invisible as the oak women. You blend into the picture, becoming part of the branches, part of the leaves. No one can find you here. As he crashes through the underbrush, you fight the urge to laugh. He is not strong, with all his bashing and crashing. You lean back into the fork of the tree, listening to the oak women soothing you. "Hush," they say. "Quiet."

Finally, he goes back to the house. In the distance, you hear the sound of breaking glass. The kitchen window, you guess, but that doesn't matter now. He can break every window and burn all your things. You don't care.

Your body is stiff and you are starting to wonder what to do. "Leave it," the oak women say. "Come with us." The first light of dawn is rising. Birds are starting to sing.

"Come on," the youngest one says impatiently. She reaches out her hand, and you take it. She smiles and tugs on your hand. It happens so easily. You stand up and look back at the small body, curled up in the fork of the tree. So thin, so beautiful. You feel the wind in your hair.

Your husband will never find you here. You will watch him from the trees. Sometimes you will drop twigs on his head. Sometimes, remembering the good times, the times when he was sorry, the times when he danced with you and treated you well, you will miss him.

But you will not be sorry, not sorry ever again. Eventually, you will forget how to lie. And then you can come back down.

Don't Look Back

A small watercolor painting hung over the fireplace. When Liz had lived in the rambling old house, one of her sketches had hung in that spot. With her eyes squinted half-closed against the late afternoon sun, Liz could almost believe that the watercolor was one of hers.

She leaned her head against the arm of the couch, where the velvet had long since been worn smooth. Amanda's golden retriever, Bristol, bumped his head against her leg, trying to get her attention, and she scratched his ears idly.

She had visited the house a year before. At the time, she had been living with Mark in San Francisco. "You're trying to live in the past," Mark had claimed when she had left to visit the old house. "You'll just make yourself unhappy. You can't go back." Lying on the couch with the afternoon sunlight shining on her face, Liz knew that Mark had been wrong. She was happy in her past. She was worried about her future.

Mark still lived in San Francisco, but Liz had moved on. For the past year, she had lived in Los Angeles. Now she was taking a job in New York, moving far away and leaving her family and friends behind.

Bristol bumped his head against Liz's leg again, and she resumed scratching his ears. "What a pair," Amanda said as she stepped into the room. The older woman set a teapot and mugs on the coffee table and sat cross-legged on the floor beside the dog. Despite her gray hair, Amanda was as casual in manner as the art students who lived in her house. "You always were that dog's favorite."

Bristol lifted his head. With an apologetic air, he moved

away from Liz, stretched, and paced to the front door. Liz frowned and sat up on the couch. "I wonder what's up," she said.

"That must be Elsa," Amanda said as she poured the tea. "She lives in your old room now."

When Liz opened the door for the dog, he pushed past her. Liz stood in the doorway, watching the golden retriever frolic around and around a girl of about eighteen. The girl was laughing and whirling as if trying to keep her face to the dog. A bright flower was stuck in the braid of her long brown hair. Under her arm, she carried a sketch pad and several slim art books.

Liz watched, remembering when Bristol had greeted her after a long day, when she had carried a sketch pad under her arm and walked home from the bus stop with a flower in her hair.

"Elsa painted the watercolor over the fireplace," Amanda said from behind Liz. "She's quite good. She's working under Professor Whittier."

"Nothing but the best for him," Liz said, her eyes still on the girl and the dog. Whittier had been Liz's professor.

Liz stepped back from the door when the girl turned toward the house. Footsteps pounded up the wooden stairs and the girl and dog burst into the room. "Hey, Amanda," Elsa began. "I won't be here for dinner."

"Slow down, kid." Amanda smiled at the girl as indulgently as she used to smile at Liz. "Say hello to Liz Berke."

"Pleased to meet you," Elsa's voice was low, as if she were not quite certain she wanted to be heard. "Professor Whittier has one of your drawings hanging in his office. It's very good." When she hesitated, Liz was painfully aware that Elsa did not know what to say and she remembered how she had felt awkward when she had met Whittier's old students, people he spoke of with respect and affection. Elsa shifted her sketchbook from one arm to the other and looked at Amanda as if for release. "I'm going out to a lecture with some friends so I won't be around for dinner, Amanda."

As Elsa hurried from the room with Bristol close behind her, Liz felt a twinge of something like regret. "Is this her first year?" she asked.

Amanda pushed a cup of tea toward Liz and nodded. "That's right. Why?"

"I don't know. When I first saw her, she reminded me of someone." Liz shrugged.

"Your lost youth, perhaps?" Amanda grinned.

"I don't know," Liz repeated, frowning. "I would have liked to talk to her, though."

Amanda laughed. "I think you overwhelmed her. All of Professor Whittier's students are dancing in your shadow, you know. You're a tough act to follow."

"Nobody says they have to follow." Liz's voice was resentful. She sat back down on the couch and sipped her tea, trying not to wish that the golden retriever's head still rested in her lap so that she could scratch the dog's ears.

Liz spent the evening with Amanda, reminiscing about the years that she had lived in the house. "It was good that you moved on, you know," Amanda said. "I remember that you almost came back here a year after you left."

"I was going to take a job as Whittier's assistant," Liz recalled. "I don't know why I didn't. Good pay, interesting work, a chance to come back. . ."

Amanda shook her head in quick denial. "I told you not to take it and for once you listened. You can't come back. There's no place for you here anymore." Though Amanda's voice was warm with affection, the words left Liz with a cold feeling: no place for her anymore.

The feeling lingered after Amanda bade her good-night and headed upstairs to the attic bedroom. In the many-shadowed hallway, Liz paused at the door to the guest bedroom listening to Amanda's footsteps ascend the stairs. Though the hour was past one, Elsa had not yet come home. Liz turned from the guest room and pushed open the door to her old room.

A bouquet of daisies, backlit by moonlight, stood on the windowsill; Liz had always had flowers in her room. The desk was littered with sketches, books, designs. An easy chair—the same easy chair that she had used or else one just as misshapen—stood by the open window, an Indian muslin bedspread flung over it to hide the rips in its upholstery.

Through the open window and across the quiet yard,

Liz heard someone whistling a fragment of song—just as she had whistled to keep back the darkness on her way home from coffeehouses, parties, late nights in the studio. Liz heard a footstep on the driveway and she fled to the guest room, listening in the darkness to the sound of Elsa's key in the lock and chiding herself for invading the student's privacy.

Liz woke early the next morning. The sunlight filtered thróugh the leaves of the tree outside the window and created shifting patterns on the ceiling. The sunlight had made shifting patterns on the ceiling of the adjacent room when she had been a student. Liz heard the creak of bedsprings in the room next door, the sound of the closet door opening. She heard footsteps on the stairs but she lay in bed, watching the light dance as the wind moved the leaves, until she heard the front door open and close. She waited until the sound of footsteps on the gravel drive had faded in the distance before she got up and joined Amanda in the kitchen for breakfast.

After breakfast, she caught the same bus she had taken each day as a student. On the bus and on the walk through the campus to Professor Whittier's office, memories plagued her. Not good memories; not bad memories; just memories: I dropped my portfolio in front of this door when I was hurrying to class, I got caught in the rain and took shelter in this building, I used that fountain to fill an old jam jar with water for a bouquet of flowers, I stood right here the first time I went to see Professor Whittier, a sketch of mine hung on the wall just around this corner.

Just around the corner, a sketch hung on the wall. Liz stopped. She recognized the woman in the portrait as Amanda and she peered at the signature. Elsa Brant. Liz could not put words to the disquieting feeling that touched her—the same uneasiness that had kept her in bed that morning.

When she raised her hand to knock on Professor Whittier's door, she could not suppress the thought: I used to do this every day. And she could not avoid the thought that followed: Elsa probably does this every day.

Professor Whittier had not changed in her absence. The glacial old man nodded slowly when she told him about the work she would be doing in New York. They talked about the changes in the school, the growth in her work, and then she could not resist asking about his students.

He shrugged. Through the years, he had remained as slow and unstoppable as a mountain of ice. "All art students are alike: lazy, self-indulgent. That hasn't changed," he said. "Only one—the girl who works in your old studio—shows any promise. Her name is Elsa Brant."

Liz had fixed her gaze on the drawing that hung behind Professor Whittier's head, a sketch of Bristol that she had completed during her sophomore year. She remembered sitting in the living room on a warm afternoon while the dog slept in a patch of sunshine, trying to catch the smooth grace of the animal in pen and ink. She remembered the moment and clung to it. She was unique. No one else could have caught that moment in just that way.

"Yes," Liz admitted quietly. "I've seen Elsa's work. She does have promise."

On her way out, Liz passed by her old studio and paused at the door. Elsa stood with her back to the corridor, facing the open window. The girl's easel held a self-portrait that was almost complete. In the painting, Elsa wore the same twisted half-smile she had worn when the dog had greeted her in the yard. Liz stepped forward, about to speak to the girl, and as she did so, realized: I always painted with the window open. She turned and fled.

"I thought you were going to stay for a while," Amanda complained as Liz stowed her suitcase in the trunk of her car. "You said you didn't plan to start driving to New York for a week or so."

"I know. I just . . ." She met Amanda's gaze. "I don't belong here anymore." She hesitated. She had been about to say—"I've been replaced"—but she had thought better of it. "You've been telling me that for years. I just now realized you were right."

Amanda looked worried. "Where are you going, then?"

"I've already called Mr. Jacobs, the man I worked for in San Jose. I'm going to be taking him to lunch." She tried to force a light-hearted note into her voice. "Oh, don't worry about it, Amanda. I'm just too restless to stay in one place just now." She hugged the older woman good-bye and got into the car. With the engine running, she reached out the car window to squeeze Amanda's hand. "I'm sorry, Amanda. I just have to..." She hesitated, uncertain of what it was she had to do. "I'll write you from New York," she said.

Liz reached the small silk-screening company in San Jose well before lunchtime. She had held her first design job here, drawing logos and designs for T-shirts.

She sat at Mr. Jacobs's desk in one corner of the workroom while the elderly man finished packing an order of T-shirts. Mr. Jacobs's pipe lay unattended in an ashtray on one corner of the desk, giving off a scent that touched old memories. Mr. Jacobs stood with his back to her, folding shirts and layering them neatly. She had offered to help, but he had turned her down, saying it was quicker to do it himself. She watched him work—a wiry old man dressed in jeans and a blue workshirt. He had always worn jeans and a blue workshirt. Liz suspected that if she returned in five years he would still wear jeans and a blue workshirt, still have just the same bald spot in his thinning gray hair. Liz tilted her chair back, resting her feet on the oak desk top, and relaxed.

As Mr. Jacobs worked, he complained about his unreliable help—high-school students who worked long enough to buy new wheels for their cars, then quit. When the car needed a new paint job, they asked to be rehired.

"I'll bet you still hire them back, don't you?" Liz accused, grinning at the old man.

"He sure does." A woman stepped from Liz's old office and answered her question. "You're supposed to be going out to lunch with your friend," the woman continued. "I said I'd pack those."

"See what kind of help I have, Liz," Mr. Jacobs said. "Libby is always ordering me around, just like you used to."

Liz put her feet back on the floor and let her chair return to an upright position. Libby wore blue jeans and had long straight hair. When she smiled at Liz, her smile was crooked—a slightly cynical line.

Mr. Jacobs scowled at the younger woman unconvincingly. "Watch yourself there. You can be replaced you know."

They went to the dinette a few blocks from the silk-screen company for lunch. Liz was uneasy and distracted. Feeling awkward, but unable to avoid the question, Liz asked about Libby. "She looks like an interesting person. Is she a good designer?"

Mr. Jacobs nodded. "She sure is. She's a good kid—I'm fond of her. She reminds me a lot of you when you first started working for me."

Liz caught a glimpse of her own face in the mirror behind the counter. Her brown hair hung straight to her shoulders and her mouth had a cynical twist. She looked away.

"She'll be moving on, soon enough, just the way you did," Mr. Jacobs was saying. "She has to grow up . . ." Liz tried to listen but she was distracted by her own reflection. The dinette seemed too crowded and noisy and Mr. Jacobs's joking words to Libby beat in Liz's head: "You can be replaced, you know. You can be replaced."

"How's that young man of yours?" Mr. Jacobs asked. The question cut through the noise of her thoughts and the noise of the dinette.

"You mean Mark," she said. She had not realized how long it had been since she had talked to Mr. Jacobs. "I haven't seen him for a while. We broke up over a year ago." She fidgeted with the silverware on the Formica countertop and when she looked up Mr. Jacobs was watching her with concern. "It's all right," she said, and her voice seemed too loud, as if she were protesting too much and too soon. "We were just going in different directions, that's all. If we had both been older and ready to settle down, it might have been different." The sudden silence in her mind reflected the words as an echo: it might have been different.

From Mr. Jacobs's office, Liz called Terry, an old friend who lived in San Francisco. She tried to keep her voice light, fighting the panic that rose in her. "Terry, can I come to visit tonight?"

"Sure, I'd be glad to see you before you head east." Terry's voice was calm. She had always served as a balance for Liz, a relaxed and soothing presence. "But I thought you were going to drive east from Santa Cruz."

"Plans have changed." Liz could hear the tension in her own voice.

"You're not chickening out on this job in New York, are you?" Terry asked. "You better not be."

In the workroom behind her, Liz could hear the rumble of Mr. Jacobs's voice, then the sound of Libby's laughter. She wanted to run away. "Please, Terry, can we talk when I get there. Please..." When Liz hung up, she slipped out the front door without saying good-bye.

At Terry's apartment, Liz tried to relax. She sat on the couch, staring at the cup of tea that her friend had given her, trying to think of a way to explain why she had been upset by meeting two women with brown hair holding jobs that she once held.

"You aren't planning on visiting Mark before you go, are you?" Terry asked. Her friend sat in an easy chair across the room, her hands clasped in her lap, her eyes intent on Liz's face. Liz knew that Terry was worried about her—but she could not help imagining another woman sitting on the couch, telling Terry about her problems while Terry listened intently.

"I'd thought of it," Liz admitted. She had imagined a reconciliation; she had imagined a mature, but tender, final farewell; she had imagined a confrontation with a dim figure—a woman with brown hair and a twisted smile.

"That wouldn't be a good idea," Terry said. "You know that."

"Yeah, I know. I just..." Liz hesitated. The dim image of the woman who followed her had grown clearer in her mind. Liz saw the woman's face—a younger version of her own. She imagined herself patting the woman on the back and saying: "Good luck. You've got a great past ahead of you, kid." She shook her head. "No," she said—half to herself, half to Terry. "I guess it wouldn't be a good idea."

In honor of Liz's visit, Terry took the next day off. At Liz's suggestion, they went to lunch at the café that had been her favorite when she had worked in the city. Just as they were leaving the restaurant, they met Dave, the editor of the magazine where Liz had been layout artist.

"Liz! I didn't even know you were in town." Dave clapped her on the shoulder. "You have to come to my party tonight. Everyone will be there." He hesitated, frowning. "Ah . . . you and Mark are still friends, aren't you?"

"Of course," she replied, a little too quickly. "It would be good to see him again." She managed an unconcerned smile. "What time should we show up?"

When they left the café, Terry put her hand on Liz's arm. "You aren't fooling me, you know. If you don't want to see Mark . . ."

"It's okay," Liz insisted. "I do want to go to the party. And I'd like to see Mark again."

"I hope you want to see him out of spite—that's a good healthy motive. I hope you want to show him how well you're doing without him." Terry was watching Liz's face. "I just hope you don't want to see him for old time's sake. You can't go back, you know."

"I know," Liz said. "I really do know."

She realized at the door of Dave's house in the hills above Oakland that she really had not known—until she saw the lady on Mark's arm. The lady's long brown hair was tied up on her head so that wisps of curls floated down around her face. Though she looked a few years younger than Liz, her mouth had a cynical twist. And seeing Mark woke Liz's old doubts: could they have worked it out? should they have stayed together?

Dave took their jackets and followed Liz's gaze to the couple. "That's Lillian," he said. "She has your old job."

"Oh, really?" Liz maintained her calm facade, but when Dave turned away, she spoke to Terry under her breath. "That's not all she has."

"If you want to leave . . ." Terry began.

Liz shook her head quickly. "It's okay." She knew by the way that Terry touched her arm that her friend realized that it was not really okay, but would not blow her cover. Liz smiled and started across the room toward the couple, stopping on her way to greet old friends from the magazine, to tell people that, yes, she had moved to bigger and better things; yes, the rumors that she was moving to New York were true; no, she had not forgotten them, not at all.

Even as she laughed and chatted, she kept an eye on Mark and Lillian and noticed when the lady left Mark to join another group of people.

"Well hello, Mark," Liz said at last. "How's life treating you?" She hugged him in greeting—they had parted as friends, after all. "You're looking good."

"Sounds like things are going well for you," he said. "From all the rumors that I've heard the job in New York will be a step up."

"It should be a challenge," she agreed. Across the room, she could see Lillian talking to Dave. "She looks like a really nice lady," Liz said. Lillian smiled at a remark, and Liz noticed again that her smile had a skewed look.

"She is." His voice had a guarded tone, and when Liz glanced at him she saw that he was watching Lillian too. "You don't remember her, do you?" She looked at him questioningly. "She was one class behind you in art school. Apparently she took a painting class with you."

Liz studied the woman's face, but could not remember having seen her before. "No, I don't remember her."

"She remembers you. Apparently she admired your work." He grinned wryly. "One of your many admirers."

Liz looked away from Lillian, meeting Mark's gaze. "I'll be in town tomorrow," she said. "I don't leave for a few days. I thought we might get together for lunch. Just to talk." She knew by Mark's expression that the question had been a mistake.

"I'd rather not," he said. "Lillian and I . . . I think she feels threatened, seeing you here. You fit back in a little too well."

"I don't want to get back together or anything. I'm no threat. I just thought . . . we're still friends and . . ." She stopped, feeling she was making a fool of herself. "We spent a lot of time together and I still care what you're doing . . ."

"You still haven't learned to let go of the past, have you?" His voice held a slight edge. "You still hang on to it."

"And you don't?" She realized as soon as she spoke that she could not explain what she meant. She could not explain that Lillian's twisted smile was just like Libby's, like Elsa's, like her own.

"I *have* let go," he said, and she did not know how to refute it.

When Terry hailed her from across the room, Liz turned away with relief to join her friend by the fireplace. Later in the evening, she started to step out on the wooden deck that overlooked the ravine behind Dave's house, and stopped with her hand on the glass door.

Mark and Lillian stood on the deck, silhouetted by moonlight. Mark's hand rested on Lillian's shoulders and as Liz watched, he lifted one hand to touch her cheek. In her mind, Liz could hear him saying: You're really very special to me, you know that?

Liz felt as if she were watching a replay of her own courtship. In the darkness beyond the figures, she imagined a long line of faces, each one framed by brown hair, each wearing a twisted smile. Behind her, she could hear music from the party; on an old album, Crosby, Stills, Nash, and Young sang: "And it seems like I've been here before . . ."

She ran away, knowing that she was running away. She persuaded Terry to leave the party. She insisted on leaving for New York the next day. Terry did not question Liz's sudden panic and Liz knew that her friend interpreted her need to be gone as stemming from a fear that she might be trapped into staying. Liz did not tell her otherwise.

As Liz drove cross-country, speeding along midwestern highways where every town looked the same, she admitted her cowardice to herself. But she kept her foot pressed to the gas pedal, staring at the road until her eyes ached and gripping the wheel to keep her hands from shaking. At a McDonald's, she ate a hamburger and gulped coffee that scorched her throat on the way down and burned in her stomach afterward. She spent one night in a roadside motel, sleeping fitfully and waking with the sensation that she was still moving, clutching the wheel and pushing down on the gas pedal. She was leaving them all behind.

A knot of resentment remained with her: Why did they follow her? Why was she chosen to be the leader, the Pied Piper with a pack of children dancing in her shadow?

* * *

She reached New York and began work, spending the first day setting up her office so that it suited her. The secretary for the art department said that Beth, the artist who had quit, would stop by and pick up the sketches that she had left behind.

Liz settled down to work at her new desk, trying to ignore the constant anger that knotted her stomach. When the door to her office opened, she looked up. The older woman who stepped inside wore her brown hair pinned back. Her mouth was twisted in an ironical grin.

"Hello," she said. "I'm Beth."

Orange Blossom Time

The Teamsters were striking again. The grocery stores were out of fruit and vegetables and were running out of canned goods. The smog hung low and mean in the east.

A woman Michael did not know carried a bushel of oranges up his front steps. When he opened the door to his one-room apartment—opened it just a crack because there had been two knifings down the street that week—she grinned at him through the narrow opening. "I brought you some oranges," she said. "I'll see you later." She swung the bushel basket off her hip and set it on the top step.

He opened the door wider as she turned away. She wore her golden hair piled on her head in an old-fashioned sort of bun. She was a small woman with a tan like no one who lived in the city should have. When she lifted a hand to smooth back her hair he noticed—with the part of his mind that noted unimportant details—a bruise on her tanned wrist.

Michael recognized her when she was halfway down the stairs to the court. He did not know her name. She lived in one of the tiny street-level apartments that had windows covered with metal grillwork to ward off burglars. Michael had lived in the apartment complex for over a year. During that time, a biker, a family of Mexicans, and a hooker had lived in that tiny apartment. A shade-loving plant that the hooker had tried to grow in the window had died from lack of light. Yet this woman had a tan like a girl on a farm.

"Hey," said Michael. "I don't understand. Why..."

"Don't worry about it," she said. "They would have gone to waste anyway."

Michael hesitated, feeling foolish. As if he had walked in during the second act of a play and was trying to piece together the plot. "I don't even know your name. I'm Michael."

"My name's Karen," she said. Michael realized as she regarded him with bright blue eyes that she did not fit. She did not fit the apartment complex; she did not fit the city. She looked like the sort of woman who would bring someone a basket of oranges. And that brought him back to the question that he had put aside earlier: Where had she gotten the oranges anyway? "I'll see you later," she said with certainty. And she walked away.

Michael was on his way back to the apartment from his part-time job at the bookstore. He was an hour later than usual—though the city's buses had continued to run on the city's emergency supply of gasoline, they had grown increasingly unreliable in the last six months.

He turned the corner into the apartment court and almost bumped into Karen. The man who lived in the apartment below Michael stood beside her, holding her wrist tightly with a dirty hand. He held a bottle in his free hand and he was saying, "Come on. We can have a drink together. I need company. I'm sick."

When Michael stopped beside them, the man bared his teeth in a sort of territorial grin. Michael could not read the expression on Karen's face. Distaste? Pity?

"Karen. I was hoping I'd run into you," Michael interrupted the man. A flicker of surprise crossed the woman's face. Michael continued, "You want to come up to my apartment and have a cup of tea? I—"

"Hey!" The man swung the bottle at Michael's head with a grunt of effort.

Michael had lived in the city since he was young. Street fighting had been a required subject at his high school, though not an officially recognized one. Not a natural fighter, in order to survive, Michael had learned to act rapidly—anticipating his enemy's moves, analyzing, and countering them.

The man was swaying, already off-balance. Michael caught the arm swinging the bottle, yanked the man forward, and struck a single, hard punch to the solar plexus. The man's grip on Karen's wrist broke and she stumbled back, rubbing her arm. The man fell forward, tripping over his own feet and twisting to one side. The bottle shattered against the asphalt and glass scattered around them. The sweet scent of cheap whiskey rose.

When Michael laid a protective hand on Karen's arm, the man scowled and started to get up, but collapsed back when he began to cough. The ragged sound began deep in his chest and seemed to tear his throat as it passed. He lay on the pavement amid bits of glass, immobilized by spasms of coughing.

Michael led Karen away, not looking back. "You're all right, aren't you?" he asked her.

"I'm fine." She hesitated, still looking a little surprised, a little puzzled. "Thanks for stopping to help. I don't expect people to do that in a neighborhood like this."

Michael hesitated, once again feeling foolish. She acted like they had never met. "I wanted to thank you again for the oranges. I was kind of out of it yesterday and—"

"Oranges?" she interrupted.

"The ones you brought me. Where did you get them anyway? All the stores I've been to in the last week have been out of everything but canned stuff."

Karen smiled tentatively. "The farmer was going to leave them to rot," she said. "I guess that must have been it."

The thought passed through Michael's mind that perhaps she was crazy, but he did not jump to conclusions. There was a basket of fresh oranges in his kitchen. "You want to come up for a cup of tea?" he asked. "Tea and oranges? I'm out of everything else."

"Tomorrow," she said. "Let's make a date for tomorrow. I just realized that there's something I have to do today." She gently freed her arm from his protective grip and he noticed that her wrist was reddened where the drunk had grabbed her and was starting to bruise.

"But you can't just walk away by yourself," he protested.

"I'll be fine," she said, and she walked away by herself.

Michael awoke early the next morning and walked to the grocery store. The windows of Karen's apartment were still dark when he left the complex. The grocery store was closed and the sign in the window read: Out of Everything. Someone who had not believed the sign had smashed the plate glass window. Through the shards of broken glass Michael could see that the shelves had been pulled down and the cash register knocked off the counter. Michael stepped closer to the door and heard a rustling in the litter of paper bags beside the counter. A furtive gray shadow ran from the shelter of the bags across the open floor. Michael watched the rat disappear into the back of the store and did not investigate further.

From a corner dispenser, he picked up a newspaper. The headlines talked about the food riots in some sections of the city, about the strike, about an epidemic of a sort of fever-flu, about the ongoing gasoline shortage.

He waited for a bus home, but after an hour he gave up and walked. The trash had not been picked up in the neighborhood for almost a month and the garbage had spilled from cans and bins into the gutter. More than once, he thought he saw a rat dart into the shadows.

Karen was waiting for him at the door to his apartment. She wore a lacy blouse that could have been from an era that matched her hairstyle. Under her arm she carried a loaf of bread—a hard-crusted long loaf with the scent of sourdough about it. "This will go better with tea," she said. "We did have a date to drink tea, didn't we?"

While the water boiled for tea, Michael sliced the bread, apologizing for the lack of butter for the bread or sugar for the tea.

"Are you from out in the country?" he asked, trying to keep any note of envy out of his voice.

"I was born in the city," she said, "but I spend a lot of time outside these days."

"Where?" he asked. "It doesn't seem like there's anywhere in the city that you can spend time in the sun anymore."

Karen had picked up a white pawn from the chess set on the coffee table. Michael had played the game regularly with another tenant in the apartment complex, but the man had moved recently. Karen examined the plastic piece in her hand, ignoring his question. "You know," she said, "when I was a kid I loved reading *Through the Looking Glass* but I never learned how to play chess."

"The book makes a lot more sense if you know how the chess pieces move." He reached out impulsively and took the tanned hand that held the pawn. "I'll teach you if you like."

"All right," she said. "I'd like that."

He noticed the bruise on the wrist of the hand that he held—dark purple marking the positions of the drunk's thumb and four fingers. The corner of his mind that cataloged such things recalled the day she had brought oranges: her hand reaching up to smooth back an escaping curl of hair and on her wrist, marked in purple, the print of a thumb and four fingers.

"Had that guy hassled you before?" he asked, suddenly protective.

"No, that was the first time I had run into him. And I could have handled it myself, I just . . ." She followed his gaze to the mark on her wrist and fell silent. "I'm used to taking care of myself."

"Some other drunk, then," he persisted. "You had a bruise like that the first time I met you. When you brought the oranges."

She continued looking down at the chessboard, where the lines ran straight and the squares were neatly ordered.

"You should be more careful," he continued. "You shouldn't wander around by yourself. You don't know what the city is like."

"I was born here," she said quietly. "I know what it's like." Gently, she freed her hand from his and set the pawn back in place. "Here. Show me how the pieces move."

She avoided his eyes and he wondered if he had overstepped the bounds of their brief acquaintance. "I didn't mean to tell you what to do," he said. "It's just . . . my younger sister was killed by a rapist when she was fifteen; my parents died in a fire set by vandals when I was twenty. The city—"

"The city can't hurt me," she interrupted. "I can leave anytime I want."

He looked at the bruise on her wrist and his voice held a note of angry concern. "Right," he said. "Two bruises in three days."

"One bruise," she said calmly. "I brought you the oranges after you hit the drunk."

"You brought them the day before."

She met his eyes and in an even tone said, "I brought them after. I travel in time." He remembered that when he first met her he had wondered about her sanity (but the stray part of his mind reserved for vagrant thoughts said—where did she get a loaf of french bread and a bushel of oranges in the city?). "If you had not come along when you did yesterday, I would have just vanished to another time, leaving that man behind." She watched him with calm eyes that could have been honest or could have been mad.

"Where did you get the oranges anyway?" he asked, because that question seemed to touch the heart of the matter.

"There were orange groves here once. The farmers would pick the oranges when most were ripe. There were always a few left. If someone were to have taken them, it wouldn't have mattered to anyone. They would have rotted anyway." She shrugged. "I took them."

"Oh," he said. And stopped, trying to think of something more to say.

"Look, why don't you just think that I'm crazy if that's easier for you," she suggested. He could tell by the tone of her voice that her indifference was feigned. "Why don't you show me how the pieces move?"

He showed her the moves and started to teach her the

rules of the game. As they played, he watched her—noting the way her hands touched the pieces and her eyes studied the board. No, she did not seem mad.

After they finished their tea, she stood to leave. "I'll be back," she said uncertainly.

"I'd like to see you again," he said. Then, still caught by confusion, he asked, "Tell me, why are you going to walk away out the door when you could just vanish?"

She smiled—for the first time since she had told him she could leave the city. She lifted a hand in farewell and vanished.

The apartment was empty and he believed her. And that night the city seemed to close in around him. He could smell the smog in the breeze that came through his window. In the apartment below, he could hear someone coughing with a painful, racking repetition. Unable to sleep, he wondered where and when Karen wandered that night.

She met him when he returned from work the next day with a bottle of red wine made of grapes grown in the Napa Valley in 1908. She explained that it was a very young wine; she had taken it from a cellar where it had been stored in 1909. The cellar was destroyed in a mudslide soon after she took the bottle, so no one missed it.

"I can't change anything back there. I can't make a difference," she explained. "If I did I couldn't travel."

"How do you know taking the wine won't change anything?" he protested. "Do you figure out all the possible repercussions of an action and . . ."

"I don't figure things out. I do what feels right. It's a different way of thinking."

He leaned forward over the coffee table, watching her closely. "You might be able to change all this." He gestured to indicate the city, the smog, the garbage, the world in general. "Just by doing some small things. Stop Ford from inventing the car by . . ."

"No, I couldn't." She reached across the table and took his hand. "If I didn't accept the world as it is, I couldn't travel."

"You won't change things," he said.

"I can't. It doesn't work that way." She squeezed his hand and said, "I'm sorry, Michael. That's the way it is."

They played chess and drank wine and he tried to teach her some of the strategy of the game. But she claimed she could not learn to look ahead any further than the next move. She shook her head when he explained traps that a good player could lay for his opponent—thinking several moves ahead.

She did not go home that night. She stayed—and when he learned she was a virgin, he was surprised. She laughed. "Who would I have slept with?" she asked him. "I started time-hopping when I was in high school. And back in time . . ." she hesitated. "I'm like a ghost back there. People look past me or through me. They don't really notice me at all." She shrugged. "And I've never told anyone else about time-hopping. I don't know why I told you, really."

He made love to her gently. Afterward, as they lay in bed together, he asked, "How old are you, anyway?"

"I was a sophomore in high school three years back according to your time. But I've been traveling around quite a bit in those years. I'd figure I'm about twenty-three."

"Your parents?"

"Killed in a gas line riot." She fell silent. "I wasn't close to them anyway. I was different."

Michael lay still, one arm around her shoulders. The lady who lay beside him could run away whenever she wanted. Run away from shortages, from smog, from plague.

"Can you take me with you?" he asked suddenly.

For a long moment, she lay silent and he almost thought that she had not heard him. "I don't know," she said at last. "You would want to make changes. You would try to mess with the laws of the Universe."

"You could try to take me."

"I'll try." She pressed close to him in the narrow bed. "Hold me. And try to come with me." He hugged her tightly, willing himself to stay with her, wherever or whenever she went.

She vanished from his arms.

He lay alone in bed, listening to the man who lived in the apartment below coughing. The air that blew in the apartment window carried the scents of the dying city.

She met him at the door with a handful of wild strawberries when he returned from his job at the bookstore. "I'm sorry it didn't work," she said. "I didn't think it would. You want to change the past and you can't do that."

"Yeah." He felt dirty and tired. He had seen a mugger attack an old woman just a few blocks from the apartment. Michael had arrived just as the young man had run away. The old woman had been crying and clutching her arm where she had been slashed with his knife.

Michael had helped her to her house and called the police from her phone. The entry hall to her apartment had smelled of stale air and grease, and while he was on the phone he could hear the old woman whimpering to herself and coughing—a dry, racking sound that ripped at her throat and lungs and made her double over in pain. He had waited with the old woman until the ambulance arrived.

Karen relaxed on his couch, leaning back and looking tanned and healthy. Michael's throat felt scratchy and sore and his eyes ached from the smog.

"Where have you been?" he asked abruptly.

"Back to when Indians lived here," she said. "Interesting people. I tried to pick up a few words of their language while I was watching the women grind acorns. I learned to grind acorns instead." She grinned and pretended to be grinding acorns. "Every day, they get up—"

"How long were you there?" he asked, knowing that he sounded angry.

"About a week." She did not try to tell him any more about Indians or acorns and he did not ask.

As he made tea, he told her about the old woman. "The city is getting worse," he said. "And it looks like this strike will go on for months."

They played chess and Michael tried not to think about the city as he played. But he could not help thinking—this lady can leave anytime. "It doesn't affect you at all, does it?" he said at last. "It doesn't matter what happens to the city at all. You can always leave."

She did not look at him. She looked down at the chessboard where the world was ordered by lines and squares. "I'm here," she said softly. "I always come back here. I watch the city where I was born decay and I cannot halt the process." Her eyes were angry and sorrowful. Michael reached out and touched her hand, but she did not respond. "I travel because I accept the world as it is. I watch and I run away." She fell silent.

"Hey, I'm sorry," Michael started. "I didn't mean to . . . I mean, you tried to take me with you, but . . ." He sat beside her on the couch. "Hey, let's get out of this apartment tonight. We can go out to dinner. I know a restaurant that's still open."

At his insistence, they went out. The wine was good; he managed to ignore the canned flavor of the vegetables. On the third glass of wine, he said, "You know what's going to happen as well as I do."

She stopped, with her glass halfway to her lips. "No, I don't. I never can see the next move."

"The city is dying—you know that. And those of us who live here will die with it. I'm dying with it. But you can leave." He watched her and thought about how she had spent the afternoon picking wild strawberries. He suppressed his anger and envy, and continued in a calm voice. "I resent that. And I'm going to resent that more and more. You're going to have to leave eventually, so you might as well leave now."

She sipped her wine, blue eyes considering him over the rim of the glass. "Would you leave me?"

His laughter scratched his sore throat and his face felt hot from the wine. "Don't be silly, Karen. We hardly know each other."

"That doesn't answer the question," she said. He did not reply. She regarded him steadily. "I wouldn't leave a friend to die alone," she said.

"Don't be silly," Michael repeated. He was sweating and the chair did not feel solid beneath him. He reached across the table to touch Karen's hand to assure himself that she was still there.

They walked back to the apartment complex, hand in hand, after waiting half an hour for a bus that did not come. The driveway of the apartment court was blocked by an ambulance. The driver stood beside the vehicle, smoking a cigarette, and the spinning light above his head illuminated his face, flashing red, red, red.

Michael asked the driver what was happening. "A drunk living in that apartment died of the fever," the driver said. "Part of the epidemic. They're going to quarantine this part of the city, I hear."

The news bulletin on the radio said that the quarantine was not just of one section of the city. The entire city was cut off, quarantined from the rest of the world.

Michael sat on the couch, his head cradled in his hands. Karen laid an arm over his shoulders and he turned to face her. He was hot again, angry. He felt suspended in a world that was disintegrating around him. "Don't—" he started, and his words were interrupted by a racking cough. The world whirled.

"Michael, I'm sorry. I want you to come with me. But . . ."

Again, the coughing, the heat, and the pain deep in his chest. She was crying and he remembered, as if from a great, dim distance, another time that she had been crying and he had reached out to her. He could not reach out.

"If I wanted to change the world for you, I could not go away," she said.

"Go away," he said dully, repeating her last words. Then in an angry tone, "All right. Go away."

She left, a quiet vanishing. The room was too hot and it kept spinning and shaking, and presently, he slept.

A cold hand on his forehead. The rim of a glass pressed to his lips. He tasted sour juice on his tongue and felt it dribbling down his chin. "Orange juice," said Karen's husky voice. "It'll help some."

He opened his eyes and in the dim light of an early morning (not knowing which morning) saw her face. Large blue eyes in a face thinner than he remembered. "What morning?" he managed to ask.

She murmured, "Your time? The morning after, I think."

Orange juice trickled down his chin and the room whirled. Like a petulant child, he turned his head from the glass and tumbled down through the levels of fever and sleep.

A scent of flowers. He opened his eyes to her face in the afternoon light now, filtered through the layer of smog over the city. Gray light. Behind her, a bouquet of flowers rested by the chess set on the coffee table. The plastic pieces were set up as if for a game, but the white queen was missing. Karen held it in her hand.

"Karen," Michael said. "I want to come with you. I don't want to care about the next move." His tongue was dry and clumsy.

She looked at him and he noticed wrinkles in the skin around her eyes. The skin of the hand that held the white queen was translucent, parchmentlike. "When you were young you figured out the chess moves. I didn't care about them. It's a different way of thinking and I can't change you, Michael." She twisted the chess piece restlessly in her hand.

"I'm getting better," he started. "Much better." He tried to lift his hand to wipe away the tears that trickled from her weary looking eyes. But his arms seemed so heavy and the room whirled around him. He closed his eyes against the gray light of afternoon and whirled down, listening to Karen's husky voice—huskier with age—saying: "I won't lie to you, Michael. You aren't getting better. The fever is fatal. . . ." Then the voice faded in the distance.

Again, the touch of a hand—feather light and cool. "Tell me about the Indians, Karen," he whispered through a dry throat. She had never told him about the Indians because he had not wanted to hear. And she told him about the taste of acorn stew and the warmth of the sun and the drink they made with manzanita berries and the way the little children played and laughed. And he whispered, "Tell me about the nicest time you've been to. Tell me."

The husky voice said, "When the orange trees are in bloom. Orange blossom time." Michael opened his eyes to his love's old face. Wrinkled. Weary-eyed. The hair that was piled on her head was gray. "I'm with you, love," she said. "I've been away many times, but I've always come back."

She lay beside him on the bed and he felt as light and as pale as the dawn light that filtered through the window. "Take me there," he said, knowing that he would never change the world—not the past, not the future. He felt her thin arms around him and felt soft grass beneath him and with his last breath he tasted orange blossoms on the breeze.

In the Islands

Though the sun was nearly set, Morris wore dark glasses when he met Nick at the tiny dirt runway that served as the Bay Islands' only airport. Nick was flying in from Los Angeles by way of San Pedro Sula in Honduras. He peered through the cracked window of the old DC-3 as the plane bumped to a stop.

Morris stood with adolescent awkwardness by the one-room wooden building that housed customs for the islands. Morris: dark, curly hair; red baseball cap pulled low over mirrored sunglasses; long-sleeved shirt with torn-out elbows; jeans with ragged cuffs.

A laughing horde of young boys ran out to the plane and grabbed dive bags and suitcases to carry to customs. With the exception of Nick, the passengers were scuba divers, bound for Anthony's Cay resort on the far side of Roatan, the main island in the group.

Nick met Morris halfway to the customs building, handed him a magazine, and said only, "Take a look at page fifty."

The article was titled "The Physiology and Ecology of a New Species of Flashlight Fish," by Nicholas C. Rand and Morris Morgan.

Morris studied the article for a moment, flipping through the pages and ignoring the young boys who swarmed past, carrying suitcases almost too large for them to handle. Morris looked up at Nick and grinned—a flash of white teeth in a thin, tanned face. "Looks good," he said. His voice was a little hoarser than Nick had remembered.

"For your first publication, it's remarkable." Nick patted Morris's shoulder awkwardly. Nick looked and acted older than his thirty-five years. At the university, he treated his colleagues with distant courtesy and had no real friends. He was more comfortable with Morris than with anyone else he knew.

"Come on," Morris said. "We got to get your gear and go." He tried to sound matter-of-fact, but he betrayed his excitement by slipping into the dialect of the islands—an archaic English spoken with a strange lilt and governed by rules all its own.

Nick tipped the youngster who had hauled his bags to customs and waited behind the crowd of divers. The inspector looked at Nick, stamped his passport, and said, "Go on. Have a good stay." Customs inspections on the islands tended to be perfunctory. Though the Bay Islands were governed by Honduras, the Islanders tended to follow their own rules. The Bay Islands lay off the coast of Honduras in the area of the Caribbean that had once been called the Spanish Main. The population was an odd mix: native Indians, relocated slaves called Caribs, and descendants of the English pirates who had used the islands as home base.

The airport's runway stretched along the shore and the narrow, sandy beach formed one of its edges. Morris had beached his skiff at one end of the landing strip.

"I got a new skiff, a better one," Morris said. "If the currents be with us, we'll be in East Harbor in two hours, I bet."

They loaded Nick's gear and pushed off. Morris piloted the small boat. He pulled his cap low over his eyes to keep the wind from catching it and leaned a little into the wind. Nick noticed Morris's hand on the tiller; webbing stretched between the fingers. It seemed to Nick that the webbing extended further up each finger than it had when Nick had left the islands four months before.

Dolphins came from nowhere to follow the boat, riding the bow wave and leaping and splashing alongside. Nick sat in the bow and watched Morris. The boy was intent on piloting the skiff. Behind him, dolphins played and the wake traced a white line through the silvery water. The dolphins darted away, back to the open sea, as the skiff approached East Harbor.

The town stretched along the shore for about a mile: a collection of brightly painted houses on stilts, a grocery store, a few shops. The house that Nick had rented was on the edge of town.

Morris docked neatly at the pier near the house, and helped Nick carry his dive bag and luggage to the house. "There's beer in the icebox," Morris said. "Cold."

Nick got two beers. He returned to the front porch. Morris was sitting on the railing, staring out into the street. Though the sun was down and twilight was fading fast, Morris wore his sunglasses still. Nick sat on the rail beside the teenager. "So what have you been doing since I left?"

Morris grinned. He took off his sunglasses and tipped back his cap. Nick could see his eyes—wide and dark and filled with repressed excitement. "I'm going," Morris said. "I'm going to sea."

Nick took a long drink from his beer and wiped his mouth. He had known this was coming, known it for a long time.

"My dad, he came to the harbor; and we swam together. I'll be going with him soon. Look." Morris held up one hand. The webbing between his fingers stretched from the base almost to the tip of each finger. The light from the overhead bulb shone through the thin skin. "I'm changing, Nick. It's almost time."

"What does your mother say of this?"

"My mum? Nothing." His excitement was spilling over. He laid a hand on Nick's arm, and his touch was cold. "I'm going, Nick."

Ten years ago, Nick had been diving at night off Middle Cay, a small coral island not far from East Harbor. He had been diving alone to study the nighttime ecology of the reef. Even at twenty-five, Nick had possessed a curiosity stronger than his sense of self-preservation.

The reef changed with the dying of the light. Different fish came out of hiding; different invertebrates prowled the surface of the coral. Nick was particularly interested in the flashlight fish, a small fish that glowed in the dark. Beneath each eye, the flashlight fish had an organ filled with bioluminescent bacteria, which gave off a cold green light. They were elusive fish, living in deep waters and rising up to the reef only when the moon was new and the night was dark.

At night, sharks came in from the open sea to prowl the reef. Nick did not care to study them, but sometimes they came to study him. He carried a flashlight in one hand, a shark billy in the other. Usually, the sharks were only curious. Usually, they circled once, then swam away.

On that night ten years before, the gray reef shark that circled him twice did not seem to understand this. Nick could see the flat black eye, dispassionately watching him. The shark turned to circle again, turning with a grace that made its movement seem leisurely. It came closer; and Nick thought, even as he swam for the surface, about what an elegant machine it was. He had dissected sharks and admired the way their muscles worked so tirelessly and their teeth were arranged so efficiently.

He met the shark with a blow of the billy, a solid blow, but the explosive charge in the tip of the club failed. The charges did fail, as often as not. But worse: the shark twisted back. As he struck at it again, the billy slipped from his hand, caught in an eddy of water. He snatched at it and watched it tumble away, with the maddening slowness of objects underwater.

The shark circled wide, then came in again: elegant, efficient, deadly.

The shadow that intercepted the shark was neither elegant nor efficient. In the beam of the flashlight, Nick could see him clearly: a small boy dressed in ragged shorts and armed with a shark billy. This one exploded when he struck the shark, and the animal turned with grace and speed to cruise away, heading for the far side of the reef. The boy grinned at Nick and glided away into the darkness. Nick saw five lines on each side of the boy's body— five gill slits that opened and closed and opened and closed.

Nick hauled himself into the boat. He lay on his back and looked at the stars. At night, the world underwater often seemed unreal. He looked at the stars and told himself that over and over.

When Nick was in the Islands, Morris usually slept on the porch of whatever house Nick had rented. Nick slept on a bed inside.

Nick was tired from a long day of travel. He slept and he came on the forbidden dreams with startling urgency and a kind of relief. It was only a dream, he told himself. Darkness covered his sins.

He dreamed that Morris lay on a dissecting table, asleep, his webbed hands quiet at his sides. Morris's eyes had no lashes; his nose was flat and broad; his face was thin and triangular—too small for his eyes. He's not human, Nick thought, not human at all.

Nick took the scapel in his hand and drew it through the top layers of skin and muscle alongside the five gill slits on Morris's right side. There was little blood. Later, he would use the bone shears to cut through the ribs to examine the internal organs. Now, he just laid back the skin and muscle to expose the intricate structure of the gills.

Morris did not move. Nick looked at the teenager's face and realized suddenly that Morris was not asleep. He was dead. For a moment, Nick felt a tremendous sense of loss; but he pushed the feeling away. He felt hollow, but he fingered the feathery tissue of the gills and planned the rest of the dissection.

He woke to the palm fronds rattling outside his window and the warm morning breeze drying the sweat on his face. The light of dawn—already bright and strong—shone in the window.

Morris was not on the porch. His baseball cap hung from a nail beside the hammock.

Nick made breakfast from the provisions that Morris had left him: fried eggs, bread, milk. In midmorning, he strolled to town.

Morris's mother, Margarite, ran a small shop in the living room of her home, selling black-coral jewelry to tourists. The black coral came from deep waters; Morris brought it to her.

Two women—off one of the sailing yachts anchored in

the harbor—were bargaining with Margarite for black-coral earrings. Nick waited for them to settle on a price and leave. They paid for the jewelry and stepped back out into the street, glancing curiously at Nick.

"Where's Morris?" he said to Margarite. He leaned on the counter and looked into her dark eyes. She was a stocky woman with skin the color of coffee with a little cream. She wore a flowered dress, hemmed modestly just below her knees.

He had wondered at times what this dark-eyed woman thought of her son. She did not speak much, and he had sometimes suspected that she was slow-witted. He wondered how it had happened that this stocky woman had found an alien lover on a beach, had made love with such a stranger, had given birth to a son who fit nowhere at all.

"Morris—he has gone to sea," she said. "He goes to sea these days." She began rearranging the jewelry that had been jumbled by the tourists.

"When will he be back?" Nick asked.

She shrugged. "Maybe never."

"Why do you say that?" His voice was sharp, sharper than he intended. She did not look up from the tray. He reached across the counter and took her hand in a savage grip. "Look at me. Why do you say that?"

"He will be going to sea," she said softly. "He must. He belongs there."

"He will come to say good-bye," Nick said.

She twisted her hand in his grip, but he held her tightly. "His dad never said good-bye," she said softly.

Nick let her hand go. He rarely lost his temper and he knew he was not really angry with this woman, but with himself. He turned away.

He strolled down the dirt lane that served as East Harbor's main street. He nodded to an old man who sat on his front porch, greeted a woman who was hanging clothes on a line. The day was hot and still.

He was a stranger here; he would always be a stranger here. He did not know what the Islanders thought of him, what they thought of Morris and Margarite. Morris had told him that they knew of the water dwellers and kept their secret. "They live by the sea," Morris had said. "If they talk too much, their nets will rip and their boats sink. They don't tell."

Nick stopped by the grocery store on the far edge of town. A ramshackle pier jutted into the sea right beside the store.

Ten years before, the pier had been in better repair. Nick had been in town to pick up supplies. For a month, he was renting a skiff and a house on Middle Cay and studying the reef.

The sun had reached the horizon, and its light made a silver path on the water. Somewhere, far off, he could hear the laughter and shouting of small boys. At the far end of the pier, a kid in a red baseball cap was staring out to sea.

Nick bought two Cokes from the grocery—cold from the icebox behind the counter. He carried them out to the pier. The old boards creaked beneath his feet, but the boy did not look up.

"Have a Coke," Nick said.

The boy's face was dirty. His dark eyes were too large for his face. He wore a red kerchief around his neck, ragged shorts, and a shirt that gaped open where the second button should have been. He accepted the Coke and took his first swig without saying anything.

Nick studied his face for a moment, comparing this face to the one that he remembered. A strange kind of calmness took hold of him. "You shouldn't go diving at night," he said. "You're too young to risk your life with sharks."

The boy grinned and took another swig of Coke.

"That was you, wasn't it?" Nick asked. He sat beside the kid on the dock, his legs dangling over the water. "That was you." His voice was steady.

"Aye." The boy looked at Nick with dark, grave eyes. "That was me."

The part of Nick's mind that examined information and accepted or rejected it took this in and accepted it. That part of him had never believed that the kid was a dream, never believed that the shark was imaginary.

"What's your name?"

"Morris."

"I'm Nick." They shook hands and Nick noticed the webbing between the boy's fingers—from the base of the finger to the first joint.

"You're a marine biologist?" asked the kid. His voice was a little too deep for him, a little rough, as if he found speaking difficult.

"Yes."

"What was you doing, diving out there at night?"

"I was watching the fish. I want to know what happens on the reef at night." He shrugged. "Sometimes I am too curious for my own good."

The boy watched him with dark, brooding eyes. "My dad, he says I should have let the shark have you. He says you will tell others."

"I haven't said anything to anyone," Nick protested.

The boy took another swig of Coke, draining the bottle. He set the bottle carefully on the dock, one hand still gripping it. He studied Nick's face. "You must promise you will never tell." He tilted back his baseball cap and continued to study Nick's face. "I will show you things you has got no chance of finding without me." The boy spoke with quiet confidence and Nick found himself nodding. "You know those little fish you want to find—the ones that glow?" He grinned when Nick looked surprised and said, "The customs man said you were looking for them. I has been to a place where you can find them every new moon. And I has found a kind that aren't in the books."

"What do you know about what's in the books?"

Morris shrugged, a smooth, fluid motion. "I read the books. I has got to know about these things." He held out his hand for Nick to shake. "You promise?"

Nick hesitated, then put his hand in the kid's hand. "I promise." He would have promised more than that to learn about this kid.

"I has a skiff much better than that," Morris said, jerking his head contemptuously toward the skiff that Nick had been using. "I'll be at Middle Cay tomorrow."

Morris showed up at Middle Cay and took Nick to

places that he never would have found alone. Morris read all Nick's reference books with great interest.

And the webbing between his fingers kept growing.

Nick bought a cold Coke in the grocery store and strolled back to his house. Morris was waiting on the porch, sitting on the rail and reading their article in the magazine.

"I brought lobsters for dinner," he said. Small scratching noises came from the covered wooden crate at his feet. He thumped on it with his heel, and the noises stopped for a moment, then began again.

"Where have you been?"

"Out to the Hog Islands. Fishing mostly. I spend most of the days underwater now." He looked at Nick but his eyes were concealed by the mirrored glasses. "When you left, I could only stay under for a few hours. Now, there doesn't seem to be a limit. And the sun burns me if I'm out too much."

Nick caught himself studying the way Morris was holding the magazine. The webbing between his fingers tucked neatly out of the way. It should not work, he thought. This being that is shaped like a man and swims like a fish. But bumblebees can't fly, by logical reasoning.

"What do you think of the article?" Nick asked.

"Good, as far as it goes. Could say more. I've been watching them and they seem to signal to each other. There's different patterns for the males and females. I've got notes on it all. I'll show you. The water temperature seems to affect them too."

Nick was thinking how painful this curiosity of his was. It had always been so. He wanted to know; he wanted to understand. He had taken Morris's temperature; he had listened to Morris's heartbeat and monitored its brachycardia when Morris submerged. He had monitored the oxygen levels in the blood, observed Morris's development. But there was so much more to learn. He had been hampered by his own lack of background—he was a biologist, not a doctor. There were tests he could not perform without harming Morris. And he had not wanted to hurt Morris. No, he did not want to hurt Morris.

"I'll leave all my notes on your desk," Morris was saying. "You should take a look before I go."

Nick frowned. "You'll be able to come back," he said. "Your father comes in to see you. You'll come back and tell me what you've seen, won't you?"

Morris set the magazine on the rail beside him and pushed his cap back. The glasses hid his eyes. "The ocean will change me," he said. "I may not remember the right things to tell you. My father thinks deep, wet thoughts; and I don't always understand him." Morris shrugged. "I will change."

"I thought you wanted to be a biologist. I thought you wanted to learn. And here you are, saying that you'll change and forget all this." Nick's voice was bitter.

"I has got no choice. It's time to go." Nick could not see his eyes or interpret his tone. "I don't belong on the land anymore. I don't belong here."

Nick found that he was gripping the rail as he leaned against it. He could learn so much from Morris. So much. "Why do you think you'll belong there? You won't fit there, with your memories of the islands. You won't belong."

Morris took off his glasses and looked at Nick with dark, wet eyes. "I'll belong. I has got to belong. I'm going."

The lobsters scratched inside their box. Morris replaced his sunglasses and thumped lightly on the lid again. "We should make dinner," he said. "They're getting restless."

During the summer on Middle Cay, Nick and Morris had become friends. Nick came to rely on Morris's knowledge of the reef. Morris lived on the island and seemed to find there a security he needed. His curiosity about the sea matched Nick's.

Early each evening, just after sunset, they would sit on the beach and talk—about the reef, about life at the university, about marine biology, and—more rarely—about Morris and his father.

Morris could say very little about his father. "My dad told me legends," Morris said to Nick, "but that's all. The legends say that the water people come down from the stars. They came a long time ago." Nick was watching Morris and the boy was digging his fingers in the sand, as if searching for something to grasp.

"What do you think?" Nick asked him.

Morris shrugged. "Doesn't really matter. I think they must be native to this world or they couldn't breed with humans." He sifted the beach sand with his webbed hands. "But it doesn't much matter. I'm here. And I'm not human." He looked at Nick with dark, lonely eyes.

Nick had wanted to reach across the sand and grasp the cold hand that kept sifting the sand, digging and sifting the sand. He wanted to say something comforting. But he had remained silent, giving the boy only the comfort of his company.

Nick lay on his cot, listening to the sounds of the evening. He could hear his neighbor's chickens, settling down to rest. He could hear the evening wind in the palms. He wanted to sleep, but he did not want to dream.

Once Morris was gone, he would not come back, Nick thought. If only Nick could keep him here.

Nick started to sleep and caught himself on the brink of a dream. His hands had been closing on Morris's throat. Somehow, in that moment, his hands were not his own. They were his father's hands: cool, clean, brutally competent. His father, a high-school biology teacher with a desire to be more, had taught him how to pith a frog, how to hold it tight and insert the long pin at the base of the skull. "It's just a frog," his father had said. His father's hands were closing on Morris's throat and Nick was thinking, I could break his neck—quickly and painlessly. After all, he's not human.

Nick snapped awake and clasped his hands as if that might stop them from doing harm. He was shivering in the warm night. He sat up on the edge of the bed, keeping his hands locked together. He stepped out onto the porch where Morris was sleeping.

Morris was gone; the hammock was empty. Nick looked out over the empty street and let his hands relax. He returned to his bed and dozed off, but his sleep was disturbed by voices that blended with the evening wind.

He could hear his former wife's bitter voice speaking over the sound of the wind. She said, "I'm going. You don't love me, you just want to analyze me. I'm going." He could hear his father, droning on about how the animal felt no pain, how it was all in the interest of science. At last he sank into a deeper sleep, but in the morning he did not want to remember his dreams.

Morris was still gone when Nick finished breakfast. He read over Morris's notes. They were thorough and carefully taken. Nick made notes for another paper on the flashlight fish, a paper on which Morris would be senior author.

Morris returned late in the afternoon. Nick looked up from his notes, looked into Morris's mirrored eyes, and thought of death. And tried not to think of death.

"I thought we could go to Middle Cay for dinner," Morris said. "I has got conch and shrimp. We can take the camp stove and fix them there."

Nick tapped his pencil against the pad nervously. "Yes. Let's do that."

Morris piloted the skiff to Middle Cay. Through the water, Nick could see the reef that ringed the island— shades of blue and green beneath the water. The reef was broken by channels here and there; Morris followed the main channel nearly to the beach, then cut the engine and let the skiff drift in.

They set up the camp stove in a level spot, sheltered by the trunk of a fallen palm tree. Morris cracked the conch and pounded it and threw it in the pan with shrimp. They drank beer while the combination cooked. They ate from tin cups, leaning side by side against the fallen palm.

"You can keep the skiff for yourself," Morris said suddenly. "I think that you can use it."

Nick looked at him, startled.

"I left my notes on your desk," Morris said. "They be as clear as I can make them."

Nick was studying his face. "I will go tonight," Morris said. "My dad will come here to meet me." The sun had set and the evening breeze was kicking up waves in the smooth water. He drained his beer and set the bottle down beside the stove.

Morris stood and took off his shirt, slipped out of his pants. The gill slits made stripes that began just below his rib cage and ended near his hips. He was more muscular than Nick remembered. He stepped toward the water.

"Wait," Nick said. "Not yet."

"Got to." Morris turned to look at Nick. "There's a mask and fins in the skiff. Come with me for a ways."

Morris swam ahead, following the channel out. Nick followed in mask and fins. The twilight had faded. The water was dark and its surface shone silver. The night did not seem real. The darkness made it dreamlike. The sound of Nick's feet breaking the water's surface was too loud. The touch of water against his skin was too warm. Morris swam just ahead, just out of reach.

Nick wore his dive knife at his belt. He always wore his dive knife at his belt. As he swam, he noticed that he was taking his knife out and holding it ready. It was a heavy knife, designed for prying rocks apart and cracking conch. It would work best as a club, he was thinking. A club to be used for a sudden sharp blow from behind. That might be enough. If he called to Morris, then Morris would stop and Nick could catch him.

But his voice was not cooperating. Not yet. His hands held the knife ready, but he could not call out. Not yet.

He felt the change in water temperature as they passed into deeper water. He felt something—a swirl of water against his legs—as if something large were swimming past.

Morris disappeared from the water ahead of him. The water was smooth, with no sign of Morris's bobbing head. "Morris," Nick called. "Morris."

He saw them then. Dim shapes beneath the water. Morris: slim, almost human. His father: man-shaped, but different. His arms were the wrong shape; his legs were too thick and muscular.

Morris was close enough to touch, but Nick did not strike. When Morris reached out and touched Nick's hand with a cold, gentle touch, Nick released the knife and let it fall, watched it tumble toward the bottom.

Morris's father turned in the water to look up at Nick and Nick read nothing in those inhuman eyes: cold, dark, dispassionate. Black and uncaring as the eyes of a shark. Nick saw Morris swim down and touch his father's shoulder, urging him away into the darkness.

"Morris!" Nick called, knowing Morris could not hear him. He kicked with frantic energy, not caring that his knife was gone. He did not want to stop Morris. He wanted to go with Morris and swim with the dolphins and explore the sea.

There was darkness below him—cool, deep water. He could feel the tug of the currents. He swam, not conserving his energy, not caring. His kicks grew weaker. He looked down into the world of darkness and mystery and he sank below the surface almost gladly.

He felt a cold arm around his shoulders. He coughed up water when the arm dragged him to the surface. He coughed, took a breath that was half water, half air, coughed again. Dark water surged against his mask each time the arm dragged him forward. He choked and struggled, but the arm dragged him on.

One flailing leg bumped against coral, then against sand. Sand scraped against his back as he was dragged up the beach. His mask was ripped away and he turned on his side to retch and cough up seawater.

Morris squatted beside him with one cold webbed hand still on his shoulder. Nick focused on Morris's face and on the black eyes that seemed as remote as mirrored lenses. "Good-bye, Nick," Morris said. His voice was a hoarse whisper. "Good-bye."

Morris's hand lingered on Nick's shoulder for an instant. Then the young man stood and walked back to the sea.

Nick lay on his back and looked up at the stars. After a time, he breathed more easily. He picked up Morris's cap from where it lay on the beach and turned it in his hands, in a senseless repetitive motion.

He crawled further from the water and lay his head against the fallen log. He gazed at the stars and the sea, and thought about how he could write down his observations of Morris's departure and Morris's father. No. He could not write it down, could not pin it down with words. He did not need to write it down.

He put on the red baseball cap and pulled it low over his eyes. When he slept, with his head propped against the log, he dreamed only of the deep night that lay beneath the silver surface of the sea.

Touch of the Bear

The spirit who takes the form of a she-bear has been sniffing around my hut for the past three nights. She cannot touch me; the bear claws that dangle from the thong around my neck are a powerful protection.

I sit in the meadow by my hut and chip the flint spearhead to create an edge. She circles me in the tall grass, her shaggy body sometimes blocking out the sun. As I work, I chant in the Old Tongue, asking why she is here. She does not answer; but when she looks at me, her red-rimmed eyes are expectant: something is coming.

She swings her heavy head to look across the meadow, and on the path from the Outside I see two spots of color, moving slowly. A shout echoes across the valley—"Hello, Sam!"—and I recognize the deep voice. My blood brother, Marshall, has returned to the valley. When I look back to the spirit, she dissolves into a gray mist that vanishes in the afternoon sun.

Setting aside my tools, I stand and bare my teeth in a smile, just as Marshall taught me long ago. The barrels of the rifles lashed to Marshall's pack gleam in the sun as he strides across the meadow toward me.

He has gained weight since last we hunted together. He is still a large man—broad-shouldered and muscular—but his muscles have become soft. Three claws—taken from the bear that he and I killed—hang from a chain around his neck.

He stands before me, grinning. "You're smart not to venture out of the Preserve, Sam," he says. "I'm glad to be back." Beneath his smile is a tension that had not been there when I saw him two years before. He swings his pack to the ground and shakes back his hair. "I need to get clear of civilization again."

The woman at his side is young, scarcely more than a girl. Her hair is the color that Marshall's was before it turned gray—the golden brown of the meadow grass in the summer. Though she is taller than I am by more than a hand's breadth, she would be considered thin and weak by the standards of my people. She has delicate features like the rest of the humans: pointed chin, small nose, no protecting brow ridges.

"This is my daughter, Kirsten," Marshall says, putting his arm around her shoulders. "Kirsten, this is Sam, the last of the Neanderthals."

She holds out her hand to me.

I know that by human standards I am a curiosity: broad-shouldered and stocky, my face too broad, my nose too flat. Some humans have judged me stupid because my brow slopes back where theirs rises in a high forehead. I am not stupid. The rich fools who brought me from the past to serve as keeper in their game preserve trained me in English. Though my voice is gruff, I speak the language well. I spoke well in my case before the World Court. The final judgment ruled me human and granted me the Preserve to repay me for being taken from my own time.

Kirsten's touch on my hand is cool, and her eyes meet mine. She is young, but she has the eyes of a shaman. A feeling of power surrounds her.

"We are here to hunt," Marshall says. "I want to hunt the cave bear." His eyes are troubled, and I know that he too remembers when we first met—two young warriors from different ends of time and he said, "I want to hunt the cave bear."

Now I understand that the she-bear spirit has been waiting for the hunt and I wonder at the anticipation that I saw in her eyes. "The omens are bad for hunting, brother," I say. "See how tall the grass is. It is too late in the spring to hunt the bear—she will be awake and alert."

"We hunted before in late spring." The tension beneath Marshall's smile has increased.

"We were younger and more foolish then."

"We can be young and foolish again."

"We can be foolish," I say.

"We must hunt." There is an undercurrent of fear in his voice. "If you don't hunt with me, I'll hunt alone."

I frown, but I do not ask why—the mood that is on him leaves no room for argument. "The moon's full tonight," he says. "We can roll the bones and let the spirits decide." I know that Marshall does not believe in the spirits; he wears the bear claws around his neck as a courtesy to me. He believes in what he calls the laws of probability—and I know that he hopes that the laws will bend in his favor tonight.

"We will roll the bones," I agree, admitting defeat. The spirits will decide and I fear I know what their decision will be.

At dusk, I leave the hut to hunt for our dinner. I take Kirsten with me.

The insects in the grass call to each other with shrill cries as I follow the stream around the edge of the meadow. We walk in silence except for the sound of Kirsten's pant legs brushing against the tall grass.

When she speaks, her voice carries the power that I can see in her eyes. "Why don't you ever leave this valley, Sam?" she asks.

I have not left the Preserve since the decision of the World Court granted me the land. "There is nothing for me Outside," I say. "I live here now."

"Do you wish you could go back to your old world?" she asks.

"The World Court would not allow it. They fear the consequences of sending me back," I say. I have wondered what would have happened if I had returned to my tribe: How would I have disturbed the flow of time in my world?

"But do you want to go back?" she asks again.

I consider her question, remembering the day I arrived in the Preserve. I was a confused youth, brought into a world I did not understand by rich men who were playing with a new toy. I learned to live without the comfort and strength of my tribe. I learned to negotiate with the spirits with no shaman to aid me. I learned my own power.

"I changed by coming to this world," I say. I shrug and

repeat, "I live here now. This valley is enough for me. I am old."

She hesitates, then says, "My father is afraid he is getting old, Sam. That's why he must hunt again."

"He is old," I say. "I am old." I do not understand these people. Though Marshall and I are blood brothers, I do not understand him.

She shrugs. "It is different for him. He must go hunting again." She is tense, but I cannot tell the source of her fear.

As we walk close by the stream, a mist rises from the water. The mist solidifies and the great she-bear paces by Kirsten's side. The spirit nuzzles Kirsten's hair and snuffles on her neck, but the woman walks on, unaware of the beast that looms over her. I stop, watching the spirit and the woman. Though Kirsten has the eyes of a shaman, she does not see. Her power is unfocused.

In the Old Tongue, the she-bear growls that she grants us permission to hunt the cave bear. I read trickery and deception in her eyes; she is a capricious spirit: sometimes generous, sometimes vindictive, but always dangerous. Kirsten frowns back at me, not knowing why I have stopped.

"Do you promise success in the hunt?" I ask the spirit in the Old Tongue.

"What?" Kirsten asks. "Who are you talking to?"

The spirit dissolves into mist without answering my question, and Kirsten repeats, "Who are you talking to?"

"I saw a spirit following you," I say. "You did not see her?"

She shakes her head, looking as doubtful as her father had when I had first told him that I must ask the spirits for permission to hunt. "Your father does not see the spirits," I tell Kirsten. "He does not believe in them. But you have the eyes of a shaman. You do not know your own power."

"A magic worker?" she says. "No, not me." She looks around her, surveying the grass and the stream. "I don't see any spirit."

"She is gone," I say.

"I didn't see anything," she insists, and follows me as I

walk beside the stream. After a moment she asks, "What kind of spirit was it?"

I motion her to silence, because I have spotted a herd of wild swine in the distance. They raise their heads as we stalk them, but they are confident that we are too far away to do them harm. In the Old Tongue I call to them, asking one of them to die. An aged boar shakes his head and steps toward us. Muttering an apology to the spirits for the use of the rifle, I lift the weapon and kill him with a single shot. The rest of the herd scatters.

Kirsten follows me to the kill. "What did you call out before you fired?" she asks.

"I asked which beast wanted to die." Kneeling by the boar's body, I untie the obsidian knife from the thong at my side. The boar's tusks are strong; his shoulders are broad. His spirit could aid me in the coming hunt. I slit his throat and his spirit slips out and stares at me with ferocious eyes. The spirit stamps its feet in the grass and nuzzles its dead body.

"Can you see the boar's spirit there in the grass?" I ask Kirsten.

She glances at me, follows my eyes, and shakes her head. "All I see is grass. If my father doesn't see your spirits, why do you think I can?"

The spirit glares at me and I call to it in the Old Tongue. It charges but I am ready. The battle is silent; the spirit roars within me and my spirit roars with it. It stamps its feet, but I surround it, holding it close as a mother holds a child.

I open my eyes and Kirsten is standing before me. She looks puzzled, worried, and she asks hesitantly, "What were you doing?"

"I have taken the spirit of the boar. When you kill an animal, you must take his spirit. Or his spirit will take yours. Your father does not understand that." I stop, still clutching the obsidian knife, my hand sticky with blood. When Marshall killed the she-bear so many years ago, he should have taken the animal's spirit. If he had she would not be stalking us now.

"You really believe that?" she asks, and her voice is young.

I shrug. "The spirits are all around us. How could I not believe?" I shoulder the carcass and we start back to the hut in silence.

"What kind of spirit was following me?" she asks again.

"A she-bear," I answer. "She says you are hers."

When we are a short distance from the hut, she speaks again. "Don't tell my father about this, all right?"

"It would not matter," I say. "Your father does not believe."

When we reach the hut, I help Marshall skin and bleed the boar while Kirsten sets up the shelter that they brought with them. Marshall talks as he works about his life in the Outside. Though he does not say so, I know that he has not been happy during the past few years. "Kirsten and I are finally trying to get to know each other," he says. "Her mother and I were divorced years ago. I never visited them much when she was a kid. But she's my only child."

I watch Kirsten setting up the shelter and beside her, the she-bear spirit walks. "Do you see the gray shadow beside your daughter?" I ask him. He frowns, squinting in the direction of his daughter, then shakes his head. "The spirit of the bear that you killed has claimed Kirsten for her own," I continue. "She is following your daughter."

"Sam—" he begins, but I interrupt.

"Just because you cannot see it, do not deny it exists," I say.

"Hey, look," he says. He lifts the bear claws from around his neck and holds them in one hand. The she-bear looks toward us with interest. "You said that these would protect me against the spirit. I'll give them to Kirsten."

"Put them back on," I say sharply. The spirit is shambling in our direction. "You need them. Your daughter is strong; she can do without." The spirit pauses as Marshall slips the chain back over his head, then turns back. I face Marshall and say, "I will teach your daughter to fight the spirit. She will learn."

That evening, we eat roast pork and drink the wine that Marshall brought in from the Outside. When Kirsten pours her wine, she spills a few drops on the ground. A gray mist swirls above the damp spot, but no spirit forms.

Marshall is yawning when the moon reaches its zenith. I pull the bones from the pouch at my side and explain to Kirsten that they are knucklebones taken from the first cave bear I killed. The three bones are rubbed smooth on one side and are marked with a notch on the other.

At my command, Marshall smooths the dust on the ground before him, facing toward the moon so that his shadow falls behind him. As he casts the bones on the ground, I chant softly in the Old Tongue, asking whether the hunt will succeed.

The bones fall with the smooth side up—all three. "The hunt will succeed," I say. Marshall smiles at me. The flickering light of the fire catches in the wrinkles under his eyes. Though he looks tired, some of the tension has left him.

"We'll have a long day's hike tomorrow," he says. "We'd better turn in."

Kirsten remains by the fire. "I'll join you soon," she says. "I'm really not tired yet." The tension returns to Marshall's face. I can see the fear that Kirsten spoke of: he fears old age; he fears the passage of time. But he goes to the shelter alone.

I crouch by the fire and fill my pipe with the tobacco that Marshall brought for me. I puff the sweet smoke thoughtfully. Smoking is the only human habit I have acquired since I was brought from the past. A pipe is a boon to a man who sits by the fire to contemplate his past and to consider his future.

"Why did you come here?" I ask Kirsten. I need to know more about this girl-woman who does not realize her own power.

"My father asked me to come," she says. I wait, asking no more. She continues, after a pause, in a lower voice. "My father found something here when he was young. I thought—" She breaks off her sentence and shrugs. "I don't really know what I'm looking for."

I nod. She is much like her father was as a youth. But where he was a raw warrior, hers is another sort of power.

"Tell me about the spirit that was following me," she asks. "Why does it follow?"

"The she-bear follows because you are powerful but you do not know your strength."

"I am not powerful," Kirsten says.

"Why do you back away from your power?" I ask. When she does not speak, I continue, "She will enter you as the spirit of the boar entered me. Unless you recognize your power, you will not be able to fight her." I blow a puff of smoke from my pipe at the gray mist that swirls beside Kirsten and the bulky shape of the spirit appears. She grumbles and snuffles, twitching her hairy ears and squinting her tiny eyes to gaze at me across the fire. "Look, there," I say to Kirsten. "The spirit is back."

Kirsten stares in the direction that I am pointing. "I can't see anything."

The she-bear interrupts me, growling in the Old Tongue that I must not teach Kirsten: the woman is hers. I growl back, asking her if she fears a fair battle. In answer, the spirit opens her mouth and rears back to her full height, towering above the fire, twice as tall as a standing man. From there, she vanishes, fading into mist.

Kirsten still gazes at the spot where I pointed and I say, "She is gone. But she will be back. You must learn to fight her. I will teach you how." But even as I say the brave words I wonder if I can teach this woman with a shaman's eyes to see what she does not want to see.

At dawn, we begin the three-day journey to the cave of the bear. Marshall is alert at breakfast and Kirsten watches him with concern. "He's taking stimulants," she tells me when Marshall is out of ear shot. "He can't keep that up all trip."

During the morning hours, we hike along the stream through the foothills, passing herds of bison and swine. We see a herd of mammoths across the valley and give them a wide berth. Toward afternoon, as we start to climb higher in the grassy hills, Marshall hikes more slowly. His shoulders sag beneath the weight of the pack, and he sweats more than the sun and heat demand. "Are you well, brother?" I ask when we stop to rest and he snaps,

"Of course. I'm fine," then tries to soften his tone with a smile. "We should worry about the youngest in the group." He gestures toward Kirsten, who has been carrying her pack steadily without complaint. She lags behind when we begin hiking again and I know the reason is her father's weariness, not her own.

We make camp earlier than I would have wished, but I am concerned for Marshall's health. At dinner, he eats only a little dried meat, and he goes to his bed while the moon is rising. "My father is burning himself out," Kirsten says. "He's relying on drugs to keep going. He's afraid to slow down."

I smoke my pipe, savoring the taste of the tobacco, and watch her face. "He says he does not know you well, that he left your mother when you were young. How is it that you know so much of him?"

She laughs, a harsh, abrupt sound. "I watched him on TV. I read his books. I saw every film he made a dozen times. Of course I know him. He's the best-loved adventurer around." She stares into the fire. "People say that I am very much like him. Maybe that's why I can't see the spirits that you do."

"You will see," I say. In a shadow some distance from the fire, the she-bear laughs. Kirsten does not look up from the flames. The spirit paces toward her and stands beside her. Kirsten makes no sign that she senses the spirit's presence. "Can you see the shadow that looms above you?" I ask.

"I see moonlight and firelight," she says. But she blinks and for a moment, I think that her eyes focus on the spirit. But she shakes her head in denial. "I can't fight what I can't see."

The next day's journey is longer and harder. We are climbing the shoulders of the mountain. Kirsten trails behind her father, intentionally slow, holding back her power and pretending to be weaker than she is. Marshall is pale. When we stop at lunch I see him take a white pill from his pack and wash it down with water from his canteen. My own legs ache from the climb; I too am growing old. But after lunch, Marshall walks with the energy of a young man.

That night at the campfire, Marshall nods as he stares into the flames. The pill has worn off. "We should not be hunting this late in the year," I say to him. "We can still turn back."

"No," he says, just as stubborn as he was as a youth. "The bones predicted success."

"Success in the hunt," I say. "But what are you hunting for?"

He stands, still a tall man, but his shoulders droop. "If you turn back, Sam, I'll go on alone."

"Your daughter—" I begin, wanting to remind him of her danger.

But Kirsten interrupts. "Not alone," she says.

He smiles at her as he turns away, a flash of teeth that makes him look almost young again. Kirsten watches him walk to the shelter and duck inside. "I can take care of myself," she says to me softly. "I fear for my father."

"You do not know how great your danger is," I say. "The spirit will take your body and leave you with nothing."

"I am different from your people. Maybe the spirit will not hurt me," she says. Her eyes are bright, as if with fever, and she does not see the spirit that prowls just outside the circle of light cast by the fire. I think for a moment that her eyes start to follow it, but she looks away. She fears to claim her power. "You could go back, Sam," she says.

I shake my head. "Marshall is my blood brother. I will stay by him."

She sits without speaking, watching the flames while the moon rises. "Let me roll the bones," she says when the moon is near the peak of its journey.

"You may not like the answer," I say, but she holds out her hand and I give her the bones.

I chant as she rolls the bones. The bones gleam white in the moonlight: three white sides up—success. The she-bear chuckles and shakes her heavy head in the darkness. Kirsten does not hear. She is studying the bones that lie in the dust. "Success in the hunt," she says. "Now if only I knew what it is I am hunting." She gives me the bones, hesitating as she places them in my hand. "Will you roll the bones, Sam?"

I shake my head. "No. I do not hunt anymore. I do not seek anything."

The next morning, the morning that we hunt the bear, I awaken at dawn. Kirsten is awake. She stands by the burned-out fire and I watch her. She stares at the slope of the mountain above us, her hands clenched into fists at her sides. Beside her, unnoticed, stands the she-bear.

The spirit vanishes when I approach. I touch Kirsten's shoulder, but she does not look at me. Watching her set face, I remember a long-ago dawn when Marshall and I gathered bear brush to burn at the entrance to a she-bear's cave. Beneath his bravado, Marshall had been afraid.

I lift the thong on which the bear claws hang from around my neck and place it around Kirsten's neck. I say, "She cannot touch you now. You are safe."

She raises a hand and runs a finger along the curving length of one claw. Her expression is a strange mixture of fear and anticipation, relief and a kind of regret. "She can't touch me, but what about you?"

"I have hunted the bear before without protection. She does not want me."

"My father—" she begins.

I interrupt. "Your father will not be able to keep you safe from something he does not believe in."

She falls silent for a moment, then says, "I'm afraid for you and for my father."

"We will take care of ourselves," I say, and she raises her hand again to touch the bear claw, feeling the sharp tip. Together we gather the bear brush for the fire.

"What did my father find here when he hunted the bear with you?" she asks.

"He found the power of the young warrior. He faced death and found strength in it."

"I wonder what I will find," she mutters.

At breakfast, Marshall is quiet. If he notices the bear claws around his daughter's neck, he does not comment. He checks his rifle once, twice, three times, and tests the edge of his spearhead.

I carry the bundle of bear brush as we climb the granite slope of the mountain, following a path that twists around boulders and through brush. I will light a fire to drive the bear from the cave, and I will stand on one side of the ledge in front of the cave. Marshall will stand—rifle and spear ready—at the other side of the ledge. Kirsten will wait on a ledge above the cave, a rifle in hand.

I follow Marshall along the narrow path to the cave. The ledge in front of the cave mouth is not much larger than the floor of my hut. The ledge ends in a sheer drop; jagged rocks lie below. The wind that swirls in and out of the cave carries the scent of bear and rotting meat.

I build the fire quietly. As I light it, I hear the sound of movement within the cave. I run to my spot, waving to Marshall to tell him: "She is coming," and I whirl to face the entrance, holding my spear ready, for I hear the bear behind me.

As she charges, I dodge to one side, ducking a half-hearted swing of her paw, made as she is turning toward Marshall. He is shouting at the beast. The animal is full-grown, almost the size of the bear spirit. Even on all fours, she towers over Marshall. Roaring, the she-bear rises on her hind legs.

The wind changes and the pungent smoke of the bear-brush fire surrounds us.

There is smoke and the roaring of a bear.

There is smoke, there is shouting, there is confusion, there is a gray mist through which I start to step to go to the aid of my blood brother.

But the mist becomes solid. The she-bear spirit stands before me, blocking my path. She swats at me with a paw, and I duck back; but I am on the edge of the cliff, and there is nowhere to run. She grins at me as she rears back on her hind legs.

"Sam!" I hear a shout from above. The spirit looks up and the bear claws that Kirsten throws rattle against the stone beside me. Even before I snatch them up, the spirit is gone. I turn and see the girl-woman on the ledge above me, facing a shadow that looms far over her.

Marshall shouts and I look to him. The bear has him. He is on the edge of the cliff. His rifle lies several feet away and he holds only his spear. As the bear swings a paw at him, he thrusts with the spear, missing but ducking away from the bear's sweeping blow. He smiles as he did when he was young—old eyes burning with the flame of a warrior. Joyous. The wrinkles are gone from his cheeks, his eyes are clear. I start toward him, then hesitate in the face of his smile.

From the ledge above, I hear Kirsten's voice. She calls to me in the Old Tongue, in a voice of power that stops me. She grins down at me. I can see both in her eyes: woman and bear. Large spirit. Sometimes vindictive, sometimes generous, sometimes angry, sometimes compassionate.

I look to Marshall. Kirsten could shoot now. The she-bear within her could turn the bear away from her father. Marshall shouts curses at the animal and thrusts again with the spear. He wears the face of a man meeting death as he wants to meet it. The bear towers above him, hesitating.

Sometimes compassionate.

The bear's paw sweeps down in a mighty blow that catches Marshall and tumbles him off the cliff. Even as he falls and the bear turns away, Kirsten is scrambling down from her ledge, almost falling herself, stumbling, almost running. She rushes down the slide of loose rock to the base of the cliff, slipping with the shifting talus, almost falling, catching herself—clumsy, quick, powerful, graceful woman-girl-bear-woman. I follow more slowly, picking my way down the slope.

Kirsten stands over her father's body, fists clenched. A thin trickle of blood flows from a scrape on her arm where she fell against a boulder. She looks up when I approach and I see the wild flicker in her eyes: woman-bear-girl-bear. "I could have stopped the bear," her voice stammers softly. "I met the spirit and she . . . and I . . . we . . ." She growled in the Old Tongue the word for merging, for union, for when two streams join to form a river. The spirit has not overpowered her; they have become one: one woman-bear, one bear-woman. "I knew then that I could stop . . ." Words catching, halting, beginning again. "I could have . . . but it was better that . . . better, but I could have stopped . . ." Her eyes fill with tears, but the wild changes—woman-bear-girl-bear—do not stop, and her fists do not relax.

I reach out and touch her shoulder, and the tears spill over. For a moment a fearful child, Marshall's only daughter, peers from the blue pools where she mourns her father and says, "He's dead, Sam. Do you think he wanted to die?" Tears spill, and she kneels by her father's battered head. I stand with my hand on her shoulder; I understand now why she had been afraid of her power. With the power, she had been able to help her father find what he sought. I understand, but that changes nothing.

We leave the bear claws around his neck, and we leave his rifle and his spear at his side. We build him a cairn, Kirsten and I, rolling and carrying rocks to surround him, to pile over him, to keep back the animals, and to protect him. I do not know who I will see each time I look at Kirsten: woman, bear, or girl-child.

When we finish, Kirsten stands over the mound of rocks. Her hands are scratched and bruised, but they are relaxed now. "I wonder if he truly wanted what he found here, Sam." Her voice is puzzled and wondering. "I wonder if he is happy now."

We make the journey back to my hut in two days; and as we walk, she becomes at ease with herself and the forest, moving quietly. Her eyes are wise and calm. She tells me I must continue to wear the bear claws around my neck, but I cannot tell whether the woman speaks or the bear. Perhaps both. She is my friend.

She speaks the Old Tongue, and the birds and the beasts listen. We dine on fish that she calls to her from the stream edge. She hears the voice of the wind and the rattling complaints of the bones of the earth.

But her quiet eyes betray her greatest strength: she is no longer afraid of her power. I do not know what she will do when she leaves my valley. What strange fishes will she call forth in the Outside? Will she ask the earth to tremble and the winds to blow a hurricane gale? Will she fill the cities with beasts? Or will she watch the humans and laugh: large, compassionate, sometimes generous, sometimes vindictive.

I do not know what the shaman-woman-bear-girl-child will do.

At my hut, she turns toward the Outside. When she lifts her pack I touch her shoulder and say, "Fortune go with you, Kirsten."

She smiles tentatively. It is a small smile, but it carries hints of great wickedness, hints of great joy and great sorrow.

"Did I do right, Sam?" she asks.

"You did what you had to do," I say. "You did well."

"Can I come back to visit, Sam?" she asks and I can see the girl-child peering from her eyes.

"Come back whenever you wish, my friend," I say, and lift my hand in farewell.

She walks toward the Outside, casting a shadow larger than herself.

On a Hot Summer Night in a Place Far Away

Gregorio is a hammock vendor in the ancient Mayan city of T'hoo, known to the Mexicans as Merida. He is a good salesman—*el mejor,* the best salesman of hammocks. He works in Parque Hidalgo and the Zocalo, T'hoo's main square, hailing tourists as they pass, calling in English, "Hey, you want to buy a hammock?"

Gregorio is short—only about five feet tall—but he is strong. His hands are strong and the nails are rimmed with purple from the plant dyes that he uses to tint the hammocks. Two of his front teeth are rimmed with gold. He is, most of the time, a good man. He was married once, and he has two little daughters who live far away in the village of Pixoy, near the city of Valladolid, on the other side of the Yucatan peninsula. Gregorio's wife threw him out because he drank too much and slept with other women. When she married another man, Gregorio left his village and traveled to Merida. He sold hammocks and lived in the nearby village of Tixkokob. Once, he went back to his village to visit his daughters, but they looked at him as if he were a stranger and they called the other man Papa. He did not go back to visit again.

Gregorio was sad when his wife threw him out, and he misses his village and his daughters, but he knows that drinking and sleeping with women does not make him a bad man. He has stopped drinking so much, but he has not stopped sleeping with women. He believes in moderation in virtue as well as vice.

Gregorio met the very thin woman in the sidewalk café beside the Parque Hidalgo. She was watching him bargain with an American couple: The bearded man in the

83

Hawaiian shirt had been determined to get a good deal, and the bargaining took about an hour. Gregorio won, though the tourist never knew it; the final price was slightly higher than Gregorio's lowest, though lower than he would usually drop for a tourist. The gringo was pleased and Gregorio was pleased.

Gregorio noticed the woman when he was tying up his bundle of hammocks. She was a thin woman with pale blond hair cropped close to her head and small breasts and long thin legs that she had stretched underneath the table. She held a notebook on her lap and a pen in one hand. She wore white pants and a white shirt and dark glasses that hid her eyes.

"Hey, you want to buy a hammock?"

She shook her head slightly. "No, *gracias*."

"*¿Porqué no?* Why not? You ever try sleeping in a hammock?"

"No." She was watching him, but he did not know what was going on behind the dark glasses. There was something strange about her face. The eyebrows, the cheekbones, the mouth—all looked fine. But there was something strange about the way that they were put together.

Gregorio set down his bundle of hammocks and looked around. It was late in the morning on a sunny Sunday. Chances were that most tourists were out visiting Uxmal or some other ancient site. He pulled out a chair. "Okay if I rest here a while?"

She shrugged again, setting her notebook on the table. Her fingers, like her legs, were long and thin. Gregorio noticed that she wore no rings. And even though there was something strange about her face, she was a good-looking woman.

He whistled for the waiter and ordered *café con leche*, coffee with milk. When it came, he poured six teaspoons of sugar into the cup and sat back in the chair. "Where are you from?"

"Here and there," she said. And then, when he kept looking at her, "California, most recently. Los Angeles."

She did not act like a Californian—Californians talked

too much and were very friendly—but he let that pass. "You on vacation?" he asked.

"More or less," she said. "Always a tourist."

They talked about the weather for a time, about Merida, about the surrounding ruins. Gregorio could not put this woman in a category. She did not seem like a tourist. She was not relaxed. Her long fingers were always busy—twisting the paper napkin into meaningless shapes, tapping on the table, tracing the lines of the checks on the tablecloth.

He asked her if she had been to visit Uxmal and Chichen Itza.

"Not this trip," she said. "I visited them before. A long time ago."

The church bell at the nearby church rang to call the people to noon mass; the pajaritos screamed in the trees. The woman sipped her café and stared moodily into the distance. She made him think of the tall storks that stand in the marshes near Progresso, waiting. He liked her; he liked her long legs and the small breasts that he knew must be hidden by her baggy shirt. He liked her silences and moodiness. Quiet women could be very passionate.

"You would sleep well in one of my hammocks," he said.

She smiled, an expression as fleeting as a hummingbird. "I doubt that."

"You will never know until you try it," he said. "Why don't you buy a hammock?"

"How much are your hammocks?"

Gregorio grinned. He quoted her his asking price, double the price he would accept. She bargained well. She seemed to know exactly when he was serious in his claim that he could accept no lower price, and she seemed, in a quiet way, to enjoy working him down to the lowest price he would accept. The hammock she bought was dyed a deep purple that shimmered in the sun.

Gregorio finished his coffee, hoisted his bundle of hammocks, and returned to work, hailing two blond gringos in university T-shirts. He lured them into a bargaining session before they realized what was what.

* * *

Tourists stroll through the Zocalo, stare up at the cathedral built from the ancient stones of Mayan temples, admire the colonial architecture of the buildings in the city. Many regard the hammock vendors as pests, like the pigeons that coo and make messes on the lintel above the cathedral door. Many tourists are fools.

The hammock vendors know what happens in T'hoo. They are a select company: only thirty men sell hammocks on T'hoo's streets, though often it seems like much more. Each man carries a bundle of hammocks, neatly bound with a cord. Each man carries one hammock loose, using it as a cushion for the cord looped over his shoulder. When he hails a tourist, he stretches the loose hammock open wide so that the tropical sun catches in the bright threads and dazzles the eyes.

Hammock vendors live at a different tempo than the tourists. They sit in the shade and talk, knowing that the luck will come when the luck comes. They can't rush the luck. Sometimes, tourists buy. Sometimes, they do not. A hammock vendor can only wander in the Zocalo and wait for the luck to come.

While they are waiting, the hammock vendors watch people and talk. The French tourists who are staying at the Hotel Caribe will never buy a hammock; they bargain but never buy. There are pretty women among the Texans who have come to study Spanish at the University of the Yucatan, but all of them have boyfriends. The tall thin woman with pale hair is always awake very early and goes to her hotel very late.

"There she is," said Ricardo, looking up from the hammocks he was tying into a bundle. "She was in Restaurant Express last night until it closed. Drinking *aguardiente*." Gregorio glanced up to see the thin woman sitting at the same table as the day before. She had a lost look about her, as if she waited for a friend who had not come.

"She was here at seven this morning," observed Pich, a gray-haired, slow-moving hammock vendor. "She needs a man."

Ricardo looked sour and Gregorio guessed that he had suggested that to the thin woman the night before without success. The hammock vendors discussed the woman's probable needs for a time, then continued an earlier discussion of the boxing match to be held that evening. The woman was of passing interest only.

Still, when Gregorio wandered on to search for customers, he passed her table and said hello. Her notebook was on the table before her, but he could not read the writing. Not Spanish, but it did not look much like English either. Though the morning sun was not very bright, she wore the dark glasses, hiding her eyes behind them. *"Buenos días,"* she said to him. *"¿Qué tal?"*

"Good," he said. He sat down at her table. "What are you writing?" He peered at the notebook on the table.

"Poetry," she said. "Bad poetry."

"What about?"

She glanced at the notebook. "Do you know the fairy tale about the princess who slept for a thousand years? I've written one about a woman who did not sleep for a thousand years."

"Why do you look so sad today? You are on vacation and the sun is shining."

She shrugged, the slightest movement of her shoulders. "I am tired of being on vacation," she said. "But I can't go home. I am waiting for my friends. They're going to meet me here."

"I understand." He knew what it was like to be homesick. She looked at him long and hard and he wondered about the color of her eyes behind her dark glasses. "Did you sleep in my hammock?" he asked her at last.

"I strung it in my hotel room."

"But you did not sleep in it?"

She shook her head. "No."

"Why not?"

She shrugged lightly. "I don't sleep."

"Not at all?"

"Not at all."

"Why not?"

"I slept at home," she said. "I can't sleep here."

"Bad dreams? I know a *curandera* who can help you

with that. She'll mix you a powder that will keep bad dreams away."

She shook her head, a tiny denial that seemed almost a habit.

"Why not then? Why can't you sleep?"

She shrugged and repeated the head shake. "I don't know."

He stared at her face, wishing that she would remove her glasses. "What color are your eyes?" he asked.

She moved her sunglasses down on her nose and peered at him over the frames with eyes as violet as the sky at dusk. Her eyes were underlined with darkness. A little lost, a little wary. She replaced her sunglasses after only a moment.

"You don't sleep really?" Gregorio asked.

"Really."

"You need a man."

"I doubt that." Her tone was cool, distant, curious. It did not match the lost look in the violet eyes he had seen a moment before. She gestured at two American women taking a table at the other end of the café. "Those two look like they need a hammock," she said.

Gregorio went to sell them a hammock.

Gregorio did not mention to the other hammock vendors that the thin woman did not sleep. Odd that he should forget to mention it—it was an interesting fact about a strange woman. Nevertheless, he forgot until he met her again, very late at night. He was wandering through the Zocalo, cursing his bad luck. He had missed the last bus to his village, Tixkokob, because he had taken a pretty young woman to the movies. But the young woman had declined to share her bed with him and he had no way home. He was in the Zocalo looking for a friend who might have a spot to hang a hammock.

He noticed the thin woman sitting alone on a bench, watching the stars. "What are you doing out here so late?" he asked.

She shrugged. "The cafés are closed. What are you doing here? All your customers have gone home."

He explained and she nodded thoughtfully and offered him a drink from the bottle of *aguardiente* that sat beside her on the bench. *Aguardiente* was a potent brandy and the bottle was half-empty. He sat beside her on the bench and drank deeply. With his foot, he nudged the paper bag that rested on the ground by her feet and it clinked: more bottles.

"I like this drink," she said slowly, her head tilted back to look at the stars. "It makes me feel warm. I am always cold here. I think, sometimes, if I found a place that was warm enough, then I would sleep."

The guitarists who seranaded tourists were putting away their instruments, grumbling a little at the evening's take. The Zocalo was almost deserted. Gregorio shifted uneasily on the bench. "I should go to Parque Hidalgo and see if Pich is still there. He would let me stay at his house."

"Keep me company a while," she said. "You can stay in my room." She glanced at him. "And don't bother looking at me like that. I plan to sit up by the hotel pool tonight. It's a good night to watch the stars." She leaned back to look at the night sky. "Tell me—have you always lived in Tixkokob?"

"I come from Pixoy. But it is better that I am not there now."

"Better for you?" Her eyes were on the sky, but he felt vaguely uncomfortable, as if she were watching him closely.

"Better for everyone," he said.

"I understand," she said. She drank from the bottle and gave it back to him. They watched the moon rise.

Her room was on the bottom floor of the Hotel Reforma. It was a small dark room, very stuffy and hot. His hammock was strung from rings set in the walls. A stack of notebooks rested on the small table beside the bed. On the dresser, there was a strange small machine that looked a little like a cassette player, a little like a radio. "What's this?" he asked, picking it up.

She took it from his hand and set it gently back on the table. The *aguardiente* made her sway just a little, like a tall tree in the wind. "My lifeline. My anchor. And maybe an albatross around my neck."

Gregorio shook his head, puzzled by her answer, but

unwilling to pursue it. The brandy was warm in his blood, and he was very close to deciding that the thin woman had invited him here because she wanted a man. He came close to her and wrapped his arms around her, leaning his head against her chest. He could feel her small breasts and that excited him.

She pushed him away with surprising strength and he fell back against the bed. She picked up her notebook and the strange small machine, tucked the bottle of *aguardiente* under her arm, and stepped toward the door. "Sleep," she said.

He slept badly. The tendrils of someone else's thoughts invaded his dreams. He wandered through a warm humid place where the light was the deep purple color of his hammock. The place was crowded with men and women as tall and thin as the thin woman. He asked them where he was, and they looked at him curiously with dark violet eyes. He wanted to go home, but when he asked if they could tell him the way, they said nothing. He was tired, very tired, but he could not rest in that place. The air was too thick and hot.

He woke, sweating, in the thin woman's room, and went to the patio to find her. The first light of dawn was touching the eastern sky, but stars were still visible overhead. She sat in a lounge chair beside the pool, speaking softly into the machine. He could not understand the words. Two empty *aguardiente* bottles were at her feet and another was on the table at her side. He sat in a chair beside her.

Fireflies were dancing over the pool. She gestured at the bottle that rested on the table and Gregorio saw that a firefly had blundered inside the bottle and seemed unable to find its way out. It crawled on the inside of the glass, its feeble light flickering. "I can't get her out," the woman said in a harsh voice blurred with brandy and filled with uncertainty. "And she can't find her way. She just keeps flashing her light, but no one answers. No one at all."

Without speaking, Gregorio took the bottle to the ornamental flower bed by the side of the pool. He took a brick from the border, lay the bottle on the cement, and tapped it lightly with the brick—once, twice, three times. A starburst of fine cracks spread from each place he struck the bottle, and when he pulled on the neck, the cracks separated and the bottle broke. The insect rose, sluggishly at first, then faster, dancing toward the other lights.

She smiled, and he could tell that the brandy had affected her. The smile was slow and full, like a flower unfolding. "She returns to her place," the woman said, blinking at the dancing lights. "Sometimes I think that I have returned home and maybe I am asleep and dreaming of this place. Sometimes I try to think that. I go for days believing that I am asleep. Then I come to my senses and I know this is real." She reached for the last bottle, but it was empty.

"Where do you come from?" Gregorio asked.

She lifted one thin arm and pointed up at a bright spot of light high in the sky. "That one."

Gregorio looked at her and frowned. "Why are you here?"

She shrugged. "Merida is as good a place to wait as any. It's warm here, warmer than most places. My friends are supposed to come get me. They're late."

"How late?"

She looked down at her thin hands, now locked together in her lap. "Very late. Just over one hundred years now." Her hands twisted, one around the other. "Or maybe they never intended to come back. That's what bothers me. I send out reports regularly, and maybe that was all they wanted. Maybe they will leave me here forever."

"Forever?"

"Or for as long as I live." She glanced at him. In the light of the rising sun, he could see her strange violet eyes—wide and mournful. "I don't belong here. I don't . . ." She stopped and put her head in her hands. "Why are they so late? I want to go home." He did not understand what she said next—the language was not English and not Spanish. She was crying and he did not know what to say or do. She looked up at him with a face like an open wound. Her violet eyes were wet and the circles beneath them stood out like bruises. "I want to go home," she said again. "I don't belong here."

"Who are you?"

She closed her eyes for a moment and seemed to gather strength to her. "The explorers brought us here," she said. "The ones in the spacecraft. They left us to gather information about your people." She looked down for a moment and he thought she would stop talking, but she looked up again. "We travel with the explorers but we are a different people. When we meet with new ways, we adapt. We learn. We take on a little bit of the other, retaining a little bit of ourselves. We blend the two." She spread her hands on her knees. "We are diplomats, translators, go-betweens for merchants. We live on the border, neither fish nor fowl, not one thing and not the other." Her hands closed into fists. "There were three of us, but Mayra died two years ago. Seena, last year. We grew tired, so tired. They left us here too long. I have lost myself. I don't know who I am.

"I should not speak, but it has been so long." She shook her head and rubbed her eyes with her slender fingers. "You will forget this. I will make you forget." She leaned back in her chair and stared at the sky. The stars were gone now, washed out by the light of the rising sun. "I send them poetry instead of reports, but still they do not come for me. Maybe they don't care. Maybe none of this matters." Her voice had a high, ragged note of hysteria. "It did not bother me at first," she said. "Not while the others were alive. Only recently. It bothers me now. I would like to curl up and sleep for days. For weeks."

Gregorio took her long thin hand in his, squeezing it gently for comfort. This woman, she needed help. And he wanted her. She was aloof and foreign and he wanted to hold her. He wanted her because of her long thin legs, like a heron's legs, her long thin hands, like the cool hands of the Madonna.

He said nothing, but he was thinking of the place that the dream had brought to his mind, the dark, warm, limestone cavern just outside the nearby village of Homun. He had been thinking about seeing the thin woman naked, swimming in the waters of the cavern, alone with him.

She looked at his face and suddenly laughed, a small

chuckle that seemed drawn from her against her will. "Sometimes, I can find my way out of my own self-pity, and I see you, son of the strange men who built those cities, goggling at me for . . . what? What do you want?" She stared at him, her violet eyes filled with amusement, then suddenly widening as if she were trying to see something in dim light. "Wait . . . where is this . . . this place . . . where?"

Her thin fingers were playing over his face as if searching for something. She reached out and ran a cool finger along the back of one hand. She had moved closer to him, her eyes wide and eager.

The quiet ones, he thought to himself. They are always the most passionate. And he imagined her clearly again, a long pale naked woman stepping into the warm water and smiling at him in invitation.

But she pulled back then, leaning back in her chair and slipping the dark glasses over her violet eyes, hiding behind the tinted lenses.

Later that day, Gregorio could not remember all that had happened out by the pool. He remembered the woman's hand in his; he remembered telling the woman that he would take her to the caves of Homun, to a very private cave he knew. But there was a curiously incomplete blurred feel to his memory.

Gregorio liked the woman, but he did not like the vague feeling that he was being tricked and he acted to prevent such a thing from happening again. In his right pocket, for clarity of mind, he carried a clear polished stone that had been thrice blessed with holy water. In his left, for good luck, he carried a jade bead that had been carved on one side with the face of Kin Ahau, the sun god who watches by day, and on the other side with the face of Akbal, the jaguar-headed god who watches by night. With these talismans he was confident. His mind would not be clouded.

The bus to Homun was hot and crowded. It dropped them on the edge of the village and Gregorio led the woman through the monte, the scrubby brush that covers much of the Yucatan, to the entrance to the cavern.

The Yucatan peninsula is riddled with limestone caverns that lead to deep dark places beneath the earth. Here and there, the caves dip beneath the water table, forming subterranean pools. Gregorio knew of such a cave, a secluded subterranean pool that was a fine place to bring cute American tourists for seduction.

A tunnel led deep into the underworld to a pool of clear water in a limestone cave. Shells—all that remained of ancient clams and oysters—were embedded in the rock. Another tunnel, extending back from the first pool, led to an even more secluded pool.

Gregorio took the woman to the most remote pool. Stalactites hung low over the pool. The air was close and humid, very hot and moist. He carried a small flashlight and shone it on the limestone to show her the way. She was smiling now, following close behind him.

Gregorio strung his hammock on the two hooks that he had set in the limestone walls long ago. As soon as he had it strung, the woman sat on the edge of the hammock and then lay back with a soft sigh.

"We can swim," Gregorio said. He was quietly stripping off his clothing.

No reply from the woman in the hammock.

He went, naked, to the hammock. She was curled on her side, one hand tucked under her cheek, the other resting on her breast like a bird who has found her nest. Her eyes were closed and she breathed softly, gently, rhythmically. He touched her cheek, warm at last, brushing a stray tendril of hair back into place, and kissed her lightly. When he touched her, he felt a bright warm sensation, like the spreading warmth of brandy but quicker, cleaner, more pure. He saw in the darkness the tall thin people, holding out their long arms in welcome. He felt content and loved and very much at home.

He did not wake her. He swam alone in the warm water, dressed, and left her there, sleeping peacefully.

In a limestone cavern at Homun, a woman sleeps like a princess in a fairy tale. Gregorio knows she is there, but few others know the way to the hidden cave and if anyone does chance to find her, Gregorio knows that the person's mind will be clouded and he will forget. Gregorio visits her sometimes, touches her lightly on the cheek and feels the warm glow of homecoming. And he watches for the day when a tall thin man who does not sleep comes to town and sits in the cafés, sitting up late as if waiting for a friend. This one, Gregorio will take to the cavern to wake the woman who sleeps so soundly, wake her with a kiss and take her home.

Sweetly the
Waves Call to Me

The harbor seal lay just beyond the reach of the waves, its dark eyes open in death. The surf had rolled and battered the body; the mottled gray fur was dusted with white sand. Gulls had been pecking at a wound in the animal's head.

Kate shifted her weight uneasily as she stared down at the body. She was alone; Michael, her lover, was still asleep at the cottage. Kate had come walking on the beach to escape the restless feeling left by a melancholy dream. She could not remember the dream; it had retreated like a wave on the beach, leaving behind feelings of loneliness and abandonment.

She raised one hand to touch the ivory pendant that dangled from a chain around her neck, a circle etched with the likeness of a seal. Michael had given her the pendant the night before—as a peace offering, she thought.

Michael had come to visit for the weekend to apologize and to forgive her—managing the seemingly contradictory acts with the competence that he brought to every task. Kate had left Santa Cruz and Michael to live for a summer in her parents' old cottage; she had needed the solitude to finish her thesis on the folklore of the sea. Michael had brought her the scrimshaw pendant to apologize for accusing her of using her thesis as an excuse for leaving him.

She did not think that she was using the thesis as an excuse. But sometimes, in the dim light of early morning when the gulls cried overhead, she was not sure. She knew that sometimes she needed him. She knew that he was solid and he was strong.

She could hear the distant roar of a truck traveling down

Highway 1. The cottage was halfway between Davenport and Pescadero—south of nowhere in particular, north of no place special. A lonely place.

Looking down at the dead body of the seal, Kate had the uneasy feeling that she was being watched. She looked up at the cliff face, then out to sea where the waves crashed. Just past the breakers, a dark head bobbed in the water—a curious harbor seal. As she stared back, he ducked beneath a wave.

She hurried back to the cottage, scrambling up the sandstone slope, following the narrow path that was little better than a wash eroded by the last rain.

The cottage was perched at the top of the bluff. The waves that pounded against the cliff threatened to claim the ramshackle building someday. The sea fog had begun a slow offensive against the cottage, the white paint was chipped and weathered, the porch sagged at one corner where a supporting post had rotted through, the wind chimes that hung from the low eaves were tarnished green.

"Bad news," Kate said as she stepped in the kitchen door. "There's a dead seal on the beach."

The kitchen was warm and bright. Michael was making coffee. "Why's that bad news?"

"Bad luck for the person who shot it," she said. "It could have been a silkie, a seal person who could change shape and become human on land. If a person kills a silkie, the sea turns against him."

Michael was watching her with an expression that had become familiar during the time that they had lived together—he did not know how seriously to take her. "You've been working on that thesis too long," he said, and poured her a cup of coffee.

She laughed and slipped an arm around his waist, leaning up against him and feeling the warmth of his body. Almost like old times. "Huh," she said, "there speaks the scientist."

"It'll be simple enough to get rid of any bad luck," he added. "I'll call the university at Santa Cruz. There's a class that recovers stranded marine mammals for dissection."

Kate released him, and sat down in one of the two

wooden kitchen chairs. The cup of coffee warmed her hands, still cold from the fog. "They don't need to get it. It'll wash out to sea at high tide tonight."

Michael frowned. "They'll want it. This is the only way that they can get specimens."

"Oh." She sipped the hot coffee. Far out at sea, over the crash of the waves, she could hear a sea lion barking. "It doesn't feel right," she said. "It seems like the body should go back to sea." Then, before he could laugh or call her foolish, she shrugged. "But I suppose it doesn't matter. In the interest of science and all."

Michael called the university and arranged to have a crew of students come to pick up the seal that afternoon, explaining that Kate would meet them, that he would be gone.

He looked at her when he hung up the phone and said, inexplicably, "Is that all right?"

"Of course, of course, it's all right," she said irritably. And when he came around the table to hug her, she realized that he had meant that he was leaving, and was that all right? She had been thinking of the seal.

When Kate stood alone on the porch, waving good-bye, she felt uneasy again, unsettled. The fog smelled of salt spray and dying kelp. Michael lifted a hand in farewell and she listened to the crunch of wheels on gravel and watched the sedan until it vanished into the fog. The engine changed in pitch when he stopped at the end of the drive, turned onto the highway, and picked up speed.

Kate realized that one hand was clinging to the pendant around her neck, and she released it. A gull shrieked in the fog and she retreated into the kitchen to work.

The papers that she spread on the kitchen table were the result of months of collecting the stories told in the Santa Cruz fishing community. There were so many stories— and so many warnings—about how one should behave around the sea.

She remembered sitting in the sun on the fishing dock while an old man mended a net and advised her: "If you cut yourself near the sea, never let the blood touch the water. Blood calls to blood. If the sea has your blood, you belong to the sea." She remembered a Scottish fisherman's widow, a sturdy old woman with bright blue eyes, had served her tea and warned: "You must not take the sea lightly. Those who take from the sea lay themselves open to the powers of the sea. And many dark creatures dwell beneath the waves."

The sea dwellers of legend were tricky. The kelpies or water horses could take human form to entice mortals into the water to drown. Mermaids and mermen could raise storms to sink ships.

But the silkies, the seal people that Kate's thoughts kept returning to, were a gentle folk. Kate leafed through one of her notebooks and found the widow's account of a young salmon fisherman who had shot a seal feeding near his boat, and had died in a storm the next month. The old widow had said that the silkies were tolerant of humans and angered only by the death of their own kind. They came ashore on moonlit nights to dance on the beach in human form. Fishermen had captured silkie maidens for wives by stealing the skin they used in their seal form; silkie men had been known to take human lovers.

Kate began listing the elements that the widow's tale had in common with traditional tales of silkies. Just before lunch, she was interrupted by the sound of tires on the gravel drive. She picked up her sweatshirt and stepped onto the porch.

Three students—two men and a woman—climbed down from the cab of the ancient pickup truck parked in the drive. "I guess you came to pick up the seal," Kate said hesitantly. With Michael gone, her uneasiness about the seal had returned. But she could not turn the students away. "I'll take you down," she said.

The day was still overcast and the wind from the sea was cold. Kate hauled her sweatshirt over her head. The cloth caught on the chain of her pendant and she yanked at the sweatshirt impatiently—too hard. The chain broke and she caught the pendant as it fell. "Damn," she muttered. Aware of the eyes of the students on her, she stuffed the pendant and chain into her pocket. "I'll take you right down," she repeated.

The students unloaded a stretcher from the back of the truck and followed Kate down the narrow path. They had to scramble over the jumble of rocks that extended from the base of the cliff to the water. At high tide, the waves crashed against the cliff, making the broad beach where the seal lay inaccessible from the path. When the moon was full and the tides reached full height, the sea swallowed both the tiny beach at the bottom of the path and the broad beach to the north.

Kate felt ill at ease with the students, unwilling to introduce herself or ask their names. These people did not belong on her beach. She stood several yards away as the two men squatted by the seal and positioned the stretcher so that they could roll the seal onto it. The woman stood at the animal's head. She shifted her weight uneasily, glanced out to sea, then back at the seal. Kate crossed her arms and hugged her sweatshirt tighter around her, suddenly cold. The woman shivered, though she was dressed more warmly than Kate.

She stepped toward Kate and caught her eye. "You must be half seal yourself to go in swimming this time of year."

Kate frowned. "Why do you figure I've been in swimming?"

The woman pointed to a set of footprints, left by bare feet, leading along the edge of the sea toward the body. The prints were almost obscured by bird tracks and boot prints.

"Not me," Kate said. "But that's odd. Those weren't here this morning. And I'm the only one who lives near here."

The woman shrugged. "Probably just a hitchhiker who stopped off the highway to walk on the beach." She looked out to sea, where the gray waves crashed against the rocks.

Kate nodded. "I suppose so." She squatted beside the footprints and peered at them closely. Just footprints in the sand; nothing unusual.

"Come on," one of the men called. The two men had picked up the stretcher and started back in the direction of the path. Kate and the woman walked in silence. Over the sound of the surf, they could hear the men talking and laughing.

"I don't see how those guys can joke about picking up bodies," the woman said. "I always feel like a grave robber."

"Yeah?" Kate glanced at the woman's face. "That's how I feel. My boyfriend called the university. I would have just as soon let the body wash back out to sea. I don't know why."

The woman nodded sympathetically. "It must be something about the ocean. And the fog. And the time of year—we're almost to the shortest day."

"The winter solstice," Kate murmured. "A bad time to mess with the ocean."

"Yeah?" The woman shot Kate a curious glance. "Why's that?"

Kate shrugged. "According to folk stories, the winter solstice is when the powers of darkness are at their strongest. It's a dangerous time."

The woman hugged her jacket closer around her, hunching her shoulders against the cold wind that blew from the sea. "You almost sound serious about that."

"I'm studying folklore and the old stories kind of get to you after a while." Kate hesitated. "It's not that I believe them. It's more like I respect them. This is old stuff. Strong stuff." She shrugged again, then fell silent.

The men lifted the stretcher into the back of the truck and the dead eyes of the seal gazed mournfully at the rusty metal of the tailgate. The woman paused before she climbed after the men into the cab. She laid a hand on Kate's arm. "Take care of yourself," she said. She hesitated as if she wanted to say more, then climbed into the cab.

The tires crunched on the gravel drive; Kate lifted a hand in farewell. She turned her back on the highway and listened to the truck shift gears when it reached the end of the drive, but she did not watch it drive away.

The fog had lifted but the sky was overcast. The horizon was marked by an almost imperceptible difference in shading between the gray-blue of the ocean and the blue-gray of the sky. The ocean was calm. A gray beast waiting at the foot of the cliff, not impatient for an end, but certain that an end would come. The setting sun was a hazy circle behind the clouds on the horizon.

Kate shifted her feet and the gravel made grinding noises. To reach the beach, a hitchhiker would have had to follow the drive to the path. If anyone had passed the cottage, she would have heard him walking in the gravel. But there had been footprints on the beach.

The sun sank out of sight. A night breeze ruffled Kate's hair and she shivered, then retreated to the cottage.

After dinner, when the warmth of the cottage had chased away thoughts of silkies and solitude, she stepped out on the porch to watch the moon rise. The lights of the kitchen glowed cheerfully through the curtains behind her. The moon would be full the following night, full and round like the ivory circle of her pendant.

She dug in her pocket to touch the smooth ivory. Her pocket was empty. Her fingers found a hole in the cloth and she cursed herself for carelessness. She must have dropped it on the path or on the beach.

No gleam of ivory rewarded her search of the path. She walked toward the broad beach, searching the sand with no luck. The tide was rising. A breaking wave washed among the rocks at the base of the cliff. When the wave retreated, she hurried across.

The dry sand of the broad beach just above where the wave had reached was marked by footprints. Bare feet. The prints led away from the path, toward the spot where she had found the seal's body.

"Hello," Kate shouted. "Is anyone out there?" No answer.

She looked back toward the jumble of rocks that separated her from the footpath. The tide was rising and the water lapped higher with each wave. Kate broke into a run, following the footprints. She took long strides and when the waves hissed under her feet she ignored the spray that splashed up to wet her jeans. Beside the rocky outcropping where she had found the seal, she stopped and scanned the beach.

There. In the shadow of the cliff at the end of the beach she saw a flickering light and a moving shadow. The light was too pale and too bright to be a campfire. A flashlight beam, perhaps.

"Hey!" Kate called. "The tide's coming in. Hey, you!"

The light remained where it was. Kate raced toward it, shouting, then saved her breath for running. When the light moved, she could see the outline of the person holding it.

She was a hundred feet away when a wave crashed against the cliff and sent an arc of spray over the flickering light. The shadowy figure moved, a darting movement too quick and graceful to be human. Like a cat. Like a sea otter. Like a seal in the water. And the light vanished.

Kate's momentum carried her three more steps. She stared at the cliff, which suddenly seemed clearly lit by moonlight. There was no one standing beneath the cliff. There was no flashlight beam. There was no nook, no cranny, no crevice where a person could hide. Just moonlight and water and a tall black cliff. Just a vanishing light and a fleet shadow.

Over the hiss of a retreating wave, Kate thought she heard a sound—a long sigh like a seal taking a breath of air after a long dive. The moonlight gleamed on a white circle on the sand before her. Her pendant. Here, far from where she had walked. She stepped forward and reached for it, aware of eyes on her. A wave rushed in to snatch the circle of ivory away before she could touch it. She groped after it in the surf, but it slipped away, lost in the foam and the moonlight.

Kate turned and ran for the path. She passed the rocky crag—her heart pounding, her breath rasping through a dry throat. The waves splashed high against the cliff and even in retreat left no dry rocks. Moonlight glistened on the swells.

A wave washed among the rocks and Kate plunged into the water, hoping to cross before another broke. The icy water sucked at her legs, dragging on her jeans. Beneath her boots, the rocks were slick with kelp and eel grass. The water was knee-deep, waist-deep. The ocean tugged at her legs, another wave broke, and a rock shifted beneath her boot. She slipped and floundered in the water, her ankle caught between two rocks. She wrenched the foot free and stood, sputtering through a curtain of wet hair. She struggled forward, hampered by wet jeans, crippled by an ankle that gave beneath her. Stumbling again, but recovering. She limped through water that was waist-deep, knee-deep. Onto a sandy bottom. Onto a tiny beach.

She collapsed on the dry sand and drew in a long shuddering breath. And another. Only when she lifted her right hand to brush the wet hair from her face did she realize that she was bleeding from a ragged gash across her palm. Cut on a rock. She staggered to her feet, and her ankle throbbed with dull persistent pain. The waves hissed in the sand, leaving an innocent line of foam.

Droplets of blood fell from her clenched fist to stain the foam.

A shadow moved beyond the breakers. A flicker of pale white light. A will o' the wisp. The eyes were still on her; she could feel them. And the loneliness that had touched her that morning had returned.

"Not me," she called hoarsely to the light. "I didn't kill her. Not me." The light dipped out of sight beneath the crest of a wave.

Kate turned away to stagger home to the sanity of a warm kitchen, a cup of tea, a hot shower. But the rush of water from the showerhead rattling against the metal walls of the shower did not cover the sound of the surf. Even as Kate washed sand from the cut on her hand, she could hear the rhythmic crashing of the waves, gentle and steady. While she was heating water for tea, a storm began with the soft touch of rain against the windows, a persistent whispering like many soft voices speaking so quietly that she could not understand them. When she caught herself listening for words in the soft rainfall, she turned on the radio.

The storm picked up in force, competing with the wailing of pop rock. The wind howled across the chimneytop. The rain lashed against the windows and blew in through the bathroom window, which was warped partly open. Kate stuffed newspaper into the gap and the paper soaked up the rain. Once soaked, the paper dripped on the floor, beating a steady counterpoint to the pealing of the wind chimes—high and furious—outside the window.

Kate paced within the kitchen, trapped but unable to sit still. Once, when the wind rattled the door, Kate thought she felt the cottage shake and she thought of mud slides and collapsing cliffs. The silkies, like the mermaids, could raise storms to shatter ships. A storm could also shatter the timbers of an old beach cottage.

The cut on her hand throbbed; her ankle ached, but she paced. She picked up the phone to call Michael, but the phone was dead. No doubt the lines were down on the highway. And if she had been able to get through, what could she have told him? That she feared for her life in a storm that the silkies had raised.

So she paced, reminding herself that the seal people were a gentle folk—not like the mermaids, not like the kelpie. She had done nothing to harm the silkies, really.

At midnight, the wind lessened and the rain eased to a gentle rhythm. As Kate lay in bed, trying to ignore the twin pains in her ankle and hand, she heard a sea lion barking from the rocks below the cliffs. It sounded much closer.

She slept uneasily and woke shivering when the wind chimes rang lightly. The rain had stopped and the sea fog had crept up the cliff to wrap itself around the cottage. She had dreamed again, though the memory of the dream was not clear. She remembered an overpowering loneliness, a fierce yearning, a hunger for something unattainable.

Kate hugged the blanket closer around her, but the chill of the fog had seeped into the cottage and into her bones. Reluctantly, she left her bed to get another blanket, crossing the cold kitchen floor to the linen cupboard and pulling a quilted comforter from the stack on the shelf.

The wind chimes jingled again, and Kate thought she heard another sound—a long sigh that could have been the wind. But it did not sound quite like the wind. The floorboards creaked beneath her as she stepped toward the door. She hesitated with her hand on the doorknob.

What did she fear, she wondered. Her mind formed an image in answer: she feared a slender manshape, standing on the porch with the fog swirling around his waist and hiding his webbed feet. The fingers of the hand that she imagined to be resting on the porch rail were joined by a thin skin. From his other hand, her pendant dangled. He smelled of the sea and a strand of eel grass clung to his shoulder. When she reached out to take the pendant, she touched his hand. It was cold—as cold as the sea.

Kate stopped with her hand on the doorknob, only half-aware that she was listening for the sound of breathing. Then she twisted the knob and jerked the door open.

Shadows of the fenceposts shifted and moved in the moonlight and drifting fog. The posts teetered this way and that, barely supporting the single strand of rusty wire that was all that remained of the fence. Nothing to hold back the sea.

The porch was empty. No webbed hand rested on the porch rail, but at the spot where she had imagined his hand lay a circle of white. With fingers that were suddenly as cold as the fog, she picked up the pendant by the chain and held it in her bandaged hand. The breeze stirred the mist and the wind chimes jingled faintly. She backed away, retreating into the kitchen, and from the doorway, she noticed a single strand of eel grass trailing across the top step. She locked the door behind her.

She did not sleep after that. With the kitchen lights blazing, she wrapped herself in the comforter and made hot chocolate. She worked on her paper and tried to ignore the ringing of the wind chimes and the crash of the waves.

In the light of dawn, with a cup of coffee in her hand, she opened the door and peered out onto the porch. The strand of eel grass still lay on the top step, and she told herself that it must have fallen from her boot when she staggered into the cottage. Just as she must have put the pendant on the railing when she broke the chain rather than stuffing it into her pocket.

She called Michael from a pay phone at a gas station, saying only that she had twisted her ankle and was coming to town to see a doctor. She arranged to meet him for dinner.

In the restaurant that evening, the traffic noises ebbed and surged like the sound of the waves. The sound distracted Kate and disrupted her thoughts as she told Michael of the storm. She did not mention her vision of the silkie, but talked of mud slides and her feeling that the cottage could collapse into the sea. Even so, she felt like a fool. In the warm café that smelled of coffee and pastry, the crashing terror of the storm seemed far away.

He gently took her bandaged hand in his hand. "Something really has you worried, doesn't it?" he asked.

She shrugged. "The ocean gets to me when I'm out at the cottage, that's all," she said. "The fog and the waves and the sea lions barking..." And the madness that lingers at the ocean's edge, she thought.

"I told you it was a lonely spot," he said.

"Not lonely so much as..." She hesitated. "I never feel quite alone anymore. And I get to imagining things. The other night, I thought I saw a light, dancing on the waves just beyond the breakers. I don't know; I guess my eyes were just playing tricks."

Michael grinned and stroked her hand. "Don't worry about your eyes," he said. "You probably did see a light. Have you ever heard of bioluminescence? There are microorganisms that glow..."

Michael explained it all—talking about red tides and marine chemistry. Kate let the reassuring words wash over her. Michael never had time for the vague, ill-defined feelings that plagued her. She listened to him, and when he was done, she managed a smile.

"You've been working on that project much too hard," he said. "Why don't you just stay in town tonight and spend the night with me?"

She stared at her coffee in silence.

"Don't be afraid to come back to me," he said softly. "You can if you want to."

She did not know what she wanted. "I have to go back tonight," she said. "I have work to do."

"Why tonight?" he asked. "Why not wait until tomorrow?"

The answer came to her mind, but she did not voice it: the moon would be full that night.

She freed her hand from Michael's grasp and held her coffee cup between her palms. "I have work to do," she repeated.

She drove back that night, speeding around the curves in the twisting road that led from Santa Cruz to her little patch of nowhere. The old Beatles song on the tape deck drowned out the whisper of the waves: "I'd like to be under the sea in an octopus's garden with you."

The full moon hung in the sky over the cottage as she rolled up the drive. She turned her key. The music stopped. And the crash of the surf filled the car.

Kate walked to the edge of the cliff. Below her, the sea shimmered in the moonlight, the swells rising and falling in a rhythm as steady as breathing. She felt eyes watching her from the ocean below.

She slipped three times as she descended the path. The third time she caught herself with her wounded hand and the cut flared with a bright new pain. Her ankle throbbed but she continued to pick her way down the slope.

The waves had not yet reached the bottom of the path. The tiny beach was a silver thread in the moonlight, extending away in either direction in a shimmering line. She stood on the silver strand and gazed out to sea.

A light danced on the wave. Loneliness swept over her as a wave swept over the sand, touching the toes of her boots with foam. Involuntarily, she took a step to follow the retreating water. The next wave lapped around her ankles and a fierce pain touched her wounded hand so that she longed to sooth it by touching it to the cold water. Somewhere in the back of her mind, she heard the echo of a voice saying: "Blood calls to blood." She took another step forward and the water lapped at her knees, dragging on the legs of her jeans.

The light danced—out of reach. The water was cold against her ankle. It eased the pain. The water could ease the stinging in her hand. If only she waded out farther.

With her bandaged hand, she gripped the pendant that hung around her neck. Michael would not believe that there was a watcher in the water. But the light was there. And the loneliness was with her. She watched the dancing light and thought about the glowing microorganisms that Michael had described. The water tugged at her legs.

"No," she said softly to the water and the light. Then louder, "No." The water tugged at her, urging, insisting. "No."

She could feel eyes on her as she trudged up the path.

Turning her back on wonder. No, turning her back on cold gray waters that would beat her against the rocks.

There was no storm that night. But she heard the sound of the waves against the cliffs—calling, calling. She slept uneasily and she dreamed of a lover: a salt-sea lover with hands like ice and the face of a prince. Between his fingers, webbing stretched; his teeth were pointed; he carried with him the scent of the sea. He loved her with a steady rocking as rhythmic as the sea, and he held her when she cried out—was it in pleasure or pain?—at the chill of his touch. She stroked his dark hair, sleek as the fur of a seal. He came to her for comfort, this silent lover whose kisses tasted of salt. He came to her to make a truce.

She woke to the scent of the sea and the sound of a gentle thumping. Half-awake, she fumbled uselessly for the pendant at her neck. It was not there, though she could not remember taking it off the night before. She left her bed, wrapping the quilt around her and stepping into the kitchen.

The door to the porch swung wide open, moving slightly in the breeze and bumping gently against the kitchen wall. She picked up her pendant from where it lay on the porch railing. She did not put it on. She did not need it. No fear was left in her.

The single wire of the old fence was strung with drops of dew, one drop on each rusty barb. The old fence should come down, she thought. It served no purpose anymore.

The waves washed against the base of the cliff; the ocean moved in its endless rhythm. Drops of her blood ebbed and surged with those waters. And the strength of the sea surged in her.

Far away, a sea lion barked. And the bright sunlight of early morning glinted on the two strands of eel grass that lay across the steps.

His Vegetable Wife

Fynn planted her with the tomatoes in the greenhouse on the first day of spring. The instructions on the package were similar to the instructions on any seed envelope. Vegetable Wife: prefers sandy soil, sunny conditions. Plant two inches deep after all danger of frost has passed. When seedling is two feet tall, transplant. Water frequently.

A week later, a fragile seedling sprouted in the plastic basin beside the tomatoes: two strong shoots that grew straight with little branching. The seedling grew quickly and when the shoots were two feet tall, Fynn transplanted the seedling to a sunny spot near the entrance to his living dome, where he would pass it on his way to the fields each day.

After transplanting the seedling, he stood beneath the green sky and surveyed his empire: a hastily assembled prefabricated living dome that marked the center of his homestead; a greenhouse built of Plexiglas slabs, tilted to catch the sun; and the fields, four fertile acres that he had tilled and planted himself. Most of the farm's tilled area was given over to cash crop: he was growing cimmeg, a plant that bore seeds valued for their flavor and medicinal properties. Row after row of dark green seedlings raised their pointed leaves to the pale sky.

Beyond the fields grew the tall grasses native to the planet, a vast expanse of swaying stalks. When the wind blew, the stalks shifted and moved and the grasses hissed. The soft sound of the wind in the grasses irritated Fynn; he thought it sounded like people whispering secrets. He had enjoyed hacking down the grass that had surrounded the living dome, churning its roots beneath the mechanical tiller, planting the straight rows of cimmeg.

Fynn was a square-jawed man with coarse brown hair and stubby, unimaginative fingers. He was a methodical man. He liked living alone, but he thought that a man should have a wife. He had chosen the seed carefully, selecting a hardy stock, bypassing the more delicate Vegetable Maiden and Vegetable Bride, selecting a variety noted for its ability to thrive under any conditions.

The seedling grew quickly. The two shoots met and joined, forming a thicker trunk. By the time the cimmeg was knee high, the Wife had reached the height of his shoulders, a pale green plant with broad soft leaves and a trunk covered with downy hairs. The sun rose earlier each morning, the cimmeg grew to waist high, filling the air with an exotic spicy scent, and the Vegetable Wife's stem thickened and darkened to olive green. The curves of her body began to emerge: swelling hips pinching in to form a thin waist; rounded breasts covered with fine pale down; a willowy neck supporting the rounded knob that would become her head. Each morning, Fynn checked the dampness of the soil around the seedling and peered through the leaves at the ripening trunk.

In late spring, he first saw her pubic hair, a dark triangle just above where the twin trunks joined to form her body. Hesitantly, he parted the leaves and reached into the dimness to stroke the new growth. The smell of her excited him: rich and earthy and warm, like the smell of the greenhouse. The wood was warm beneath the hair and it yielded slightly to his touch. He moved closer, moving his hands up to cup the breasts, running his thumbs over the unevenness that promised to become nipples. The rustle of the wind in her leaves made him look up.

She was watching him: dark eyes, a suggestion of a nose, a mouth that was little more than a slit, lips barely parted.

He backed away hastily, noticing only then that he had broken the stalks of several leaves when he stepped in to fondle the trunk. He touched the broken leaves guiltily, then reminded himself that she was only a plant, she felt no pain. Still he watered the Wife generously that day, and when he went to work in the cimmeg fields, he hummed to himself so that he would not hear the grasses whispering.

The instructions had said that she would ripen at two months. Each morning, he checked on her progress, parting the leaves to admire the curves of her body, the willowy stalk of her neck, the fine bright gleam of her eyes. She had a full body and a softly rounded face. Though her eyes were open, her expression was that of a sleepwalker, an innocent young girl who wanders in the darkness unaware.

The expression excited him as much as her body, and sometimes he could not resist pushing close to her, running his hands along the gentle curve of her buttocks and back, stroking the fine dark hair that topped her head, still short like a little boy's hair, but growing, maturing like the rest of her.

It was late spring when he first felt her move under his touch. His hand was on her breast, and he felt her body shift as if she were trying to pull away. "Ah," he said with anticipation, "it won't be long." Her hand, which had formed recently from a thickened stalk, fluttered in the wind as if to push him away. He smiled as she swayed in a puff of wind and her leaves rustled.

That afternoon, he brought a thick rope, looped it around her ankle, and knotted it carefully in place. Smiling at her angelic face, framed in dark hair, he spoke softly. "Can't have you running off. Not now that you're almost ripe." He tied the other end of the rope firmly to the frame of the dome, and after that he checked on her three times each day, rather than just once.

He cleaned the inside of the dome for the first time in months, washing the blankets of his bachelor bed, opening the windows to banish the mustiness. He could look out the open window and see her swaying in the breeze. Sometimes, she seemed to be struggling against the rope, and when she did that he checked the knots to make sure they were secure.

The cimmeg grew tall, its sharp glossy leaves catching the sunlight and glittering like obsidian blades. Her leaves withered and fell away, leaving her naked olive green body exposed to the sun and to his gaze. He watched her carefully, returning from the fields several times each afternoon to check the knots.

He woke one morning to find her crouched at the end of her tether, pulling at the knot with soft fingers that bled pale sap where the coarse rope had cut her. "Now, now," he said, "leave that alone." He squatted beside her in the dust and put his hand on her sun-warmed shoulder, thinking to reassure her. She turned her head toward him slowly, majestically, with the stately grace of a flower turning to face the sun. Her face was blank; her eyes, expressionless. When he tried to embrace her, she did not respond except to push at his shoulders weakly with her hands.

Excitement washed over him, and he pushed her back on the hard ground, his mouth seeking her breast where the rough nipple tasted like vanilla, his hand parting her legs to open the mysteries of that dark downy triangle of hair.

When he was done, she was crying softly, a high faint sound like the singing of the small birds that nested in the tall grass. The sound woke compassion in him. He rolled off her and buttoned his pants, wishing that he could have been less hasty.

She lay in the dust, her dark hair falling to hide her face. She was silent, and he could hear the wind in her hair, like the wind in the tall grass.

"Come now," he said, torn between sympathy and annoyance. "You are my Wife. It can't be that bad."

She did not look at him.

He cupped her chin in one hand and tilted her head so that he could see her expression. Her face was serene, expressionless, blank. He patted her shoulder, reassured by her expression. He knew she felt no pain; the instructions had said so.

He untied the rope from the frame of the dome and brought her inside. By the window, he set a basin of water for her. He secured the rope to the leg of the bed, leaving the tether long enough so that she could stand in the window or the doorway and watch him work in the fields.

She was not quite what he expected in a wife. She did not understand language. She did not speak language. She paid little attention to him unless he forced her to look at him, to see him. He tried being pleasant to her—bringing her flowers from the fields and refilling her basin with cool clean water. She took no notice. Day and night, she stood in the window, her feet in the basin of water. According to the instructions, she took her nourishment from the sun and the air and the water that she absorbed through pores in her skin.

She seemed to react only to violence, to immediate threats. When he made love to her, she struggled to escape, and sometimes she cried, a wordless sound like the babble of the irrigation water flowing in a ditch. After a time, her crying came to excite him—any response was better than no response.

She would not sleep with him. If he dragged her to bed, she would struggle free in the night, and when he woke she was always at the window, gazing out at the world.

He beat her one afternoon, when he returned from the fields and caught her sawing at the rope with a kitchen knife. He struck her on the back and shoulders with his belt. Her cries and the sight of the pale sap excited him and he made love to her afterward. The rough blankets of his bed were sticky with her sap and his sperm.

He kept her as a man keeps a Vegetable Wife, as a man keeps a wild thing that he has taken into his home. Sometimes, he sat in the dome and watched darkness creep over his homestead as he listened to the wind in the grasses. He watched his Vegetable Wife and brooded about all the women who had ever left him. It was a long list, starting with his mother, who had given him up for adoption.

One day, a government agent came in a copter to inspect the cimmeg fields. Fynn did not like the man. Though Fynn directed his attention to the cimmeg, the government agent kept glancing toward the dome. The Wife stood in the window, her naked skin glistening in the sun, smooth and clear and inviting. "You have good taste," said the agent, a young man dressed in khaki and leather. "Your Wife is beautiful."

Fynn kept his temper with an effort.

"They're quite sensitive, I hear," said the young man.

Fynn shrugged.

The apple tree that he had planted near the dome entrance bore fruit: a basketful of small hard green apples. Fynn had crushed them into a mash and fermented a kind of applejack, a potent liquor smelling of rotten apples. Late in the afternoon after the agent had left, he sat beneath the apple tree and drank until he could barely stand. Then he went to his Wife and dragged her away from the window.

Fynn whipped his Wife for flaunting her nakedness. He called her a tramp, a whore, a filthy prostitute. Though the sap flowed from the welts on her back, her eyes were dry. She did not fight back, and her passivity inflamed him. "Goddamn you!" he cried, striking her repeatedly. "Goddamn you."

He grew tired and his blows grew softer, but his fury was not abated. She turned on the bed to face him, and his hands found her throat. He pressed on her soft skin, thinking somehow, in the confusion of drunkenness, that strangling her would somehow stop the whispers that he heard, the secrets that were everywhere.

She watched him, impassive. Because she absorbed air through the skin, the pressure at her throat did not disturb her. Nevertheless, she lifted her hands and put them to his throat, applying slow steady pressure. He struggled drunkenly, but she clung to him until his struggles stopped.

He was quiet at last, quiet like a plant, quiet like a tree, like the grasses outside. She groped in his pocket and found a jackknife. With it, she cut away the rope that bound her. The skin of her ankle was scarred and hardened where the rope had rubbed her.

She stood in the window, waiting for the sun. When it warmed the earth, she would plant the man, as she had seen him plant seeds. She would stand with her ankles in the mud and the wind in her hair and she would see what grew.

Good-Bye, Cynthia

The closet is filled with boxes and the boxes are filled with things that I have almost forgotten. Two chunks of clear acrylic, molded to imitate quartz pebbles—my sister and I had stolen them from the bases that supported the "Cars of the Future" display at the 1965 New York World's Fair. Two troll dolls, still dressed in the tunics that my sister and I had sewn for them. Two aluminum medallions from the county fair engraved with our names: the inscription on the heart says Janet; the inscription on the four-leafed clover, Cynthia. Two charm bracelets that Aunt Mary brought us from Hawaii: the letters that dangle from mine spell out ALOHA; Cynthia's says HAWAII.

My mother comes up behind me and peers over my shoulder. "Oh," she says. "Your charm bracelets. How pretty. I'd almost forgotten them."

It is very convenient that the pronoun "you" is both singular and plural. Five years after Cynthia went away, my mother stopped mentioning her name or acknowledging that I had once had a sister. One day I came home from school to find that my mother had bought a new coverlet and bolsters for the twin bed that had been Cynthia's, converting it into a day bed that served as a couch. She had taken Cynthia's picture from the mantel and removed Cynthia's books from the bedroom shelves. Each year, on the frame of the kitchen door, Cynthia and I had marked off our heights in pencil; my mother had erased Cynthia's share of the marks. My mother had erased Cynthia.

I close my hand around the charm bracelets to hide

116

them from my mother's view, but she has forgotten them already. My mother tried hard to forget.

"I'd like you to sweep the dead leaves from the garage roof," she says. "If you sweep them off the roof, I can rake them up from the lawn."

I tuck the bracelets back into the shoe box, hiding them away. Unlike my mother, I don't want to forget.

When I was in first grade and Cynthia was in third grade, she told me stories about the lady from outer space. "She comes from planet X," Cynthia would say. "And she flies in a spaceship."

Cynthia knew constellations and stars on a first-name basis. In the summer sky, she could find all the constellations: Cassiopeia, Scorpio, Draco, Sagittarius, and many more with names that seemed so exotic. She pointed out stars: Antares, the reddish heart of Scorpio; Polaris, the North Star. She knew where and when to look for falling stars and satellites. And she knew all about alien spaceships.

She had learned about the constellations and planets from the leader of her Girl Scout troop. Her information about spaceships had come from less reputable sources—the tabloid newspapers that my mother brought home from the supermarket, science fiction books from the library, and late-night TV movies. But the sources didn't matter; Cynthia believed in the space lady and I believed in Cynthia.

Whenever our parents argued, Cynthia told me stories about spaceships. Our parents' angry voices drifted up the stairs, like poisonous gas that filled the house and made breathing difficult. My mother's voice was high, with an edge like broken glass; my father's voice was a low intermittent roar, like a truck gunning its engine.

I don't remember what they were fighting about. Money, most likely. They always fought about money: money to fix the washing machine, money to pay for swimming lessons at the YMCA, money for new clothes, money for braces that Cynthia didn't want. Always money.

Cynthia spoke quickly, breathlessly, drowning out the voices. "Up on the moon, where the space lady lives, they don't have any money. Instead of money, they have rocks.

And whenever anyone needs more rocks, they just go outside and get some. So everyone always has plenty."

"Where do they live?" I asked.

"In caves," she said.

"I wouldn't want to live in a cave."

"These are moon caves," she said. "Not like earth caves at all. They grow lots of plants to give off oxygen and there are flowers everywhere."

Sometimes, I dreamed of the space lady and her flower-filled caverns on the moon. In my dreams, her face was very much like my mother's face. She wore a long green dress covered with glittering sequins. Cynthia said that the space lady was coming to take us away to another planet. I wished that she would hurry.

My mother is cleaning the house before putting it up for sale. Ever since she and my father got divorced, I've been telling her that this house is just too big for one person. Finally, she has agreed that it is time to sell. I drove out from the city to help her, and for the past three days, I've been weeding the garden and mowing the lawn, fixing the back fence and knocking cobwebs from the rafters in the garage. The house looks better than it has in years.

I climb the ladder to the garage roof. The willow that grows beside the house has littered the wooden shingles with leaves and fallen branches. As I sweep the debris into the rain gutter, the wooden shingles creak and snap underfoot. "Now don't fall," my mother calls from below. The window of my old bedroom lets out onto the garage roof. I peer in through the dirty glass and see my old bed, the open closet.

On warm summer nights, Cynthia and I used to slide the window open and slip silently out onto the splintery shingles. We would lie on the roof and watch the stars.

I remember watching a meteor shower one night in August. We counted twenty-eight shooting stars, each one worth a wish. Each time a bright streak crossed the sky, I wished for a pony, but I didn't think I would really get one.

Cynthia told me that the falling stars weren't really stars at all. Each falling star was a rock falling down to earth and burning up in the atmosphere as it fell. "Except for some of them," she said. "Some of them are spaceships bringing people from other planets down to earth."

"There." I pointed out a meteor that left an especially brilliant trail. "I bet that one's a spaceship."

"Maybe," she said. "You might be right." We watched as a few more meteors left trails across the sky. "They can't land right here," she told me. "Too many people. They don't like landing where people can see them."

Cynthia claimed that the only way to get the space lady to land was to signal to her with a flashlight from the top of a big hill. Our house was on the edge of a development. Just behind us was a big hill where range cattle still grazed. Cynthia thought that this hill would be perfect for the space lady's landing. "You can come with me when I go to signal her," she told me graciously.

As I sweep away the leaves and debris, I can look from the garage roof and see the big hill. It is still free of houses: in an area prone to mud slides, the land was considered too steep for construction. The hillside looks a little mangy; new growth, watered by the early autumn rains, sprouts in irregular patches among last year's golden brown grass. Near the hilltop, a cluster of coast live oak trees provides a spot of shade. On the steepest slopes, I can see dusty brown streaks where bicycle-riding kids have worn trails through the vegetation.

I clean the rain gutters, dragging out matted tangles of leaves and branches. "That's great," my mother says as I finish the job. "Just great." She looks weary and a little frazzled, an expression that has become habitual over the years. She has always been an active woman, but now her energy seems somehow unhealthy, almost feverish, as if she continues to work only because her body will not allow her to rest. She holds the ladder steady as I climb down from the roof, and I notice her hand on the metal. Just below the skin, thick blue veins snake across the back of her hand. The skin is wrinkled and spotted. She has grown old, and her body betrays her.

"I need your help moving some things in the garage," she says. "I want to get out one of the steamer trunks so I can pack the linens inside it."

The trunk is nearly hidden beneath cardboard boxes, stacks of yellowing newspapers, paper bags filled with rags and scraps of cloth. With great effort, I move the boxes and extract the trunk, a heavy black chest large enough to hold a body or two.

"I'll clean it out later," my mother says, but as I stand there, she lifts the lid and pokes idly through the contents: old papers, books, clothing that's long since out of fashion. "Here," she says, pulling out a large book bound in dark green fabric. "You should take that to your father. It's his college yearbook."

I accept the yearbook reluctantly. I saw my father rarely, and I'm not eager to drag this book around until the next time we get together for dinner. "Why don't you mail it to him?"

"I'm not mailing it," my mother says irritably. "I want nothing to do with him."

"All right, all right." They started divorce proceedings the year after I graduated from college. They had stayed together for the sake of the children, but it had never been a good marriage. In all my memories, I can't find a single moment of spontaneous affection between my mother and father: I can't remember a casual hug, a kiss, a joke. I remember only arguments: about money, about my father's drinking, about where to go on vacation, and then, while on vacation, about where to stay and what road to take. My father always drove and he would never stop to ask directions. Yet somehow, it would always be my mother's fault when we got lost. Little things—they argued incessantly about little things.

The arguments finally drove Cynthia out. That summer, we kept talking about going to the hill to signal for the space lady, but we always put it off. First, Cynthia wanted to wait until after her Girl Scout troop went for their overnight camping trip. Then I insisted we wait until after the Fourth of July, so we could watch the fireworks. Then we waited until the neighbor's cat had her kittens—I didn't want to miss that.

As the summer wore on, I found one excuse after another. I was hoping that we might make it to the beginning of school without having had a chance to climb the hill in the night. I didn't want to admit to Cynthia that I was scared: afraid of the dark, afraid of the teenage boys who rode their old bicycles around the hill all day and smoked cigarettes in the shelter of the oaks, afraid of the cows that grazed in the dying grass, afraid of the space lady herself. I hoped that autumn would come early and the weather would turn cold and wet. Even Cynthia would not insist on climbing the hill in the mud and the rain.

But one week before the first day of school, my parents had a fight that lasted for hours. We could not make out the words for the most part, but sometimes a phrase would penetrate the walls of our bedroom.

"You'll wake the children." My mother's voice, high and anxious.

"Damn the children." My father, a subterranean rumbling, blurred by drink.

More words, lost in the distance. My father was saying something about how stupid and impossible my mother was. My mother, desperate and shrill, was defending herself. I hid my head beneath the covers, but I could still hear their voices. I covered my ears, but even when I could not hear, I could feel the tension in the air. An invisible wire connected me to my parents. The wire carried messages, like the blurred voices that traveled along the string of a tin-can telephone. The sense was lost, but the feeling was conveyed: pain, anger, frustration, and fear. They weren't arguing about money; they were arguing about broken promises. The messages came through the floor, through the walls, and I could not escape.

Finally, I heard my father leave the house, start the car, and drive away. For now, the argument had ceased, but I knew that it wasn't really over. It did not end—it never ended. The anger was hidden beneath the ashes, ready to flare again when someone stirred the fire.

I heard my mother come upstairs. Quietly, she opened the door to our room. Both Cynthia and I pretended to be asleep, breathing softly and evenly, our eyes lightly closed. Through my eyelids, I could see the light from the open door, see my mother's shadow cross the room. She leaned over my bed and tucked the blanket under my chin. Then I heard her footsteps move away, heard the door close.

Several minutes later, Cynthia whispered to me. "Janet?"

I thought about pretending to be asleep, but decided that I wouldn't be able to fool Cynthia. "What?"

"I'm going up the hill tonight. You coming?"

"I can't," I said. "Don't go."

She didn't reply. I heard her getting dressed. The beam of her Girl Scout flashlight flickered across the walls as she searched for her sneakers. I wished that she would say something, but Cynthia wasn't about to dare me to do something I didn't want to do. She didn't call me chicken or tell me that I was stupid. "I wish you wouldn't go," I whispered.

"I've got to." She stood beside my bed, dressed in jeans and a T-shirt. She carried her sneakers in one hand and her flashlight in the other. "Good-bye," she said. "I'll say hello to the space lady for you. Promise you won't tell them where I've gone."

"I promise," I said. And she slipped out the door.

I imagined her walking down the stairway, stepping on the edge of each tread so that the boards wouldn't creak. As quietly as I could, I opened the bedroom window and climbed out on the garage roof. It was scary going out on the roof alone, but I wanted to wave to Cynthia. From the end of the driveway, she waved back.

I watched the sky for a while, waiting to see the spaceship land. I guess I must have fallen asleep. When I opened my eyes, the moon was down and I was soaked with dew. I crawled back inside, into my own bed.

In the morning, Cynthia did not come back. When my mother asked me where Cynthia was, I said I didn't know. I said she must have left while I was asleep. My mother called the police and they searched for her. There were pictures of Cynthia in the newspapers and flyers posted in the windows of the supermarket: Have you see this child? Missing: Cynthia Jacobs, Age 9. The flyers showed a solemn-eyed little girl in a Girl Scout uniform, staring steadily into the camera.

My parents did not fight as loudly after that, but the tension between them grew stronger. I felt it, and their silence did not fool me. I understood why Cynthia had gone. During dinner, my mother would talk to me and my father would talk to me, but they would never talk to each other. I felt torn and confused and I wished that I had gone with Cynthia.

My mother and I finish cleaning the garage and I spend some time going through the boxes in my closet, sorting my old possessions into three piles: one for the garbage, one for the Salvation Army, and the smallest one to take with me. It is late when my mother and I sit down to a dinner of hastily prepared hamburgers. We don't talk much over the meal; I don't have much to say to my family. So much was always left unspoken. But somehow, this night, I feel there are things that I must tell her.

"You know, looking through all that stuff in the closet reminded me of Cynthia," I say.

My mother gets a wary look, haunted around the eyes. She has pushed the memory of Cynthia away. She does not want to hear this, but I have to tell her. "I think that wherever Cynthia is now, she's happy," I say. "I really do." I don't tell her that I can still feel a connection with Cynthia; a tenuous thread binds us together. I know Cynthia is happy. I would feel it if she were sad.

Though my mother urges me to spend the night, I leave that evening. I tell her that I have things to do in the city and that I like to drive at night. Both excuses happen to be true. I take a box filled with souvenirs from the closet and I wave good-bye to my mother as I drive away.

A few blocks from the house, on a cul-de-sac where there are few streetlights, I park my car. A dog barks in a nearby house, and then falls silent. Crickets chirp in the grass and I can hear the rhythmic hiss of a lawn sprinkler in the distance. The air smells of wet grass, the aroma of the suburbs. From the car, I take a flashlight and a shoe box filled with things from the closet.

Climbing the hill is easier now than it was when I was a child. My flashlight beam picks out urban detritus on the grassy slope: a broken plastic water pistol, discarded in the weeds; a red reflector, fallen from someone's bicycle; a crumpled cigarette pack.

At the crest of the hill is a flat granite stone. I sit on the stone and unpack the box. One acrylic pebble, stolen from the World's Fair and more valuable because of the dishonesty required for its acquisition. One charm bracelet that says HAWAII. A medallion in the shape of a four-leafed clover. A troll doll with orange hair and green glass eyes, dressed in a clumsily stitched felt tunic. I place these things on the rock and lie down beside them, looking up at the stars.

I can pick out a few constellations: Scorpio, the Big Dipper, Draco. Staring at the stars and the sliver of a moon, I drowse off and dream of the shooting stars that fell when I was a child. Each one was so bright and magical; each one, a visitor from another world. One is brighter than the rest: it slashes across the darkness, leaving a blue-white streak that lingers in my eyes and makes me blink. When I open my eyes, my sister is with me.

Cynthia is wearing jeans and a T-shirt, and she is still just a kid. "You're the same age you were when you left," I say.

She explains that the space lady's ship travels faster than light. Cynthia has been all over the galaxy and yet she is still just a little over ten years old. She has remained still while the rest of us moved on, frozen in time like an insect in amber.

"I brought some things for you," I say. "I found them in the closet back home."

She smiles at the collection on the stone beside me, then picks up the acrylic pebble and rolls it from hand to hand. "Moon rocks," she said. "That's what I thought these were. I know better now." She set it back down on the stone. "You keep them. I don't need this stuff where I am. Keep it for me."

"Where have you been?" I ask her, and she tells me about the caverns on the moon, about colonies on other planets, about distant stars. She says that she named a constellation after me, but it's only visible from a planet orbiting Vega.

She says that I can come with her when she goes, but she says it sadly, as if she knows my answer before I speak.

"Mom thinks you're dead," I tell her, and she nods. "I can't go," I say. "But I'm glad you're happy. I'm really glad."

We sit together for a while. I put my arm around her shoulders and she seems so small and thin. My big sister Cynthia, just a little kid now.

I wake just before sunrise. My back is stiff from lying on the rock; my clothes are wet with dew. I gather up the bracelet, the pebble, the medallion, and the troll doll, and I put them back in the shoe box. I walk down the hill and the light of the rising sun brings tears to my eyes.

Prescience

Katherine knew the future: she read it in the tarot cards, in the lines on a person's palm, in tea leaves, in horoscopes, in the way a man sat in a chair, in the way a woman placed her money on the counter when she paid for the fortune. She kept a dream journal, and her dreams, all too often, came true.

Though her predictions were accurate, her customers were usually dissatisfied. The futures that Katherine saw were never happy. In calm and measured tones, she told them of coming disasters: broken marriages, lost jobs, spoiled vacations, disappointments in love. People rarely returned for a second reading.

It was just after noon, and Katherine sat on a high stool at the counter of the occult store where she worked. The shelves behind her were filled with the paraphernalia of magic: vials of graveyard dust, bottles of holy water, canisters filled with mandrake root, powdered bone, and incense. Her boss had gone out to lunch and she was eating a container of low-fat yogurt.

The string of bells that hung on the doorknob jingled and a man walked into the store. She glanced at him, then returned to her yogurt. Generally, the customers did not wish to be observed too closely. This one prowled among the bookshelves for a time, then finally approached the counter.

"Hello," he said. "I'd like to have my fortune read."

She looked up and met his eyes. Of course, she remembered his face. Last night, she had dreamed exactly this: he came into the shop, she read his palm, and then he asked her out for coffee.

"Can't be done," she said briskly. "Our fortune-teller's gone. She ran off with the carnival."

"Don't you read palms?"

"Nope. Sorry. Can't help you."

He didn't look like a bad sort. But already, she knew too much about him. By the way he held his shoulders and the tilt of his head, she knew he was lonely and a little nervous about being in the shop. He had nice eyes: dark and a little wistful. But she knew better and she refused to be drawn in. She didn't need to see the lines on his palm to know that he was trouble. She could see the clouds and predict the coming storm. Going out with him would be a disaster.

"Sorry," she said again. "It's really too bad."

She looked down at her yogurt, not wanting to know any more. "Awfully sorry," she said, and kept her eyes down until she heard the bells jingle and knew that he was gone.

After lunch, she had a cup of jasmine tea. When she placed the cup in the sink to wash it, she thoughtlessly glanced in the bottom, where the loose tea leaves had accumulated. His face was there, plain enough for anyone who knew how to see it.

Her boss was a toad of a man, a squat Hungarian who burned incense to gain power over women. He read palms, and whenever he could, he grabbed Katherine's hand and examined the lines of her palm. His hands were sweaty and he always held on a little too long.

"You're afraid," he said. "Your heart and your life lines cross—a sign of uncertainty." She peered unwillingly into her own palm. It seemed to her that there were more lines each day, crisscrossing her palm like bird tracks in the sand. The lines made her nervous: too many decisions, too many choices, too many fates. "I think you are afraid of men," he said.

She snatched her hand away and went to tidy the canisters of herbs. She saw him staring at her from across the shop, but she ignored him. He was harmless enough. She never saw him in her dreams.

*   *   *

Two in the morning: she woke up and scrambled for the light, for a pen, for her dream journal. It was important to note the details quickly, before they blurred and lost their definition. She wrote, "A coffee shop on Haight Street. The dark-haired man across the table takes my hand and asks me something. I can't hear him because the pounding of my heart is too loud. I am terrified, overcome by panic."

She hesitated, groping for more details. With details, she can protect herself.

"I am wearing my favorite silver bracelet and a peasant blouse. There's a cup of coffee on the table in front of me. He strokes my hand gently; I like his touch on my skin."

She scratched out the last line and got out of bed long enough to put her peasant blouse on the floor beside the door. The next day, she would give it to the Salvation Army. The bracelet, she would send to her sister in Texas as a present.

Even so, she lay awake for a long time before she could sleep again.

Katherine peered at the lines on her customer's palm. This woman had beautiful hands, with well-manicured nails. Compared to Katherine's, her palm was wonderfully clear: the lines were beautifully defined, expressways with highway markers and street signs to tell the way. On Katherine's palm, the lines resembled the trails left by rabbits in a meadow: faint tracks where the grass was beaten down, crossing and recrossing one another in nonsensical fashion.

Katherine followed the woman's love line and said that she would soon fall in love. The woman smiled, but Katherine tried to talk her out of it.

"I hate being in love," Katherine said. "It's like some kind of disease. It grabs you and turns your mind to jelly. Love always makes me stupid. Frankly, if I were you, I'd try to get out of it."

Katherine caught her boss watching her from the other side of the shop. He was frowning.

The woman blinked at Katherine, startled by her vehemence.

"Your heart line is strong," Katherine said, returning to the reading and dispensing with further editorial comment.

After work, she walked down Haight Street, heading up to the post office to mail the bracelet to her sister. She hated to give the bracelet up, but she knew better than to play games with fate.

As she walked past a coffee shop, she saw the man inside. He sat alone at a table, drinking coffee and reading the paper. Her eye registered the details that she did not want to know. From the way he held his coffee cup, she knew that he was protective and a little possessive. The angle of his newspaper revealed that he was shy, but he covered that up with outward show of sociability. He was slow to express his emotions. He was uncomfortable in his body.

She hurried past, carrying her small package as if it held a bomb.

Because she knew the future, she often started saying good-bye before she said hello. In the blank hours before she fell asleep, she rehearsed farewell speeches. She was very skilled at saying good-bye. She could toss it off as if it didn't really matter: "It's been nice." "So long." "See you around."

That night, she sent out for Chinese food. It came with two fortune cookies. The first one said: "Nothing ventured, nothing gained." The second said: "Watch your step." She burned both scraps of paper in the incense burner by her bed. The smoke from the fortunes smelled faintly of jasmine.

A dream: the dark-haired man was walking toward her, and she wanted to run away. She turned and ran, but she was running in slow motion, as if she were running through glue. She woke drenched in sweat and wrote the dream down, cursing the lack of detail.

She was working at the counter when her boss grabbed her hand and pried it open.

"You are avoiding something," he said. "But you can't avoid it much longer. The energy has to go somewhere." She was dimly aware that he was stroking her hand and smiling.

"What should I do?" she murmured, half to herself.

He grinned at her as if he had thought she would never ask. "Put yourself in my hands," he said. "I know what to do." His grip on her wrist tightened.

She pulled away and stared him down with glacial eyes.

Whenever she was upset, she walked on the beach, trying to read the messages that the waves painted on the sand. She could not read the waves, and she liked that. People were too easy. They wore their futures on their faces, out where everyone could see. She could not help but read them, whether she wanted to or not.

The sandpipers ran ahead of her, leaving footprints on the sand, but the waves always washed them away, wiping the beach clean again.

She was concentrating on the waves, and she looked up just in time to see him walking toward her. He was looking out to sea, where the sunset was smearing the clouds with color. She turned and ran, but the loose sand slowed her down.

She dreamed: she sat with him on a green park bench and held his hand. He looked at her and said, "I love you," and then he kissed her. And she knew, sure as anything, that he would leave her.

She could not sleep again that night. She sat up and read the tarot cards, thinking of him. In the cards, she found heartbreak, betrayal, and pain.

It is not good to read your own cards, she reminded herself. The accuracy is suspect. She shuffled and read again. Entrapment, confusion, destruction.

Yet again: happiness, contentment, peace. Too many futures.

She shuffled repeatedly and laid the cards out on the table, searching in the brightly colored pictures for patterns in which she could believe.

At dawn, she reluctantly went for a stroll in Golden

Gate Park, where the morning sun was just beginning to burn off the fog.

She found him on a green park bench, feeding popcorn to the pigeons. They flocked around him, running after the kernels that he tossed. Their footprints in the dust made an intricate pattern of crisscrossing lines. It was impossible to tell where the prints left by one bird left off and the prints of another began. She stood for a moment and watched him.

He looked at her—a quick sidelong glance—and then returned to the pigeons before she could meet his eyes. Still, he did not speak.

"What bothers me is the inevitability of it all," she said. "Is my life a paint by numbers? Doesn't knowing the future set me free? Apparently not."

He looked at her, bewildered. "What?"

He didn't look so dangerous, really. A bold pigeon climbed onto his tennis shoe and reached for the popcorn in his hand. He squinted a little because the sun was in his eyes.

"Nice morning," she said, and he nodded.

"About that reading," she said and, against her better judgment, she took his hand. "Don't say it," she told him before he could open his mouth. "Just don't say it."

Then she stole a quick look at her own palm. It seemed that the heart line was a little stronger and that maybe the life line did not cross it at all.

"I still think you'll leave me," she said softly. She looked up and met his eyes. He was confused. She was doing things in the wrong order again. It wasn't time to say good-bye. Not yet.

"All right then," she said. "I'll risk it."

And then, despite it all, she kissed him.

Clay Devils

Dolores dreams of the devil one night. The devil of her dream is one of the many devils who live in the *malpais*, the bad lands outside the village. He is tall with a craggy face and a body covered with coarse dark hair, like the hair of a goat. Dark red horns grow from his head.

He leers at her, and his teeth are long and yellowed, like the teeth in a coyote skull that she once saw in the desert. He reaches for her with his long claws, but she wakes before he can catch her.

Tomas, her husband, and Esperanza, her daughter, are still sleeping when she slips silently from beneath the blanket and pulls on her thin cotton dress. The sun's first pale light is shining between the loosely woven branches that form three walls of the kitchen, a small shelter built on the back of the one-room adobe house. Dolores opens the door to the wooden chicken coop, and the two chickens, skinny birds that never grow fat, ruffle their feathers and peer nervously out the door.

In the hearth, a few coals from last night's fire still glow. She fans them to life and feeds them with tinder, saving the cost of a match. By the time Tomas wakes up, she has ground cornmeal on the grinding stone, cooked tortillas for breakfast, and packed a lunch of tortillas and beans for her husband to take with him to the fields where he will spend the day working.

Tomas uses a gourd bowl to scoop water from the aluminum can that stands just outside the kitchen. He splashes his face, dries it on his shirt, then stands for a moment in the kitchen doorway, gazing out at the hills. A

few drops of water, caught in the hairs on his arm, glisten
in the sunlight like bits of broken glass by the roadside.

"Soon, the American will come," he says without looking
at her.

Dolores, like many of the women in her village, makes
clay toys and whistles that her husband sells to tourist
shops in the city market. One man—an old American—
was particularly pleased with Dolores's work: clever whistles shaped like doves, like owls, like chickens, like dogs
baying at the moon; miniature clay men and women,
dressed like the people of her village. The American had
asked Tomas whether Dolores made other clay figurines,
and Tomas, eager to do business, had said yes, she made
many beautiful figures. The American had arranged with
Tomas to come to their village to see the beautiful things
that Dolores made.

"Yes, says Dolores, putting another tortilla to cook. "In
a few days, I will fire the toys and paint them."

Tomas nods. He is a good-looking young man and
Dolores knows that he wants to do well at business. He
has never been content to work in the field—he complains
that the afternoon sun makes his head hurt and using a
short-handled hoe to knock down weeds makes his back
ache. He wants to wear black store-made pants, rather
than the homemade white trousers that village men wear
when they work in the fields.

Esperanza toddles from her bed to stand by her mother,
and Dolores gives her a warm tortilla to eat.

"Today, I will make many figurines," Dolores says, and
Tomas nods his approval. Soon, he takes his lunch and
goes to the fields to work.

The clay, which Tomas helped Dolores carry from the
river, is wrapped in black plastic to keep it damp. Warmed
by the sun, the clay feels good in her hands. It smells of
the river; aromas of dark secrets and ancient places.
Dolores kneads the clay like dough, squeezing out air
bubbles that would make her pottery burst in the firing.
After kneading the clay smooth, she breaks a handful away
from the rest and begins smoothing it into shape, trying to
think of something to make that will please an American.

Esperanza plays in the dirt and sings to herself, a series of notes without a tune. The chickens scratch in the dusty weeds, searching for insects to eat. On the roof, doves make small mournful sounds, grieving for some long forgotten loss.

The house is on the very edge of the village, and Dolores looks out onto the rolling pine-covered hills of the *malpais*, where devils live. Without thinking, Dolores shapes a little man with a craggy face, deep-set eyes, and horns that curl from his forehead.

When Dolores was a little girl, only a little older than Esperanza is now, her grandfather warned her about the devils in the *malpais*. 'Don't go walking there alone," he said. "Or the devils will take you with them to Hell." Grandfather said that he heard the sounds of a devil snuffling around the house on the night that Pedro, Dolores's favorite brother, died of fever. When Dolores's father got drunk and could not work, grandfather blamed the devils. When Dolores was stung by a scorpion, grandfather knew that the devils were at fault. When she was a little girl, Dolores had feared the devils. She knew that they were responsible for the bad things that happened in the village.

Now, a grown woman, she refuses to be afraid of a clay doll that she can twist in her hands. She gives her toy devil grasping talons and a gaping smile that shows his sharp teeth. She bends his legs so that he is dancing and tilts his head back so that he is laughing. A silly devil, a child's toy.

Dolores puts him in the sun to dry and begins working another handful of clay. She finds herself making another laughing devil. This time, she gives him a guitar to strum with his long sharp claws, so that he may play while his brother dances. Together, they dry in the sun. Another devil, a trumpet player, joins them.

She does not like the look of the three devils, lying on their backs in the sun and laughing, probably at something evil. But she leaves them and hurries to make other figures: a whistle shaped like a frog and one shaped like a dove; a clay burro with its neck outstretched to bray; five clay goats and a man to tend them.

Finally, when the sun is high overhead, she wraps the

rest of the clay in the black plastic, gives Esperanza a tortilla to eat, and begins her other chores: carrying water from the public fountain, gathering firewood from the *malpais*, pulling weeds from her small garden. She puts beans to soak for the evening meal and sweeps the dirt floor of the house with a twig broom.

Just before Tomas comes home, she checks her pottery. The figures are warm to the touch. The afternoon sun is red on the devils, touching the dark clay with light the color of blood. The laughing figure makes her uneasy, but she is not a little girl, to be so easily frightened.

When Tomas comes home, she shows him the figures. He picks up one of the devils—in the afternoon sun, the clay has already stiffened. He examines the figure casually, just as he might examine a whistle or a clay burro. "The American will like these," he predicts. And he pokes the devil lightly in the belly, as if tickling the small figure. "Oh, how he dances." Tomas's presence banishes her uneasiness and she smiles at her own fears.

That night, when Esperanza is sleeping, Tomas makes love to Dolores. The night is warm and they throw back the thin blanket. Their bed frame is built of wooden packing crates, and the slats creak beneath their shifting bodies, a rhythmic song that keeps time to her soft moans. With his arm around her, she falls asleep and has no dreams.

A few days later, she fires the pottery in a pit that she has dug on a barren patch of ground near the house. When she lights the wood and straw, flames cackle and the wood snaps like gunfire. The heat of the fire touches her face, hotter than the afternoon sun, and Esperanza crows with delight, clapping her hands to see the flames. Black smoke from the straw rises like thunderclouds.

Dolores goes about her chores while the fire burns: carrying water to her garden, fetching firewood to replace the wood she has burned, going to the market to buy a little rice, a little chili. Late in the afternoon, the fire has burned low. With a green branch, she rakes away the ashes, uncovering the blackened figurines. Soot-colored dove whistles nestle in the ashes; baying dogs lift their blackened heads. Two goats have broken, cracking when

the air trapped within the clay expanded in the heat of the
fire. But the devils are intact. Silently, they play their
instruments with their inhuman hands, laughing and dancing on the smoking ground.

The next day, she paints the figures with the bright
paints that Tomas brought her from the city. She leaves
the devils until last, then gives them red horns and yellow
teeth and flashing golden eyes. The bright colors shimmer
in the afternoon sun, and the devils leer at her as she
works, staring with their bulging eyes.

The American is a thin gray-haired man in a brightly
flowered shirt and pale brown pants. His face and the top
of his head, visible through his sparse hair, are reddened
from the sun. He speaks Spanish well, and he is very
polite.

He is a very clean man: his hands are pale and soft.
Dolores notices that his fingernails are as clean and as
neat as a woman's. He picks up a dove whistle with his
soft hand and looks at it, turning the toy this way and
that.

Tomas stands beside the American, his legs wide apart,
his thumbs hooked in the waistband of his trousers. "They
are very good," Tomas says. "Very beautiful." He is like a
nervous rooster, strutting for show.

Dolores stands back, keeping her eyes down, her hands
hidden in her apron. She is wearing her best dress, the
newer of the two she owns, but she is ashamed of her
looks. Her own fingernails are broken and stained with
clay.

The American says nothing. He puts the dove down and
picks up the dancing devil. One by one, he examines each
of the devils. "The others are pleasant, but nothing special," he says at last, dismissing the other toys with a wave.
"But these show imagination. I know a few folk art collec-
tors in America who . . ." He stops without finishing his
sentence. "I will buy these," he says, pointing to the
devils. "And I would like to see more."

Before he leaves, he and Tomas shake hands. They will
do business.

* * *

That evening, Tomas buys tequila with money from the American. Other men from the village come to hear him brag of his success. Dolores watches from the doorway of the house.

The men sit on the rusting hulk of an old car that was abandoned on the edge of the *malpais*. The car's wheels were stolen long ago. Now the car rests on its belly, and men perch on its rusted hood. They drink tequila and laugh loudly. The light from the setting sun paints them red. Their shadows stretch away into the *malpais*.

Dolores dreams that night of devils. One is feathered like a rooster and he struts through the dream, puffing out his chest and preening his shiny horns. Another has a bulging belly, like an old sow with a litter. His ears are hairy, like the ears of a pig, and his horns curl like goat horns.

Tomas has little to say at breakfast. His eyes are red and weary looking, and he complains that his head hurts. He pushes Esperanza away when she comes to kiss him good morning. "Make more devils," he tells Dolores before he goes to the fields.

She comforts Esperanza and makes devils of clay. In her hands, the fat devil becomes fatter. Her fingers smooth the round curve of his belly, a pig's belly supported by spindly legs. His ears droop mournfully as he dries in the sun. He is a ridiculous devil, a child's toy, but somehow she cannot laugh at him.

From a handful of clay, she makes the strutting rooster devil, with his puffed out chest and his nose like a beak. The devil looks foolish, but Dolores is uneasy. The devils stink of dark and ancient places, and she remembers her grandfather's tales.

"Never call the evil one by name," her grandfather told her. "If you do, you will call him to you and give him power."

She pats the clay, molding the delicate shapes of devil's horns and wondering what her grandfather would say about these toys. A breeze blows from the *malpais* and she feels ill, weak, and feverish.

* * *

Tomas insists on bringing the devils into the house that evening. He sets them on a shelf beside the bed, pokes the fat one in the belly, and laughs.

Again, Tomas and his friends sit on the old car and drink tequila. Dolores goes to bed, but she does not sleep. She can hear Tomas talking and the laughter of his friends. And she hears other sounds—small sounds, like mice searching for grains of corn on the dirt floor. She lies awake, knowing that the devils are moving on the shelf, their claws scratching against the wood.

She is awake when Tomas stumbles into the house. He brings his bottle of tequila with him: she hears the clink of glass as he sets the bottle down by the bed, the rustle of clothing as he takes off his shirt. He lies beside her in the bed, and she turns toward him. His breath stinks of tequila, and he pulls her toward him, pressing his lips against her throat. He makes love to her in the darkness, but she thinks of the devils, watching from the shelf. The bed sings, but she is silent. At last, Tomas sleeps.

While her husband and daughter sleep, Dolores listens to the devils moving on the shelf. In the morning, the devils are quiet, standing as if they had never moved. That morning, on her way to fetch water from the public fountain, Dolores stops at the house of the *curandera*, the village healer and herbalist.

Doña Ramon's house and yard have a pungent smell from the drying herbs in the rafters and the growing herbs in the yard. Esperanza stays close by her mother, her eyes wide, a little fearful of Doña Ramon.

Dolores tells Doña Ramon of the American who wants devils, of her terrible dreams, and of the sounds she hears at night.

The old woman nods. "These devils will bring you bad luck," she says. "When you make them, you give the devil power. You call the devils from the *malpais* to your house."

"What can I do?" Dolores asks.

"Stop making devils."

"The American wants devils," Dolores says.

"Then you will have bad luck."

That afternoon, Dolores makes whistles shaped like doves and owls and coyotes and frogs, simple toys that will make children happy and will bring no devils to her house. As she works, Esperanza plays beside her in the mud, making round balls of clay and patting them flat to make mud tortillas.

When Tomas comes home that evening, he examines Dolores's new pottery. There is not a single devil. "The American told you to make devils," he says to her. "Why do you make these toys?"

"I do not like the devils," Dolores tells him softly. "They will bring bad luck."

Tomas scowls. "These devils will bring us money. And money will bring us luck."

She shakes her head. "The *curandera* told me that these clay devils will bring real devils from the *malpais* to our house."

Tomas laughs. It is wicked, hurting laughter with no joy in it. "Why do I have such a stupid wife?" he asks. "There are no devils in the *malpais*. Those are stories to scare children."

Dolores shakes her head again, suddenly stubborn. "I can't make devils," she says. "I—"

Tomas strikes without warning, an open-handed slap that nearly knocks her down. "Why do I have such a stupid wife?" he shouts. "The American wants devils and you will make devils." When he strikes her again, Dolores falls to her knees and clutches her head, weeping. He stands over her for a moment, his hand raised as if to strike again. When she looks up at him, he scowls at her, the expression of a young boy who has been denied something he wants. "You must make devils," he says. "Then we will have money, and we can buy you a new dress." Reluctantly, she nods her head. Then he tells her to dry her tears and helps her to her feet.

That night, Tomas drinks with his friends, finishing the tequila that he bought with the American's money. Dolores dreams of a bat-winged devil who dances on a platform of human skulls, a feathered devil who clutches two weeping children in its talons; a snake devil who has caught a naked woman in his coils.

The next morning, Dolores makes devils: the snake with the captive woman; the bat-winged dancer; the bird devil and the children. Her head aches and she is weary before the day is half over.

When Tomas comes home, he sees her work and smiles. "These will bring money," he says, but she does not answer. He puts them on the shelf with the others and, because there is no more tequila, his friends do not come to visit. He sits alone on the rusting car and drowses in the setting sun. Dolores watches from the kitchen door; she does not like seeing him sitting so near the *malpais* when the night is coming. She goes to him. "Come in the house," she says. "It is not good to be out here."

He smiles, and his face looks unfamiliar in the red light of sunset. "You shouldn't fear the devils," he says. "The devils will make us rich. The devils will buy you new dresses and build us a new house."

She takes his hand and he follows her into the house, obedient as a sleepwalker. They go to bed and he sleeps; Esperanza sleeps. And Dolores hears whispering.

"Dolores," they say. "We will make you strong. We will give you money. We will give you power." Tiny voices, dry as the wind from the desert. "Listen to us."

Tomas turns in his sleep, and Dolores hears him moan softly, as if crying out in a dream. He is a weak man, susceptible to the devils' promises. They have promised him riches, then tempted him with drink. He is weak, but she is strong. She hears the whispering voices, but she does not listen.

In the faint light of early dawn Dolores leaves her bed and carries the devils out to the edge of the *malpais*. She lines them up side by side on the hood of the old car. They stare at her with bulging eyes, threaten her with their claws.

She takes a large stick from the ground and clubs the snake devil who holds the woman captive, smashing the unfired clay into pieces. The light of the sun warms her as she lifts her club to strike again.

A Falling Star Is a Rock
from Outer Space

A falling star dropped precipitously from the sky over San Francisco, slicing through the hazy air with a trail of blue-white fire. Mrs. Laura Jenkins stared out her kitchen window, transfixed in the act of scrubbing a pot. The kitchen window looked out toward the pair of soft gray-green hills known as Twin Peaks. The falling star appeared over the Twin Peaks radio tower and slashed across the sky, heading toward her house.

Make a wish, Mrs. Jenkins thought, but no wish came to mind. Only an ill-defined feeling of loss and longing. She did not know what, exactly, to wish for.

Looking out at the deep blue evening sky, Mrs. Jenkins remembered another falling star, long ago. Andrea had been ten, and Mrs. Jenkins had accompanied her daughter's Girl Scout troop on a weekend camping trip. On a crisp cold evening, Mrs. Jenkins and Andrea were out gathering firewood. In the west, the sky was a deep royal blue, darkening to black overhead. When a falling star streaked across the darkness with a burst of fire, Mrs. Jenkins called out, "Make a wish! Quick, before it fades."

Andrea, wise beyond her years, shook her head contemptuously. "That's silly," she said. "It's a piece of rock falling to earth from outer space. How could it grant a wish?"

Then Andrea scampered back to the campfire with an armload of wood, leaving her mother to blink at the first stars in the evening sky.

Mrs. Jenkins was a timid woman, pale and frail boned, but beneath that weakness was a stubborn streak. Mrs. Jenkins didn't know how, but it seemed likely to her that a falling star could grant a wish. At least, the magic of falling stars seemed no less unlikely than many other things that people accepted without question. Things like wristwatch calculators and astronauts on the moon and horoscopes and UFOs. If people could believe in those things, Mrs. Jenkins felt she had the right to believe in falling stars. No matter how much her daughter scoffed.

Mrs. Jenkins pulled her flannel bathrobe more tightly around her. She dropped a few ice cubes into a tumbler and poured herself some Old Bushmills Irish whiskey. The ice cubes crackled on a high brittle note, like shards of frozen laughter. With the first sip of whiskey, Mrs. Jenkins felt, as always, a touch of guilt. Ever since Andrea had moved away to New York, where the lights and career prospects were brighter, Mrs. Jenkins had relied on the relaxing influence of alcohol. Mr. Jenkins, a fast-talking used-car salesman, had departed long ago: one year after the birth of their daughter, he had walked down to the corner market for a six-pack, and he had never returned. Mrs. Jenkins lived alone in a two-bedroom flat, the top floor of a Victorian house that had been divided into apartments.

Whiskey soothed her restless thoughts of Andrea and helped her sleep. Whiskey kept her company, whiskey held her hand and gave her comfort, whiskey kept her warm in a cold world. She needed the whiskey when the flat seemed so large and empty and New York seemed impossibly far away.

On Monday, the morning after the falling star, Mrs. Jenkins found a strange hair in her bathroom sink. It was a long red-gold hair that coiled around the drainhole like a snake ready to strike. Mrs. Jenkins's own hair was short, curly, and brown touched with gray. She picked up the strange hair on a tissue and frowned at it.

Mrs. Jenkins was the only person who used her bathroom and she cleaned it carefully once a week. There was no explanation for the red-gold hair. Yet there it was, glinting in the morning sun, a puzzle, an anomaly.

She had no time to consider the strange hair. She had to hurry to her job as school librarian at Putnam Avenue School, where she had worked for the past thirty years.

She threw the hair into the trash and dismissed it from her mind.

She took the bus to work. The bus was crowded with kids on their way to school, men and women on their way to work. Mrs. Jenkins sat in an aisle seat, her purse in her lap, her hands folded over it protectively. An old man wandered down the aisle, stopped beside Mrs. Jenkins's seat, and reached up to grab the strap just over her head. He was raggedly dressed in an old sport coat and jeans, he desperately needed a shave, and he smelled strongly of Old Spice and faintly of urine. But he smiled at Mrs. Jenkins, and she, without thinking, smiled back. The look in his eyes was vague and unfocused. "Did you see the light in the sky last night?" he said conversationally to Mrs. Jenkins.

"The falling star," she said. "Yes, I did."

The old man swayed with the movement of the bus. "An alien spaceship," he said softly. "Coming in for a landing." His tone was gentle and matter-of-fact. "I saw it fall from the sky and go down the storm drain. Just like that. Right down into the sewers." He nodded, still smiling at her in a dreamy way. "Most people don't know that the aliens live in the sewers. The government denies it. But I saw them land."

"Of course," said Mrs. Jenkins nervously. She always tried to be agreeable to crazy people. She turned her head and pretended to be looking out the window for her stop.

"Watch out for them," said the man behind her back.

When her stop came, she fled the bus and did not look back until she was safely at the door to the school. Something about the man and his interpretation of the falling star had disturbed her, but she put it out of her mind.

That evening, when she returned from work, she opened the cupboard to get a can of soup and discovered that all the graham crackers were gone. The empty box lay on its side, brown wax paper wrappers crumpled within. She had purchased the graham crackers to make a pie crust, and she remembered using only half the box. She picked up the empty box and shook it uneasily. Even if she had finished off the box of crackers, surely she would have

thrown the package away. She would not have left it empty
on the shelf. It was as odd and as inexplicable as the hair
in the sink. Finally, she threw the empty box away and
closed the cupboard tightly, as if closing something in.

Over the next few days, she kept losing things. A
package of gum vanished from her bedside table. Potato
chips and peanuts disappeared from the kitchen cupboard.
The packages remained, but the food was gone. And not
just food, but other things as well: a wave-rounded fragment of green glass that she had found on the beach; a
cheap kerchief made of silky material printed with a bold
floral pattern; a gaudy rhinestone brooch that she had
bought on a whim. On Wednesday, when she came home
from work, it seemed to her that the things on her
dressing table—her hairbrush, her perfume, her jewelry
box and knickknacks—had been rearranged subtly, nudged
this way and that.

On Wednesday night, she watched the late-night news
on television and drank a nightcap. Lately, she had been
bothered by small sounds at night: the floors creaked as if
someone were walking softly in the hallway; she heard
rustling, as if cloth were shifting in the wind. Once she
thought she heard someone tapping at the window, but it
was only a tree branch tapping against the glass. She was
constantly on edge, plagued with the same sort of anxiety
she had felt when Andrea was very small. As she lay in
bed at night, she listened, though she did not know what
she was expecting to hear.

But she did nothing except turn on the television to
drown out the silence. She could think of nothing to do.
Mentioning her anxiety to Andrea would only worry her
daughter and make her think that her mother was getting
old and foolish. There was no use doing that.

Mrs. Jenkins became seriously alarmed on Thursday
morning, when she found evidence that someone had
made a peanut-butter-and-jelly sandwich during the night.
On the kitchen counter she found an open jar of peanut
butter, an open jar of strawberry preserves, a knife liberally
coated with peanut butter and jelly, and a scattering of
bread crumbs. She blinked at the mess in the morning
light. Could she have fixed herself a midnight snack and

forgotten? But even at midnight she wouldn't have been so sloppy.

She put away the peanut butter and jelly and wiped the counter clean, but she glanced uneasily over her shoulder as she left the kitchen.

At work that day she was distracted. She read aloud to the kindergarteners, as she did each Thursday morning—a weekly treat for the children and a welcome break for the teachers. Her selection was a fairy tale about a princess who was kind to a frog who later turned out to be a prince. But she was distracted and her words lacked their usual conviction.

Later that morning, she spilled a cup of coffee on her desk, and while she was mopping it up with paper towels from the bathroom, she snagged her nylons on an open desk drawer. By noon, her head was aching and she snapped at two fourth grade girls who were loudly arguing about whether a stegosaurus could beat a brontosaurus in a fight. She told the kids that both dinosaurs were vegetarians and would not fight in the first place.

"Something wrong?" asked Annie Clark, the college student who helped in the library on a part-time basis.

"Just a headache," Mrs. Jenkins murmured. "I haven't been feeling well lately."

Annie insisted that Mrs. Jenkins take two aspirins. For the rest of the afternoon, Annie hushed the children whenever they started to get noisy.

At three o'clock, half an hour before school let out, Mrs. Jenkins sat at her desk and checked in the magazines that had arrived that week, tucking each one into a plastic cover and stamping it PROPERTY OF PUTNAM AVENUE SCHOOL. It was a simple mindless task that kept her from thinking too much about the strange occurrences at her apartment. She hesitated with a science fiction magazine in hand and inspected the cover. The picture showed a spaceship descending in the night sky over a city. The spacecraft was fire-engine red, sleekly streamlined, and equipped with sweeping tail fins. It left a trail of blue-white light across the glossy black sky. Mrs. Jenkins stared at it for a moment, remembering the falling star and thinking about aliens who lived in the sewers and crept in through the plumbing. It would have to be a very small alien, she thought, to fit through a drainpipe.

"Are you feeling all right, Mrs. Jenkins?" asked Annie with concern.

Mrs. Jenkins jerked her eyes away from the picture guiltily, startled by Annie's question. She had not heard the younger woman approach. "I'm fine," Mrs. Jenkins said defensively. "Just fine."

Annie shrugged, smiling at the older woman. "It's just that there's a nasty flu going around. You'd better take care of yourself."

Mrs. Jenkins nodded testily. "I take care of myself," she muttered, and continued her work, avoiding Annie's eyes.

That evening, as she rode the bus home from work, she felt uneasy. She walked very slowly from the bus stop, delaying the moment that she had to enter her house. She checked the mail: a letter from Andrea and a junk mail advertisement addressed to someone named Beth Bettbett. She took both letters upstairs.

The deadbolt offered a reassuring resistance when she turned her key in the lock of the front door. The lock was secure—no one could get in and surely she had nothing to worry about. Quietly, she closed the front door behind her and prowled through the apartment, searching for signs of an intruder.

The apartment was laid out in a linear fashion, with room following room like the boxcars on a train. All the rooms—her bedroom, the bathroom, the living room, the kitchen, and Andrea's old bedroom—led off a single badly lit hallway that ran the length of the flat. A door near the end of the hallway let onto the backstairs, which led down to the garbage cans and a tiny weed-choked back patio. Just beyond the back door was Andrea's old room—an afterthought, a tiny cozy room that was just large enough for a twin bed, a chest of drawers, and a small writing desk.

Mrs. Jenkins's bedroom was just as she had left it: warm, cozy, reassuring. The kitchen was clean: no crumbs, no mess. Outside the kitchen window, a sparrow perched on the branch of an ancient pine that grew in the adjacent yard. The sky was the pale soft gray of goose down. It was

February and the brief California winter was giving way to spring. For a moment, in the midst of her nervousness, Mrs. Jenkins felt something different stirring: a sense of anticipation and welcome. She had always loved spring, and the monotony of rainy winter days had left her eager for the sun.

She dropped the letters on the kitchen counter and went to check the back door. The deadbolt was in place and the door was secure. But when she glanced toward the back room, Andrea's bedroom, her nervousness returned. It was silly, of course. Foolish to think that anyone might be hiding back there.

She listened at the door. No sound came from within. She laid her hand on the knob, hesitated, then jerked the door open suddenly.

The room was filled with silence, dust, and Andrea's cast-off possessions. On the shelves were high-school year-books, a collection of Nancy Drew mysteries, and a few old picture books. In the closet hung Andrea's prom dress and an old ski jacket—out of style but too good to discard. On the desk was a transistor radio with a broken tuning knob. Andrea's ancient security blanket, a worn piece of flannel with a faded print of red roses on blue, lay folded neatly at the foot of the bed. On top of the blanket, looking as if they belonged here, were the rhinestone brooch, the rounded green glass, and the lost kerchief.

Mrs. Jenkins snatched up her possessions. She felt like an intruder, but she had always felt a little out of place in Andrea's room. She forced herself to look around, examining the faded rock groups that smiled from posters on the walls. The air held a faint scent that she could not identify: vanilla, perhaps, or cinnamon. The door to the closet was ajar. When she glanced into the darkness, she thought she saw movement behind the prom dress. She waited, listening for a sound. When she heard nothing, she backed out of the room and closed the door firmly behind her.

For dinner, she made herself a small salad and reheated part of a casserole she had made earlier in the week. Over the meal, she read Andrea's letter, a cheerful note that talked about her work in a New York advertising agency and about the miserable weather in New York. As always,

Andrea sounded quite cheerful, practical, and very, very distant.

For dessert, Mrs. Jenkins had chocolate ice cream. It had been a difficult week and she felt she deserved a reward. She left her daughter's letter on the kitchen counter with the unopened advertisement, poured herself a nightcap, and sat down in the living room to watch the late-night movie.

She went to bed late and dreamed that she heard a baby crying. In the dream, she wandered through her apartment, searching for the source of the sound, but could not find it. She was alone in her apartment with the constant cry of an unhappy child.

She woke feeling confused, disoriented. She showered, wrapped herself in her robe, and wandered into the kitchen. The shaft of morning light spotlighted the ice cream carton. It lay on its side in a pool of melted ice cream, as dark and thick as blood in the morning sun. Mrs. Jenkins reached for the junk mail advertisement with a hand that trembled.

The letter had been torn open, as if by eager fingers. Brightly colored brochures spilled from the envelope. Mrs. Jenkins pulled one out at random. For $9.95, the brochure said, she could have a picture book personalized for her child. The picture on the brochure showed a little girl wearing a T-shirt that proclaimed her name to be Sue. Sue was reading a picture book titled *My Secret Friend* and the little girl in the book was named Sue. In the space on the order form marked "Your child's name here:" someone had scrawled BETH."

Outside the kitchen window the sky was blue and the sun was shining, but Mrs. Jenkins could not stop shivering. Her hair, still wet from the shower, dripped down the collar of her robe to send a cold trickle down her back. Moving quickly, she swept the advertisements off the counter and threw them away. She wiped up the melted ice cream and put the carton in the trash. Then she fled the kitchen, dressing quickly and hurrying to work.

On the bus to work, she eyed a disheveled old woman who wore three sweaters over her flowered dress. The shopping bag at the woman's feet was stuffed with clothing and the woman was talking loudly to the disinterested businessman who sat beside her, trapped in his seat by the crowd on the bus. The woman was telling him about the aliens who came to her apartment and stole her things. They came at night, she told him; they came out when everyone was asleep and nobody noticed but her.

Mrs. Jenkins watched, wondering if this woman had started by forgetting things, misplacing things, until at last she no longer remembered where she was or what she was doing.

The last time that Andrea had been out to visit, she had asked Mrs. Jenkins if she were still comfortable living alone. A simple question, an innocent question, but suddenly Mrs. Jenkins was worried about its implications: rest homes, senior citizens' clubs, places for women who could not take care of themselves.

Mrs. Jenkins was very glad when the bus reached her stop.

At work, she could not concentrate. She felt a little sick to her stomach, a little dizzy and disoriented. At noon, she told Annie Clark that she had a touch of the flu, and she went home early.

With the afternoon sunlight streaming in the windows, her apartment seemed cheerful and homey. Sunshine cast a glowing rectangle on her bedroom carpet. The bathroom and living room were just as she had left them.

She stopped in the door to the kitchen. Her stomach tightened. On the counter lay the advertisement that she had thrown away. She knew for certain that she had thrown it away—on one corner of the brochure was a smear of chocolate from the ice cream carton in the trash. Beside the brochure, a stuffed toy watched her with bright blue-glass eyes. She picked it up and smoothed back its soft fur with a hand that trembled. It was a sweet little toy, a plump white kitten with white plush fur. She remembered buying it for Andrea's ninth birthday. She had known, even as she took the kitten from the shelf in the toy store, that the stuffed toy was too babyish for Andrea, too cute, too sweet. But Mrs. Jenkins was drawn to it, and she bought it at the same time that she bought the chemistry set that Andrea really wanted.

Andrea had opened the chemistry set with cries of delight. The kitten she accepted politely and set on her bookshelf where it had grown dusty over the years. Mrs. Jenkins had never once seen Andrea take the kitten from the shelf and stroke its fur.

Mrs. Jenkins stood in the kitchen and held the stuffed toy in her hand. The chill that had touched her spine did not go away. She placed the toy on the counter and she backed from the room.

She had never noticed before how badly lit the hallway was. No windows here, and only a little light filtered in through the open kitchen door. She tiptoed down the hall until she stood outside the door to Andrea's room. Through the door she could hear the faint sound of a transistor radio playing a scratchy rendition of a rock-and-roll tune. She put her hand on the cold metal doorknob, listening intently. Her stomach ached and she was angry. Finding the kitten made her feel sad and lonely and somehow the sadness and loneliness had become an anger that centered somewhere in her stomach.

"Listen," she said softly. Then more loudly, as if she were scolding a room filled with boisterous children, "Listen to me!" She could hear an hysterical edge in her voice, but could not control it. "You'd better get out of here, you hear me?" She listened for a moment. Over the staticy music she thought she heard something else: a small sigh as if someone on the other side of the door had let out a breath.

"I don't know who you are or how you got in here, but I'm telling you that I'm putting a lock on this door," she said. "A good strong lock that opens only from the outside. So you'd better get out of here while you can." She rattled the doorknob and the radio abruptly fell silent. "You'd better get out of here."

She fled the apartment. When she returned, an hour later, she carried a hammer, holding it in her hand like a club. Tucked under her arm was a brown paper bag from the hardware store.

The hallway was quiet, a brooding stillness. Mrs. Jenkins went directly to Andrea's door. There too the hallway was quiet: no radio, no muffled breathing.

The lock was a simple sturdy mechanism. A steel rod about half an inch thick slid into two metal rings that attached to the door and two metal rings that attached to the doorframe. The young man at the hardware store had assured Mrs. Jenkins that the lock would make any door quite secure.

Dust motes danced in the stream of afternoon light that shone through the kitchen door. Mrs. Jenkins waited, listening. Only silence.

She held the steel rings up to the door. With a sharp pencil, she marked the places where the screws would go. Eight screws, each an inch long. She tapped starting holes with hammer and nail, then screwed the hoops into place. The wood of the frame was hard and the pressure of the screwdriver against her palm raised a blister. But she persisted even when the blister popped, ignoring the pain and forcing the screws into the wood. She was breathing heavily by the time she finished.

She slid the steel rod neatly into the hoops. She rattled the knob and tugged on the door, but the lock held firm. She left it then and tried to go about her normal evening routine. She made herself some dinner, even though she wasn't really hungry, settled down with *The New York Times Book Review*, and tried to read the reviews of children's books.

The apartment was not quiet. She could hear the rush of traffic on the nearby street; it ebbed and flowed like rushing water in a river. She turned on the radio and classical music filled one corner of the room. But beneath the rumble of passing cars and the dancing tune on the harpsichord, she could sense the silence, the great angry darkness. She poured a nightcap, but even the whiskey could not hold back the brooding silence.

It began to rain. Raindrops tapped against the windows, as if seeking a way in. The tires of cars hissed on the wet streets. Mrs. Jenkins found that she had started a review for the third time and she still did not remember what it said.

She took out her umbrella, her raincoat, and her plastic rain hat, and she went to the movies. A musical comedy was playing at a theater down the block. In the darkness of

the theater she felt safe: bright pictures moved on the
giant screen, enormous faces sang about love, and everything worked out right in the end. But when the movie
was over, she had to go home.

The light bulb on the landing had burned out and she
fumbled for her keys. As she stood in front of the door, she
heard music and laughter, but assumed the noise came
from her downstairs neighbors, three students who tended
to be noisy.

She opened the door to her apartment and blinked in
the sudden glare of the hallway light. The radio in her
bedroom was blaring a pop hit—something about love and
betrayal. A muffled television voice told a joke she could
not hear and a laugh track roared with amusement.

She ran toward the living room, dropping her umbrella
in the hall and leaving the front door open, thinking only
of turning off the television and stopping the laughter.

A blizzard of paper scraps covered the living room floor,
drifting around the couch and piling up beside the legs of
the coffee table like snow beside fence posts. Last Sunday's newspaper had been torn into tiny pieces and scattered
like a New York snowstorm, white touched with gray.

The oven timer was buzzing, a raucous nagging tone.
The blender, an ancient Osterizer, was stuck on purée and
it whined on a high thin note. All the heating elements of
the stove were cherry red, and the kettle was whistling
with agonized desperation, as if it had been howling for
hours with no hope of relief. As Mrs. Jenkins stood in the
doorway, unwilling to venture into the snowdrifts of paper,
the toaster popped and the laugh track guffawed. A breeze
from the open window caught a few paper scraps, swirling
them in a miniature tornado, picking up other scraps and
tossing them high in the air. Mrs. Jenkins heard the front
door slam closed and her breath came quickly, almost in
sobs.

"I'm sorry," she said suddenly. Her hands were clasped
in front of her and she was almost crying. "I'm sorry.
Please stop it." Then louder. "Stop it! I said I'm sorry!"
Then shouting so that she could be heard over the laughter, the whistling, and the buzzing, "Goddamn it—I'm
sorry!"

The lights went out. The laughter fell silent, along with the whine of the blender and the buzz of the timer. The whistling of the kettle persisted for a minute, deepening from its panicked wail to a bass note, fading to a whimper, and then to nothing.

Mrs. Jenkins stood in the darkness, listening to the sound of her own breathing. She heard a faint rustling and something soft—maybe a paper scrap blown by the breeze—brushed past her ankle. Nothing else happened.

She reached for the light switch beside her and flipped it up and down. No response. The apartment's circuits had overloaded and a fuse had blown, a minor emergency that Mrs. Jenkins could deal with.

Tentatively she stepped into the living room, shuffling her feet through the newspaper scraps. Nothing harmed her. She could see the outline of the television set in the faint glow of a streetlight shining through the window. She fumbled for the set's on/off switch and pushed it to off. Carefully she made her way into the kitchen where she turned off the blender, the oven timer, and all the heating elements on the stove.

She turned quickly away from the stove, half-expecting to find someone watching her from the living room. The room was empty. She listened but heard nothing except the rapid beating of her own heart. She groped in the kitchen drawer for spare fuses, a candle, and matches. On her way to the fuse box she caught a glimpse of her own reflection in the living room window. In the wavering candlelight, her face was pale, her eyes were wide, and the irises were ringed with white.

She changed the fuse. When she threw the circuit breaker, the lights in the hallway came on and the radio deejay announced the next tune. She went to the bedroom, turned off the radio, and sat for a moment on the bed. The bright lights hurt her eyes and her ears still rang with the remembered buzzing of the oven timer.

She forced herself to stand and walk down the hall to Andrea's room. The steel bar had been shoved to one side, unbolting the door. Slowly, she slipped the bar out of the hoops completely, leaving the door free to open. She put the bar in the kitchen drawer where she kept the fuses.

Her purse lay in the doorway where she had dropped it. She picked it up, shook off the bits of paper, and took out the box of Milk Duds that she had bought at the theater. About half were left. She put the box on the kitchen counter and returned to her bedroom.

Her head ached and the sickness in her stomach had grown worse. She felt feverish as she undressed and put on her nightgown. She lay on the bed and picked up a magazine, planning to read for a while before going to sleep.

She woke with her stomach in a knot. The bedroom light was still on. Her stomach twisted and she ran to the bathroom where she vomited into the toilet again and again, continuing to retch helplessly even after her stomach was empty. For a time, she lay on the bathroom floor, welcoming the coolness of the linoleum. She roused only to vomit.

She woke sometime later and pulled the blanket closer around her, shivering with a sudden chill. Vaguely she wondered where the blanket had come from; it hadn't been there a minute ago. Her fingers worried at a hole in the flannel as she drifted in and out of sleep. Finally, she woke enough to realize that she might be more comfortable in bed. She pulled the blanket around her shoulders like a cape and staggered back down the hall to her bedroom, pausing now and then to lean against the wall. The hall seemed very long, but at last she reached her room and collapsed on the bed.

She drifted in and out of sleep for the rest of the night. Once she woke and wished she had a glass of water so that she could wash the taste of vomit from her mouth. The next time she woke, she discovered a glass of water on her bedside table. She sipped it gratefully and did not question its presence.

In the morning, she woke briefly, then drifted back to sleep. She slept sporadically, and each time she woke she found a gift on the table beside her: a glass of orange juice from the pitcher in the refrigerator; a cup of hot mint tea sweetened with honey; two slices of toast, still warm from the toaster; the stuffed white kitten with its blue-glass eyes.

Late in the afternoon, she fell sound asleep again and slept through until morning. She woke early, feeling ravenous, and wandered into the living room. The paper scraps had been swept into a paper bag and a jam jar on the kitchen table was crammed full of dandelions and yellow mustard flowers, gathered, she suspected, from the back patio. The box of Milk Duds was empty.

The rain had stopped and the sky was clearing: pale blue with a border of white lace clouds. A rainbow curved over the radio tower on Twin Peaks.

She thought about what it would be like to be young, lonely, and far from home. Then she smiled at the bouquet of ragged flowers. Children could be thoughtless, but they meant well.

The apartment was quiet, but it seemed filled with a kind of warmth, a cozy feeling, like the sound of a cat purring or the touch of sunshine on bare skin. Mrs. Jenkins threw away the empty Milk Duds box, added more water to the jar of flowers, and fixed herself some scrambled eggs for breakfast. As she worked, she hummed to herself, a tuneless happy sound.

She folded the blanket that had covered her when she lay on the bathroom floor, recognizing the worn sky blue flannel as Andrea's security blanket. Mrs. Jenkins left it at the door to Andrea's room. Inside the room, the transistor radio played softly.

When she went out to get a Sunday paper, Mrs. Jenkins stopped by the corner market to buy another carton of chocolate ice cream and a box of graham crackers.

With Four Lean Hounds

We start with a thief: slim, wiry girl with ash-gray hair and eyes the color of the winter sky. No one knew how old she was and no one cared. Old enough to beat; just barely old enough to bed.

Tarsia was running from an angry baker. The loaf tucked under her arm was still warm. She dodged between the stalls of the market, heading for a spot where she knew she could climb the tumbledown wall that ringed the city. From there she could run surefooted across slate roofs, hide among the chimneys. A creature of the wind and sky, she could escape all pursuit.

She heard the whistle of the guard's warning and the pounding of his running feet. Ill luck: he was between her and the wall. Behind her, the baker shouted curses. She changed course abruptly, ducking into the mouth of an alley and—too late—realized her mistake.

The walls were slick stone. Though she climbed like a monkey, she could not scale them. The alley's far end had been blocked by a new building. A dead end.

She heard the guard's whistle echoing down the cold stone walls and remembered the feel of the shackles on her wrist. Her bones ached in memory of the cold jail.

A jumble of papers that the wind had blown against the alley's end rustled. A rat peered out at Tarsia—a grizzled old grandfather rat who watched her with an arrogant air of unconcern, then turned tail and darted into a hole that had been hidden in the shadows. It was a dark, dank hole just the width of a small thief's shoulders.

Tarsia heard the footsteps at the mouth of the alley and, like a sensible thief with a healthy concern for her skin, she dropped the loaf and squeezed into the hole. Her shoulders scraped against the damp stone. A creature of rooftops and light, she wiggled down into the darkness.

On her belly, she groped her way forward, reminding herself that rats were only bats without wings. As a child of the rooftops she knew bats. But she could hear her heart beating in the narrow stone passage and she could not lift her head without bumping it. She inched forward, telling herself that surely the drain led into a larger passage; it could not just get smaller and darker and damper.

A cold blast of air fanned her face, carrying scents of still water, damp stone, and sewage. At last, she could raise her head. She felt a soft touch on her ankle—a tiny breeze rushing past—with only a hint of fur and a long tail.

She heaved herself out of the drain into a larger space, quick and clumsy in her eagerness to move. She stepped forward in the darkness, stepped into nothing and stumbled, clutching at an edge she could not see, slipping and falling into a moment she did not remember.

A thunder of wings from the pigeons wheeling over-head, the scent of a charcoal fire—damp, dismal smell in the early morning—drifting from a chimney. The slate roof was cold beneath Tarsia's bare feet and the wind from the north cut through her thin shirt. In one hand she clutched the damp shirt she had taken from a rooftop clothesline. She was listening.

She had heard a sound—not the rattle of the latch of the door to the roof. Not the pigeons. Perhaps only the wind?

There again: a rumbling like drumbeats and a wild sweet whistling like pipes in a parade. From behind a cloud swept the chariot of the Lady of the Wind. She brought the sunshine with her. She wore a silver crescent moon on her forehead and a golden sun shone on her breast. Ash-gray hair floated behind her like a cape. Four lean hounds—winds of the North, South, East, and West—ran laughing through the sky at her side.

The Lady looked down at Tarsia with wise eyes, smiled, and held out her hand. Tarsia reached out to touch her.

* * *

Tarsia's head ached and her feet were cold. She opened her eyes into darkness, leaving behind the bright dream of a memory that had never been. Tarsia had watched the caravan that carried tribute to the Lady leave the city, heading north, but she had never seen the Lady.

The hand with which Tarsia had clung to the edge was sore and stiff; when she touched it to her lips, it tasted of blood. She lay half-in and half-out of a cold stream that tugged at her feet as it flowed past.

She could not go back, only forward. She felt her way slowly, always keeping her hand on the wall and always sniffing the air in hopes of scenting dust and horses—city smells. She heard a rumbling sound ahead that reminded her of cartwheels on cobblestones, and she quickened her pace.

The tunnel opened into a cavern—a natural formation in the rock of the earth. Patches of fungus on the walls glowed golden, casting a light dimmer than that of the moon.

The giant who lay in the center of the cavern was snoring with a rumbling like cartwheels. He slept in a cradle of rock, molded around him, it seemed, by the movements of his body. The air that blew past the giant, coming from the darkness beyond, carried the scents of grass and of freedom.

A giant blocked her way and she was only a small thief. She had never stolen from the house of the wizard or the stall of the herb-seller. She knew only the small spells that helped her break the protection of a household.

The giant had an enormous face—broad and earth colored. He shifted in his sleep and Tarsia saw the chain on his ankle, bound to a bolt in the floor. The links were as thick as her leg; the rusted lock, the size of her head. She wondered who had imprisoned him and what he had done to deserve it. She tried to estimate the length of the chain and judged it long enough to allow him to catch anyone trying to sneak past.

The shifting breeze ruffled his hair and the rumbling stopped. Nostrils flared as he sampled the air. "I smell you," he said slowly. "I know your scent, witch. What do you want with me now?" He spoke as if he knew her.

Tarsia did not move. One hand rested on the rock wall; one hand uselessly clutched her knife. The giant's eyes searched the shadows and found her.

"Ah," he said. "The same eyes, the same hair, the same scent—not the witch, but the witch's daughter." He grinned and Tarsia did not like the look in his eyes. "You were a long time in coming."

"I'm no one's daughter," she said. Giants and witches— she had no place in this. Her mother? She had no mother. "I'm just a poor thief from the city. And I want to get back."

"You can't get past me unless you free me, witch's daughter," he said.

"Free you?" She shook her head in disbelief. "How? Break the chain?"

The giant scowled. "A drop of your blood on the lock will free me. You must know that." His voice was unbelieving. "How can you hope to win your mother's throne when you don't even know—"

"Who is my mother?" she interrupted, her voice brittle.

"You don't know." He grinned and his voice took on the sly tone she had heard from strong men who did not often have to be clever. "Free me and I'll tell you." He pulled his legs under him into an awkward crouch, his head bumping the cavern's ceiling. "Just one drop of blood and I'll let you go past. Even if the blood does not free me, I'll let you go."

"Even if it does not free you?" she asked warily.

"You doubt yourself so much?" He shrugged. "Even so."

She stepped forward, wary and ready to dart back to the passage. With her eyes on the crouching giant she nicked the scrape on her hand so that the blood flowed fresh and a drop fell onto the rusted lock. She backed away. The giant's eyes were fixed on the lock and on the smoke that rose from the lock, swirling around the chain.

She reached the far side of the cavern while the giant watched the lock, and from that safety she called out sharply, "Who is the witch who bound you here, giant? Keep your part of the bargain. Who—?"

"There!" the giant said. With a triumphant movement, the giant tugged the chain and the lock fell free.

"Who is the witch?" Tarsia called again.

"Thank you for your help, witch's daughter." He stepped past her, into the darkness where the ceiling rose higher. "I will go now to play a part in bringing the prophecies to pass."

"But who is my mother?" she shouted. "You said you would tell me."

He grinned back over his shoulder. "Who would be strong enough to chain a son of the earth? No one but the Lady of the Wind." He stepped away into the darkness.

"What?" Tarsia shouted in disbelief, but her voice echoed back to her. She could hear the giant striding away in the darkness and her mind was filled with the thunder of wings, with the baying of four lean hounds. She ran after the giant, knowing that she could not catch him but running in spite of that knowledge. The scent of fresh air and growing things grew stronger as she ran. "Wait," she called, but the giant was gone.

The air smelled of newly turned earth. She ran toward a bright light—sunlight of late afternoon. She could see the marks left by the giant's fingers where he had torn the rock aside and pushed his way out. His feet had ripped dark holes in the soft grass and the prints led down the rolling hills to the river that sparkled in the distance. She thought that she could see a splash in the river—tiny and far away—which could have been a giant splashing as he swam.

Sometimes stumbling, sometimes sliding in the grass, she ran down the hills, following the footprints. Ran until her legs slowed without her willing it. She trudged along the riverbank as the shadows grew longer. She was heading north. The mountains lay to the north, and the Lady's court was in the mountains.

The light was failing when she stopped to rest. She sat down just for a moment. No more than that. Shivering in the chill twilight, she tumbled into a darkness deeper than the tunnels beneath the city.

A scent of a charcoal fire—damp dismal scent in the early morning—but Tarsia did not stand on the cold slate of the roof. The wind that carried the scent of smoke blew back her hair and the sound of wings was all around her.

She stood at the Lady's side in the chariot and the four hounds of the wind ran beside them. Far below, she saw the gray slate rooftop and the fluttering clothes on the line. Far below, the ancient towers of the city, the crumbling walls, the booths and stalls of the marketplace.

"This is your proper place, my daughter," the Lady said, her voice as soft as the summer breeze blowing through the towers. "Above the world at my side." The Lady took Tarsia's hand and the pain faded away.

Tarsia heard a rumbling—like the sound of cartwheels on a cobbled street. Far below, she saw the towers shake and a broad, earth-colored face glared up at them. Shaking off the dust of the hole from which he had emerged, the giant climbed to the top of the city wall in a few steps. He seemed larger than he had beneath the earth. He stood on top of the old stone tower and reached toward them. Tarsia cried out—fearful that the giant would catch them and drag them back to the earth. Back down to the smoke and the dust.

The scent of smoke was real. Tarsia could feel the damp grass of the riverbank beneath her, but she was warm. A cloth that smelled faintly of horse lay over her.

She forced her eyes open. A riverbank in early morning —mist sparkling on the grass; a white horse grazing; smoke drifting from a small fire; a thin, brown-haired man dressed in travel-stained green watching her. "You're awake," he said. "How do you feel?"

Her head ached. She struggled to a sitting position, clutching the green cape that had served as her cover around her. Wary, used to the ways of the city, she mumbled, "I'll live."

He continued watching her. "You're a long way from anywhere in particular. Where are you going?" His accent matched that of traders from the South who had sometimes visited the city.

She twisted to look behind her at the hills. She could not see the city, and she wondered how far she had come in the winding tunnels. "I came from the city," she said.

"I'm going away from the city." More alert now, Tarsia studied the white horse. It looked well fed. The saddle that lay beside the animal was travel worn, but she could tell that it was once of first quality. The cloak that covered her was finely woven of soft wool. A lute wrapped in similar cloth leaned against the saddle.

"I'm a minstrel," the man said. "I'm traveling north."

Tarsia nodded, thinking that when a person volunteered information it was generally false. No minstrel could afford a saddle like that one. She looked up into his brown eyes—noting in passing the gold ring on his hand. She knew she could trust him as a fellow thief. As far as she could trust a thief. She was not sure how far that was, because she had always preferred to work alone.

"I was planning to head north too," she said. "If you take me with you, I can help you out. I can build a fire that doesn't smoke . . ." She looked at the smoldering fire and let her words trail off. She knew she looked small and helpless in the cloak and she hoped that her face was pale and smudged with dirt.

"I suppose I can't very well leave you here," he said, sounding a little annoyed. "I'll take you as far as the next town."

She got to her feet slowly, taking care to appear weak. But she made herself useful—poking the fire so that the sticks flamed. She toasted the bread that the minstrel pulled from his pack and melted cheese on thick slices.

She helped him saddle the white horse. On a pretext of adjusting the saddlebags, she slipped her hand inside and found a money pouch. Swiftly, she palmed one, two, three coins—and slyly transferred them to her own pocket for later examination. Even if he only took her to the next town, she would profit by the association.

As they traveled alongside the river, she rode behind him on the horse. "How far north are you going?"

"To the mountains," he said and began to pick a tune on his lute.

"To the court of the Lady of the Wind," she guessed, then suppressed a smile when he frowned. Where else would a minstrel go in the mountains? She amended mentally; where else would a thief go? "Could I come with you?"

"Why?"

She shrugged as if reasons were not important. "I've never been to a court before. I've heard the Lady is very beautiful."

The minstrel shook his head. "Beautiful, but wicked."

"I can pay my way," Tarsia said, wondering if he would recognize the look of his own coins.

But he shook his head again and the tune he was playing changed, mellowing to music that she remembered from her childhood. She could not remember the words except for the refrain about the beautiful Lady and the four lean wind hounds at her side. The Lady was the sister to the sun and daughter of the moon.

When the minstrel sang the refrain, it had a sneering, cynical tone. The lyrics were about how the Lady had bound the spirits of the Earth, the Water, and the Fire, how she had captured the four winds and bound them in her tower, about how the world would be unhappy until the four winds were free.

"That isn't the way that I remember the song," Tarsia said when the minstrel finished.

He shrugged. "In my country, we pay the Lady no tribute. Our lands have been dry and our crops have been poor for five long years. We do not love the Lady."

Tarsia remembered the parade that was held each year in the Lady's honor when the tribute was sent. The city was noted for its silverwork, and each year, the best that the artisans had produced was sent to the mountain court. And the winds blew through the towers and brought rain for the farmers around the city walls.

Last year, at the end of a day of picking the pockets of parade spectators, Tarsia had climbed the city wall and watched from above the gate while the caravan headed north, winding between farmers' huts and green fields. On her high perch, she had been chilled by the wind— but glad to be above the crowd. The last horse in the caravan had carried a silver statuette of the Lady gazing into the distance with one hand resting on the head of a hound. Tarsia had felt a kinship with the Lady then—alone and proud, above the world.

"Why don't you pay tribute?" she asked the minstrel. "Are you too poor?"

"Too proud," he said. "Our king will not allow it."

"How foolish!"

The minstrel smiled wryly. "Maybe so. The whole family is foolish, I suppose. Idealistic and stiff-necked."

"So the people of your land will die of pride."

He shook his head. "Perhaps. Perhaps not. Maybe something will happen." He sighed. "I don't know, though—the king seems inclined to rely on luck. He seems to think the prophecy will come to pass."

Tarsia frowned. "Why are you going to the Lady's court if you don't like her?"

"A minstrel doesn't worry about magic and winds." He started to play another song, as if to avoid further discussion. The notes echoed across the slow green waters of the river and the steady beat of the horse's hooves provided the rhythm. He sang about an undine, a river nymph who took a human lover, then betrayed him to the waters, letting the river rise to drown him.

Trees with long leaves trailed their branches in the water. The path twisted among the gnarled trunks. They wandered deeper into the shade and the river seemed to take the sunlight into itself, letting it sparkle in swirling eddies but never allowing it to escape. On the far side of the river, the bank rose in a fern-covered cliff, decked with flowers.

"Pretty country," Tarsia said.

"Treacherous country," said the minstrel. "If you tried climbing the cliff you'd learn that those flowers mark loose rock, ready to give beneath your hand or tumble down on you."

At dusk, they were still in the wood and the trees all looked the same. They made camp in an inviting glen, but the tiny fire that Tarsia built seemed to cast little light. Tarsia thought she heard rustling in the trees and once, while she was toasting bread and cheese for dinner, thought she glimpsed a flicker of white in the distance over the

river. She wrapped herself in the minstrel's extra cloak
and curled up alone by the side of the fire.

For a moment she thought that she was in the cavern
beneath the city: it was dark and cold. But the wind that
beat against her face smelled of flowing water and growing
things, and above her, she could see the stars. The Lady
stood beside her, a proud, silent presence.

They had escaped the giant and Tarsia realized that the
giant alone was no threat to the Lady. They dipped closer
to the earth, and Tarsia could see the winding water of the
river, glittering in the moonlight. She could see a tiny spot
of light—her own fire—and she thought she could see the
minstrel on the ground beside it. So far below.

She thought of him coming to the Lady's court to steal
and she wished she could invite him into the chariot
beside her. So cold and alone he looked, as she had felt so
many times on the wall in the city of towers.

"You are above all that now," whispered the Lady at her
said. "You are the daughter of the moon, sister to the sun."

The lapping of the water and the soft nickering of the
horse woke her. The water sounded near, very near. She
sat up and blinked at the sheen of moonlight on the water,
just a few feet away from her. The horse stood at the limits
of his tether, pulling away from the rising waters. Blinking
again, Tarsia could see the slim figure of a woman dressed
in white, standing in the water. At the sound of Tarsia's
movement, the woman looked at her with mournful eyes.

She held out her hands to Tarsia and water dripped
from the tips of her long fingers. Moonlight shimmered on
her, just as it shimmered on the water. From her delicate
wrists, silver chains that seemed to be fashioned of moonlight extended to the water.

Tarsia drew her legs away from the water, stood up and
backed away. The water nymph stretched out her hands
and almost reached Tarsia. The young thief could hear
words in the sound of the lapping water: "Come to me,
touch me, touch the river." Tarsia laid a hand on the horse,
ready to vault to its back and run.

The moonlight touched a spot of darkness in the water—

the minstrel's cloak. The water was around his neck and
still he slept peacefully. His cloak drifted about his shoulders, moving with the water, half tangled around the tree
against which he leaned. To reach the minstrel, Tarsia
would have to touch the river and approach the woman of
water. But no one would know if she ran away to her
mother's court.

"Let me go, daughter of the moon," whispered the
water. The breeze that rustled the leaves by Tarsia's head
seemed to be chuckling.

"Let him go and I'll free you," Tarsia bargained desperately.
"But let him go first." She did not know how to free the
nymph. The watery hands reached for her and she wanted
to leap onto the horse and run.

"Free me, and I will let him go," hissed the voice of the
lapping water.

"But I can't . . . I don't know how. . . ."

A whisper in the night: "Give to me of yourself, daughter of the moon."

In the moonlight, Tarsia could see the minstrel's head
fall back into the water and a swirl of silver bubbles rise.
She stepped forward, ready to push the water nymph
aside. Tarsia's eyes were wet: tears of frustration, anger,
sorrow, pain. A single tear escaped, trickled down her face
and fell into the river. Just one.

Tarsia grabbed the minstrel's cloak and his arm and
roughly dragged him toward the riverbank. At the sound
of a long sigh, she looked up to see the moonlight chains
on the water woman's arms fade. The nymph raised her
hands to the sky in an exultant gesture and the river
sighed, "Thank you, daughter of the Lady." The slim
figure melted into the river, becoming one of the sparkling
ripples in the current. The minstrel coughed and began to
move.

Tarsia lit a fire to dry him out, draping the dry cloak
over his shoulders. She did not need it for warmth. She
felt strong—no longer a thief, but daughter to the Lady.

"How did you plan to get along without me to build
fires?" she asked the minstrel.

He shrugged his slim shoulders beneath the cloak. "I
trust to luck to get me by. Luck and destiny." His eyes

were bright with reflected moonlight. "Sometimes they serve me well."

The next day's ride took them out of the river canyon into the golden foothills. A boy tending a flock of goats by the river stared at them in amazement. "No one ever comes by that path," he said.

Tarsia laughed, cheered by the sight of the mountains ahead. "We came that way."

"What about the undine?" the boy asked.

"What about the undine," she said, still laughing as they rode past. "We sent her on her way."

They walked the horse along the river's edge just past the goat herd. Ahead, they could see the buildings of a small town. The sun shone on Tarsia's face and she saw the mountains, craggy peaks where the snow never melted. "Take me with you to the Lady's court," she asked the minstrel suddenly. "I know why you're going there, and I want to come."

He looked startled. "You know? But . . ."

She laughed. "Do you think I'm half-witted? No minstrel could afford a horse like this one or a fine leather saddle. I knew you were a thief when we first met." She shook her head at the incredulous look on his face. "I know you are going to the Lady's court to steal."

"I see," he said slowly. "But if I'm a thief, why do you want to come with me?" He studied her face intently.

For a moment, she considered telling the truth. But she was city bred, not trusting. "I want to see which of the stories about the Lady are true," she said. "Besides, I can help you." She could imagine herself at her mother's side, rewarding the minstrel with gold and jewels for bringing her there, and she smiled.

"It's a dangerous place," he said.

"If you don't take me, I will go alone," she said. "If you take me, I'll pay my way. I'll pay for tonight's lodging."

He nodded at last. "If you wish, I'll take you. But it's your choice."

The breeze whispered in the tall grass of the riverbank. "The wind is encouraging us," Tarsia said.

"The wind is laughing at us," said the minstrel.

In the inn that night, Tarsia and the minstrel were the

center of a group of villagers. The boy with the goats had told what path they had followed. "You came past the undine," the innkeeper said in amazement. "How did you do it?"

Tarsia told them, leaving out only the water nymph's sigh of farewell. "So the river is free of the Lady's bond," said a sour-faced farmer. "She will not be happy." And the corners of his mouth turned up in a grim smile.

"Softly, friend," advised the innkeeper. "You would not want to be overheard. . . ."

"We live in the shadow of her rule," grumbled the farmer. "But maybe that will come to an end. My boy said he saw the footprints of a giant heading toward her court. These folks say the undine is free. Maybe the Lady . . ."

"Only one of the Lady's own blood can free the winds," interrupted the innkeeper. "And she has no children."

"They say she had a daughter once," said the minstrel quietly. "I studied the ancient stories as a student of the lute. They say that the child was captured in a battle with a neighboring city. The child was killed when the Lady would not release the winds to ransom the girl."

"And the Lady mourned for her daughter?" Tarsia added tentatively.

The crowd of villagers laughed and the minstrel raised his eyebrows. "I doubt it. But the stories don't really say."

A loose shutter banged in the rising wind outside the inn. The group of villagers that had gathered around Tarsia while she had been telling of the water nymph dispersed to other tables.

"Some say that the winds that the Lady allows to blow carry tales back to her," the minstrel told Tarsia softly. "No one knows for certain." The shutter banged again and the conversations around them stopped for a moment, then resumed in hushed tones.

"The land here was green once," said the minstrel. "The people have become bitter as the land has become dry."

The minstrel began to pick the notes of a slow, sweet tune, and Tarsia went to the bar to bargain with the innkeeper for their night's lodging. She took one of the minstrel's coins from her pocket and it flashed silver in the firelight. The innkeeper weighed it in his hand and turned it over to examine both sides.

"A coin of the south," he said, then peered more closely at the profile etched on one side.

The notes of the song that the minstrel was playing drifted across the room, over the sounds of conversation. He was picking out the sad ballad about the Lady that he had played the day before. The innkeeper glanced at him sharply, then looked back at the coin. He seemed to be listening to the sound of the wind prowling around the windows.

"You are heading into the mountains from here?" he asked.

"Yes," Tarsia said cautiously. She knew that he was no friend of the Lady.

He handed her back the coin. "Good luck," he said. "Eat supper as you like, and you may sleep in the loft above the stable."

She frowned at him without comprehension. "What do you mean? Why?"

He seemed to study the minstrel's face in the dim light. "Consider it as payment for ridding the river of the undine." He smiled at her for the first time, and took her hand to fold her fingers around the coin. "Good luck."

She pocketed the coin and returned unhappily to the minstrel's side. She did not like bargains she did not understand. Like the giant, the innkeeper seemed to think that she knew more than she did.

"Did you make a deal?" the minstrel asked.

She sat down on the bench beside him, frowning. "We're sleeping in the stable loft. No payment—he didn't even argue."

"I see." The minstrel nodded across the room to the innkeeper and the older man waved back, a gesture that was almost a salute.

"There are things on which one does not bargain, little one," said the minstrel. "You'll have to learn that."

That night they bedded down in sweet-smelling hay. Outside, the wind bayed like a pack of hounds on the hunt, and Tarsia lay awake. She listened to the minstrel's steady breathing and thought about the mountains and the court of the Lady. But she did not want to sleep and dream.

When she turned restlessly in the hay, the minstrel blinked at her. "Lie down and go to sleep."

"I can't," she grumbled back, into the darkness that smelled of horses.

"What's wrong?" he asked.

"I'm cold," she said, and it was true—even with his extra cloak around her, she was shivering.

He raised himself on one elbow wearily, and lifted his cloak to invite her to lie beside him. She snuggled against his chest and he touched her cheek lightly. "What's worrying you?" he asked. "Do you want to turn back?"

"It used to be so simple," she said, half to herself. "I used to be just a thief in the city, climbing on the city wall and laughing at people who were foolish enough to let me pick their pockets. So simple . . ."

"What are you now?" Though his voice was soft, the question had edges.

The winds bayed and she shivered. "No one. No one at all."

The minstrel rocked her gently in his arms and she listened to his steady breathing as he slept beside her. She slept, but not easily.

The Lady's hand was warm on Tarsia's. Far below, the small thief could see the village: toy huts set on a golden hillside. The mountains rose ahead of them: cold, gray, and forbidding.

"We don't need them," the Lady said in her soft voice. "It doesn't matter that they hate me."

The wind was in Tarsia's face and the stars wheeled about her and she was high above them all. No one could touch her here. No one could put her in shackles or chase her into the sewers. She had come home.

She was quiet when they left town the next morning. The same boy who had met them on the river path was grazing his goats on the hillside. "There are robbers in the mountains," he called to them. "They'll get you if you go up there." The boy was cheerful at the prospect. "There's a dragon, too. The Lady bound him there. If the robbers don't get you, the dragon will find you and ..."

The minstrel urged the horse through the center of the boy's herd and the goats scattered, bleating as they ran.

The horse picked its way carefully up the dry slopes. Toward dusk, the grass gave way to rough rock and the animal began stumbling in the dying light. At Tarsia's suggestion, they dismounted and led the horse. To shake the saddle-weariness from her legs, Tarsia ran ahead, dodging around rocks and scrambling up boulders, feeling almost as if she were at home on the walls of the city. She climbed a rock face and peered over the edge at the minstrel, considering surprising him from above. She saw a movement—a flash of brown—on the trail ahead of him, movements in the brush on either side.

"Hold it there." The man who stepped from behind a boulder had an arrow pointed at the minstrel. Other men closed in from behind.

"I have nothing of value," said the minstrel casually. "Nothing at all."

"You've got a horse," said the leader of the robbers. The man had a soft, lilting accent like the minstrel's. "And I think we need it more than you do." The man lifted the minstrel's money pouch from his belt. Grinning, he hefted the pouch in his hand and gazed at the minstrel's face. "Damn, but your face looks familiar. Do I know you ..." His voice trailed off.

"I'm going to the court of the Lady. I need the horse to get there," the minstrel said.

"A man of the South going to visit the Lady," the leader wondered. "Strange. Since our foolish king has refused to pay tribute to the Lady, few from the South venture into her mountains." As he spoke, he fumbled with the minstrel's pouch, pouring a stream of coins into his hand. "Nothing of value," he said then. "Just pretty gold and silver." The robber held a coin up to the light of the dying sun—just as the innkeeper had held it up—and he whistled long and low. He glanced at the minstrel's face and Tarsia could see his teeth flash in a grin. "Did I say our king was foolish? Not so foolish as his son." The leader tossed the coin to another man in the circle. "Look. We've got a prince here."

The coin was tossed from hand to hand—each man inspecting the minstrel and the coin, the coin and the minstrel. Tarsia, peering over the edge, tried to remember the profile on the coin, briefly glimpsed in a dim light. She tugged a coin from her pocket and compared the cold metal etching with the minstrel's face. They matched.

"We follow our destiny and our luck," the minstrel—or the prince?—was saying. "I am on a mission at my father's request."

The leader's grin broadened and he tossed a coin into the air so that it flashed gold as it tumbled back to his hand. "Bringing tribute," the leader said.

"No." The winds were silent and the voice of the prince—once, the minstrel—was calm. "I have come to free the winds."

Tarsia leaned against the rock and listened to the rhythm of her heart—beating faster and faster. She heard the leader laugh. "What do you expect the Lady to say to that?"

"I may have to destroy the Lady. But the winds must be free. For the sake of the land you have left behind, you must let me go."

"You appeal to the honor of a thief?" the leader said. "You are foolish indeed. And foolish to think that you alone can destroy our Lady."

The prince looked up then, just as if he had known all along where Tarsia was hidden, then looked back to the leader. But his words were echoing in Tarsia's mind: "destroy the Lady . . ." And in her mind, the winds howled. The prince was not alone: the giant had been seen climbing toward her court and the undine was free. Tarsia leaned against the rock for support and listened to the men argue about what to do with the minstrel—no, the prince. She had to remind herself he was a prince. They could hold him for ransom, deliver him to the Lady for a reward, kill him on the spot, feed him to the dragon. She followed, a little above them and a little behind them as they walked to the dragon's cave, still arguing. She heard the horse nicker softly as they stood at the cave entrance. The man who held the animal's reins was right below her hiding place, paying more attention to the argument than to the horse.

Tarsia sprang. Landed half-on and half-off the white horse's broad back, gripping its mane and pounding its sides with her heels. The animal leapt forward—was it by the horse's inclination or her direction? she was not sure—toward the prince. The horse reared as she strove to turn it, dancing in place and throwing its head back, startled past the capacity of even a well-trained horse to bear. Tarsia fought for control, only partly aware of the men who dodged away from the animal's hooves in the dim light of twilight. She could not see the prince.

A crackling of flame, a scent of sulfur, and the mountain was no longer dark. Small thief—she had never dabbled in magic, never met a dragon. If she had imagined anything, she had imagined a lizard breathing fire.

A lightning bolt, a fireworks blast, a bonfire—but it moved like an animal. Where it stepped, it left cinders and when it lifted its head she stared into the white glory of its eyes. A sweep of its tail left a trail of sparks. Half-flame, half-animal—or perhaps more than half-flame.

She could see the prince, standing in its path. The child of fire opened its mouth and for a moment she could see the jagged lightning of its teeth.

"Child of fire," Tarsia called to it, "If I free you will you lead me to my mother?"

The crackling warmth assented with a burst of heat and a flare of flame.

Tarsia's heart was large within her and she was caught by confusion—burning with shame and stung by betrayal. She saw the prince through a haze of smoke and anger. The coins she had stolen from him were in her hand and she wanted to be rid of them and rid of him. "I give of myself to you, child of fire," she said, and hurled them into the flames. Three points of gold, suddenly molten.

The heat of her pain vanished with them. She burned pure and cold—like starlight, like moonlight, like a reflection from the heart of an icicle.

The dragon beat his wings and she felt a wave of heat. He circled the mountain, caught an updraft and soared higher. His flame licked out and lashed the granite slope beneath him before he rose out of sight.

In the sudden silence, Tarsia fought the horse to a standstill. The prince stood alone by the cave. The world was tinted with the transparent twilight blue of early evening in the mountains, touched with smoke and sprinkled with snow.

"You didn't tell me you wanted to free the winds," Tarsia said. Her voice still carried the power it had had when she spoke to the dragon. "You didn't tell me you were a prince."

"I could only trust you as much as you could trust me, daughter of the wind."

"Ah, you know." Her voice was proud.

"I guessed. You freed the undine," he said.

"Had you planned to use me to destroy my mother?" she asked. "That won't work, prophecy or no. I'm here to help my mother, not to destroy her." She urged the horse up the canyon, following the mark left by the dragon's fire. She did not look back.

Up the mountains, following the trail of burned brush and cinders, kicking the horse when it stumbled, urging it to run over grassy slopes marked by flame. The moon rose and the horse stumbled less often. Alpine flowers nodded in the wind of her passing. On the snowbanks, ice crystals danced in swirling patterns.

The towers of the Lady's castle rose from the center of a bowl carved into the mountain. A wall of ice rose behind the towers—glacial blue in the moonlight. The ice had been wrought with tunnels by the wind and carved into strangely shaped pillars. Tarsia rode over the crest of the ridge and started the horse down the slope toward the gates when she saw the giant by the towers.

She felt the strength within her, and did not turn.

As Tarsia drew nearer she saw the figure in the ice wall—the slim form of the undine. She smelled the reek of sulfur and the ice flickered red as the dragon circled the towers.

The gates had been torn from their hinges. The snow had drifted into the courtyard. The stones had been scorched by fire.

Tarsia pulled the horse to a stop in front of the grinning giant. "So you've come to finish the job," he said.

"I have come to see my mother," Tarsia answered, her voice cold and careful.

"I hope you know more than you did when I talked to you last," said the giant.

"I have come to talk to my mother," she repeated. "What I know or what I plan to do is none of your concern." Her voice was cold as starlight.

The giant frowned. "Your mother's men have fled. Her castle is broken. But still she holds the winds in her power. She stands there where we cannot follow." The giant gestured to the tallest tower. Tarsia noticed that the wind had scoured a bare spot in the snow at the tower's base. "Visit her if you will."

Tarsia left the white horse standing by the tower door and climbed the cold stairs alone. She could feel a breeze tickling the back of her neck and tugging at her clothes. She was cold, so cold, as cold as she had been the morning she stole the loaf of bread.

A slender figure was silhouetted in the doorway against the sky. "So you have come to destroy me," said a voice that was at the same time silky and sharp.

"No," Tarsia protested. "Not to destroy you. I came to help you."

She looked up into the gray eyes. The Lady was as beautiful as Tarsia's vision: slim, gray-eyed, ashen haired, dressed in a gown as white as a cloud. In her hand, she held on leash four hounds. They were silver in the moonlight and their bodies seemed to shimmer. Their eyes were pools of darkness and Tarsia wondered what the winds of the world thought about. Where would they wander if they were not on leash? The breeze tugged at her hair and she wondered why they needed to be bound.

Tarsia stared into the Lady's eyes and the Lady laughed— a sound like icicles breaking in the wind. "I see myself in your eyes, Daughter. You have come to help." She reached out and touched the girl's shoulder, pulling the young thief to her. Her hand was cold—Tarsia could feel its chill to her bones.

The wind beat in Tarsia's face as she stood beside the

Lady, looking down at the giant and the snowbank, silvered by moonlight. The dragon swooped down to land nearby and the glow of his flames lent a ruddy cast to the snow.

"We are above them, Daughter," said the Lady. "We don't need them."

Tarsia did not speak. Looking down, Tarsia saw the piece of chain still dangling from the giant's arm and remembered wondering why he had been bound.

"You are waiting for the coming of the one who will destroy me?" called the Lady. "You will wait forever. Here she stands. My daughter has joined me and we will be stronger together than I was alone. You will be cast back to your prisons."

The dragon raised its fiery wings in a blaze of glory. The giant stood by the gate, broad face set in a scowl. The undine flowed from one ice pillar to another—her body distorted by the strange shapes through which she passed.

"All who have risen against me will be chained," said the Lady.

"That need not be," said Tarsia, her voice small compared to her mother's. Then she called out to the three who waited, "Will you promise never to attack us again? Will you vow to—"

"Daughter, there can be no bargains," said the Lady. "No deals, no vows, no promises. You must learn. Those who betray you must be punished. You have power over them; you cannot bargain with them."

The Lady's voice gained power as she spoke—the cold force of a winter wind. Not angry, it was cold, bitter cold. Like the bitter wind that had wailed around the towers of the city—alone, lonely, proud. Like the gusts that had chilled Tarsia when she slept on the city wall. Like the chill in the dungeon when she was chained and unable to escape.

Tarsia looked at the hounds at her mother's feet: shimmering sleek hounds with eyes of night. Why must they be chained? She looked at the Lady: sculpted of ivory, her hair spun silver in the moonlight.

"Go," Tarsia told the hounds. "Be free." The words left her body like a sigh. And the power that would have been hers, that had been hers for a time, left her with the breath. With her sharp knife and an ease born of a magic she did not understand, she reached out and slashed the leashes that held the hounds. Beneath her, the tower trembled.

The hounds leapt forward, laughing now, tongues lolling over flashing teeth, sleek legs hurling them into the air, smiling hounds looking less like hounds and more like ghosts, like silver sand blown by the wind. The Lady's hair whirled about her. She lifted white arms over her head, reaching out to the faraway moon. Tarsia watched and knew that she would never be so beautiful, never be so powerful, never would the winds heel to her command.

The tower trembled and the scent of sulfur was all around and crystals of snow beat at Tarsia's face. She felt herself lifted—or thrown—and caught and tumbled like a coin through the air.

Somehow, someone shut out the moon and stars.

A scent of a charcoal fire—damp dismal smell in the early morning—and . . . damn, she thought. Will I never be free of this? She forced her eyes open.

"You're awake," said the prince. "How do you feel?"

She had been angry, she remembered. And she had been cold with a frozen bitterness. Now she felt only an emptiness where once the power had dwelled within her. She felt empty and light.

She looked back at her mother's castle. A ruin: scorched stones marked with the handprints of the giant, dusted with snow and tumbled by the wind. The ice had crept over the ruin, cracking some stones. Tarsia shivered.

She struggled to her feet and stepped away from the castle, toward the village. Ahead, she could see snow crystals whirling on the surface of a drift. The grass around her feet shifted restlessly in the breeze. She looked at the prince and thought of all the things that she wanted to explain or ask—but she did not speak. The wind flirted with the hem of her skirt and tickled the back of her neck.

"I'll take you with me to my land if you bring the winds along," the prince said. His gaze was steady, regarding her as an equal.

"I can't bring them," she said. "I'm not their mistress."

"They will follow," said the prince. "You're their friend."

The breeze helped him wrap his cape around her and the winds made the flowers dance as the prince and the thief rode away from the ruins.

On the Dark Side of the Station Where the Train Never Stops

This is the story of how Lucy, the fireborn, became the North Star. It happened last month.

(What do you mean—the North Star was there the month before last? I'll bet you believe in dinosaurs too. Take my advice—don't.)

I'll start the story in an Irish pub in the heart of New York—a pub full of strangers and dark corners and the smell of good beer. Beer had seeped into the grain of the place and you could scarcely get away from the scent, any more than you could get away from the sound of laughter and the babble of voices. The locals were puzzled by the strangers in their pub, but the Irish have always recognized the fey. The fireborn and the shadowborn are fey without a doubt.

It was a party and Lucy was there. Of course she was there: Lucy always found the parties or the parties found Lucy, though sometimes it was hard to say which.

Lucy was fireborn and a bag lady. No sweet-lipped heroine she. A chin like a precipice, a nose like a hawk, a voice like a trumpet, and eyes of a wintery blue.

Lucy was charming the bartender, asking him for a full pint measure, rather than the half-pint he usually drew for a lady. The rings on Lucy's battered hands caught the dim glow of the lights. Lucy herself glowed, just a little, with stored radiance. A glitter from her buttons, a sheen from her gray hair. Her eyes sparkled with the light of distant stars.

She was explaining to the barkeep with a straight face, ". . . but you can see for yourself that I'm not a lady."

The barkeep grinned. "So tell me who you all are and what you're all doing here."

"We've always been here," she said.

"In my pub?"

"No—but around and about. Under the city and over the city and such." She waved a hand in a grand gesture to include the world. "Everywhere."

The barkeep nodded. It was difficult to disagree with Lucy when she fixed you with her blue eyes. He drew her a pint.

I will tell you a little more than Lucy told the barkeep, just so you'll be satisfied with the truth of it all. Lucy and her friends are the people who run the world. Often people confuse them with bums, hobos, and bag ladies. People don't know. Lucy and her friends are the people with the many small-but-important jobs that you know so little about: the man who invented ants; the strange-minded dark-dweller who thought that boulders should be broken down into sand and sand shaped back into boulders again; the woman who puts curious things in unlikely places—like the gold lamé slipper you saw by the road the other day.

Some say that Lucy and her friends are gods and some give them names like Jupiter, Pluto, Mercury, Diana. I do not agree. They are people—longer-lived and more important people than most, but people nevertheless.

Lucy took her beer and drifted away from the bar. She wandered—talking to people she knew and people she didn't and people she might like to know. She drifted toward a dark corner where she heard a voice that interested her. And so, she met the man in the shadows.

A cap like a ragpicker, boots like a rancher, a shirt with holes it is better not to discuss—he was one of the shadowborn. No matter what you have heard, they are not all bad, these shadowborn. Not all bad, though their minds are a little twisted and their bones are in the wrong places. Sometimes, they are very interesting people.

He had a nice laugh, and many a meeting has been based on no more.

"Hello," said Lucy to the laughter in the darkness. "My name's Lucy."

"I'm Mac," he said.

"And what's your excuse for being here?" she asked.

He laughed again—an interesting chuckle, more interesting because it held a hint of shadow. "I'm in the business of inventing the past and laying down proof that it really was."

(Now there's a secret of the fireborn and the shadowborn. The world is really only a few years old. Some say five years; some say three. It really doesn't matter that I tell you this. You won't believe it anyway. People rarely believe important truths.)

"What do you do, Lucy?" he asked.

"I'm a firecatcher on the Starlight Run," she said—and it sounded very important when she said it. Well, firecatcher is an important job, I suppose. Someone has to catch the light of distant stars and guide it down to Earth. But really, the Solar Run and the Lunar Ricochet Run (with the tricky reflection) are more important to folks on Earth. The Starlight Run is simply longer and lonelier.

Lucy had been put on the Starlight Run younger than a firecatcher usually was. She had many people fooled into thinking that she was stronger and smarter and tougher than she was. She was on the Starlight Run, and there are many ways that a firecatcher can make that run and be lost forever.

(You want to know how and when and why? Who are you to ask for explanations of things that even people of power don't understand? And explanations will do you no good anyway. Trust me.)

"Interesting job," Mac said. "Not an easy one." And Lucy grinned and set her pint on the table as if she would stop for a while. You know how it is when you meet someone who seems like a friend? You don't know? You should. But even if you don't, just trust me: that's how it was. He seemed like a friend.

"Hey, Lucy," a firecatcher called from the bar.

Lucy laid a hand on the shadowborn's shoulder and said, "I've got to talk to that one. I'll be back." And she ran away to talk and never did get back to the shadows. Parties can be like that.

And that night, Lucy left the city, running up and away

to the far-off stars. And after a time, she came back. She went away, and she came back. And each time she came back, the world seemed a little brighter and the space between the stars a little darker. But she was a firecatcher and she went away and she came back, and there was another party.

The gathering was in the phantom subway station at Ninety-first Street, where the train never stops anymore. The old station was lit by fireballs that Lucy had placed in the rafters. Laughter and voices echoed from the tiled walls.

"You seem a little tired tonight, Lucy," said Johnson, a jovial man who knew everyone's business but managed to keep it all to himself. He lived by the stone lions at the public library and had the look of a fireborn but (some said) the twisty mind of a shadowborn. He was not all sparkle—he governed the sky over the city and some of that sky was clouds.

"l am tired," Lucy said. "Could you do me a favor?"

"What's that?"

"Make it cloudy tomorrow night. l need a holiday."

Johnson frowned. "It's not in the schedule."

She watched him silently. Did I tell you—it's hard to say no to Lucy.

"All right, I'll fix it," he said at last. "We'll have rain."

"Thanks," she said and her eyes studied the crowd.

"Who are you looking for?" Johnson asked.

"Looking for trouble. What else?" Then her eyes stopped on a shadowy alcove beneath a stairway. "I think I found it." She grinned at Johnson and started to turn away.

"Hey, hold on," said Johnson, laying a hand on her shoulder. "He's a shadowborn and—"

"I talked to him at a party a while back," she said. "He seemed interesting. I always wanted a friend in dark places. Besides . . ." She let the word trail away, she shook the restraining hand from her shoulder, and she headed for the stairway. There never was any explaining Lucy's "Besides . . ." And explanations would do no good anyway. She headed for the shadows.

On the edge of the bottom step of the stairs, a spot of

white fluttered in the darkness. Another spot of white crouched nearby.

"Hello, cat," Lucy said to the crouching whiteness, but the young animal was intent on the white scrap of paper that twitched on the stairs.

There was no wind.

Lucy watched and the paper moved—a slight twitch and a bit of a tumble. The cat's eyes grew wider and she inched forward. Again, the scrap moved, fluttering like a bird with a broken wing. The cat flattened herself to the floor, staring.

Not a breeze. But the paper fluttered again and the cat pounced. She held the scrap down with one paw and waited for it to struggle. And waited. Batted at it gently with the other paw.

Lucy heard the darkness ahead chuckle, and she chuckled too. She had a nice laugh, or so folks said. Despite her nose and her chin and her voice, she had a nice laugh. She raised a hand in the darkness and the glitter from her rings became brighter. Still, it was difficult to see him in the dim light and easy to see that he liked it that way.

A cap like a ragpicker, boots like a rancher. Lucy grinned and he grinned back.

"Give up," she said to the cat. "It's not what you think."

"Things hardly ever are," said the man in the shadows. He looked back at the cat and the bit of paper fluttered away, flying like a bat to disappear in the darkness.

The sound of a train in the distance interrupted further discussion. The train never stopped at the Ninety-first Street station—not anymore. But it passed through with a rush of displaced air and a shriek of metal wheels on metal tracks and a headlight like a blaze of glory. The light flashed over peeling advertisements and mosaic tiles obscured by graffiti and empty spaces and a wide-eyed cat who crouched low to the floor.

The rumbling train passed, leaving a great silence behind. Then party guests emerged from behind pillars and from shadowy corners.

Lucy sat in the alcove beneath the stairs. "So what have you been up to, Mac? I haven't seen you since the party in the pub."

"Manufacturing things that never were," he said. "I've been over on the East Side, laying in a fossil bed that should complicate the history of life by more than a little. All sorts of inconsistencies. They'll be confused for weeks. Serves them right for trying to find explanations where there aren't any."

"There's nothing wrong with explanations," she said.

"Ha! They only muddy things," he said. "If only people would accept fossils as interesting art forms. Or the bones of dragons." He shrugged. "What can you expect? They wear lab coats and never see past one kind of truth to another kind. So what have you been doing, Lucy?"

"Going on the Starlight Run." She grinned and her eyes sparkled. "I'm off again, day after tomorrow."

"It's a dark and lonely run," he said.

"Ah, but it's worth it," she said. And she told him about the Starlight Run and about how she dodged through time to jump vast distances and how she caught the light. And he talked to her about the dark ways beneath the city. I can't tell you all that was said.

But they weren't just talking. This was something else and it's hard to say just what. No, there was no crackle of sparks, no ozone in the air. But there was a bright chill that was not just the chill of the unused air of an ancient subway station. There was a tension that was something more than the tension of a party.

Lucy, the fireborn, and Mac, the shadowborn, talked and chuckled. Around them, the party died down. The fireballs were fading when Mac said, "Hey, I'll show you the project I've been working on."

They walked hand in hand. He found his way confidently through the darkness and their footsteps echoed in the tunnels. They stepped into a cavern—she could tell by the change in the echoes. Lucy lifted her hand and her rings glittered with light.

They stood at the edge of a pit. Mac waved at the bones below. "I'm having trouble with this one," he said. The skull looked vaguely crocodilian; the rest was a jumble of bones. "I don't mind making a creature that can't walk, but this one won't even stand. I was playing with the joints and ways of putting them together and—" He stopped, shaking his head.

Lucy frowned, looking down at the bones. "Let's see," she said. She reached a hand toward the pit and the bones began to glow. The heavy skull seemed to shift a little in its resting place, then a shining replica of the head lifted free. The beast raised itself slowly, bone by glowing bone. Each bone was a duplicate of the jumble in the pit.

The beast—a giant lizard of a sort—hesitated, its belly on the ground, its legs bent at an awkward angle. "Thigh bones should be shorter," Mac muttered.

The glowing bones shifted and the beast held its head higher. "Larger feet," he said, and the bones that formed toes stretched and flexed. The beast twitched its tail impatiently. "The back's too long," Lucy said, and shortened a few vertebrae. The beast shook its heavy head, and glared up at them with its empty eyes. "I wish it didn't have so many teeth," she said.

"Leave the teeth," Mac said. "It needs teeth."

The beast gathered its legs beneath itself, still staring at them. It lifted its head farther up and its mouth gaped wider. "I don't like the teeth," Lucy said. And the glow began to fade from the pit. The beast lay down to sleep, as if it had never lived.

Mac and Lucy sat side by side on the edge of the pit. "Why does it need teeth?" she asked.

He shrugged. "The world requires them."

"Not that many," she said. "Not always."

"Just that many," he said. "Always."

Only the faintest glimmer remained on the bones. Still, they sat on the edge, holding hands.

There are things that happen between men and women— even those of the fire and the shadow. Some have names: friendship and love and lust and hatred. Some have no names—being complex mixtures of the named ones with additions of other elements, like curiosity and happiness and wine and darkness and need.

This was one of the second kind of thing. But who knows which and at the time it did not seem to matter. Don't worry too much about the particulars—as I said before, who are you to know how and when and why?

But understand that Lucy, the firecatcher on the Starlight Run, woke up on a hard bench in the phantom subway station.

Hadn't there been a softer surface the night before—with a hint of sheets and pillows and warmth? Maybe. The memory was blurred and she could not say. She was puzzled, for she had not often gone to bed with warmth and awakened in darkness.

It was all very sudden; it was all very odd—and I suppose that's where the story really begins. With sudden chill and darkness. Lucy lifted a hand and tossed a fireball into the empty station. The white cat watched from a tunnel that led to the Outside. "Odd," Lucy said. "Very odd."

Best not get into her thoughts at this point, for her thoughts were neither as coherent nor as polite as "Odd." Best that I let Lucy retain some of her mystery and simply say that she wandered through the tunnel to the Outside and that her feet left glowing prints on the tile floor and her hand left bright marks on the wall where she touched it.

She blinked in the light of the Outside. (Surely you didn't think I'd tell you of the secret ways beneath the city, did you? You were wrong.)

Business people—men and women in neat suits—hurried past her with averted eyes. They saw only a bag lady in a disheveled dress. People do not see all that is there. People do not see much.

Now, Lucy was a mean and stubborn woman. Folks who knew her well did not cross her, because they knew that she didn't let go of an idea or a discontent. She would take it and shake it and worry it—usually to no avail, but that didn't stop her. She did not like dangling ends and she would tie herself in knots to get rid of them.

Johnson, who always knew where to be, lounged in a nearby doorway. Lucy looked at him and he shook his head before she could even speak.

"Very odd," Lucy said again, though I know that was not what she was thinking. She glanced back at the tunnel behind her and she frowned.

Johnson fell into step beside her as she headed for the East Side. "You're heading for trouble," he said.

"Why should today be different from any other day?" she asked and kept on walking.

"So he stole your heart, eh?" Johnson said after a moment. "The shadowborn can be—"

"You know better than that," Lucy interrupted. "I'm just puzzled. I know we were friends and it doesn't seem . . ."

"Very friendly," Johnson completed the trailing sentence. "Hey, he's a shadowborn. He's different."

"Yeah?" Lucy shook her head. "I don't understand."

"You don't understand and they don't understand. It always amounts to a lack of understanding." He walked beside her for a while, then said, "So you're going to try to track down an explanation?"

"I am."

"Don't be disappointed if he doesn't have one," Johnson warned her.

"He must know where he went and who he is," Lucy grumbled.

"Maybe not. But good luck," he said, and he stopped walking.

Lucy continued through the city alone. The day was overcast; Johnson had kept his word and there would be no starshine that night.

In the tunnels on the East Side, Lucy found Mac directing the placement of fossils by several shadowy figures. One skeleton had a lizardlike head with too many teeth. "Hey, I wanted to talk to you," she said. "I—"

"I thought you might want to," he said. "It's simple really."

"Oh, yeah?"

"I thought we should maybe just be friends."

"Yeah? Well, that's all right, but . . ." she began, but he was gone. Directing the positioning of a complex skeleton with legs all out of proportion to its body. Then he was back.

"Yeah, friends. Things get too complicated otherwise," he said. He looked at her, but she could not see his eyes in the shadows.

"Well, it seems to me that things don't need to be complicated. . . ." But he was gone again, grumbling at the workman who was laying down the creature's neck, explaining with words and gestures that the neck had to be placed as if the animal had fallen naturally, not as if some ham-handed workman had laid . . .

Lucy left quietly.

There was a tension in the city that afternoon, a current, a flow of power. It was the kind of day when the small hairs on the backs of your hands stand on end for no reason.

Lucy wandered the city and visited friends. "People don't act like that," she told her friend Maggie. "Not without a good reason."

Maggie shrugged. Maggie specialized in sidewalks and streets that went where no one expected them to go. "Maybe he has a reason." Her voice was soft, like the hiss of tires on pavement, going nowhere. "Maybe he prefers the company of his own kind. Or maybe he prefers no company at all. Or maybe he was never there at all. You can see things in the shadows sometimes."

"He really was there," Lucy said to her friend Brian. She met him in the park in the late afternoon. He was putting away his torches and Indian clubs after a long day of juggling. Brian juggled the lightning on rainy nights.

"Maybe he just wants to be friends," Brian suggested. "Well, cheer up. I'll teach you to juggle."

But the round balls always tumbled to the ground and Lucy could not laugh as she had laughed every other time that Brian had tried to teach her.

"So what is it about him?" Brian asked at last, sitting down in the grass.

"It's not him," Lucy said, sitting down beside him. "It's people. People shouldn't act that way."

"They do."

"Not us," she said. "*They* do." She gestured at the people strolling through the park. A girl sat on a bench nearby and the sun was shining on her hair. A man with sky blue eyes walked past the young woman and for a moment their eyes met. Lucy saw it and Brian saw it. But the man walked on past and the sunlight faded from the woman's golden hair. "They're like that," Lucy said. "They don't see past the surface. But this shadow-born . . . he's one of us."

"Maybe not," Brian said. He reached for her hand and she started when he touched her—just a small shiver. Then she took his hand and they watched the sunlight fade and the shadows stretch away across the park. But she left when darkness came.

There was a thunderstorm over the city that night and great flashing streaks of lightning split the overcast sky. Rumbles of thunder shook the buildings and made bums and bag ladies seek the cover of doorways and bus shelters.

But Lucy was a mean and stubborn woman. She walked through the storm and did all the things that should bring luck and power.

She threw three copper coins in a certain fountain at midnight.

She put seven pennies, standing on edge, between the bricks of a certain wall.

She turned her jacket inside out, like a woman who has been led astray by pixies and means to break the spell.

She found a four-leaf clover in the wet grass of the park and tucked it behind her left ear.

At dawn, Johnson found her sitting in the park in the wet grass. "Do me a favor?" she asked without looking up. "Can you make it rain tonight?"

He shook his head slowly. His face was set in a frown and his hands were deep in his pockets. "It won't do you any good," he said. She did not look up at him. "You can't just stay and look and wait." He waited a moment, but she did not speak. "You really are upset, aren't you?"

She plucked another daisy from the grass beside her. "He was a· friend. I didn't think I could lose a friend so easily."

"Tomorrow night, the stars must shine," he said unhappily.

"It's a long and lonely run," she said slowly. And at last she looked up at him. He could not read her expression. "But I have until twilight."

"It's no good, Lucy. You're looking for an explanation and—"

"I'm looking for trouble," she said with a touch of her old tone. "I'll find it."

And the sun rose over the city and began to burn away the fog. Lucy went back to the tunnels on the East Side. (Trust me: you couldn't follow the directions there if I gave them.) Her footsteps echoed in the darkness. The construction site was empty and the corridors were dark and silent. She went looking for trouble and she did not find it.

She ended up back at the phantom subway station, alone and unhappy. But she was a firecatcher and a lady of some power. Even tired and hurt, she had some power. She traced a figure in the air, outlined it with light. A cap like a ragpicker, boots like a rancher, a shirt with undiscussable holes. Face in shadow, of course.

"You know, I don't understand," she said to the figure. "And I don't think you do either." A train rumbled through the station and the figure disappeared for a moment in the brighter glow of the headlight. Lucy did not move. A slight tremor went through the glowing shape, like a ripple in a reflection, starting at the battered boots and ending at the stained cap. "I'm confused, and I don't like being confused." She glared at the figure for a moment. It did not move, did not speak.

She walked away, leaving a trail of glowing footprints. At the entry to the tunnel (Still want to know where the tunnels are, don't you? Ha! You'll never find out now.), she looked up at the night sky, toward the Little Bear, her particular constellation.

She walked across town to the library, where she knew Johnson would be. "I came to say good-bye," she said.

"You're leaving on the Run?"

She nodded. "It's a tricky run," she said and her voice was young and soft. "I may not be back."

Johnson tried to take her hand but she stepped back and laid a hand on the head of one of the lions. "It's all right," she said. "I just need a different point of view for a while. I'll be fine. I might be back later."

Johnson shook his head. "Hey, if I see that shadowborn, what do you want me to—"

"Don't say a word," she said. "Don't explain a thing."

She stood with one hand on the head of the lion and she

looked up toward the Little Bear, a constellation that had always seemed to be missing a star. And she began to fade—her hair changing from the color of steel to the color of twilight, her face losing its craggy reality, her body losing its harsh line. And in a moment, she was gone and away on the Starlight Run.

She hasn't come back yet. That's why you can't see many stars in the city—they're short a firecatcher still. She became a star herself, sitting up in the far-off, throwing gobs of light down at the world. (And if you want to know how she became the North Star, ask the man who lives by the lions. He may tell you, if you have the right look about you. Or he may not.)

What do you mean—the North Star was always there? Haven't you been listening? The world is not as it seems. Ask any poet. Ask any bag lady. Ask anyone who sees in the twilight and knows of the fireborn and the shadows.

Down in the tunnels and secret ways of the city, the white cat mated with a black tom and produced litters of kittens who pounce and play with paper scraps that dance and flutter but never live. A faintly glowing figure still waits in the phantom subway station for a train that will never stop.

And Mac? You want to know what happened to the shadowborn? It's possible that he never was at all. But if he was, then probably he still is and probably he is happy and probably he has never found the light sculpture that leans against the dark wall of the phantom subway station. Probably.

So that's the story and you can draw your own conclusions. But one warning: If you have a streak of the shadow in you, don't follow the North Star. She may lead you astray. Lucy can be like that—she can hold a grudge.

And if you do have the shadow in you, don't worry. I made the whole thing up. There—feel better? All right? All right.

In the Abode
of the Snows

In a hospital room with white walls, Xavier Clark held the hand of his dying mother. The chill breeze from the air-conditioner made him think of the snow-covered peaks of the Himalayas: Annapurna, Machhapuchhare, Dhaulagiri, Nilgiri. Places he had never been. His mother's shallow breathing could have been the whispering of snow crystals, blown by mountain breezes across a patch of ice. The veins beneath her pale skin were faintly blue, the color of glacial ice.

His mother's eyes were closed, and he knew she was dying. With each passing year, she had grown more frail, becoming as brittle as the delicate teacups that she kept locked in the china cabinet. Her hair had grown paler, becoming so ethereal that her scalp showed through no matter how carefully she combed and arranged the white wisps.

His mother's breathing stopped, and he listened, for a moment, to the quick light sound of his own breathing and the pounding of his own heart. Closing his eyes, he clung to his mother's hand and savored a faint uneasy feeling of release, as if his last tie to earth had been cut and he could soar like a balloon, leaving the ordinary world behind.

Xavier returned from the hospital to his mother's house. Though he had lived in the house for all of his forty years, he still thought of it as his mother's house. Even when his father had been alive, the house had been his mother's. His father had always seemed like a visitor, stopping at the house to rest and write between expeditions to Nepal.

When Xavier was five, his father had died in a snowslide

on the eastern slope of Dhaulagiri. When Xavier tried to remember his father, he could picture only the broad-shouldered man that he had seen in out-of-focus book-jacket photos, a lifeless black-and-white image.

More clearly than Xavier remembered his father, he remembered his father's possessions: an elaborately carved prayer wheel that reeked of incense, a small rug on which two dragons curled about one another in an intricate pattern, a brass bowl that sang when struck with a wooden rod, wooden masks with great empty eyes and grimacing mouths, round brass bells the size of his fist attached to a strip of brightly colored tapestry. Upon receiving word of his father's death, Xavier's mother had taken all these exotic treasures, wrapped them in newspaper, and packed them in a steamer trunk that she pushed into a corner of the attic. As a child, Xavier had yearned to look at his father's belongings, but the steamer trunk was locked and he had known better than to ask his mother for the key.

His mother had never talked of his father after his death. She never remarried, raising Xavier herself, living frugally on the proceeds of his father's insurance policies and on royalties from his books.

As a teenager, Xavier bought copies of his father's three books: *Adventures on the Roof of the World, Land of Yak and Yeti,* and *The Magic of Nepal.* He hid the books from his mother and read them in his room when he was supposed to be doing his homework. On the map in the flyleaf of one book, he traced his father's journeys in red pen. In his sleep, he muttered the names of mountains: Machhapuchhare, Annapurna, Dhaulagiri, Nilgiri. He remembered the names of Himalayan rivers, fed by monsoon rains and melting snows. He knew the names of his father's porters—the Sherpas who accompanied the mountaineering expeditions—better than he knew the names of his own schoolmates.

He was a shy teenager with few friends. After graduating from high school, he attended the local college and majored in biology. He had planned to base his thesis on observations of mountain sheep in the Rockies, but just before he was due to leave, his mother had taken ill. He canceled his trip and spent the summer observing waterfowl in a local pond, writing a thesis on the behavior of coots in an urban environment.

At college graduation, he was offered a job as wildlife biologist in the Idaho National Forest. Upon receiving the good news, his mother suffered the first in a series of heart attacks. He accepted a position as biology teacher at the local high school and stayed home to nurse her.

Living in his mother's house with the silent memories of his father's glorious past, he had become a secretive and solitary man. His clothes hung loosely on his body, like the skin of a reptile preparing to molt. His students joked about him, saying that he looked like one of the thin dry lizards that he kept in the classroom's terrarium. He had grown prematurely old, never leaving town because his mother was never well enough to travel and never well enough to be left alone.

In the empty house, the evening of his mother's death, Xavier was truly alone for the first time in decades. He felt strangely hollow—not lonely, but empty. He felt light, insubstantial, as if the slightest breeze could carry him away. He could do anything. He could go anywhere. He thought about his father's trunk and went to the attic.

The trunk had been pushed to the farthest corner, tucked under the eaves—behind a broken lamp, a dressmaker's dummy stuck with pins, a box of Xavier's old toys, and an overstuffed armchair with torn upholstery in which generations of mice had nested. The trunk was locked and, for a moment, Xavier hesitated, considering retreat. Then he realized that the house and all its contents were his. With a screwdriver and hammer, he attacked the trunk's rusty hasp and tore it free of the lid.

On top of the newspaper-wrapped bundles in the trunk lay a package wrapped in brown paper and decorated with Nepali stamps. Xavier carefully unwrapped the package and found a leatherbound notebook filled with spidery handwriting that looked curiously like his own.

Xavier opened the book and read a page: "I have decided to leave the expedition and press on alone, following the Kali Gandaki to its source. In the bleak northern hills, I am certain I will find the man-ape that the Sherpa call the yeti. Winter is coming and many will call me foolish, but I cannot turn back. I miss my wife and son, but I like to think that my son, if he were here, would understand. I cannot turn back. The mountains will not let me."

Mingling with the dusty air of the attic, Xavier thought he smelled incense, a foreign smell that awakened unfamiliar urges. Kneeling beside the trunk, with his father's journal in his hands, he felt, in some strange way, that he had made a decision. He knew that he would not return to school for the fall term.

In a new backpack, purchased at the local sporting goods store, Xavier packed field notebooks, camera, and many rolls of film. He bought a kerosene stove and tested it in the backyard, boiling water for tea in a lightweight aluminum pot. He bought a plane ticket to Katmandu by way of Bangkok and converted $5,000 cash into traveler's checks. He studied a book titled *Nepali Made Simple*, memorizing simple phrases. He haunted the local college library, reading all the accounts of yeti sightings that he could find.

Mountaineers described the beast as inhumanly tall and covered with shaggy hair. Some said it was nocturnal, prowling the barren slopes between the treeline and the permanent snows. Some said it was like a monkey; others, like a bear. Tibetans and Nepalis credited the beast with supernatural powers: its bones and scalp were valued as objects of great power.

He read his father's journal, lingering over descriptions of the terrain, the mountains, the wildlife. His father's books had maintained a heroic tone: men battled the wilderness, always fought fair, and usually triumphed. The journal gave a more realistic account: describing stomach upsets and bouts with dysentery, complaining of lazy porters, recording bribes given minor officials for quicker service. The journal told of superstitions: Tibetans believed that shamans could transform themselves into birds, that finding a hat was unlucky, that dogs howling at dawn were an inauspicious omen. Xavier read all this with great enthusiasm.

At night, Xavier dreamed of cold slopes, scoured clean

by endless winds. He was filled with a feverish longing for the high country, where the snows never melt. He would find the yeti, track its movements, study its biology. He would finish the task that his father had begun and return to his mother's house to write of his success.

On his first day in Katmandu, Xavier wandered the narrow streets of the alien city, marveling at how strange and yet how familiar it seemed. It matched his father's descriptions, yet somehow, on some level, it seemed quite different.

A shy Hindu boy with a red tika dot painted on his forehead stared at Xavier from a dark doorway. The child wore no pants and his dark skin reflected a little light from the street, a subtle sheen on thin legs, thin buttocks. In the shade provided by a shrine to Ganesh, the elephant-headed son of Vishnu, a street dog rested and licked her sores.

The market smelled of incense, strong spices, and cow manure. Xavier shooed away the vendors who tried to sell him tourist trinkets, the rickshaw drivers who asked in broken English where he was going, the black market money changers who offered him a good rate, a very good rate, for American dollars. He was caught by the feeling that something was about to happen, something sudden and strange, something exotic and unanticipated. He stared about him with impassioned hungry eyes, watching for a secret signal that the adventure began here.

In a small square, bedsheets and other laundry flapped from the second floors of the surrounding houses. The wooden frames of the windows had been ornately carved sometime in the last three centuries. The faces of Hindu deities and demons stared from a complex background of twisting human bodies, vines, and flowers. In the square below, heaps of yellow grain dried in the autumn sun. Small children kept guard, stopping noisy games to chase away cows and dogs and pigs.

In a small street stall frequented only by Nepalis, Xavier ate lunch, crouching uncomfortably on a wooden bench just barely out of the street. The high clear piping of flutes played by flute sellers mingled with the honking of rickshaw horns and the jingling of bicycle bells.

Though the Nepalis ate with their hands, the shopkeeper insisted on giving Xavier a tarnished and bent fork and on showing the American how to sprinkle hot peppers on his *daal baat*, the rice and lentil dish that served as the staple of the Nepali diet. The shopkeeper, a wizened man in a high-crowned brimless hat, sat beside Xavier on the bench and watched him eat.

"You come from England?" the shopkeeper asked Xavier.

"No, from America."

"You going trekking?"

"Well, yes," he said. "I plan to go up past a town called Jomsom. I . . ." He hesitated, then plunged on. "I have read that yeti have been seen in that area."

"Ah, you wish to find the yeti?"

"Very much."

The shopkeeper studied him. "Westerners do not have the patience to find the yeti. They hurry, hurry, and never find what they look for."

"I have all the time in the world," Xavier said.

The shopkeeper folded his hands in his lap, smiled, and said, "You will need a guide. My cousin, Tempa, can take you where you need to go."

Xavier ate and listened to the shopkeeper praise the virtues of his cousin Tempa. Sitting in the open stall, he looked up at the thin strip of sky visible between the houses. A single bird flew over, heading northwest. Xavier watched it vanish from sight and knew, with the same certainty that had caused him to quit his job and come to Nepal, that he would go northwest to the Himalayas, to the high country where anything could happen.

On the fourth day on the trail, Xavier and Tempa were caught in a violent hailstorm that transformed the path into a running stream that splashed merrily around Xavier's boots. The water quickly penetrated the waterproof oil that Xavier had applied to the boots in Katmandu. His socks were soon soaked and his feet ached with the cold.

In a low stone hut that served as teahouse and provided primitive accommodations, they found shelter. The group of ragged porters that huddled by the fire looked up when Xavier ducked through the low doorway. The teahouse was filled with woodsmoke and the scent of unwashed clothing. The small fire that burned in the center of the single room seemed to provide more smoke than warmth.

Xavier blinked as his eyes adjusted to the dark interior. Not elegant accommodations, but better than a tent and no worse than the teahouses that had sheltered them for the past three days. Xavier propped his pack against the wall and hung his rain parka on a nail that jutted from the wooden doorframe.

The proprietress, a Tibetan woman, offered him *rokshi*, locally distilled wine, and he accepted gratefully. The clear liquor smelled faintly of apples and tasted overwhelmingly of alcohol. The first mouthful seared his mouth and throat with a bright, almost painful warmth that spread slowly to his chest. He sat on a wooden bench by the door and slowly unlaced his wet boots.

Tempa was already deep in conversation with the porters who crouched by the fire. He looked up at Xavier, his eyes reflecting the firelight. "They say that snow has fallen in the pass to the north," Tempa said to Xavier. "And a big storm is coming."

Xavier shrugged, pulled off his boots, and gingerly wiggled his toes. Since the very first day, Tempa had been complaining about the weight of his pack, the length of each day's hike, the perils of bad weather. "Not much we can do about the weather," he said.

Tempa frowned. "Big storm," he said. "Too late in the season to go on. Tomorrow, we go back."

Xavier shook his head and frowned at Tempa, trying to assume an air of authority. "Go back? We've just started. If there's a storm, we'll wait it out."

"Too cold," Tempa said. "Winter is here."

"Tomorrow, we go on," Xavier said. His father had written of stubborn porters and of the need to show them who was boss. "Do you understand? I'm not ready to go back."

Tempa returned unhappily to his friends by the fire. Xavier relaxed, loosened the collar of his damp flannel shirt, and leaned back against the stone wall of the teahouse. The warmth of the *rokshi* spread throughout his body. Outside, the rain had stopped and a rooster was crowing. Xavier closed his eyes and listened to the soft whispering of water flowing down the trail, the gentle clucking of the chickens that searched for edible insects in the scrubby weeds that grew just outside the teahouse door. The breeze that blew through the door smelled of mountains that had been washed clean by the rain. He took a deep breath, but caught a whiff of another scent, something stronger than the woodsmoke or the *rokshi*—an animal scent. He looked up to see an old man standing in the hut's open doorway.

Though the afternoon breeze was cold, the old man wore no shirt or jacket, only a loose loincloth of an indeterminate color. The cloth may once have been white, but it had become an uncertain shade of gray: the color of dust, of woodsmoke, of ashes and grime. The man's long gray-streaked hair was wound in a topknot. The ancient face was stern—a high forehead, a nose like a beak. Around the man's neck hung a string of round beads, each one a different shade of off-white. Xavier stared at the beads, recognizing them from a description in his father's journal. Each of the 108 beads had been carved from the bone of a different human skull. At the man's belt dangled a carved ivory *phurba*, the ritual dagger carried by all shamans of Bon, the ancient animistic religion that had preceded Buddhism in the Himalayas.

In one hand, the man carried a metal bowl, which he held out to the Tibetan woman. She beckoned him in and he squatted beside the fire.

"*Namaste*," Xavier said, the traditional Nepali greeting that meant "I salute you." His voice was suddenly unsteady. Here was adventure—a traveling shaman visiting the same teahouse.

The old shaman stared at Xavier, but did not return his greeting.

Xavier beckoned to Tempa. "Who is the old man?" he whispered.

Tempa's small vocabulary deserted him when he did not find it convenient to speak English. Now, occupied with a glass of *rokshi* and eager to return to his friends, Tempa shrugged. *"Ta chaina."* I don't know.

"Where is he from?"

Tempa frowned, seemingly reluctant to say anything about the old man. "He lives alone." Tempa waved an arm toward the hills.

"A hermit," Xavier said.

Tempa shrugged and returned to his friends.

The Tibetan woman served dinner, scooping a serving of rice into the old man's bowl and moistening the grain with a spoonful of *daal*. The old man silently accepted the offering. The woman dished out a similar dinner for the others.

After his third glass of *rokshi* and a plate of *daal baat*, Xavier had relaxed. The old man, he noticed, ate alone, squatting in a corner of the hut. With *rokshi*-induced courage, Xavier went to the corner and endeavored to begin a conversation with the old man.

"Rokshi?" Xavier said to the old man, and then he signaled the woman for another glass. The old man studied Xavier with impassive black eyes, then accepted the glass.

"Timiko ghar ke ho?" the old man asked Xavier. *"Timi kaha jane?"* Where are you from? Where are you going?

Xavier replied in halting Nepali. I come from America. Then he waved a hand to indicate his destination, pointing northward toward the high cold mountains that filled his dreams. *"Meh-teh hirne,"* he said. Which meant, more or less, I look for the yeti.

The old man took Xavier's hand in a strong grip and peered into the American's face with sudden intensity. He spoke rapidly in Nepali, but Xavier could not follow his words. When Xavier shrugged, looking bewildered, the old man called to Tempa, who sat with the other porters by the fire. Tempa responded in Nepali.

The old man broke into a grin, his stern face collapsing into wrinkles. He reached out a withered hand and cupped Xavier's chin, lifting the biology teacher's face as a doting grandmother might lift the face of a shy child. The old man threw back his head and laughed at something that he saw in Xavier's face. He released his hold on Xavier, and said something, but the only word Xavier could catch in the rapid string of Nepali was "*meh-teh*." Something about yeti.

Xavier smiled uneasily, wondering how his father would have handled a situation like this. "What's all that about?" Xavier asked Tempa. Reluctantly, Tempa left his friends and came to squat beside Xavier and the old man.

"He wants to know where you are going," Tempa said. "I tell him you look for the yeti."

Xavier nodded and smiled at the old man.

The old man said something else in rapid Nepali. Xavier shook his head and asked him to speak more slowly.

Still grinning, the old man repeated himself, pausing after each word and accompanying his words with gestures. Xavier couldn't follow everything that the old man said, but he thought he caught the gist of it: The old man had seen the yeti many times. He was a powerful shaman and he had hunted the yeti many times.

Xavier poured the old man another cup of *rokshi* and asked him to tell about the yeti. Beside the fire, three porters played a noisy game of cards. Outside the door, by candlelight, the Tibetan woman washed the dinner dishes. Inside the smoky teahouse, Xavier leaned close to the old man, ignoring his animal scent, and listened to tales of the yeti.

The yeti looked like men, only different, the old man explained slowly. They hunted at night, and they were very strong. With only his hands, a yeti could kill a yak, break the neck. (The old man brought his hands together like a man snapping a stick.) The yeti is fierce and cunning.

Xavier, with hand gestures and halting Nepali, asked the old man how he hunted such a fierce beast. With a dirty finger, the old man tapped his temple and nodded sagely. He called out to the woman, and she brought a stoneware crock and two tin cups. The old man filled the cups with a ladle and offered one to Xavier. "*Yo chang ho,*" the old man said. This is *chang*.

Xavier had heard of *chang*, a thick beer brewed with rice and barley. Unwilling to offend the old man, he sipped the thick beverage. It tasted like a mixture of sour porridge and alcohol, but after the first few sips, it wasn't too bad.

The old man tapped the cup and told Xavier that he hunted the yeti with *chang*. He launched into a long explanation which Xavier followed with difficulty. To catch a yeti, it seems, the old man found a village where a yeti had been bothering people, stealing their crops and killing their goats. On a night when the moon was new, the old man left a pot of *chang* in the path where the yeti would find it. The yeti drank the *chang* and fell asleep, and in the morning, the old man captured it easily. Yeti, said the old man, like *chang*.

More *chang*, more labored discussion of the habits of the yeti. Xavier grew accustomed to the smoke that filled the room. At some point, the Tibetan woman lit a candle, and the flickering light cast enormous shadows that danced on the walls. The old man's face, illuminated by the candle, seemed filled with sly amusement. Sometimes, it seemed to Xavier that the old man was laughing at him beneath the words, teasing him with some private joke. But the room seemed small and cozy and Xavier's Nepali improved with each glass of *chang*. It was a good life, a good place to be. Xavier lost track of how many cups of *chang* he drank. The old man seemed like a good friend, a faithful companion.

Somehow, Xavier found himself telling the old man about his father and his search for the yeti. Groping for words in Nepali, he tried to explain that he needed to find the yeti, to finish what his father had started. He tried to explain how he felt about the mountains. In a mixture of Nepali and English, he tried to describe his dreams of mountains and snow.

The old man listened intently, nodded as if he understood. Then he spoke softly, slowly, laying a hand on Xavier's hand. I can help you find the yeti, he said to Xavier. Do you want to see the yeti?

Drowsy from *chang*, half-mesmerized by the candle-light, Xavier took the old man's hands in both of his. "I want to find the yeti," he said in English.

The old man fumbled for something in the pouch that

dangled at his belt. He displayed his findings to Xavier on the palm of a withered hand: a small brown bone etched with spidery characters. The bone was attached to a leather thong. It was made of yeti bone, the old man explained. Very powerful, very magical.

Xavier reached out and touched the small dried object. It was warm to the touch, like a small sleeping animal. The old man smiled. His dark eyes were caught in a mesh of wrinkles, like gleaming river pebbles in a bed of drying mud.

The old man nodded, as if reaching some conclusion, then looped the leather thong around Xavier's neck. Startled, Xavier protested, but the old man just smiled. When Xavier lifted the pendant, as if to remove it, the old man scolded him in Nepali.

They had more *chang* to celebrate, and Xavier's memories were fuzzy after that. He remembered the old man reassuring him that he would see the yeti. He remembered lying down on a bamboo mat by the fire and pulling his still damp sleeping bag over himself.

In his dreams, he fingered the bone that hung around his neck. He dreamed of studying the mark of a bare foot on the side of a snowy mountain. In the dream, he squatted to measure the length, the width. Suddenly, without surprise, he realized that his own feet were bare. His feet ached from the cold of the snow, and he was hungry, very hungry.

He blinked awake in the pale morning light. He could hear the hollow clanging of metal bells: a mule train was passing on the trail. The wood smoke that drifted through the hut's open door reminded him of the cold mist that filled the mountain gorges of his dreams. His head and belly ached, and he remembered drinking too much *rokshi*, too much *chang*.

The other bamboo mats were empty. The Tibetan woman crouched by the hearth, poking the fire that burned beneath the blackened teakettle. The porters were gone; the old man was gone. Confused by lingering dream images, Xavier sat up and felt the leather thong around his neck. The bone was there. He ran a fingernail over the rough surface and felt more confident. His throat was sore and his voice was hoarse when he asked the woman where his porter, Tempa, had gone.

The woman shook her head. *"Ta chaina,"* she said. I don't know.

Xavier struggled from his sleeping bag and stumbled out of the hut, making for the boulder-strewn slope that served as a latrine. The wind numbed his face and the gray world outside the hut seemed less substantial than his dreams. The sky was overcast; the mountains, hidden by distant haze. The ground underfoot was composed of mottled gray and brown pebbles, swept clean by the steady wind from the north. The trail, a faint track marked by the dung of pack mules and the scuff marks of hikers' boots, led northward.

Xavier stopped beside a large boulder. He noticed a large raven, perched on a distant rock, watching with interest as he pissed. "What do you want?" he said crossly to the bird. The bird regarded the man with bright curious eyes, shrieked once, then took flight, leaving him alone, blinking at the gray sky.

Xavier made his way back to the hut. Tempa was gone. When he asked the Tibetan woman again, she shrugged and said something about Tempa leaving very early in the morning. The porter had taken some of Xavier's possessions along with his own: Xavier's wool gloves and hat, the wool socks that had been drying by the fire, and the rupee notes that Xavier kept in his jacket pocket.

Xavier contemplated the desertion with mixed feelings. He could pursue the thieving porter, but if he turned back, he would miss his chance to search for the yeti. He was seized by uncertainty. Perhaps the weather was turning bad and he should turn back. Could he find his way without a guide? Should he abandon his provisions and trust to local supplies for his food?

At the same time, he was glad at the thought of traveling on alone. The porter had seemed skeptical of Xavier's plans from the first day on the trail. Tempa had, Xavier felt, lacked the proper spirit of adventure.

In the end, it was Xavier's memory of the old man's words that decided him. "You will see the yeti," said the old man. How could Xavier turn his back on such a prophecy?

Taking a loss, Xavier sold most of his remaining supplies to the Tibetan woman. He added the rest to his own load. When he left, his pack was heavier by about twenty pounds. Though he knew that his shoulders would be aching by noon, he whistled as he walked, relishing the thought of being alone in the desolate reaches of the Himalayas.

North of Ghasa, past the village of Tukche, the valley broadened. No trees grew on the great gray slopes. On the lee side of large boulders grew stunted bushes and patchy grasses, tough plants with foliage as dusty as the rocky slopes. Shaggy goats, snatching a thorny lunch in one such patch, stared at Xavier as he passed, their golden eyes faintly hostile. The children who tended the herd, two ragged boys with unruly hair and snotty noses, silently watched the white man with indifferent curiosity.

Once, a flock of ravens took flight from the hillside beside him, wheeling above him to darken the sky like a flight of demons. One raven from the flock kept pace with him for a time: flying ahead to perch on a *mani* wall, a jumbled construction built of flat stones carved with Buddhist prayers. As Xavier approached, the bird called out in a croaking guttural voice, then flew to a boulder a few hundred yards down the trail. Each time Xavier drew near, the bird flew on a little farther, then stopped by the trail, as if waiting for the man to catch up.

The wind blew constantly, kicking up the dust and carrying along leaves and twigs. It blasted the boulders and scoured the *mani* stones, as if trying to wipe the carved letters away. It chapped his lips, dried his throat, and rubbed dust into his skin and hair.

The trail followed the Kali Gandaki, a chilly turbulent river with waters as gray as the rounded granite boulders that lined its bank. In the valley, the river widened, flowing in a network of channels that merged and separated like the veins and arteries of a living animal. The trail wandered beside one of the channels. Beside the water, sparse red-brown grass grew, gray soil showing between the blades.

Without his wool cap, Xavier's ears were unprotected and the rushing of the wind blended with the rushing of the river and the shrill cries of insects in the grass. As he traveled north, signs of passing travelers grew fewer: the mark of boot in the mud; a few hoofprints; ancient horse droppings, long since dried to dust. The trail sometimes disappeared altogether, leaving Xavier to wander by the stream, searching for another sign to show him the way.

A few trees had grown there, reached maturity, then died. Their skeletons reached for the sky, twisted by the nagging wind and crippled where peasants had chopped away branches for firewood. The landscape had a dream-like quality, as if this were a place that Xavier had imagined for himself. Dry branches rattled in the dry breeze. He was not startled when a raven flew from a twisted tree, laughing when the wind lifted it aloft. It seemed right for the raven to be there, to laugh, to fly ahead as if showing him the way.

The village of Jomsom was an unwelcome intrusion on the landscape, a cluster of low-lying stone houses inhabited by people who had been blasted into passivity by the constant wind. The streets and houses were gray and lifeless, and he passed through as quickly as he could.

A few miles beyond Jomsom, the trail forked: one branch led to Muktinath, a destination popular with trekkers. Xavier took the other branch, the ill-marked track that led to the north. A few miles down the trail, he stopped by the Kali Gandaki, clambering down the steep bank to the rushing water. Though the air was still cold, hiking had warmed him. The wind had eased and the sun was out. He stripped to the waist, draping his shirt over a rock and putting his watch beside it. He splashed the river water on his face, his chest, and up over his back, gasping when the cold water struck his skin, shaking his head like a wet dog.

He was toweling dry when he heard the harsh cry of a raven. The black bird was perched on the boulder beside his shirt. Xavier saw the raven peck at something on the rock, and he shouted, waving at the bird. The raven took flight, and Xavier saw that it carried his watch in its beak. The bird circled, the watch glinting in its beak. Then the wind caught the bird and it soared away over the woods, vanishing from sight.

Xavier did not miss the watch as much as he expected to. As the day passed, he grew accustomed to a timeless existence. He stopped to eat lunch when he was hungry, rested when he was tired. He camped out that night, stopping between villages beside the Kali Gandaki and using his mountain tent for the first time. He dreamed bright crystalline dreams: he was on a steep ice slope, pursuing a dark shape that remained always just a few steps ahead. He chased the dark shape to the edge of a precipice and slipped on the ice, realizing as he fell that the fleeing darkness was his own shadow.

When he woke, the ground was white with frost, and his breath made clouds that the wind swept away. At dusk the next day, he reached the village of Samagaon. The villagers eyed him with great suspicion: strangers were a rare sight so far from the trekking route.

With Tempa's theft, Xavier's supply of rupees had dwindled. He found only one teahouse, and the proprietor, a Gurkha soldier who had returned to his home village, scoffed at the American's traveler's checks, puffing his cheeks out and saying that the checks might be no good, he couldn't tell.

Xavier considered the matter, then offered to trade some of his equipment for cash and food. The man did not want a wool sweater or down jacket, but he inspected the kerosene stove carefully. On the spur of the moment, Xavier decided he could do without a stove. He demonstrated it carefully, filling the fuel tank with kerosene and lighting the burner. It coughed once or twice, then roared with a steady blue flame that lit one corner of the dark smoky tea shop. In limited Nepali, Xavier praised the stove: "*Ramro cha. Dheri ramro.*" It's good, very good. His voice was hoarse from days of silence.

While Xavier bargained, two ragged little girls watched from behind the skirts of the man's wife. They stared with wide round eyes, trying to absorb this curiosity, this white man far from the places that white men were found. The shopkeeper came from a long line of traders, and he drove a hard bargain. In the end, Xavier traded for rice, lentils, curry powder, and 200 rupees cash—a fraction of the stove's value, but he could carry no more food and the shopkeeper claimed that he had no more cash. Xavier spent the night on the shopkeeper's floor, ate a hurried breakfast of corn porridge sweetened with honey, and headed north.

He sang as he walked, a tuneless melody that seemed to ebb and flow like the rushing of the river. His beard was growing in, and when he saw his reflection in a still pool, he laughed at himself, a rough-looking character with a dirty face and good crop of stubble.

Early in the morning, he could see the mountains. But as the day progressed, clouds obscured the view, forming what looked like a new uncharted range of snow-covered peaks, billowing masses of pale gray cloud mountains.

Early in what he supposed to be the afternoon, the overcast sky grew darker. He reached a river crossing: the Kahe Lungpa, a swollen stream that tumbled down from the high peaks to meet the Kali Gandaki. The bridge over the river was down. Water rushed past one shattered wooden support, causing the rotten boards to shiver in the current. Perhaps the bridge had washed out during the monsoon storms. The crossing was far from any village and no doubt the few travelers who passed this way did not have the resources or time to repair or replace the bridge, but simply forded the river.

For a moment, he stood on the bank, gazing at the roaring stream. In one book, his father told of fording snow-fed rivers barefoot, preferring, he wrote, "the momentary discomfort of crossing barefoot to the prolonged chafing of sodden boots." Xavier reluctantly removed his boots, shivering in the cold breeze. He tied the boots to the pack, slipped on a pair of rubber thongs, rolled up the legs of his jeans, and stepped down into the water, knowing that if he hesitated, he would turn back.

The first few steps were painful, but the cold water numbed his feet, making the pain more bearable. The river dragged at his legs, trying to shift the rounded stones beneath his feet. He took his time, making sure that each foot was planted before trusting his weight to it, taking one slow step after another. Time had no meaning: he could have been walking through the water for an hour or a minute, he would not have known the difference.

He was halfway across when the first snowflakes fell. The pain returned to his feet: a sharp hurt that seemed to extend deep into his bones. He tried to move more quickly, but his feet could no longer feel the rocks beneath him. He stumbled, caught himself, then slipped again and fell, twisting to one side and catching himself on his arm. The river snatched at the pack; the current yanked it to and fro. Xavier clung to the pack's straps, struggling to regain his footing and to hoist the waterlogged pack from the river. He staggered forward, floundering, gasping from the shock of the cold water, almost losing his thongs, dragging himself onto the far bank and flinging his pack beside him.

From the scraggly bushes on the riverside, a raven laughed hysterically. Xavier ignored the bird, breathing in great gasps and clutching at the damp grass that grew on the bank. After a moment, he rolled over to check his pack. Only then did he realize that the river had snatched the boots from his pack, as well as soaking his food, and drenching his sleeping bag.

For a moment, he lay on the ground, unwilling to move. His feet ached from the cold, his hands trembled. Then he felt for the carved bone pendant around his neck. The old man had said he would see the yeti. The reassurance comforted him. He forced himself to sit up and figure out how to get warm.

A pair of damp wool socks provided some protection for his feet; his wool sweater blocked some of the wind. He warmed himself with exercise, searching for driftwood in the bushes that grew along the river. When he was moving, his arms and legs did not tremble as violently.

An hour's search yielded a small stack of sticks, none bigger around than a finger, and a few damp logs, driftwood cast on shore by the river. His teeth chattering, he searched for tinder, scraps of dry material small enough to catch quickly. But the snow had dampened the leaves and grasses, leaving nothing dry.

The wind grew stronger, slicing through his wet clothing and making him shiver uncontrollably. With his pocketknife, he whittled a few thin splinters from a stick, heaping them together in the shelter of a bush. He built a small teepee of sticks over the tinder and hunched over it.

The first match went out immediately. The head of the second match—wretched Nepali matches—broke off without catching. The third matched burned reluctantly. When he held the flame beside his heap of shavings, two slivers of wood smoldered for a moment, but the red glow faded as soon as the match went out.

Xavier's hands shook as he carefully arranged grass beside the wood shavings. The grass, like the wood, would not burn. Desperate for warmth, he patted his pockets, searching for a scrap of paper. In his wallet, he found his traveler's checks, bone dry and warm from his body heat. They were worthless in the woods, and he hesitated only for a moment before crumpling a $50 check. He arranged the splinters of wood over the dry paper.

The check burned well, but it was small and it burned out before the wood caught. He sacrificed two more, holding his hands out to protect the tiny flame from the wind. The checks whispered as they burned, tiny crackling voices that spoke of distant places and hidden secrets. When he added the fourth and fifth check, the wood caught, flames moving reluctantly from stick to stick. He propped a driftwood log near the fire where it would dry, and made himself as comfortable as he could, sitting with his back in the bushes to protect it from the wind. He draped his wet sleeping bag over his lap where the fire would warm it.

The night was long. Despite the cold, he dozed off now and then, waking only to cough, a hoarse grating sound in the darkness. When he woke, he found himself clutching the bone. He dreamed of chasing the yeti through the pale gray crevices of cloud mountains. He woke to feed the fire, then returned to dreams.

After a time, the darkness and the cold no longer seemed alien. They were threatening, but familiar. It seemed natural to wake in the darkness, struggling for warmth.

In the morning, he hiked in rubber thongs. He coughed constantly. Once, on the outskirts of a village, a little girl who was tending a herd of goats greeted him timidly. He tried to reply, but the sound that came from his mouth was only a rough croaking, noise with no meaning like the clatter of rocks in a rock slide. He tried to smile, wanting to show the child that he meant no harm, but she scampered up the slope with her goats.

He hiked on for three days. Some of his food spoiled and he knew that food would be scarce farther north. But somehow, for some inexplicable reason, he was happy. The wool socks grew tattered and encrusted with mud, but his feet grew used to being cold. His beard grew thicker and he washed less frequently, growing accustomed to the grime on his face and hands. He hurried through villages, avoiding people. When he was greeted, he nodded, but remained silent.

He passed through the village of Dhi in the early evening, walking quickly through the darkness. Rather than making him eager for human company, solitude left him wishing for more solitude. A dog barked wildly from inside a house, a near hysterical baying. Xavier grinned savagely and kept walking. He despised the laundry flapping from the lines and the heaps of dung beside the trail. He slipped through the village, nodding a greeting to a woman filling a metal jug at a stream. She dropped the jug and stared at him. Though she called out, he did not stop, but kept walking away into the darkness to seek the mountains.

As he hiked, he listened to the wind, to the river's voice, to the chatter of ravens. The sound seemed to flow through him, bringing him peace. Though the weather grew colder, he did not worry.

He made camp a day's walk from Dhi by the confluence of the Mustang Khola and a smaller stream that was unnamed on his map. The wind was constant there, sweeping around the boulders and scouring the rocks. In a small hollow between two house-size boulders, he pitched his tent.

The first night, he heard the howling of wolves in the distance. At midnight, he woke when snow began to fall, a gentle flurry that drifted against the tent. In the morning, he found the tracks of wolves in the snowflakes that powdered the ground near his fire ring.

During the first few days, he explored his surroundings. He saw fat short-tailed mice scampering among the rocks. Wild sheep, the blue Himalayan *bharal*, grazed by the stream. Xavier climbed upstream, following sheep trails among the boulders.

Half a day's scramble up the stream, he found a small cave, tucked among the rocks. From the look of the cave, it had once been inhabited—by a hermit, a holy man, or a *sennin*, a mountain lunatic. Three fire-blackened rocks formed a triangular hearth; a mound of brush in the back provided a scratchy bed. Beneath the cave, the valley broadened into a small meadow: tough, red-brown grass poked through the light snow. The cave's entrance offered a view of the river valley better than any he had found elsewhere.

He moved his gear to the cave just before the second snowfall and made his bed in the brush heap in the back. He grew adept at cooking over a small fire: the smoke made his eyes itch, but he grew used to that. In the cave, his sleep schedule changed. Daylight reflecting from the snow hurt his eyes, and so he slept through the brightest part of the day, then woke at twilight to watch the wolves chase the blue sheep through the moonlit valleys. He dreamed during those long daylight sleeps. In his dreams, the old man came to him and told him that he would see the yeti.

Somehow, he was certain that his goal was near. This valley had the flavor of the fantastic: the wind muttered of secrets; the boulders watched him as he slept. Sometimes, he believed that he would soon understand the language of the raven that perched outside his cave each evening. He knew this place as a man knows the landscape of his own dreams, and he knew that the yeti was here.

He woke and slept, woke and slept, watching the valley for signs of the unusual. His hair and beard grew long and wild. He discarded his tattered wool socks and his feet grew tough and calloused. His skin chapped in the wind. In the sand by the river, he discovered the mark of a broad bare foot; on a thorny bush, he found a red-gold tuft of hair. A few signs and a feeling, nothing more, but that was enough.

His supplies ran low, but he was reluctant to leave the valley to find more. He ate wild greens and trapped short-tailed mice in an old food tin and roasted them over the fire. Once, he found a *bharal* that had been killed by wolves, and he used his pocketknife to hack meat from the carcass.

In his dreams, the valley was filled with moving shadows that walked on two legs, shambling like bears, shaggy and slope browed. When he woke, his dreams did not fade, but remained as sharp and clear as the world around him. He dreamed of the raven, but somehow the bird was more than a raven. The black bird was the old man who had given him the bone. The old man wanted something in return.

Xavier never went out by day.

At last, his food ran out completely. He captured one last mouse, charred its body in the fire, and picked its bones clean. By moonlight, he walked to the village of Dhi. The trail made him nervous; it was too well trodden. The first smell of woodsmoke made him stop. He heard barking dogs in the distance.

On the edge of the village, he paused to drink in a still pool. He was startled by his own reflection. His eyes were wild and rimmed with red; his face was covered with thick red-brown hair. He crouched in the field near a house, unwilling to go closer. Stacked in racks by the house were ears of corn, dried by the wind and the sun.

Hunger drove him forward, but something held him back. He did not belong here. The sky was growing light when he moved at last. He stood below the racks and reached up to pull corn free—one ear, two ears, a dozen, two dozen. He was tying them up into a bundle when he heard a sound.

Ten feet away stood a ragged boy, barefoot in the chilly morning. His face was smudged with dirt and already his nose was running. His eyes were wide, and they grew wider when Xavier looked at him. "*Meh-teh*," he whispered, backing away from Xavier, then turning to run. "*Meh-teh!*"

Xavier ran too, losing one of his thongs in the rocks by

the trail, abandoning the other. The raven led him on, laughing overhead. He ran back to his cave.

He roasted an ear of corn in the fire. It was charred and tough, but he ate it with relish. He slept for a long time, dreaming of the old man and the raven, two who were one. He knew that he belonged in this place. Each night, he went to the village and stole food. When the dogs barked, people ran from their huts, carrying torches and knives and shouting *"Meh-teh! Meh-teh!"*

One day soon, he knew he would find a pot of *chang* in the path. The raven told him so in a dream. When he found the *chang*, he would drink it and fall asleep. The villagers would capture him and the old man who was the raven would take his scalp. That was the way of things.

He was happy.

Rachel in Love

It is a Sunday morning in summer and a small brown chimpanzee named Rachel sits on the living room floor of a remote ranch house on the edge of the Painted Desert. She is watching a Tarzan movie on television. Her hairy arms are wrapped around her knees and she rocks back and forth with suppressed excitement. She knows that her father would say that she's too old for such childish amusements—but since Aaron is still sleeping, he can't chastise her.

On the television, Tarzan has been trapped in a bamboo cage by a band of wicked pygmies. Rachel is afraid that he won't escape in time to save Jane from the ivory smugglers who hold her captive. The movie cuts to Jane, who is tied up in the back of a jeep, and Rachel whimpers softly to herself. She knows better than to howl: she peeked into her father's bedroom earlier, and he was still in bed. Aaron doesn't like her to howl when he is sleeping.

When the movie breaks for a commercial, Rachel goes to her father's room. She is ready for breakfast and she wants him to get up. She tiptoes to the bed to see if he is awake.

His eyes are open and he is staring at nothing. His face is pale and his lips are a purplish color. Dr. Aaron Jacobs, the man Rachel calls father, is not asleep. He is dead, having died in the night of a heart attack.

When Rachel shakes him, his head rocks back and forth in time with her shaking, but his eyes do not blink and he does not breathe. She places his hand on her head, nudging him so that he will waken and stroke her. He does not move. When she leans toward him, his hand falls to dangle limply over the edge of the bed.

In the breeze from the open bedroom window, the fine wisps of gray hair that he had carefully combed over his bald spot each morning shift and flutter, exposing the naked scalp. In the other room, elephants trumpet as they stampede across the jungle to rescue Tarzan. Rachel whimpers softly, but her father does not move.

Rachel backs away from her father's body. In the living room, Tarzan is swinging across the jungle on vines, going to save Jane. Rachel ignores the television. She prowls through the house as if searching for comfort—stepping into her own small bedroom, wandering through her father's laboratory. From the cages that line the walls, white rats stare at her with hot red eyes. A rabbit hops across its cage, making a series of slow dull thumps, like a feather pillow tumbling down a flight of stairs.

She thinks that perhaps she made a mistake. Perhaps her father is just sleeping. She returns to the bedroom, but nothing has changed. Her father lies open-eyed on the bed. For a long time, she huddles beside his body, clinging to his hand.

He is the only person she has ever known. He is her father, her teacher, her friend. She cannot leave him alone.

The afternoon sun blazes through the window, and still Aaron does not move. The room grows dark, but Rachel does not turn on the lights. She is waiting for Aaron to wake up. When the moon rises, its silver light shines through the window to cast a bright rectangle on the far wall.

Outside, somewhere in the barren land surrounding the ranch house, a coyote lifts its head to the rising moon and wails, a thin sound that is as lonely as a train whistling through an abandoned station. Rachel joins in with a desolate howl of loneliness and grief. Aaron lies still and Rachel knows that he is dead

When Rachel was younger, she had a favorite bedtime story. *Where did I come from?* she would ask Aaron, using the abbreviated gestures of ASL, American Sign Language. *Tell me again.*

"You're too old for bedtime stories," Aaron would say. *Please,* she would sign. *Tell me the story.*

In the end, he always relented and told her. "Once upon a time, there was a little girl named Rachel," he would say. "She was a pretty girl, with long golden hair like a princess in a fairy tale. She lived with her father and her mother and they were all very happy."

Rachel would snuggle contentedly beneath her blankets. The story, like any good fairy tale, had elements of tragedy. In the story, Rachel's father worked at a university, studying the workings of the brain and charting the electric fields that the nervous impulses of an active brain produced. But the other researchers at the university didn't understand Rachel's father; they distrusted his research and cut off his funding. (During this portion of the story, Aaron's voice took on a bitter edge.) So he left the university and took his wife and daughter to the desert, where he could work in peace.

He continued his research and determined that each individual brain produced its own unique pattern of fields, as characteristic as a fingerprint. (Rachel found this part of the story quite dull, but Aaron insisted on including it.) The shape of this Electric Mind, as he called it, was determined by habitual patterns of thoughts and emotions. Record the Electric Mind, he postulated, and you could capture an individual's personality.

Then one sunny day, the doctor's wife and beautiful daughter went for a drive. A truck barreling down a winding cliffside road lost its brakes and met the car head-on, killing both the girl and her mother. (Rachel clung to Aaron's hand during this part of the story, frightened by the sudden evil twist of fortune.)

But though Rachel's body had died, all was not lost. In his desert lab, the doctor had recorded the electrical patterns produced by his daughter's brain. The doctor had been experimenting with the use of external magnetic fields to impose the patterns from one animal onto the brain of another. From an animal supply house, he obtained a young chimpanzee. He used a mixture of norepinephrinbased transmitter substances to boost the speed of neural processing in the chimp's brain, and then he imposed the pattern of his daughter's mind on the brain of this young chimp, combining the two after his own fashion, saving his daughter in his own way. In the chimp's brain was all that remained of Rachel Jacobs.

The doctor named the chimp Rachel and raised her as his own daughter. Because the limitations of the chimpanzee larynx made speech very difficult, he instructed her in ASL. He taught her to read and to write. They were good friends, the best of companions.

By this point in the story, Rachel was usually asleep. But it didn't matter—she knew the ending. The doctor, whose name was Aaron Jacobs, and the chimp named Rachel lived happily ever after.

Rachel likes fairy tales and she likes happy endings. She has the mind of a teenage girl, but the innocent heart of a young chimp.

Sometimes, when Rachel looks at her gnarled brown fingers, they seem alien, wrong, out of place. She remembers having small, pale, delicate hands. Memories lie upon memories, layers upon layers, like the sedimentary rocks of the desert buttes.

Rachel remembers a blond woman who smelled sweetly of perfume. On a Halloween long ago, this woman (who was, in these memories, Rachel's mother) painted Rachel's fingernails bright red because Rachel was dressed as a gypsy and gypsies liked red. Rachel remembers the woman's hands: white hands with faintly blue veins hidden just beneath the skin, neatly clipped nails painted rose pink.

But Rachel also remembers another mother and another time. Her mother was dark and hairy and smelled sweetly of overripe fruit. She and Rachel lived in a wire cage in a room filled with chimps and she hugged Rachel to her hairy breast whenever any people came into the room. Rachel's mother groomed Rachel constantly, picking delicately through her fur in search of lice that she never found.

Memories upon memories: jumbled and confused, like random pictures clipped from magazines, a bright collage that makes no sense. Rachel remembers cages: cold wire mesh beneath her feet, the smell of fear around her. A man in a white lab coat took her from the arms of her hairy mother and pricked her with needles. She could hear her mother howling, but she could not escape from the man.

Rachel remembers a junior high school dance where she wore a new dress: she stood in a dark corner of the gym for hours, pretending to admire the crepe paper decorations because she felt too shy to search among the crowd for her friends.

She remembers when she was a young chimp: she huddled with five other adolescent chimps in the stuffy freight compartment of a train, frightened by the alien smells and sounds.

She remembers gym class: gray lockers and ugly gym suits that revealed her skinny legs. The teacher made everyone play softball, even Rachel who was unathletic and painfully shy. Rachel at bat, standing at the plate, was terrified to be the center of attention. "Easy out," said the catcher, a hard-edged girl who ran with the wrong crowd and always smelled of cigarette smoke. When Rachel swung at the ball and missed, the outfielders filled the air with malicious laughter.

Rachel's memories are as delicate and elusive as the dusty moths that dance among the rabbit brush and sage. Memories of her girlhood never linger; they land for an instant, then take flight, leaving Rachel feeling abandoned and alone.

Rachel leaves Aaron's body where it is, but closes his eyes and pulls the sheet up over his head. She does not know what else to do. Each day she waters the garden and picks some greens for the rabbits. Each day, she cares for the rats, bringing them food and refilling their water bottles. The weather is cool, and Aaron's body does not smell too bad, though by the end of the week, a wide line of ants runs from the bed to the open window.

At the end of the first week, on a moonlit evening, Rachel decides to let the animals go free. She releases the rabbits one by one, climbing on a stepladder to reach down into the cage and lift each placid bunny out. She carries each one to the back door, holding it for a moment and stroking the soft warm fur. Then she sets the animal down and nudges it in the direction of the green grass that grows around the perimeter of the fenced garden.

The rats are more difficult to deal with. She manages to wrestle the large rat cage off the shelf, but it is heavier than she thought it would be. Though she slows its fall, it lands on the floor with a crash and the rats scurry to and fro within. She shoves the cage across the linoleum floor, sliding it down the hall, over the doorsill, and onto the back patio. When she opens the cage door, rats burst out like popcorn from a popper, white in the moonlight and dashing in all directions.

Once, while Aaron was taking a nap, Rachel walked along the dirt track that led to the main highway. She hadn't planned on going far. She just wanted to see what the highway looked like, maybe hide near the mailbox and watch a car drive past. She was curious about the outside world and her fleeting fragmentary memories did not satisfy that curiosity.

She was halfway to the mailbox when Aaron came roaring up in his old jeep. "Get in the car," he shouted at her. "Right now!" Rachel had never seen him so angry. She cowered in the jeep's passenger seat, covered with dust from the road, unhappy that Aaron was so upset. He didn't speak until they got back to the ranch house, and then he spoke in a low voice, filled with bitterness and suppressed rage.

"You don't want to go out there," he said. "You wouldn't like it out there. The world is filled with petty, narrow-minded, stupid people. They wouldn't understand you. And anyone they don't understand, they want to hurt. They hate anyone who's different. If they know that you're different, they punish you, hurt you. They'd lock you up and never let you go."

He looked straight ahead, staring through the dirty windshield. "It's not like the shows on TV, Rachel," he said in a softer tone. "It's not like the stories in books."

He looked at her then and she gestured frantically. *I'm sorry. I'm sorry.*

"I can't protect you out there," he said. "I can't keep you safe."

Rachel took his hand in both of hers. He relented then, stroking her head. "Never do that again," he said. "Never."

Aaron's fear was contagious. Rachel never again walked along the dirt track and sometimes she had dreams about bad people who wanted to lock her in a cage.

Two weeks after Aaron's death, a black-and-white police car drives slowly up to the house. When the policemen knock on the door, Rachel hides behind the couch in the living room. They knock again, try the knob, then open the door, which she had left unlocked.

Suddenly frightened, Rachel bolts from behind the couch, bounding toward the back door. Behind her, she hears one man yell, "My God! It's a gorilla!"

By the time he pulls his gun, Rachel has run out the back door and away into the hills. From the hills she watches as an ambulance drives up and two men in white take Aaron's body away. Even after the ambulance and the police car drive away, Rachel is afraid to go back to the house. Only after sunset does she return.

Just before dawn the next morning, she wakens to the sound of a truck jouncing down the dirt road. She peers out the window to see a pale green pickup. Sloppily stenciled in white on the door are the words: PRIMATE RESEARCH CENTER. Rachel hesitates as the truck pulls up in front of the house. By the time she decides to flee, two men are getting out of the truck. One of them carries a rifle.

She runs out the back door and heads for the hills, but she is only halfway to hiding when she hears a sound like a sharp intake of breath and feels a painful jolt in her shoulder. Suddenly, her legs give way and she is tumbling backward down the sandy slope, dust coating her red-brown fur, her howl becoming a whimper, then fading to nothing at all. She falls into the blackness of sleep.

The sun is up. Rachel lies in a cage in the back of the pickup truck. She is partially conscious and she feels a tingling in her hands and feet. Nausea grips her stomach and bowels. Her body aches.

Rachel can blink, but otherwise she can't move. From where she lies, she can see only the wire mesh of the cage and the side of the truck. When she tries to turn her head, the burning in her skin intensifies. She lies still, wanting to cry out, but unable to make a sound. She can only blink slowly, trying to close out the pain. But the burning and nausea stay.

The truck jounces down a dirt road, then stops. It rocks as the men get out. The doors slam. Rachel hears the tailgate open.

A woman's voice: "Is that the animal the county sheriff wanted us to pick up?" A woman peers into the cage. She wears a white lab coat and her brown hair is tied back in a single braid. Around her eyes, Rachel can see small wrinkles, etched by years of living in the desert. The woman doesn't look evil. Rachel hopes that the woman will save her from the men in the truck.

"Yeah. It should be knocked out for a least another half hour. Where do you want it?"

"Bring it into the lab where we had the rhesus monkeys. I'll keep it there until I have an empty cage in the breeding area."

Rachel's cage scrapes across the bed of the pickup. She feels each bump and jar as a new pain. The man swings the cage onto a cart and the woman pushes the cart down a concrete corridor. Rachel watches the walls pass just a few inches from her nose.

The lab contains rows of cages in which small animals move sleepily. In a sudden stark light of the overhead fluorescent bulbs, the eyes of white rats gleam red.

With the help of one of the men from the truck, the woman manhandles Rachel onto a lab table. The metal surface is cold and hard, painful against Rachel's skin. Rachel's body is not under her control; her limbs will not respond. She is still frozen by the tranquilizer, able to watch, but that is all. She cannot protest or plead for mercy.

Rachel watches with growing terror as the woman pulls on rubber gloves and fills a hypodermic needle with a clear solution. "Mark down that I'm giving her the standard test for tuberculosis; this eyelid should be checked before she's moved in with the others. I'll add thiabendazole to her feed for the next few days to clean out any intestinal worms. And I suppose we might as well deflea her as well," the woman says. The man grunts in response.

Expertly, the woman closes one of Rachel's eyes. With her open eye, Rachel watches the hypodermic needle approach. She feels a sharp pain in her eyelid. In her mind, she is howling, but the only sound she can manage is a breathy sigh.

The woman sets the hypodermic aside and begins methodically spraying Rachel's fur with a cold, foul-smelling liquid. A drop strikes Rachel's eye and burns. Rachel blinks, but she cannot lift a hand to rub her eye. The woman treats Rachel with casual indifference, chatting with the man as she spreads Rachel's legs and sprays her genitals. "Looks healthy enough. Good breeding stock."

Rachel moans, but neither person notices. At last, they finish their torture, put her in a cage, and leave the room. She closes her eyes, and the darkness returns.

Rachel dreams. She is back at home in the ranch house. It is night and she is alone. Outside, coyotes yip and howl. The coyote is the voice of the desert, wailing as the wind wails when it stretches itself thin to squeeze through a crack between two boulders. The people native to this land tell tales of Coyote, a god who was a trickster, unreliable, changeable, mercurial.

Rachel is restless, anxious, unnerved by the howling of the coyotes. She is looking for Aaron. In the dream, she knows he is not dead, and she searches the house for him, wandering from his cluttered bedroom to her small room to the linoleum-tiled lab.

She is in the lab when she hears something tapping: a small dry scratching, like a windblown branch against the window, though no tree grows near the house and the night is still. Cautiously, she lifts the curtain to look out.

She looks into her own reflection: a pale oval face, long blond hair. The hand that holds the curtain aside is smooth and white with carefully clipped fingernails. But something is wrong. Superimposed on the reflection is another face peering through the glass: a pair of dark brown eyes, a chimp face with red-brown hair and jug-handle ears. She sees her own reflection and she sees the outsider; the two images merge and blur. She is afraid, but she can't drop the curtain and shut the ape face out.

She is a chimp looking in through the cold, bright windowpane; she is a girl looking out; she is a girl looking in; she is an ape looking out. She is afraid and the coyotes are howling all around.

Rachel opens her eyes and blinks until the world comes into focus. The pain and tingling have retreated, but she still feels a little sick. Her left eye aches. When she rubs it, she feels a raised lump on the eyelid where the woman pricked her. She lies on the floor of a wire mesh cage. The room is hot and the air is thick with the smell of animals.

In the cage beside her is another chimp, an older animal with scruffy dark brown fur. He sits with his arms wrapped around his knees, rocking back and forth, back and forth. His head is down. As he rocks, he murmurs to himself, a meaningless cooing that goes on and on. On his scalp, Rachel can see a gleam of metal: a permanently implanted electrode protrudes from a shaven patch. Rachel makes a soft questioning sound, but the other chimp will not look up.

Rachel's own cage is just a few feet square. In one corner is a bowl of monkey pellets. A water bottle hangs on the side of the cage. Rachel ignores the food, but drinks thirstily.

Sunlight streams through the windows, sliced into small sections by the wire mesh that covers the glass. She tests her cage door, rattling it gently at first, then harder. It is securely latched. The gaps in the mesh are too small to admit her hand. She can't reach out to work the latch.

The other chimp continues to rock back and forth. When Rachel rattles the mesh of her cage and howls, he lifts his head wearily and looks at her. His red-rimmed eyes are unfocused; she can't be sure he sees her.

Hello, she gestures tentatively. *What's wrong?*

He blinks at her in the dim light. *Hurt,* he signs in ASL. He reaches up to touch the electrode, fingering skin that is already raw from repeated rubbing.

Who hurt you? she asks. He stares at her blankly and she repeats the question. *Who hurt you?*

Men, he signs.

As if on cue, there is the click of a latch and the door to the lab opens. A bearded man in a white coat steps in, followed by a clean-shaven man in a suit. The bearded man seems to be showing the other man around the lab. ". . . only preliminary testing, so far," the bearded man is saying. "We've been hampered by a shortage of chimps trained in ASL." The two men stop in front of the old chimp's cage. "This old fellow is from the Oregon center. Funding for the language program was cut back and some of the animals were dispersed to other programs." The old chimp huddles at the back of the cage, eyeing the bearded man with suspicion.

Hungry? the bearded man signs to the old chimp. He holds up an orange where the old chimp can see it.

Give orange, the old chimp gestures. He holds out his hand, but comes no nearer to the wire mesh than he must to reach the orange. With the fruit in hand, he retreats to the back of his cage.

The bearded man continues, "This project will provide us with the first solid data on neural activity during use of sign language. But we really need greater access to chimps with advanced language skills. People are so damn protective of their animals."

"Is this one of yours?" the clean-shaven man asks, pointing to Rachel. She cowers in the back of the cage, as far from the wire mesh as she can get.

"No, not mine. She was someone's household pet, apparently. The county sheriff had us pick her up." The bearded man peers into her cage. Rachel does not move; she is terrified that he will somehow guess that she knows ASL. She stares at his hands and thinks about those hands putting an electrode through her skull. "I think she'll be put in breeding stock," the man says as he turns away.

Rachel watches them go, wondering at the cruelty of

these people. Aaron was right: they want to punish her, they want to put an electrode in her head.

After the men are gone, she tries to draw the old chimp into conversation but he will not reply. He ignores her as he eats his orange. Then he returns to his former posture, hiding his head and rocking himself back and forth.

Rachel, hungry despite herself, samples one of the food pellets. It has a strange medicinal taste, and she puts it back in the bowl. She needs to pee, but there is no toilet and she cannot escape the cage. At last, unable to hold it, she pees in one corner of the cage. The urine flows through the wire mesh to soak the litter below, and the smell of warm piss fills her cage. Humiliated, frightened, her head aching, her skin itchy from the flea spray, Rachel watches as the sunlight creeps across the room.

The day wears on. Rachel samples her food again, but rejects it, preferring hunger to the strange taste. A black man comes and cleans the cages of the rabbits and rats. Rachel cowers in her cage and watches him warily, afraid that he will hurt her too.

When night comes, she is not tired. Outside, coyotes howl. Moonlight filters in through the high windows. She draws her legs up toward her body, then rests with her arms wrapped around her knees. Her father is dead, and she is a captive in a strange place. For a time, she whimpers softly, hoping to awaken from this nightmare and find herself at home in bed. When she hears the click of a key in the door to the room, she hugs herself more tightly.

A man in green coveralls pushes a cart filled with cleaning supplies into the room. He takes a broom from the cart, and begins sweeping the concrete floor. Over the rows of cages, she can see the top of his head bobbing in time with his sweeping. He works slowly and methodically, bending down to sweep carefully under each row of cages, making a neat pile of dust, dung, and food scraps in the center of the aisle.

The janitor's name is Jake. He is a middle-aged deaf man who has been employed by the Primate Research Center for the last seven years. He works the night shift. The personnel director at the Primate Research Center likes Jake because he fills the federal quota for handicapped employees, and because he has not asked for a raise in five years. There have been some complaints about Jake—his work is often sloppy—but never enough to merit firing the man.

Jake is an unambitious, somewhat slow-witted man. He likes the Primate Research Center because he works alone, which allows him to drink on the job. He is an easygoing man, and he likes the animals. Sometimes, he brings treats for them. Once, a lab assistant caught him feeding an apple to a pregnant rhesus monkey. The monkey was part of an experiment on the effect of dietary restrictions on fetal brain development, and the lab assistant warned Jake that he would be fired if he was ever caught interfering with the animals again. Jake still feeds the animals, but he is more careful about when he does it, and he has never been caught again.

As Rachel watches, the old chimp gestures to Jake. *Give banana*, the chimp signs. *Please banana*. Jake stops sweeping for a minute and reaches down to the bottom shelf of his cleaning cart. He returns with a banana and offers it to the old chimp. The chimp accepts the banana and leans against the mesh while Jake scratches his fur.

When Jake turns back to his sweeping, he catches sight of Rachel and sees that she is watching him. Emboldened by his kindness to the old chimp, Rachel timidly gestures to him. *Help me*.

Jake hesitates, then peers at her more closely. Both his eyes are shot with a fine lacework of red. His nose displays the broken blood vessels of someone who has been friends with the bottle for too many years. He needs a shave. But when he leans close, Rachel catches the scent of whiskey and tobacco. The smells remind her of Aaron and give her courage.

Please help me, Rachel signs. *I don't belong here*.

For the last hour, Jake has been drinking steadily. His view of the world is somewhat fuzzy. He stares at her blearily.

Rachel's fear that he will hurt her is replaced by the fear that he will leave her locked up and alone. Desperately she signs again. *Please, please, please. Help me. I don't belong here. Please help me go home.*

He watches her, considering the situation. Rachel does not move. She is afraid that any movement will make him leave. With a majestic speed dictated by his inebriation, Jake leans his broom on the row of cages behind him and steps toward Rachel's cage again. *You talk?* he signs.

I talk, she signs.

Where did you come from?

From my father's house, she signs. *Two men came and shot me and put me here. I don't know why. I don't know why they locked me in jail.*

Jake looks around, willing to be sympathetic, but puzzled by her talk of jail. *This isn't jail. This is a place where scientists raise monkeys.*

Rachel is indignant. *I am not a monkey. I am a girl.*

Jake studies her hairy body and her jug-handle ears. *You look like a monkey.*

Rachel shakes her head. *No. I am a girl.*

Rachel runs her hands back over her head, a very human gesture of annoyance and unhappiness. She signs sadly, *I don't belong here. Please let me out.*

Jake shifts his weight from foot to foot, wondering what to do. *I can't let you out. I'll get in big trouble.*

Just for a little while? Please?

Jake glances at his cart of supplies. He has to finish off this room and two corridors of offices before he can relax for the night.

Don't go, Rachel signs, guessing his thoughts.

I have work to do.

She looks at the cart, then suggests eagerly, *Let me out and I'll help you work.*

Jake frowns. *If I let you out, you will run away.*

No, I won't run. I will help. Please let me out.

You promise to go back?

Rachel nods.

Warily he unlatches the cage. Rachel bounds out, grabs a whisk broom from the cart, and begins industriously sweeping bits of food and droppings from beneath the row of cages. *Come on,* she signs to Jake from the end of the aisle. *I will help.*

When Jake pushes the cart from the room filled with cages, Rachel follows him closely. The rubber wheels of the cleaning cart rumble softly on the linoleum floor. They pass through a metal door into a corridor where the floor is carpeted and the air smells of chalk dust and paper.

Offices let off the corridor, each one a small room furnished with a desk, bookshelves, and a blackboard. Jake shows Rachel how to empty the wastebaskets into a garbage bag. While he cleans the blackboards, she wanders from office to office, trailing the trash-filled garbage bag.

At first, Jake keeps a close eye on Rachel. But after cleaning each blackboard, he pauses to sip whiskey from a paper cup. At the end of the corridor, he stops to refill the cup from the whiskey bottle that he keeps wedged between the Saniflush and the window cleaner. By the time he is halfway through the second cup, he is treating her like an old friend, telling her to hurry up so that they can eat dinner.

Rachel works quickly, but she stops sometimes to gaze out the office windows. Outside, moonlight shines on a sandy plain, dotted here and there with scrubby clumps of rabbit brush.

At the end of the corridor is a larger room in which there are several desks and typewriters. In one of the wastebaskets, buried beneath memos and candybar wrappers, she finds a magazine. The title is *Love Confessions* and the cover has a picture of a man and woman kissing. Rachel studies the cover, then takes the magazine, tucking it on the bottom shelf of the cart.

Jake pours himself another cup of whiskey and pushes the cart to another hallway. Jake is working slower now. As he works he makes humming noises, tuneless sounds that he feels only as pleasant vibrations. The last few blackboards are sloppily done, and Rachel, finished with the wastebaskets, cleans the places that Jake missed.

They eat dinner in the janitor's storeroom, a stuffy windowless room furnished with an ancient grease-stained couch, a battered black-and-white television, and shelves of cleaning supplies. From a shelf, Jake takes the paper bag that holds his lunch: a baloney sandwich, a bag of barbecued potato chips, and a box of vanilla wafers. From behind the gallon jugs of liquid cleanser, he takes a magazine. He lights a cigarette, pours himself another cup of whiskey, and settles down on the couch. After a moment's hesitation, he offers Rachel a drink, pouring a shot of whiskey into a chipped ceramic cup.

Aaron never let Rachel drink whiskey, and she samples it carefully. At first the smell makes her sneeze, but she is fascinated by the way that the drink warms her throat, and she sips some more.

As they drink, Rachel tells Jake about the men who shot her and the woman who pricked her with a needle. He nods. *The people here are crazy,* he signs.

I know, she says, thinking of the old chimp with the electrode in his head. *You won't tell them I can talk, will you?*

Jake nods. *I won't tell them anything.*

They treat me like I'm not real, Rachel signs sadly. Then she hugs her knees, frightened at the thought of being held captive by crazy people. She considers planning her escape: she is out of the cage and she is sure she could outrun Jake. As she wonders about it, she finishes her cup of whiskey. The alcohol takes the edge off her fear. She sits close beside Jake on the couch, and the smell of his cigarette smoke reminds her of Aaron. For the first time since Aaron's death she feels warm and happy.

She shares Jake's cookies and potato chips and looks at the *Love Confessions* magazine that she took from the trash. The first story that she reads is about a woman named Alice. The headline reads: "I became a go-go dancer to pay off my husband's gambling debts, and now he wants me to sell my body."

Rachel sympathizes with Alice's loneliness and suffering. Alice, like Rachel, is alone and misunderstood. As Rachel slowly reads, she sips her second cup of whiskey. The story reminds her of a fairy tale: the nice man who rescues Alice from her terrible husband replaces the handsome prince who rescued the princess. Rachel glances at Jake and wonders if he will rescue her from the wicked people who locked her in the cage.

She has finished the second cup of whiskey and eaten

half Jake's cookies when Jake says that she must go back to her cage. She goes reluctantly, taking the magazine with her. He promises that he will come back for her the next night, and with that she must be content. She puts the magazine in one corner of the cage and curls up to sleep.

She wakes early in the afternoon. A man·in a white coat is wheeling a low cart into the lab.

Rachel's head aches with hangover and she feels sick. As she crouches in one corner of her cage, the man stops the cart beside her and locks the wheels. "Hold on there," he mutters to her, then slides her cage onto the cart.

The man wheels her through long corridors, where the walls are cement blocks, painted institutional green. Rachel huddles unhappily in the cage, wondering where she is going and whether Jake will ever be able to find her.

At the end of a long corridor, the man opens a thick metal door. A wave of warm air comes from the doorway. It stinks of chimpanzees, excrement, and rotting food. On either side of the corridor are metal bars and wire mesh. Behind the mesh, Rachel can see dark hairy shadows. In one cage, five adolescent chimps swing and play. In another, two females huddle together, grooming each other. The man slows as he passes a cage in which a big male is banging on the wire with his fist, making the mesh rattle and ring.

"Now, Johnson," says the man. "Cool it. Be nice. I'm bringing you a new little girlfriend."

With a series of hooks, the man links Rachel's cage with the cage next to Johnson's and opens the doors. "Go on, girl," he says. "See the nice fruit." In the new cage is a bowl of sliced apples with an attendant swarm of fruit flies.

At first, Rachel will not move into the new cage. She crouches in the cage on the cart, hoping that the man will decide to take her back to the lab. She watches him get a hose and attach it to a water faucet. But she does not understand his intention until he turns the stream of water on her. A cold blast strikes her on the back and she howls, fleeing into the new cage to avoid the cold water. Then the man closes the doors, unhooks the cage, and hurries away.

The floor is bare cement. Her cage is at one end of the

corridor and two of its walls are cement block. A doorway in one of the cement block walls leads to an outside run. The other two walls are wire mesh: one facing the corridor; the other, Johnson's cage.

Johnson, quiet now that the man has left, is sniffing around the door in the wire mesh wall that joins their cages. Rachel watches him anxiously. Her memories of other chimps are distant, softened by time. She remembers her mother; she vaguely remembers playing with other chimps her age. But she does not know how to react to Johnson when he stares at her with great intensity and makes a loud huffing sound. She gestures to him in ASL, but he only stares harder and huffs again. Beyond Johnson, she can see other cages and other chimps, so many that the wire mesh blurs her vision and she cannot see the other end of the corridor.

To escape Johnson's scrutiny, she ducks through the door into the outside run, a wire mesh cage on a white concrete foundation. Outside there is barren ground and rabbit brush. All the other runs are deserted until Johnson appears in the run beside hers. His attention disturbs her and she goes back inside.

She retreats to the side of the cage farthest from Johnson. A crudely built wooden platform provides her with a place to sit. Wrapping her arms around her knees, she tries to relax and ignore Johnson. She dozes off for a while, but wakes to a commotion across the corridor.

In the cage across the way a female chimp is in heat. Rachel recognizes the smell from her own times in heat. Two keepers are opening the door that separates the female's cage from the adjoining cage, where a male stands, watching with great interest. Johnson is shaking the wire mesh and howling as he watches.

"Mike here is a virgin, but Susie knows what she's doing," one keeper was saying to the other. "So it should go smoothly. But keep the hose ready."

"Yeah?"

"Yeah. Sometimes they fight. We only use the hose to break it up if it gets real bad. Generally, they do okay."

Mike stalks into Susie's cage. The keepers lower the cage door, trapping both chimps in the same enclosure.

Susie seems unalarmed. She continues eating a slice of orange while Mike sniffs at her genitals with every indication of great interest. She bends over to let Mike finger her pink bottom, the sign of estrus.

Rachel finds herself standing at the wire mesh, making low moaning noises. She can see Mike's erection, hear his grunting cries. He squats on the floor of Susie's cage, gesturing to the female. Rachel's feelings are mixed: she is fascinated, fearful, confused. She keeps thinking of the description of sex in the *Love Confessions* story: When Alice feels Danny's lips on hers, she is swept away by the passion of the moment. He takes her in his arms and her skin tingles as if she were consumed by an inner fire.

Susie bends down and Mike penetrates her with a loud grunt, thrusting violently with his hips. Susie cries out shrilly and suddenly leaps up, knocking Mike away. Rachel watches, overcome with fascination. Mike, his penis now limp, follows Susie slowly to the corner of the cage, where he begins grooming her carefully. Rachel finds that the wire mesh has cut her hands where she gripped it too tightly.

It is night, and the door at the end of the corridor creaks open. Rachel is immediately alert, peering through the wire mesh and trying to see down to the end of the corridor. She bangs on the mesh. As Jake comes closer, she waves a greeting.

When Jake reaches for the lever that will raise the door to Rachel's cage, Johnson charges toward him, howling and waving his arms above his head. He hammers on the mesh with his fists, howling and grimacing at Jake. Rachel ignores Johnson and hurries after Jake.

Again Rachel helps Jake clean. In the laboratory, she greets the old chimp, but the animal is more interested in the banana that Jake has brought than in conversation. The chimp will not reply to her questions, and after several tries, she gives up.

While Jake vacuums the carpeted corridors, Rachel empties the trash, finding a magazine called *Modern Romance* in the same wastebasket that had provided *Love Confessions*.

Later, in the janitor's lounge, Jake smokes a cigarette, sips whiskey, and flips through one of his own magazines. Rachel reads love stories in *Modern Romance*.

Every once in a while, she looks over Jake's shoulder at grainy pictures of naked women with their legs spread wide apart. Jake looks for a long time at a picture of a blond woman with big breasts, red fingernails, and purple-painted eyelids. The woman lies on her back and smiles as she strokes the pinkness between her legs. The picture on the next page shows her caressing her own breasts, pinching the dark nipples. The final picture shows her looking back over her shoulder. She is in the position that Susie took when she was ready to be mounted.

Rachel looks over Jake's shoulder at the magazine, but she does not ask questions. Jake's smell began to change as soon as he opened the magazine; the scent of nervous sweat mingles with the aromas of tobacco and whiskey. Rachel suspects that questions would not be welcome just now.

At Jake's insistence, she goes back to her cage before dawn.

Over the next week, she listens to the conversations of the men who come and go, bringing food and hosing out the cages. From the conversations, she learns that the Primate Research Center is primarily a breeding facility that supplies researchers with domestically bred apes and monkeys of several species. It also maintains its own research staff. In indifferent tones, the men talk of horrible things. The adolescent chimps at the end of the corridor are being fed a diet high in cholesterol to determine cholesterol's effects on the circulatory system. A group of pregnant females is being injected with male hormones to determine how that will affect the offspring. A group of infants is being fed a low-protein diet to determine adverse effects on their brain development.

The men look through her as if she were not real, as if she were a part of the wall, as if she were no one at all. She cannot speak to them; she cannot trust them.

Each night, Jake lets her out of her cage and she helps him clean. He brings treats: barbecued potato chips, fresh fruit, chocolate bars, and cookies. He treats her fondly, as one would treat a precocious child. And he talks to her.

At night, when she is with Jake, Rachel can almost forget the terror of the cage, the anxiety of watching Johnson pace to and fro, the sense of unreality that accompanies the simplest act. She would be content to stay with Jake forever, eating snack food and reading confessions magazines. He seems to like her company. But each morning, Jake insists that she must go back to the cage and the terror. By the end of the first week, she has begun plotting her escape.

Whenever Jake falls asleep over his whiskey, something that happens three nights out of five, Rachel prowls the center alone, surreptitiously gathering things that she will need to survive in the desert: a plastic jug filled with water, a bag of food pellets, a large beach towel that will serve as a blanket on the cool desert nights, a discarded shopping bag in which she can carry the other things. Her best find is a road map on which the Primate Research Center is marked in red. She knows the address of Aaron's ranch and finds it on the map. She studies the roads and plots a route home. Cross-country, assuming that she does not get lost, she will have to travel about fifty miles to reach the ranch. She hides these things behind one of the shelves in the janitor's storeroom.

Her plans to run away and go home are disrupted by the idea that she is in love with Jake, a notion that comes to her slowly, fed by the stories in the confessions magazines. When Jake absentmindedly strokes her, she is filled with a strange excitement. She longs for his company and misses him on the weekends when he is away. She is happy only when she is with him, following him through the halls of the center, sniffing the aroma of tobacco and whiskey that is his own perfume. She steals a cigarette from his pack and hides it in her cage, where she can savor the smell of it at her leisure.

She loves him, but she does not know how to make him love her back. Rachel knows little about love: She remembers a high-school crush where she mooned after a boy with a locker near hers, but that came to nothing. She reads the confessions magazines and Ann Landers's col-

umn in the newspaper that Jake brings with him each
night. From these sources, she learns about romance. One
night, after Jake falls asleep, she types a badly punctuated,
ungrammatical letter to Ann. In the letter, she explains
her situation and asks for advice on how to make Jake love
her. She slips the letter into a sack labeled "Outgoing
Mail," and for the next week she reads Ann's column with
increased interest. But her letter never appears.

Rachel searches for answers in the magazine pictures
that seem to fascinate Jake. She studies the naked women,
especially the big-breasted woman with the purple smudges
around her eyes.

One night, she finds a plastic case of eyeshadow in a
secretary's desk. She steals it and takes it back to her cage.
The next evening, as soon as the center is quiet, she
upturns her metal food dish and regards her reflection in
the shiny bottom. Squatting, she balances the eye shadow
case on one knee and examines its contents: a tiny makeup
brush and three shades of eye shadow—Indian Blue,
Forest Green, and Wildly Violet. Rachel chooses the
shade labeled Wildly Violet.

Using one finger to hold her right eye closed, she dabs
her eyelid carefully with the makeup brush, leaving a
gaudy orchid-colored smudge on her brown skin. She
studies the smudge critically, then adds to it, smearing the
color beyond the corner of her eyelid until it disappears in
her brown fur. The color gives her eye a carnival bright-
ness, a lunatic gaiety. Working with great care, she matches
the effect on the other side, then smiles at her reflection,
blinking coquettishly.

In the other cage, Johnson bares his teeth and shakes
the mesh. She ignores him.

When Jake comes to let her out, he frowns at her eyes.
Did you hurt yourself? he asks.

No, she says. Then, after a pause, *Don't you like it?*

Jake squats beside her and stares at her eyes. Rachel
puts a hand on his knee and her heart pounds at her own
boldness. *You are a very strange monkey,* he signs.

Rachel is afraid to move. Her hand on his knee closes
into a fist; her face folds in on itself, puckering around the
eyes.

Then, straightening up, he signs, *I liked your eyes better before*.

He likes her eyes. She nods without taking her eyes from his face. Later, she washes her face in the women's restroom, leaving dark smudges the color of bruises on a series of paper towels.

Rachel is dreaming. She is walking through the Painted Desert with her hairy brown mother, following a red rock canyon that Rachel somehow knows will lead her to the Primate Research Center. Her mother is lagging behind: she does not want to go to the center; she is afraid. In the shadow of a rock outcrop, Rachel stops to explain to her mother that they must go to the center because Jake is at the center.

Rachel's mother does not understand sign language. She watches Rachel with mournful eyes, then scrambles up the canyon wall, leaving Rachel behind. Rachel climbs after her mother, pulling herself over the edge in time to see the other chimp loping away across the windblown red cinder rock and sand.

Rachel bounds after her mother, and as she runs she howls like an abandoned infant chimp, wailing her distress. The figure of her mother wavers in the distance, shimmering in the heat that rises from the sand. The figure changes. Running away across the red sands is a pale blond woman wearing a purple sweatsuit and jogging shoes, the sweet-smelling mother that Rachel remembers. The woman looks back and smiles at Rachel. "Don't howl like an ape, daughter," she calls. "Say Mama."

Rachel runs silently, dream running that takes her nowhere. The sand burns her feet and the sun beats down on her head. The blond woman vanishes in the distance, and Rachel is alone. She collapses on the sand, whimpering because she is alone and afraid.

She feels the gentle touch of fingers grooming her fur, and for a moment, still half-asleep, she believes that her hairy mother has returned to her. She opens her eyes and looks into a pair of dark brown eyes, separated from her by wire mesh. Johnson. He has reached through a gap in the fence to groom her. As he sorts through her fur, he makes soft cooing sounds, gentle comforting noises.

Still half-asleep, she gazes at him and wonders why she was so fearful. He does not seem so bad. He grooms her for a time, and then sits nearby, watching her through the mesh. She brings a slice of apple from her dish of food and offers it to him. With her free hand, she makes the sign for apple. When he takes it, she signs again: *apple*. He is not a particularly quick student, but she has time and many slices of apple.

All Rachel's preparations are done, but she cannot bring herself to leave the center. Leaving the center means leaving Jake, leaving potato chips and whiskey, leaving security. To Rachel, the thought of love is always accompanied by the warm taste of whiskey and potato chips.

Some nights, after Jake is asleep, she goes to the big glass doors that lead to the outside. She opens the doors and stands on the steps, looking down into the desert. Sometimes a jackrabbit sits on its haunches in the rectangles of light that shine through the glass doors. Sometimes she sees kangaroo rats, hopping through the moonlight like rubber balls bouncing on hard pavement. Once, a coyote trots by, casting a contemptuous glance in her direction.

The desert is a lonely place. Empty. Cold. She thinks of Jake snoring softly in the janitor's lounge. And always she closes the door and returns to him.

Rachel leads a double life: janitor's assistant by night, prisoner and teacher by day. She spends her afternoons drowsing in the sun and teaching Johnson new signs.

On a warm afternoon, Rachel sits in the outside run, basking in the sunlight. Johnson is inside, and the other chimps are quiet. She can almost imagine she is back at her father's ranch, sitting in her own yard. She naps and dreams of Jake.

She dreams that she is sitting in his lap on the battered old couch. Her hand is on his chest: a smooth pale hand with red-painted fingernails. When she looks at the dark screen of the television set, she can see her reflection. She is a thin teenager with blond hair and blue eyes. She is naked.

Jake is looking at her and smiling. He runs a hand down her back and she closes her eyes in ecstasy.

But something changes when she closes her eyes. Jake is grooming her as her mother used to groom her, sorting through her hair in search of fleas. She opens her eyes and sees Johnson, his diligent fingers searching through her fur, his intent brown eyes watching her. The reflection on the television screen shows two chimps, tangled in each other's arms.

Rachel wakes to find that she is in heat for the first time since she came to the center. The skin surrounding her genitals is swollen and pink.

For the rest of the day, she is restless, pacing to and fro in her cage. On his side of the wire mesh wall, Johnson is equally restless, following her when she goes outside, sniffing long and hard at the edge of the barrier that separates him from her.

That night, Rachel goes eagerly to help Jake clean. She follows him closely, never letting him get far from her. When he is sweeping, she trots after him with the dustpan and he almost trips over her twice. She keeps waiting for him to notice her condition, but he seems oblivious.

As she works, she sips from a cup of whiskey. Excited, she drinks more than usual, finishing two full cups. The liquor leaves her a little disoriented, and she sways as she follows Jake to the janitor's lounge. She curls up close beside him on the couch. He relaxes with his arms resting on the back of the couch, his legs stretching out before him. She moves so that she is pressed against him.

He stretches, yawns, and rubs the back of his neck as if trying to rub away stiffness. Rachel reaches around behind him and begins to rub his neck gently, reveling in the feel of his skin. The thoughts that hop and skip through her mind are confusing. Sometimes it seems that the hair that tickles her hands is Johnson's; sometimes, she knows it is Jake's. And sometimes it doesn't seem to matter. Are they really so different? They are not so different.

She rubs his neck, not knowing what to do next. In the confessions magazines, this is where the man crushes the woman in his arms. Rachel climbs into Jake's lap and hugs him, waiting for him to crush her in his arms. He blinks at her sleepily. Half-asleep, he strokes her, and his moving hand brushes near her genitals. She presses herself against him, making a soft sound in her throat. She rubs her hip against his crotch, aware now of a slight change in his smell, in the tempo of his breathing. He blinks at her again, a little more awake now. She bares her teeth in a smile and tilts her head back to lick his neck. She can feel his hands on her shoulders, pushing her away, and she knows what he wants. She slides from his lap and turns, presenting him with her pink genitals, ready to be mounted, ready to have him penetrate her. She moans in anticipation, a low inviting sound.

He does not come to her. She looks over her shoulder and he is still sitting on the couch, watching her through half-closed eyes. He reaches over and picks up a magazine filled with pictures of naked women. His other hand drops to his crotch and he is lost in his own world.

Rachel howls like an infant who has lost its mother, but he does not look up. He is staring at the picture of the blond woman.

Rachel runs down dark corridors to her cage, the only home she has. When she reaches the corridor, she is breathing hard and making small lonely whimpering noises. In the dimly lit corridor, she hesitates for a moment, staring into Johnson's cage. The male chimp is asleep. She remembers the touch of his hands when he groomed her.

From the corridor, she lifts the gate that leads into Johnson's cage and enters. He wakes at the sound of the door and sniffs the air. When he sees Rachel, he stalks toward her, sniffing eagerly. She lets him finger her genitals, sniff deeply of her scent. His penis is erect and he grunts in excitement. She turns and presents herself to him and he mounts her, thrusting deep inside. As he penetrates, she thinks, for a moment, of Jake and of the thin blond teenage girl named Rachel, but then the moment passes. Almost against her will she cries out, a shrill exclamation of welcoming and loss.

After he withdraws his penis, Johnson grooms her gently, sniffing her genitals and softly stroking her fur. She is sleepy and content, but she knows that they cannot delay. Johnson is reluctant to leave his cage, but Rachel takes him by the hand and leads him to the janitor's lounge. His presence gives her courage. She listens at the door and hears Jake's soft breathing. Leaving Johnson in the hall, she slips into the room. Jake is lying on the couch, the magazine draped over his legs. Rachel takes the equipment that she has gathered and stands for a moment, staring at the sleeping man. His baseball cap hangs on the arm of a broken chair, and she takes that to remember him by.

Rachel leads Johnson through the empty halls. A kangaroo rat, collecting seeds in the dried grass near the glass doors, looks up curiously as Rachel leads Johnson down the steps. Rachel carries the shopping bag slung over her shoulder. Somewhere in the distance, a coyote howls, a long yapping wail. His cry is joined by others, a chorus in the moonlight.

Rachel takes Johnson by the hand and leads him into the desert.

A cocktail waitress, driving from her job in Flagstaff to her home in Winslow, sees two apes dart across the road, hurrying away from the bright beams of her headlights. After wrestling with her conscience (she does not want to be accused of drinking on the job), she notifies the county sheriff.

A local newspaper reporter, an eager young man fresh out of journalism school, picks up the story from the police report and interviews the waitress. Flattered by his enthusiasm for her story and delighted to find a receptive ear, she tells him details that she failed to mention to the police: one of the apes was wearing a baseball cap and carrying what appeared to be a shopping bag.

The reporter writes up a quick humorous story for the morning edition, and begins researching a feature article to be run later in the week. He knows that the newspaper, eager for news in a slow season, will play a human-interest story up big—kind of a *Lassie, Come Home* with chimps.

Just before dawn, a light rain begins to fall, the first rain of spring. Rachel searches for shelter and finds a small cave formed by three tumbled boulders. It will keep off the rain and hide them from casual observers. She shares her food and water with Johnson. He has followed her closely all night, seemingly intimidated by the darkness and the howling of distant coyotes. She feels protective toward him. At the same time, having him with her gives her courage. He knows only a few gestures in ASL, but he does not need to speak. His presence is comfort enough.

Johnson curls up in the back of the cave and falls asleep quickly. Rachel sits in the opening and watches dawn light wash the stars from the sky. The rain rattles against the sand, a comforting sound. She thinks about Jake. The baseball cap on her head still smells of his cigarettes, but she does not miss him. Not really. She fingers the cap and wonders why she thought she loved Jake.

The rain lets up. The clouds rise like fairy castles in the distance and the rising sun tints them pink and gold and gives them flaming red banners. Rachel remembers when she was younger and Aaron read her the story of Pinnochio, the little puppet who wanted to be a real boy. At the end of his adventures, Pinnochio, who has been brave and kind, gets his wish. He becomes a real boy.

Rachel had cried at the end of the story and when Aaron asked why, she had rubbed her eyes on the backs of her hairy hands. *I want to be a real girl,* she signed to him. *A real girl.*

"You are a real girl," Aaron had told her, but somehow she had never believed him.

The sun rises higher and illuminates the broken rock turrets of the desert. There is a magic in this barren land of unassuming grandeur. Some cultures send their young people to the desert to seek visions and guidance, searching for true thinking spawned by the openness of the place, the loneliness, the beauty of emptiness.

Rachel drowses in the warm sun and dreams a vision that has the clarity of truth. In the dream, her father comes to her. "Rachel," he says to her, "it doesn't matter what anyone thinks of you. You're my daughter."

I want to be a real girl, she signs.

"You are real," her father says. "And you don't need some two-bit drunken janitor to prove it to you." She knows she is dreaming, but she also knows that her father speaks the truth. She is warm and happy and she doesn't need Jake at all. The sunlight warms her and a lizard watches her from a rock, scurrying for cover when she moves. She picks up a bit of loose rock that lies on the floor of the cave. Idly, she scratches on the dark red sandstone. A lopsided heart shape. Within it, she awkwardly prints: Rachel and Johnson. Between them, a plus sign. She goes over the letters again and again, leaving scores of fine lines on the smooth rock surface. Then, late in the morning, soothed by the warmth of the day, she sleeps.

Shortly after dark, an elderly rancher in a pickup truck spots two apes in a remote corner of his ranch. They run away and lose him in the rocks, but not until he has a good look at them. He calls the police, the newspaper, and the Primate Research Center.

The reporter arrives first thing the next morning, interviews the rancher, and follows the men from the Primate Research Center as they search for evidence of the chimps. They find monkey shit near the cave, confirming that the runaways were indeed nearby. The reporter squirms on his belly into the cave and finds the names scratched on the cave wall. He peers at them. He might have dismissed them as the idle scratchings of kids, except that one of the names matched the name of one of the missing chimps. "Hey," he calls to his photographer, "Take a look at this."

The next morning's newspaper displays Rachel's crudely scratched letters. In a brief interview, the rancher had mentioned that one of the chimps was carrying a bag. "Looked like supplies," he had said. "They looked like they were in for the long haul."

On the third day, Rachel's water runs out. She heads toward a small town, marked on the map. They reach it in the early morning—thirst forces them to travel by day. Beside an isolated ranch house, she finds a faucet. She is filling her bottle when Johnson grunts in alarm.

A dark-haired woman watches from the porch of the house. She does not move toward the apes, and Rachel continues filling the bottle. "It's all right, Rachel," the

woman, who has been following the story in the papers,
calls out. "Drink all you want."

Startled, but still suspicious, Rachel caps the bottle and,
keeping her eyes on the woman, drinks from the faucet.
The woman steps back into the house. Rachel signals to
Johnson, telling him to hurry and drink. She turns off the
faucet when he is done.

They are turning to go when the woman emerges from
the house carrying a plate of tortillas and a bowl of apples.
She sets them on the edge of the porch and says, "These
are for you."

The woman watches through the window as Rachel
packs the food in her bag. Rachel puts away the last apple
and gestures her thanks to the woman. When the woman
fails to respond to the sign language, Rachel picks up a
stick and writes in the sand of the yard. "THANK YOU,"
Rachel scratches, then waves good-bye and sets out across
the desert. She is puzzled, but happy.

The next morning's newspaper includes an interview
with the dark-haired woman. She describes how Rachel
turned on the faucet and turned it off when she was
through, how the chimp packed the apples neatly in her
bag and wrote in the dirt with a stick.

The reporter also interviews the director of the Primate
Research Center. "These are animals," the director explains angrily. "But people want to treat them like they're
small hairy people." He describes the Center as "primarily
a breeding center with some facilities for medical research." The reporter asks some pointed questions about
their acquisition of Rachel.

But the biggest story is an investigative piece. The
reporter reveals that he has tracked down Aaron Jacobs's
lawyer and learned that Jacobs left a will. In this will
Jacobs bequeathed all his possessions—including his house
and surrounding land—to "Rachel, the chimp I acknowledge as my daughter."

The reporter makes friends with one of the young
women in the typing pool at the research center, and she
tells him the office scuttlebutt: people suspect that the

chimps may have been released by a deaf and drunken janitor, who was subsequently fired for negligence. The reporter, accompanied by a friend who can communicate in sign language, finds Jake in his apartment in downtown Flagstaff.

Jake, who has been drinking steadily since he was fired, feels betrayed by Rachel, by the Primate Research Center, by the world. He complains at length about Rachel: they had been friends, and then she took his baseball cap and ran away. He just didn't understand why she had run away like that.

"You mean she could talk?" the reporter asks through his interpreter.

Of course she can talk, Jake signs impatiently. *She is a smart monkey.*

The headline reads: "Intelligent chimp inherits fortune!" Of course, Aaron's bequest isn't really a fortune and she isn't just a chimp, but close enough. Animal rights activists rise up in Rachel's defense. The case is discussed on the national news. Ann Landers reports receiving a letter from a chimp named Rachel; she had thought it was a hoax perpetrated by the boys at Yale. The American Civil Liberties Union assigns a lawyer to the case.

By day, Rachel and Johnson sleep in whatever hiding places they can find: a cave; a shelter built for range cattle; the shell of an abandoned car, rusted from long years in a desert gully. Sometimes Rachel dreams of jungle darkness, and the coyotes in the distance become a part of her dreams, their howling becomes the cries of fellow apes.

The desert and the journey have changed her. She is wiser, having passed through the white-hot love of adolescence and emerged on the other side. She dreams, one day, of the ranch house. In the dream, she has long blond hair and pale white skin. Her eyes are red from crying and she wanders the house restlessly, searching for something that she has lost. When she hears coyotes howling, she looks through a window at the darkness outside. The face that looks in at her has jug-handle ears and shaggy hair. When she sees the face, she cries out in recognition and opens the window to let herself in.

By night, Rachel and Johnson travel. The rocks and sands are cool beneath Rachel's feet as she walks toward her ranch. On television, scientists and politicians discuss the ramifications of her case, describe the technology uncovered by investigation of Aaron Jacobs's files. Their debates do not affect her steady progress toward her ranch or the stars that sprinkle the sky above her.

It is night when Rachel and Johnson approach the ranch house. Rachel sniffs the wind and smells automobile exhaust and strange humans. From the hills, she can see a white van marked with the name of a local television station. She hesitates and considers returning to the safety of the desert. Then she takes Johnson by the hand and starts down the hill. Rachel is going home.

Recycling Strategies
for the Inner City

I see the metal claw lying in the gutter among the broken bottles and litter, and I recognize it immediately: a piece of an alien spaceship. Before I pick it up, I glance in both directions to make sure no one is watching. The only person nearby is a hooker waiting for a john, and she is watching the cars drive past. A young couple is walking by, but they are looking away, determined to ignore both the hooker and me. They, like so many other people, don't really want to see what's around them.

I scoop up the alien artifact. The claw has three digits, joined together at a thick stalk. The end of the stalk is rough, as if it had broken off a larger piece. Though the day is foggy, the metal is warm to the touch. When I touch the claw, I feel its digits flex in response, but when I examine it more closely, it lies still.

I add the claw to the treasures in my pink plastic shopping bag, and I hurry to the hotel where I live. Harold is at the front desk when I come in. He's wearing the same dingy white shirt, burgundy tie, and frayed blue suit jacket he always wears. I think he believes that the suit jacket gives him an air of respectability. Harold calls himself the hotel manager, but he's really just the desk clerk. He's a middle-aged man with delusions of grandeur.

He looks up when I walk in. "Your social worker was looking for you today," he grumbled. "She said you had missed your last two appointments." Harold doesn't look at me when he speaks. He looks past me, at a point somewhere over my head.

"I must have forgotten," I tell him. A month ago, I was assigned to a new social worker, a bright young woman

247

just out of graduate school. I suspect that she is an agent of the CIA. The one time that I mentioned the aliens to her, I caught a look in her eyes, a flicker of joyous discovery. She hid her elation, but not before I noticed.

"She left this." He holds out a slip of industrial green paper. It is an official notification that I have an appointment with the city Department of Social Services tomorrow.

I take the paper, drop it in my shopping bag, and head for my room. On my way through the lobby, I pass Mr. Johnson, Mrs. Danneman, and Mrs. Goldman. They sit in the grimy armchairs in the lobby, watching people walk by the hotel's front windows. I nod to them and smile, but they do not respond. They stare past me, like zombies who are trying to remember what life was like. I may be old, but I hope I will never be that close to dead. I punch the button for the elevator.

On the top floor of the hotel, the hallway stinks of other people's food: tomato soup heated on illegal hot plates, greasy burgers from the take-out place on the corner, Chinese food in soggy cardboard containers. Down the center of the hall, there's a long strip of bright red carpet that covers the path where the gray wall-to-wall carpet has worn through. The runner is wearing too: a trail of footprints and dirt marks the center and the edges are starting to fray.

I carry my shopping bag down the hall to my room—a cozy cubicle furnished with a single bed, a battered chest of drawers, and a chair upholstered in turquoise blue vinyl. The room is small, but I've made it my own. Along the walls, I've stacked cardboard boxes filled with the things that I've collected. The paper bags that hold my other treasures fill most of the floor space. A narrow path leads from the door to the chair.

I make my way to the chair and set my shopping bag on the worn gray carpet. This is the best part of the day. Now I sort the treasures I have found, putting each one where it belongs: the buttons go into the bag of buttons, the bottle caps into the box of bottle caps, the broken umbrella into the stack of broken umbrellas. The green slip from the Department of Social Services goes in the trash.

There is no proper place for the metal claw. I set it on

the arm of the chair. I will put it with the other spaceship parts, when I find more.

The government does not want people to know about the alien spaceships. They deny all reports of UFOs and flying saucers. The government is good at hiding the things people would rather not see: the old men and women in the lobby, the hookers on the corners, the aliens who visit our world.

But I know about the aliens. Late at night, I sit on the narrow metal balcony of the fire escape outside my window and I watch the sky. The city lights wash out the stars, but there are other lights in the sky: planes landing at the San Francisco airport, police helicopters on patrol, and, of course, the alien spaceships, small sparks that dance just above the buildings of downtown. Sometimes, I can barely see them. I have to squint my eyes and concentrate, staring into the darkness until at last they become clear.

It was drizzling, night before last, when I tried to communicate with the aliens. I had been watching one particular alien spaceship through the rain-streaked window. Its faint wavering light reminded me of fireflies that I had seen as a child. The light blinked on and off, on and off: a dash, a series of dots. I knew it had to be a message, but I could not translate the signal.

The light came lower, hovering just above the buildings a few blocks away. I left the window and stood by my door, flicking the light switch so that the bare bulb in the ceiling went on and off, on and off, repeating the pattern I had seen. I didn't know how the aliens responded; from my post by the light switch I could not see out the window. As I was repeating the pattern for the third time, I heard the wailing of a siren and the muffled thunder of a police helicopter. I abandoned the light switch and hurried to the window.

The helicopter was circling nearby. The roving beams of its spotlights reflected from the raindrops, forming bright shafts of light that seemed to connect the copter to the ground. The spotlights moved in a frantic, erratic pattern, rippling over the cars, the alleys, the walls of buildings.

Sirens in the street, bright lights flashing blue and red and blue and red, the rattle of gunfire, a distant explosion— I backed away from the window, suddenly frightened. I turned off my light and crawled into bed, pulling the covers up under my chin. I hadn't meant to lure the spaceship in too close. I hadn't meant to cause trouble. For a long time, I lay awake, listening to the sirens.

The next day, Harold said that there had been a drug bust down the street. "Thank God they're doing something to clean up the neighborhood," he said to Mrs. Goldman, who wasn't listening.

Harold believes what he reads in the newspapers. He doesn't know about the aliens. He doesn't see the world as it really is.

With the alien claw on the arm of my chair, I lie in my bed, trying to sleep. My room is not a quiet place. The bathroom faucet drips, a delicate tap, tap, tapping in the darkness. The wheezing of buses and the rattling of Muni trains drift up to my window from the street below. My next-door-neighbor's TV rumbles through the walls—he's a little deaf, and he keeps the sound turned up loud.

On this particular night I notice a new noise: a furtive scrabbling that stops each time I move. I sit up in the bed and look around, thinking it might be a rat. I've seen rats on the stairs, nasty gray shadows that flee at the sound of footsteps.

The metal claw is no longer on the arm of the chair. I wait, remaining very still. Finally, by the pale moonlight that filters through my window, I see the claw crouching among the bags and boxes. As I watch, it begins to move again, pulling itself along with its three digits and dragging its broken stalk across the carpet. I shift my weight, the bed creaks, and the claw stops, freezing in position.

It seems so frightened and helpless, crouching on the floor in the darkness. "It's all right," I say to it softly. "Don't worry. I won't hurt you. I'm your friend." I remain very still.

Eventually, the claw moves again. I hear a soft rustling as it pushes between the paper bags. I hear it rattling among the broken umbrellas. I fall asleep to the gentle clicking as its digits flex and straighten, flex and straighten again.

In the morning, I see the claw sunning itself in the pale morning light that comes in the window. When I was a girl on my grandfather's farm, the morning light was yellow—like the corn that grew in the fields, like the sunflowers on the edge of the garden. But the city light is gray. I remember reading somewhere that different stars cast light of different colors. I wonder what color light the claw is used to.

During the night, the claw has improved itself. It has six legs now—the original three and three more that look like they were constructed from the ribs of a broken umbrella. When I sit up in bed, the claw scurries away, seeking refuge among the boxes and bags. I watch it go.

It's comforting to have something alive here in my room. I had a kitten once, a scrawny black alley cat that I found hiding under a dumpster in an alley. But Harold found out about it and told me cats weren't allowed. When I was out, he got into my room and took the kitten away. I don't think he could catch the claw and take it away. I'll bet that the claw would hide so well that he wouldn't even see it.

I get up and wash my face. In a cracked cup, I make myself a cup of instant coffee, using hot water from the bathroom tap. I eat a sweet roll from a bag of day-old donuts that I bought from the shop on the corner. As I eat my breakfast and get dressed, I talk softly to the claw that I know is hidden somewhere among my things. "No one will find you here," I tell the claw. "I'll make sure of that. You'll be okay with me."

The claw does not respond, but I know it's there, hidden and silent. I finish dressing, take my shopping bag, and go out to see what I can find.

The day is cold and a bitter wind has swept the gutters almost clean. Though I search for hours, I can't find any other spaceship parts. I find other things: a few aluminum cans, a rhinestone brooch with a broken pin, a stray button from someone's coat. Near a construction site, I find a one-foot length of cable made up of many strands of copper wire. But nothing else from the spaceship. Finally, late in the afternoon, I return to my room.

The claw has been busy while I was out. In the narrow space between the bed and the bags of things, it has built a metal framework from the narrow ribs of broken umbrellas. In my absence, it seems to have gained confidence. As I make my way to the chair, it continues working.

The framework forms a cylinder that is maybe six feet long and two feet across. As I watch, the claw neatly snips another rib from a broken umbrella. Carrying the strip of metal in its two front feet, it makes its way to the end of the cylinder, then begins to weave the strip in with the others, pushing it over and under the crisscrossing strips of the framework. It's a clever little machine, busy about its own business. I wonder if it even notices that I'm home.

I set the shopping bag on the floor at my feet and begin to sort through my acquisitions. Boldly, the claw comes over to investigate these additions to my collection. It examines the cable closely, gently separating the individual copper strands. I watch for a moment and then put my hand down by the floor, wiggling my fingers as if coaxing a cat to come nearer. The claw abandons the cable and turns toward my hand, approaching cautiously. It touches me delicately with two of its digits, hesitates, then clambers onto my outstretched hand.

My hands are still cold from being outside. The claw radiates a comforting warmth, like the glow of a wood fire. Moving slowly, I bring it to my lap. It folds its legs beneath it, snuggling down. I stroke it gently and the claw responds by vibrating pleasantly, like a cat purring.

"Were you lonely before I found you?" I ask the claw. "Were you lost and all alone?"

The claw just keeps on purring. I can feel its heat through the fabric of my dress. The warmth soothes my aching legs. It feels so right to hold the claw and just sit.

"You must have been frightened," I say. "It's much better when someone's with you."

I stroke the claw, knowing that I should get up and heat up some soup on the hot plate. But I'm not hungry now, though I haven't eaten since the sweet roll I had for breakfast. Through my window, I watch the sky grow darker. I relax, reluctant to move, and I consider the framework that the claw has constructed.

It could be something dangerous, I suppose, but I rather doubt that. The claw seems like a friendly creature. I study the structure and think about what it might be. Back in school, I remember experimenting with a worm called the planaria. If you cut off a piece of a planaria, the piece will grow into a whole planaria again. All you need is a piece, and the piece recreates the rest.

Suppose that the alien spaceship was like a planaria. Each part of it contained all the information about the whole thing. Break off one piece, and that piece would go about reconstructing the rest. I consider the framework that the claw has built.

"I'll tell you what I think," I say to the claw. "I think you are rebuilding the spaceship that blew up."

The claw shows no interest in my theories. After a time, it scrambles off my lap and gets back to work, busily weaving the copper wire in and out through the framework it has built. Every now and then, it selects a metal button from the box of buttons, threads the wire through the holes in the button, and then continues its weaving. I can see no pattern to its selection or placement of buttons. That night, I lie awake, listening to the rustlings of the claw as it searches among my things and assembles them into an alien pattern.

I wake to the rattle of aluminum. The claw is hard at work. Flattened aluminum cans fill the gaps in the framework, held in place by a lacework of copper wire. Pearl buttons and rhinestone brooches, scavenged from my bags and boxes, sparkle among the cans. The claw scrambles over the surface, tirelessly weaving copper wire over the can that it is adding. It looks so natural there: like a spider on its web.

I don't want to leave. I'm afraid that if I leave, the claw will be gone when I come back. I sit on the edge of the bed to watch it work. As I watch, it hesitates for a moment, and then leaves its work to rest on the floor at my feet. When I reach out to touch it, it clambers onto my hand and lets me put it in my lap. For a time, it sits in my lap and purrs, then it returns to work.

I feel sad, watching the claw build the craft that will take it away. Eventually, I go out on my usual rounds, unwilling to watch any longer.

It is a cold, bleak day, and I find nothing of interest. A few aluminum cans, a few bottle caps. Maybe the claw can use them to complete its work. I carry them back to the hotel.

My social worker is waiting for me in the lobby, perched uncomfortably on the dingy sofa. She sits between Mrs. Goldman and Mr. Johnson. She is talking brightly about something, but they are ignoring her, lost in their own hazy thoughts. She catches me before I can slip past.

"I'm so glad to see you," she said. "I was quite worried when I missed your appointment. I asked the manager to check your room." She glanced at Harold, but he was busy with his papers, refusing to look up. "You know, we really must clean up all that trash beside your bed."

I stare at her. "What are you talking about?"

"All those cans and things. It's really a health hazard. I've already arranged to have someone come in tomorrow and—"

"You can't do that," I protested. "Those are my things."

"Now just relax," she said, her voice dripping with understanding. "It really isn't safe. Imagine if there were a fire. You'd never be able to get out of your room with all that clutter. It's really best—"

"If there were a fire, we'd all roast like marshmallows," I say, but she isn't listening.

"—best if we clean it all up for you. I wouldn't be doing my job if I didn't—"

I back away from her and flee to my room. Fortunately, she doesn't follow. Even if she isn't an agent of the government, she is dangerous. She wants to teach me to overlook things, to look past things, to ignore the world. She thinks there is only one way of looking at the world— her way. I don't agree.

* * *

I rush into my room and close the door. The spaceship fills the space between the bed and the boxes. A hinged lid, like the lid of a pirate chest, stands open, poised to close. I put my hand on the tail section. I can feel a faint trembling, as if something were humming inside. The claw crouches beside the lid, waiting.

"You'd better get out of here," I tell the claw. "They're closing in on us. They'll lock us both up."

I open the window so that the spaceship can take off. When I stand back, nothing happens. The claw just sits by the lid, remaining motionless.

"Look, you'd really better leave," I say. It doesn't move. I sit in the chair and watch it, frustrated by its inaction. From the TV next door, I hear the *Star Trek* theme song.

The claw climbs to the armrest of the chair. With two of its legs, it takes hold of my finger. Gently, it tugs on my hand, trying to move me in the direction of the cylinder.

"What do you want?" I ask, but it only tugs again, more strongly this time.

I pick up the claw in my other hand and go to the spaceship. The hollow place inside it is just my height and just wide enough for my shoulders. The claw had arranged some old sweaters inside: it looks soft and rather inviting.

Maybe I wasn't quite right the other night when I was thinking about planaria. I should have thought a little longer. Consider, for instance, the difference between a horse and a car. A horse has a mind of his own. You develop a relationship with a horse. If you like the horse and the horse likes you, you get along; if not, you don't. A horse can miss you. If you leave a horse behind, the horse can come looking for you. A car is just a hunk of metal—no loyalty. If you sell your car, you may miss it, but it won't miss you.

Suppose, just suppose, that someone somewhere built a spaceship that was more like a horse than a car. A spaceship that could rebuild itself from pieces. That someone went away and left the spaceship behind—died maybe, because otherwise why would anyone leave behind such a wonderful spaceship? And the spaceship waited for a while, and then came looking for its creator, its master. Maybe it couldn't find its original master—but it found someone else. Someone who wanted to travel. The claw is purring in my hand.

I take off my shoes and step gingerly into the opening. Carefully, I slide my legs into the cylinder. At my feet, I can feel the warmth of the hidden engines. The claw curls up beside me, snuggling into the crook of my neck.

"Ready?" I ask. Reaching up, I close the lid. And we go.

Bones

This is a true story, more or less. In the history books, you can find Dr. John Hunter, a noted surgeon and naturalist. London's Royal College of Surgeons maintains his museum, an amazing collection of eighteenth-century oddities and natural curiosities.

Charlie Bryne is in the history books too. He came to London from Ireland in 1782. Advertised as the World's Tallest Man and the Descendant of Irish Kings, he exhibited himself as a curiosity and a freak.

The history books tell of their meeting—but now I'm getting ahead of myself. I must start long before that.

On a cold winter evening, when the ground was white with frost, Charlie Bryne sat on a stool by the peat fire. Though the boy was only ten years old, he was already as tall as a grown man. His mother, a youthful widow, sat close by, her shawl pulled up around her shoulders and a glass of whiskey in her hand. The firelight shone on her face, making her cheeks rosy and her eyes bright.

"Tell me the story, Mum," Charlie asked. "Tell me how I got to be so big."

She smiled at him fondly. "Ah, you know the tale as well as I do, Charlie. You have no need for me to tell it."

"I've forgotten. Tell me again," he pleaded.

"All right—just once more. Fill my glass and we'll have the story." He refilled her glass from the jug and she settled herself more comfortably in her chair.

"It was a year after a young horse threw my husband and broke his back," she began. "I was a widow with a fine farm, and many a bachelor farmer would gladly have had me to wife. But I was happy to be on my lone, and I would have none of them." She pushed back her dark hair with her hand, smiling at the memory. "Old Sean Dermot died that autumn, and I went to the wake. As it came about, I stayed too late, and I was walking home after dark. 'Twas a lonesome road I had to travel—and I was tired, so I took a shortcut, the path that ran beside the Giant's Boneyard."

She shook her head at her own foolishness. The Giant's Boneyard was a lonely, haunted spot. In a field too rocky for planting, wild grasses grew thick and green around great boulders of unusual shapes. People said that the boulders were the bones of a giant, a king of Ireland who had died a hundred years before, while fighting to protect his people from invaders. Some said that he had promised, with his dying words, to return if ever Ireland needed him. Some said he walked at night, strolling through the field that held his bones. In any case, most people avoided the place after dark.

"The moon was a sliver in the sky, hanging low and giving just enough light for me to see. I was only halfway across the field when I saw a blue light, a beautiful light, the color of the Blessed Virgin's robes. I was not foolish enough to go running after fairy lanterns. I kept to the path, hurrying toward home, but the light danced across the field toward me. And then I saw it clearly."

She clasped her hands before her, and leaned toward Charlie. He caught his breath, watching her. "The blue light shone from a golden crown on the head of an enormous man. A powerful man—stronger than the blacksmith in the village, taller than the tallest I had ever seen. He was handsome, but his eyes were dark and fierce. When he looked at me, I froze, bound to the spot and unable to run."

She fixed her gaze on Charlie, as if to show him how it felt, and he shivered. "He spoke to me sweetly, saying that I would bear him a son. His son would have the old blood in his veins, and he would save Ireland. Then he took me by the hand and led me to a spot where the grass was soft. There he lay with me, taking his pleasure as a man does with a woman. In the morning, I woke with the sun in my eyes, beside the boulder they call the Giant's Skull." She leaned back in her chair. "Nine months later, you were born. You were the biggest baby the midwife had ever laid her eyes upon. And you've kept growing ever since. You take after your father, sure enough."

Charlie nodded, gazing into the fire. "Have you ever seen my father again?"

"That I have not," she murmured. "But I know you for his son."

"Then I must save Ireland? When must I do this?"

"That I don't know. When the time comes, surely it will be clear to you."

Charlie frowned at the fire, his expression fierce. "I will do what I must do," he said. "If only I can figure out what that is."

Charlie wasn't his mother's son, though he sat at her knee and fetched her whiskey. He was a child of the woods and the wild fields—growing up outdoors as much as in. Summer and winter alike, he ran barefoot, coming home to his mother's house with dusty feet and brambles in his hair.

He was a strange lad—with a peculiar, dreamy air about him that made some think he was dim-witted. But he wasn't stupid—he just paid attention to other lessons. Reading and writing seemed unimportant when he could look out the window and see the flowers growing in the fields, hear the birds singing. He understood the mathematics of bird nests, the poetry of cloud formations, the penmanship of snail tracks left on the cold stones of the churchyard wall.

He had a way about him. Animals liked him: the wildest horse would consent to be shod when Charlie held its head. Cows bore their calves more easily if he were standing by. Over the years, the widow Bryne's farm prospered: her fields were fertile and her hens laid more eggs than any in the village. Her cows gave the richest milk and bore their calves with never a bit of trouble.

Charlie lived with his mother, helping to tend her prospering farm. When he was just sixteen, he was taller than the tallest man in the county. At twenty, he measured eight feet tall, and he was still growing. And always he wondered when he would be called upon to save Ireland.

One sunny day, he was drowsing in the Giant's Boneyard, his back against the boulder known as the Giant's Skull. Leaning against the sun-warmed surface, he listened to the wind in the grass and the high thin peeping of the little birds that searched for seeds in the meadow. A lark flew from the grass and came to perch on the boulder. When Charlie held out his hand, the bird flew to him. With one finger, he gently rubbed the bird's head. When Charlie stopped his petting, the lark tilted back its head, sang a liquid trill, then pushed off his finger and took flight.

Charlie watched the bird fly, then plucked a blade of grass from a clump beside him and chewed on the sweet stem. The earth beneath him was warm; the sun shone on his face. He belonged in this meadow the way the boulders belonged. It seemed to him sometimes that he should stay here always, letting the grass grow over him, its roots tickling the surface of his skin as it tickled the granite boulders.

The wind carried the sound of voices. Some neighboring farmers had stopped their work in a nearby field to have a bit of lunch. Their deep voices blended with the distant songbirds and the humming of bees in the wildflowers. Charlie let the sounds wash over him.

"Patrick's gone to England," said one man. Charlie recognized the voice of Mick, an elderly farmer. Patrick was his oldest son. "He said he'll come home rich or not at all."

"Not at all, more than likely," muttered his companion. John, Charlie guessed from the voice, another neighbor. "Have you ever known a young lad to come home? My wife has borne me five strong sons. The Lord took two of them, and they are happy with the angels in heaven. But the other three are in England. I think the ones that are with the angels are more likely to come home than the ones that are in London."

"Aye, that's God's truth," Mick agreed sadly. "I've never known a one to come home to till his father's farm."

A pause, punctuated by the gurgling of beer pouring from the jug.

"Every night, as I go to sleep, I wonder who will till this land when I'm gone," John said softly. "'Tis not such a large plot—barely enough to feed us—but it was my father's farm and his father's before him." John stopped talking long enough to take a draught of beer, then continued. "'Tis a sad thing when a man with five sons has no one to help him with the plowing."

"It ain't right," Mick said. "It ain't right that the best of our children run away to England, never to return."

John laughed, a dry humorless sound. "Aye, we need to protect ourselves. The blasted English have given up fighting with swords. Instead they lure the children away with sweet promises and gold. Treacherous bastards."

"Aye," Mick agreed sadly. "That they are."

The men were silent for a moment, and then John spoke again. "I see you looking over there at those boulders. Old stories won't help you now."

Mick's voice was soft. "I think sometimes about the old king, rising up from his bones. If he were to come before us, I'd tell him to bring the children home. Go to London and bring our sons and daughters back to us."

John snorted. "If you're looking for magic to save you, you're more foolish than I thought. There's no magic there—just boulders and tall green grass. The magic faded long ago."

Charlie frowned. John was an unhappy man—bitter, tired, as dried up as the land he cultivated. Charlie understood why all his sons left and why all his daughters married young.

"Ah, well," Mick said. "All the wishing in the world won't till the field. I think we'd best get back to work."

The voices faded, leaving only the humming of the bees and the wind in the grasses. Charlie tilted his head to the sun and thought.

Thinking made Charlie uneasy. But he could not help considering Mick's words. For some time, he had felt that something was wrong, an uneasy and uncomfortable sensation in his belly. He had watched his neighbors' sons and daughters leave their fathers' farms and go to England, saying they would return. The land called out to them, wishing them back again, but they did not come back.

And he dreamed of a day when the children were all gone; old men and women tilled the farms, weeping for their sons and daughters who had run away, never to return.

Maybe he fell asleep in the sun. Without being aware of it, he may have quietly slipped over the thin line between sleep and wakefulness, lying there in the grass. The sun was low in the sky and the boulders cast long shadows across the meadow.

He heard footsteps and looked up. A tall man wearing a crown regarded him sadly. Charlie scrambled to his feet. He recognized his father, though the man did not entirely match his mother's description. The king's eyes were not fierce, but mournful and sad. He wasn't really handsome: his face was broad and pleasant, rather like Charlie's own. His gray beard was touched with green, as if strands of moss grew among the hairs. He wore armor made of tarnished metal plate, joined by strips of leather. Small, soft-petaled flowers sprouted among the lacings. His crown gave off a weak blue light, like the strange fluorescence that glows from rotting wood.

The king sat down heavily on a nearby boulder. "Your turn has come, my son," he said. His tone was melancholy; his voice, a soft rumble. "You must go to England and bring the sons and daughters of Ireland home."

Charlie nodded eagerly. "I know," he said. "I'll bring them home."

The king stared at the ground. "There is still magic here, though some do not have eyes to see it." He studied Charlie. "You must come back to this place, when your task is done. You belong here. You are part of the magic and power. This is the place you must die and be buried."

Charlie frowned. He saw no need to talk about what would happen when he died. He was young and strong and eager to do what his father wanted. "Yes, yes," he said. "I understand."

The king reached for the scabbard that hung at his side and pulled out a sword. It was as tarnished as the armor, but jewels gleamed on its hilt. "Here is my sword. Perhaps it will help you." He looked at the weapon doubtfully.

"It was my father's before me, and it still has some magic in it."

Charlie took hold of the hilt and bowed to his father clumsily.

It was dark when Charlie woke. The grass was damp with dew, and where the sword had been was a plain straight staff of hawthorn wood. When Charlie picked it up, the white blossoms and green shoots sprouted from the dry wood, as if spring had come in the space of a minute. Charlie frowned and brushed the blossoms away but they sprouted again. At last, he gave up and left them be, carrying a staff adorned with small white flowers that smelled of spring.

Every August, not far from Dublin, farmers gathered at the Donnybrook Fair to race horses, sell cattle, drink whiskey, and get into fights. That year, on the last day of the fair, the sky was gray and a misty rain was falling. The hard-packed soil of the fairground was slick and muddy.

Joe Vance hunched his shoulders against the dampness and pushed through the crowd, down the aisle of hastily constructed booths and sagging tents. The country people seemed oblivious to the rain: they were playing pitch-and-toss, gawking at the Punch and Judy show, listening to the hideous wail of the organ-grinder's instrument and laughing at the antics of his flea-bitten monkey.

Vance had spent the morning trying to entice passing farmers into a simple sporting game. He had three shells and a dried pea: to win, a farmer had only to guess which shell hid the pea. But the crowd had been reluctant to play. For five hours, Vance had been sitting in the drizzle and calling to the crowd without a penny to show for it. Vance suspected that some other thimble rigger must have passed through recently, and the locals were wise to the trick. All in all, Vance was sick of the country and eager to return to London, where a sharp had a chance to earn a guinea or two.

Vance was almost to the end of the aisle when he saw a clump of people gathered around a young man. The young man seemed to be standing on a box; he towered over the tallest man in the crowd. On his shoulder, a meadowlark perched, looking just as calm as you please. As Vance watched, the small bird tipped back his head and sang a high sweet trill, followed by a glorious burst of song. The liquid notes cut through the babble of the crowd and the wailing of the organ.

"Is the bloody bird tame?" Vance asked a man in the crowd, but the man just shrugged. Vance pushed his way closer. He had seen caged finches fetch a pretty penny among the London gentry, and they did nothing but chirp and flutter. A man might turn a profit if he had a supply of tame larks.

Just as Vance reached the front of the crowd, the bird finished its song and took flight. The young man on whose shoulder it had perched smiled after it and took a step, as if to follow. With a shock, Vance realized that the man was not standing on a box at all. With his bare feet planted firmly on the muddy earth, he stood at least two feet taller than any other man in the crowd. He was a country lad, dressed in rough homespun cloth that was marked with the dust of the road. In one hand, he held a wooden staff that was decorated with white flowers.

Vance forgot the lark and the hope of profits that had flown with the bird. "God save me, man—how bloody tall are you?" Vance asked, staring up.

The young man glanced down at Vance and shrugged. "Tallest in Derry County."

"Tallest I've ever laid eyes on," Vance said. "How old are you?"

"Twenty years this summer."

"Bloody remarkable," Vance muttered. He squinted, measuring the man with his eyes. Londoners were always willing to pay to see a curiosity. "Must be eight feet tall, if you're an inch. What's your name, lad?"

"Charlie Bryne."

"My name's Joe Vance, Charlie, and I'm pleased to meet you. You're a likely lad, Charlie, a very likely lad. I must confess, I've never met a one like you before. A marvel in your own right."

Charlie's eyes were a brilliant innocent blue, as pale and clear as the summer sky. "Where are you from?" he asked.

"From London, the finest city in all the world."

Charlie studied Vance. "Tell me—are there many Irishmen in London?"

"Irishmen? Why, I'd wager half a crown that there are more Irishmen in St. Giles Rookery than in all of County Derry," Vance said enthusiastically. "You'd never be homesick in London."

Charlie's face was guileless, the sweet face of a fool. "I want to go to London," he said.

Vance smiled at the way that fate was playing into his hands. His luck, it seemed, had finally turned. "I knew it when I laid eyes on you, Charlie. I knew you for a man with a spirit of adventure, an itching to see the world. And you're in luck, Charlie, tremendous luck." Vance moved closer, reaching up to place a hand on Charlie's shoulder. "I'll take you there, lad. You see, I'm a manager. I find people with special talents, and I help 'em along. Groom 'em, so to speak. Back in London, I managed Bruisin' Peg. You may have heard of her?"

Charlie shook his head.

"Best lady prize fighter in all London. When Peg was in the ring, you could hear the screaming for miles around. Pity she had to retire." Vance felt it unnecessary to mention that her decision to retire had been precipitated by a broken leg and a clout on the ear that had left her half deaf. He had abandoned her in a low London boardinghouse, with enough money to pay a week's rent. It had seemed like an opportune time to leave town with the rest of the profits. "I'll take you to London, lad," Vance continued. "It'll be a wonderful opportunity for you, a wonderful opportunity."

And so it happened that Charlie came to be on board a bluff-bowed brig that sailed from Dublin to England. Late at night, on the first night of the crossing, Tom Dorland was on deck, having been awakened by the lice that infested his bedding and clothes. He strolled in the open air, grateful that the cold and the motion had quieted the insects, but knowing that they would rouse again if he returned to his narrow bunk.

A half moon, high in the sky, illuminated the deck, casting a silver light on the boxes and barrels and bundles that were lashed to the railings. The wind had died and the ship was barely moving through the water. Tom leaned on the railing, staring out to sea.

"'Tis a pleasant evening," a deep voice said from the shadows beside a large box.

Tom glanced toward the voice, frowning into the shadows. "Seems a chilly night to be sleeping out in the air," he said.

"Too many people in the cabin," the man said.

Tom nodded. The passenger's cabin was a dank shelter on the foredeck. When the ship was fully booked, as it was for this passage, the small space became impossibly crowded.

"How long will it take to reach London?" the man asked.

Tom looked up at the stars. "If we don't get a wind, we could be on the sea for days."

"Ah," the man in the shadows said. "Is that so?" Tom heard the creaking of the deck and saw a large shadow detach itself from the others. A very large shadow—the man was taller than Tom by more than two feet. Tom stared up at the giant—another crewman had told him of the tall man who had come aboard as a passenger, but Tom had assumed that the other sailor's talk was exaggerated.

"You're a big 'un," Tom managed at last.

"I'm my father's son," the giant said, leaning on the railing beside Tom. The big man shook his head, staring out at the calm waters. "I have urgent business in London."

Tom shrugged. "If you want to get there quickly, you have my blessing," he said disrespectfully. "Call up a wind and blow us there in a hurry."

The giant did not take offense at Tom's tone. "A wind," he mused. "A wind to blow us away from Ireland." He moved his hand and Tom noticed, for the first time, the staff he carried. The giant frowned at it, then waved it tentatively out over the rail, swinging it in a circle. A breath of fresh wind puffed against Tom's face. The giant waved the staff again, smiling now. The wind filled the sails and gently pushed the ship toward the shore of England.

* * *

London was larger than Charlie had expected. So many people, bustling here and there with their own business to attend to. He would have been lost in a minute without Joe Vance. He followed the little man down narrow winding streets, ducking to avoid the wooden signs that hung over shop doorways. Vance threaded his way through the commotion with ease, dodging coaches and hackneys, pushing past fruit sellers with baskets and barrows, sidestepping odorous puddles of offal and horse dung. Charlie was hard-pressed to keep up. He saw an Irishwoman selling oranges on the street corner, her black shawl wrapped tight about her shoulders to keep off the cold. He wanted to stop and chat with her, but Vance rushed on and Charlie feared he would lose his guide. He noticed a young Irish girl selling flowers. But he could not stop to talk, he had to hurry to follow Vance. People stared at him as he passed, called to their friends and pointed to him.

Vance turned from a narrow street into an even narrower alley. The thin strip of evening sky that showed between the tenements was gray with fog; the air was damp and cool. Laundry, strung between the buildings, hung limp in the still air. A group of boys was playing marbles at the far end of the street. Two pigs slept in a scatter of straw in the gutter. As Charlie passed, the larger animal lifted its head and sniffed the air, its small eyes regarding the giant with a dim sort of recognition.

The alley led to a small courtyard where tall buildings blocked out all but the smallest square of gray sky. Vance stepped into a hallway that reeked of varnish from the cane shop next door and called up the stairs. The woman who came down shrieked when she saw him—a cry of surprise and delight, mixed with a little bit of chiding. "Well, it's Joe Vance, blast your eyes. Where have you been, you no-good scoundrel."

While Vance and the woman talked, Charlie waited in the courtyard, staring up at the patch of sky. He heard them murmuring about someone named Peg, and Vance said "God rest her soul," in an insincere voice. But Charlie paid no attention.

He felt tired and confused. On the ship, he had begun to feel ill at ease, missing the solid warmth of Irish soil beneath his feet. When he had complained to Vance, the little man had attributed the complaint to seasickness and said that the feeling would go away when he reached solid ground again. But the sickness had remained, a hollowness in his belly, like the emptiness of hunger without the hunger pains. He wore shoes now—Vance had insisted on that when they reached Dublin—and he longed for the touch of honest soil beneath his feet.

"Charlie, come along, lad. Mary will set us up with the rooms we need," Vance called to him.

Vance seemed familiar with the house. The woman showed them a furnished sitting room and a bedroom that attached to it. The bedroom was dark and cold, but Charlie just shrugged when Vance asked him what he thought. He barely looked at the rooms, knowing that he would not be in London for so very long. He would gather the Irish, and then be on his way. So it was not worth quibbling about the look of the rooms.

Vance engaged the rooms and then hurried Charlie along, saying that they had many things to do that day. They went to a tailor shop and Vance had Charlie measured for a suit of clothes. Then they went to the office of the *Morning Herald* where Vance placed an advertisement and ordered handbills to post. "Make 'em say 'The tallest man in the world,'" Vance told the clerk. "'Eighth wonder of the world.'"

While Vance was talking to the clerk, Charlie stepped outside. He looked down the narrow street. In the distance, he saw the open sky and a spot of green. He left Vance behind, drawn to the greenery.

The River Thames flowed through London, bringing water to the city and carrying away the sewage and refuse. Charlie walked down the street and found himself on steps leading down to the river. A tall tree grew on the riverbank, providing a restful spot in the gray stone of the city. In the tree, a bird was singing.

Charlie sat on the stone steps. A sea gull landed beside him and cocked its head from side to side, studying him with one yellow eye and then the other. Charlie smiled at the bird, then tilted his head back so that the sun shone on his face. The river water lapped gently against the bottom step, whispering comforting words in a language all its own. He rested there, soaking up the warmth of the sun and feeling a portion of his strength returning to him.

Sean was a mudlark, one of the filthy crew who made their living by scavenging bits of saleable refuse from the mud of the River Thames. When the tide was out, he and his two brothers waded into the dirty water, foraging for bits of rope and old iron to sell to the ragman, or for lumps of coal that their mother could burn.

Sean was seven years old, and he had been mudlarking since he was six. His father, a laborer on the docks, had died after being crushed between two barges. With Sean's father's death, the family had fallen on hard times. His mother did char work when she could get it, and all the children scavenged.

On warm days, it was not so bad to wade in the river: they could clamber from the water and let the sun warm them every now and again. But when the wind blew, there was no comfort for them—just cold mud and cold water and a gray and cheerless sky.

On that sunny day, Sean and his brothers had been both lucky and unlucky. Over by the docks where some men were repairing a ship, they found a dozen copper nails, worth a half-penny for the lot. That was good luck—but bad luck came with it. Sean had stepped on one of the nails, running it deep into his foot. When the sailors chased them away from the docks, he could scarcely run for the pain. Even now, hours later, his foot throbbed with a hot pain and he hobbled after his brothers, walking on his heel to avoid touching the wound to the mud.

"Look there," David, his oldest brother, called. "By the river steps." The tallest man Sean had ever seen was lounging in the sun on the stone steps that led down to the water. "Come on," David said. "Let's go talk to him."

The three boys approached cautiously, marveling at the size of the man. Their mother had told them stories of the giants who lived in Ireland in the early days. This man might have emerged from such a story.

Sean was in shallow water just a few yards away from the giant when the man opened his eyes. "Good day, sir," said David, the boldest of the three. "Have you a penny for some poor lads?"

The giant blinked at them. "A penny?" He shook his head. "Not so much as a penny, though Joe Vance says that I will be a wealthy man soon enough."

Encouraged by such an amiable response, Sean stepped closer. "You're very big," he said. "Are you a giant, like the ones in the stories?"

The man nodded. "My father was a giant. I suppose I'm one too." He held out his hand. "Come up out of the water if you like." He took Sean's hand and lifted him from the water. "There now," he murmured. "Sit down here."

Sean limped up the steps to sit beside the giant. His brothers hung back, gaping at him from the safety of the river. But the giant seemed friendly enough.

"What have you done to your foot?" the giant asked him.

"Stuck it with a nail," Sean said, bending his leg and twisting his foot around so he could examine the wound in the sole. The skin around the puncture had turned a deep purple. The chill of the river water had numbed the foot somewhat, but when Sean tried to wipe the mud away from the wound, he winced at the stabbing pain.

The giant's hand closed over Sean's, engulfing the boy's hand and foot both. "Don't poke at it, lad. Let it be, and perhaps I can help." The giant's hand was warm and it seemed to soothe the pain.

The boy gaped up at the giant. "Are you a doctor?"

The giant shook his head. "Not a doctor. But it seems I sometimes have a healing way about me." He wet his lips. Suddenly, for all his size, he looked like he was not so much older than Sean. "My father gave me a magic sword," he said softly, jerking his head toward a stout wooden staff that leaned against the steps beside him. "It has a power to it. You can touch it if you like."

Sean reached out and fingered the white blossoms that grew from the wooden shaft.

"Do you come from Ireland?" the giant asked.

Sean shook his head. "My mother came from Ireland. I have never been there."

"Ah," the giant said. "But still you are Irish by blood."

He nodded slowly. "I have come to take the Irish back home. You'll be coming with me."

Young as he was, Sean knew the way of the world. He frowned at the giant. "We can't go to Ireland," he said. "We don't have money for the fare."

The giant studied him solemnly, as if this were the first time that he had thought of the fare. "Bran the Blessed once waded across the water between England and Ireland. He could have carried the Irish home—but he was a bigger giant than I am." He hesitated, frowning. "Maybe we could walk."

Sean shook his head. "We can't walk across the sea."

The giant looked mournful, and Sean cast about in his mind, trying to think of something that might help. "Moses parted the waters," he said. His mother made a practice of telling them stories from the Bible, on nights when she was not too tired. "Maybe you could do that."

The giant studied the Thames. He lifted his staff and waved it at the water, as if pushing it back. "Go back," he rumbled. "Show me some dry land."

The water obeyed sluggishly, drawing back away from the base of the steps to reveal the black muck of the bottom. It stopped a few feet from the steps, and the giant waved again, as if herding a reluctant cow. "Go on now. Move yourself." The water drew back another two feet, forming a smooth green-brown wall that was as smooth and shiny as glass. Sean's brothers stood ankle-deep in the mud, gazing at their own feet in amazement.

"Charlie! Where are you, you blasted Irishman? Charlie!" Hearing an angry voice, the giant lowered his staff. The waters flowed back into place and lapped quietly at the base of the steps. Sean slipped off the steps and returned to the safety of the river. A small man appeared at the top of the steps and shouted again at the sight of the giant. "Where have you been, Charlie?"

"Right here by the river," the giant said with quiet dignity. "Just talking to these lads. They're from Ireland."

Vance glared at Sean and his brothers. "Half the mud-larks in London are Irish," he grumbled. "Come on now, Charlie. We have business to attend to."

"They are my people, Joe. I'll be taking them back to Ireland presently."

Vance nodded impatiently, but softened his tone. "Certainly you will, Charlie. But now we must be going."

Sean watched the giant go. It wasn't until he followed his brothers that he realized that his foot no longer ached. That night, he sat by the fire and searched for the wound. But the sole of his foot was smooth and unblemished, with nary a puncture, a hole, or a scrape.

There are no gardens in Covent Garden. The square that bore that name was in the heart of London's West End, in the shadow of St. Paul's Church and not far from the decaying tenement houses of St. Giles Rookery, a slum inhabited by the Irish. By day, costermongers, people selling fruit and vegetables, filled the square. As they called out their wares, their cries competed with the braying voices of would-be entertainers: a juggler who sent sharp knives dancing through the air, a Welshman who swallowed live mice and snakes, a man with a monkey that danced on its hind legs to the music of a hand-cranked organ, another with a chicken that walked a tightrope.

In nearby Drury Lane, gentlemen wagered on the cockfights. In the coffeehouses, gamblers favored games that depended on the spin of a wheel or the toss of the dice, playing roulette and faro, brag and basset, crimp and hazard and rolypoly. For those gamblers with money to spare at evening's end, the south side of the square offered Mother Needham's and Mother Cole's, well-known among London's brothels.

An Irishwoman named Kathleen had a stall in Covent Garden. Her face was pretty enough—she had even features and her eyes were the color of the ocean caught in a tidepool. But most people didn't notice her eyes or her face. Instead, their gazes lingered on the hump that rose from her back like the pack on a peddler. Kathleen was born with a twist in her back, and with this she made her living.

She read palms and told fortunes. Her stall was not far Tom King's Coffeehouse where gentlemen gambled, and many a gambler came to touch her hump for luck. Sometimes they asked her if they should gamble that night. She would study their palms and give them advice. "Not tonight, Your Grace. There's a bad look to the moon and the luck is not with you." "Stick to the wheel. The dice will be against you." Maids, out shopping for fresh fruit, would give her a penny to tell them about handsome young men. "His heart is false, dearie," she told them. "Look elsewhere for your true love."

On a sunny morning, she sat on a stool outside her stall, letting the warmth of the day soak into her bones. The weather had changed from foul to fair, and the changes made her hump ache with a deep abiding pain. She had smeared on a salve that a patterer had claimed would heal any misery, but the ache remained.

Above the cries of farmers hawking their vegetables, she heard a trill of birdsong. She looked to see if someone had caged birds to sell. The men with caged birds and the boys with nests to sell were the first and sometimes the only signs of spring in London.

When she heard the song again, she looked up and saw a songbird perched on the pole that supported her rain cover. He tilted back his head and loosed another sweet song.

"Look there," an apple seller cried. When she looked toward the voice, she saw a man who towered above the rest of the crowd. He wore the garb of a country lad and carried a walking staff decorated with hawthorn blossoms.

"That's right, look sharp, lads," said the small man who walked beside the giant. "My name's Joe Vance and this is Charlie Bryne, the Irish giant, descendant of kings. I'll wager you've never seen his like before. Tell your friends to come and see him. On display every day except Sunday."

While the small man shouted his pitch, the tall man glanced at the crowd, clearly a little bewildered by all the noise and confusion around him. If it hadn't been for his size, he would have looked like a schoolboy, visiting the big city for the first time.

When Kathleen smiled at him, he smiled genially back. "Good day to you," she called to him. "Would you have your fortune told, Charlie Bryne? No charge for the descendant of kings." Telling his fortune for free would be worth her while, she knew, attracting attention to her and bringing her business after he was gone.

He came to her, the crowd moving aside before him like wheat before the wind. "Where in Ireland are you from?" he asked, his voice a deep grumbling that blended with the noise of the crowd.

"My parents came from County Cork," she said. "But I have been in England since I was just a babe."

He held out his hand and she took it. His skin was warm and rough, like a boulder that had been warmed by the sun. The lines on the palm were etched deep, like cracks in a granite boulder.

"Someone is looking for you," she said. "You have a secret he wants."

"I have no secrets," Charlie said.

"Someone wants something you have. There will be pain and sorrow, and you will die far from home."

He shook his head stubbornly. "That cannot be," he rumbled. "I promised my father that I would return to Ireland." He smiled down at her. "I will take you with me."

Vance called to Charlie then, shouting across the crowd. He squeezed Kathleen's hand gently. When he walked off through the crowd, the songbird followed, circling the giant. After he left, Kathleen realized that her hump no longer ached. For a time, she was free of the pain.

The clock on the mantel struck eight and Joe Vance moved into the crowd. "That's the end of today's visiting hours, ladies and gentlemen. Come again tomorrow. The amazing Irish giant will be accepting visits from the gentry from eleven to three and from five to eight each day. Tell your friends."

Charlie stood by the fire and watched the crowd leave the room, glad to see them go. For the past four hours, he had answered the same questions over and over again: he was twenty years old; he stood eight foot two inches in his stocking feet; his foot was fifteen inches long.

He was uncomfortable in his new suit. The tailor had

cut it too tight in the chest and shoulders. Whenever Charlie took a deep breath, the seams threatened to split. Joe Vance had advised him to breathe shallowly.

Joe Vance sat in one of the chairs by the fire and spilled a handful of coins onto a kerchief that he had spread on the hearth rug. He was counting out Charlie's share: one-quarter of the take. Vance took the rest. He had explained to Charlie that out of this share he took care of all the necessities of business—paying the rent, arranging to have young boys hand out advertisements in the streets and so on.

Firelight reflecting from the coins sparkled in Vance's eyes. He finished counting and pushed a small stack of coins toward Charlie. Charlie picked up the coins and jingled them in his hand.

"There you go, lad—enough money to keep you busy for the night, eh?" Vance grinned at Charlie and slipped the rest of the take into his money pouch. "Now I'll be off—I have business to attend to." He winked at Charlie and hurried off.

In the dark bedroom, Charlie took off his new suit and his new shoes, and put on his comfortable old homespun clothes. The hawthorn flowers that bloomed on his staff perfumed the room with the fresh scent of spring. He took the staff in hand and set out to find the Irish and do his father's bidding.

Night was settling over London as he left his rooms and made his way down the dark alley toward Covent Garden. Here and there, an oil lamp in a doorway illuminated the threshold of a shop. Charlie kept to one side of the narrow street, ducking beneath the hanging wooden shop signs. A few industrious shopkeepers had scattered cobblestones in front of their doorways. The stones, embedded in the hard-packed dirt of the alley, hurt Charlie's bare feet.

The street opened into a square crowded with stalls and people. The air was loud with the cries of sellers: "Chestnuts, penny a score!" "Apples! Fine 'ating apples!" "Oysters, three for a penny. Fine and fresh. Oysters!"

A candle cast an uncertain light over a vegetable stall. The hot coals of the chestnut seller's stall shone with a

hellish glow, painting the passersby as ruddy as devils.
The oyster seller's makeshift stall was beneath a streetlamp.
The wick in the oil-filled globe cast a puddle of feeble
yellow light. The flickering light distorted people's faces,
making them looked pinched and angry.

Three gentlemen hurried through the square—swell
gamblers by the look of them, on their way to a coffeehouse or a bordello. A young girl, no more than eight
years old, trotted after them, calling out, "Please, gentlemen,
do buy my flowers. Do buy a bunch please." As she passed
the oyster seller's stall, the child lost her footing, tripping
over a pothole in the street. She bumped into the stall and
fell, dropping her flowers and knocking half a dozen
shellfish into the street.

She was in the mud, scrambling after her fallen bouquets, when the oyster seller swore and lifted his hand to
cuff her. In the flickering light, his face looked frozen and
masklike, as if all human feeling had left him.

"Here now," Charlie called out. He stepped between
the man and the child. "She didn't mean you any harm."

The oyster seller glared up at Charlie. "Blasted Irish
whelp," he muttered, but he lowered his hand and stepped
back, putting his stall between himself and the giant,
clearly fearful.

Turning to the little girl, Charlie found her on her knees
in the mud, gathering up her flowers. The blossoms were
muddy and battered, and the child was weeping as she
tried unsuccessfully to brush the filth from the bouquets.
He squatted beside her. "Now, lass," he murmured, not
knowing what to say. "Come now, don't cry."

She ignored him, continuing to inspect her flowers
through her tears. Charlie studied her a moment, then
held out his staff, where the hawthorn flowers still bloomed.
"Look here, lass. You can pick a new bouquet right here."

She glanced up and Charlie helped her to her feet.
"There's a lass," he said, still holding out his staff. His legs
were tired from squatting, and so he plucked the child
from the mud and lifted her, supporting her on one arm.
He held the staff in his other hand, where she might easily
reach the blossoms. "Pick a bouquet," he urged her.

A few passersby, intrigued by Charlie's size, had stopped

to watch him argue with the oyster seller. They lingered to watch the girl pluck flowers from the giant's staff. She picked a bunch and bound them together with a dirty bit of string that she pulled from some hidden pocket in the rags that served as her clothes. She picked another bunch, larger than the first. The watching crowd grew larger. Though clearly the staff should have been plucked bare, it was as thick with flowers as ever.

The girl picked a third bunch of flowers, working awkwardly with her right hand while her left arm cradled an enormous bouquet. Her arms were full when the giant set her down, and yet the staff still bore a crown of white blossoms. As the little girl passed among the crowd, selling flowers to people who marveled at how sweet and fresh they were, the crowd watched Charlie expectantly, awaiting his next trick.

"'Tis a miracle," murmured an elderly Irish apple seller. She wore her shawl over her graying hair and clenched a pipe in her teeth.

"It's nothing but a conjurer's trick," said a dapperly dressed young gentleman. "A very clever one, I admit. How do you do it, man?"

Charlie blinked at him, a little confused. "What do you mean?"

"Where did the flowers come from?" the man asked impatiently.

"From the soil of Ireland," Charlie said, giving as honest an answer as he knew how.

The man snorted in disbelief. "They never give away a trick," he said to the lady beside him. Before Charlie could speak again, the man reached out and took the staff from Charlie's hand to examine it. When the staff left Charlie's hand, the flowers wilted. Their petals showered to the ground, like an early snowfall. When Charlie took the staff back, the blossoms returned, fresh flowers opening where no buds had even been visible.

"Trickery," the man said, and pushed away through the crowd, the lady on his arm.

"Let us have another trick," said a lad in the crowd. He was a ragged young man, bold because he was surrounded by his mates, who were as ragged and dirty as he was. "Conjure us something."

Charlie looked around at the crowd, not knowing what to do. "I don't know any tricks. I have come here from Ireland to bring the Irish home."

"Home to Ireland?" The bold lad made a rude sound, and his companions laughed. "I'd sooner go to blazes than go to Ireland."

"But you must go home," Charlie said. "The land, it needs you back."

"The land needs me," one of the lad's companions scoffed. "And what about what I need?"

"The land will give you what you need," Charlie said, confident as could be.

Another of the young men laughed. "I need a fine suit of clothes and a gold watch. Will the land give me that?"

The first lad shouted, "I need a coach and four fine horses. Will the land give me that?"

"I need a house in the country!"

"I need a roast goose for dinner!"

"I need five gold guineas!"

Charlie shouted above them. "These are not the things you need. You don't understand. I have come to take you back where you belong. You must listen to me."

But the crowd would not listen. Their pleasure seemed to border on hysteria: half of them were drunk; the others would like to be. Their laughter was not genuine and easy; it had a frantic edge to it.

"Do not waste yourselves in this foul city where you can't see the sky." Charlie's voice boomed over the babble of the crowd. "Come back to the island where you were born! Come with me!"

"And who are you to tell us what we must do?" shouted the first lad.

"I am my father's son," Charlie bellowed above the noise. "My father was a king. He sent me here."

"A king, you say?" The ragged lad laughed. "King of the beggars!"

Charlie protested, shaking his head. "No, a king of Ireland. He fought and—"

"King of the Vagabonds!" another young man cried.

"King of the Fools!" shouted a third.

"Aye, that is it," cried the first lad, taking up the shout. "King of the Fools! That is what we have." They surged around him, laughing and pulling at him, like a flock of starlings harrying a raven. "King of the Fools!"

They crowned him with a garland of watercress, snatched from a vegetable seller. They dressed him in a rude cape of flour sacking, grabbed from the protesting baker. They would have done more, but a policeman came to stop the merriment, and the lads left Charlie sitting in the mud not far from Kathleen's stall.

Kathleen found him there when she stepped out to see what all the noise was about. Charlie was leaning against a wall on the edge of the square, the flour sacks around his neck, the garland drooping over one eye. He still clung to his staff.

Kathleen took pity on him, helping him from the mud, taking the garland from his head, using her kerchief to wipe the muck from a cut he had somehow gotten beneath his eye.

"What is it you did, to make those rowdy boys treat you so rudely?" she asked him.

He shook his head, obviously still bewildered by it all. "I only told them that I had come to bring them home to Ireland."

Kathleen dabbed at his wound, making exasperated sounds beneath her breath. He was like a big child, he was. "Bring them home to Ireland? You'll have to tie them up and put them in a box for that. They'll not go willingly."

He shivered in the cold of the night fog, shaking his head. "I don't understand these people. This place has changed them. This place makes people hard, scarcely people at all."

She shook her head. "They're people, right enough. People trying to make their way in a hard cruel world."

"'Tis a cold place, London. I have not been warm since I left Ireland," Charlie muttered.

He looked so mournful and hangdog. She cast about for a way to cheer him. "There are ways to warm yourself, Charlie. I'll show you a way out of the cold. We'll stop a bit at the Black Horse Tavern. You'll find more Irish there, right enough."

The Black Horse Tavern was crowded and noisy, ringing with the shouts of drunken young costermongers playing at cards, dice, and dominoes. A whore who had paused to warm herself with gin was laughing at a bawdy joke; a pimple-faced apprentice stared at her half-exposed breasts and grinned. The air was close with the greasy aroma of roasting mutton.

Kathleen found them a place to sit at a rude wooden table and waved a hand to a serving man. "Gin will warm you," she muttered. "It'll warm you as you've never been warmed before."

The man brought them two glasses of gin, and she sipped at one. The liquor stung her lips and the biting aroma brought tears to her eyes, but it warmed her. A glass or two, and the pain in her hump would ease, the ache in her bones would subside. The gin was medicinal, she reckoned, and that was why she drank it. "It's a foul drink, but it eases a person," she said to Charlie.

Charlie tasted it gingerly. "It has more of a bite than whiskey," he said. "But it does warm me."

"That it does," she said. She leaned forward, resting her elbows on the table and looking up at Charlie, wondering what to do with him. An overgrown schoolboy, that's what he was. "Why don't you go home, Charlie? Go home to your mother's farm. You don't belong here."

He downed the rest of the glass of gin and shook his head. "My father told me I must bring the Irish home. I cannot go home alone."

Kathleen shook her head. "The Irish will never go home. We all talk of the green hills and how we long for them, but we remember the famines and the hardships as well. We won't go back."

"But you must," he said, his tone urgent. He had another glass of gin, and told her of falling asleep in the Giant's Boneyard. He told her of how his father came to him and told him what to do. "He gave me his sword," Charlie said, gesturing with the staff. "It's a magic thing. On the ship that carried me from Ireland, I waved my staff

and a wind came to blow us to England." He leaned
forward, his face already flushed from the gin. "And when
I waved it over the river, the waters parted, leaving a path
of dry land."

Kathleen sipped her gin and listened, watching his
broad daft face. He was an innocent and a lunatic, that was
clear enough. But she could not help thinking about the
stories that her mother had told her when she was a little
girl. Legends of giants and heros and magical swords.
Charlie's story began like an old tale—the enchanted son,
the magic sword, the quest.

As Charlie talked, he drank gin, downing glass after
glass. With each glass, his words grew louder and made
less sense. He was growing agitated. "And the Irish will
follow me to the side of the sea," he said, his voice loud
enough to cut through the noise of the tavern. "And I will
wave my staff and the waters will part before me." He
stood up, knocking over his bench and stretching his
hands apart to show how the waters would open to let him
through. "We will march across the empty seabed, walking back to the land where we belong."

"Sit down, Charlie," Kathleen said. "Calm yourself."

Around him, the costermongers and apprentices were
staring and laughing.

"Come with me," he called to them, spreading his
arms. "Come with me, my people. I will lead you back to
Ireland." The gin had released a passion in him, and he
shouted to be heard over the laughter and the rude
shouts. "Follow me," he called to them. "Follow me back
to Ireland."

Kathleen watched him sway just a little, made unsteady
by the gin. He lifted his staff, and apprentices scrambled
aside for fear of a clouting. Charlie strode into the gap, his
head held as proudly as a king. He lifted his staff high, and
the crowd parted, leaving him a path that he accepted as
his due. "Follow me," he called, his voice slurred with
drink. Kathleen stood to pursue him. The poor fool would
never find his way home alone. But the crowd closed in
behind him, leaving her to struggle slowly toward the
door.

*   *   *

The night air was cold and Charlie was woozy from the gin. He found himself on the street, puzzled that no one had come after him. Surely in the tavern, when they had made way before him, they had planned to follow. But when he looked back, no one was there, not even Kathleen.

He had not meant to drink so much. But the gin had touched the empty spot that had been in his gut since he left Ireland, providing him with warmth and comfort.

When the wind blew, he shivered and shuffled in the direction that he thought might lead to his rented rooms. His head seemed to have grown large and unwieldy: his feet seemed very far away and very slow in responding to his desires. He managed to walk just a few blocks before he sat down beneath a streetlamp for a little rest. Benumbed by gin, he fell asleep in the gutter.

On the far side of the street, a pair of whores trudged past, carefully picking their way through the garbage and filth from chamberpots. It was getting late, and law-biding citizens were at home in bed, their doors barred against cutthroats and robbers.

A dog ventured from the mouth of an alley where it had been feeding on scraps of garbage. The animal walked with a peculiar lurching gait, its right hind leg having been broken years before by the well-placed kick of a carriage horse. The bone had healed crooked, and the leg no longer touched the ground.

The dog sniffed Charlie. His suit smelled of roasting meat and gin, aromas from the Black Horse Tavern. Attracted by the man's body heat, the dog curled up by Charlie's side and went to sleep. In his sleep, Charlie moved a hand to encircle the dog.

For a time, the man and dog slept peacefully. A burning wick in the oil-filled globe that served as streetlamp cast a dim yellow light on Charlie's face. He smiled in his sleep.

Charlie was dreaming. In his dream, there was music: the singing of larks and the laughter of children filled the air. He was leading a triumphant procession made up of all the Irish who had left the island to seek their fortune in England. He was bringing them home, and they were all dancing after him. The girl who sold flowers was dancing with the rude lad who had called Charlie King of Fools.

The girl's rags flapped around her legs and her bonnet had fallen back on her head. She and her partner were pale from lack of sun and thin from bad food, but already the sunshine was putting roses in their cheeks again. Everyone was dancing: the prostitute from the tavern; the old woman who sold apples; the mudlarks and the ragged Irish beggars from the streets of London.

Charlie danced at the head of the procession, laughing at the way the old apple seller capered. Overhead, the sky was blue, and the sun was on his face. The earth was warm beneath his bare feet. He led them through the country roads to his mother's farm, past the fields filled with growing grain, out to the Giant's Boneyard, where he lay down in the fragrant grass. He belonged here, among the bones of his father. With his head pillowed on his arm, he closed his eyes. In the distance he could hear people laughing and singing.

Someone was calling to him: "Charlie. Charlie Bryne. You can't just lie there like a great lump. Rouse yourself, man. Wake up."

Charlie blinked his eyes. Kathleen was shaking him awake. "Wake up, you gin-soaked lump," she grumbled at him. "The cold will be the death of you if you lie here all night."

Charlie squinted up at her. "What happened?" he mumbled. "Where did all the people go?" He stared at the houses around him—tall, gray, and foreboding in the dim light.

"I've been looking for you," Kathleen was saying. "I knew you couldn't find your way alone. Now where is it you're living?"

Charlie sat up, groaning with the effort. Disturbed by the movement, the dog that lay beside him stood up, shook itself, and wagged its tail tentatively. Absentmindedly, Charlie reached over and rubbed the animal's ears.

"I lay down to rest for a time," Charlie said. "I felt mortally tired, Kathleen."

"Mortally drunk, more like it. You put away enough gin to fell an ox."

The dog leaned against Charlie's side, a small patch of warmth in the chilly night. Charlie's hand stroked the animal idly. "They didn't follow me, Kathleen. It seemed to me they would."

Kathleen reached out and touched his shoulder. "Go back home, Charlie. If you stay here, you'll die in the gutter with a bellyful of gin."

He straightened his shoulders. "The old blood runs in my veins. I'll bring my people back to Ireland." Then the edge of doubt crept into his voice for the first time. "You believe me, Kathleen. Don't you?"

"You must get on home," she said in a weary voice. "Tell me where you live and I'll walk you there."

" 'Tis right by a cane shop on a narrow street where a man can scarcely see the sky," Charlie said. "Not so far from Covent Garden."

"I know the one," Kathleen said. She held her hand out to him, coaxing him as if he were a wayward child. "Come along, Charlie. I'll take you home."

"It isn't my home," Charlie said stubbornly. " 'Tis a place I live, nothing more."

"True, but it's a warm place to sleep, and for tonight you'd best settle for that," she said. "Now come with me."

Leaning on his staff, Charlie staggered to his feet. The dog moved away, wagging its tail in earnest. When Charlie stood, Kathleen's head did not reach his chest. He looked down at her and placed a hand on her shoulder, seeking the warmth of contact with another person as much as the support. Charlie and Kathleen started off down the street, and the dog followed Charlie, trotting easily on all four legs.

Charlie sat in a chair by the fire. He had been on his feet all afternoon, answering questions from the gentry and showing off his size. His head ached with a blinding pain. For the past few days, the world seemed to close in around him when his head ached; his vision narrowed and blackness nibbled at the edges, like the premature coming of night. He closed his eyes for a moment.

"Hey there, lad," Vance said. Charlie heard Vance pull another chair close to the fire and sit down. "You all right?"

"I'm cold."

Charlie heard Vance poke the fire and toss some more coal on the grate. He could see the light of the fire dancing on the inside of his eyelids and feel the heat on his hands. But the warmth did not seem to penetrate the skin. The fire could warm the surface, but his bones were cold. Only the sun and earth of Ireland could warm him deep down. The sun of Ireland or a glass of British gin.

Each night, he went out to the streets to preach to the Irish. There were some who came to hear him each night, a few who believed in him. The old apple seller called him a saint and brought her ailing granddaughter to him for healing. The little flower seller sought him out—but that may have been for practical reasons; she could count on him for a supply of fresh blossoms. The rude young men called him a conjurer, a madman, a fool. The coster-mongers laughed at him. He offered to show them that he could make the river waters part, but no one would follow him to the riverside. Each evening ended the same way: in the tavern, drinking gin with Kathleen.

He blinked and Vance came into focus. The little man was leaning forward in his chair, peering into Charlie's face with a considering air. "You've been drinking too much, lad. Gin will be the death of you."

"This country will be the death of me," Charlie muttered.

"Right you are, lad." Vance was not paying attention. He was counting the take. When he handed Charlie his share, he frowned a little.

"Now don't spend it all on gin," Vance said. "You'd do well to stay home tonight."

Charlie stared at Vance. He did not like the man's proprietary tone. "I will go or stay as I please," he said slowly.

Vance stopped in the act of gathering up the coins. "Well sure, Charlie, of course you will. I was just saying, as a friend, that you—"

"I go to the ginhouses to find my people," Charlie interrupted. "I find them there, drinking gin to warm their bones. They miss the soil of Ireland, though they do not know that's what it is they're missing. They feel the hollowness, just as I feel it, and they drink gin to fill it. I go there to find them and bring them home." He stood up and glared down at Vance.

Vance studied the giant with cold, blank eyes. "Just take care not to sleep in the gutter, lad. Your cough's getting worse."

Charlie's shoulders slumped a little. His head ached and the power had gone from him. "Right you are, Joe. I'll not sleep in the gutter. I'm sorry, Joe."

Now that's enough of Charlie Bryne. Let's consider John Hunter, a man of science, as different from Charlie Bryne as a man could be. We can begin at Kathleen's stall in Covent Garden, on a chilly morning just a few weeks after she met Charlie.

The wind off the Thames blew through Kathleen's wool shawl and made her hump ache. A burly Scot dressed in a fine wool coat passed her stall and glanced into the shadows where she sat.

"You there," he said. "Have you seen the man with the dancing monkey? I'm looking for him."

"I have not seen him this morning." She studied the gentleman, wondering if she might earn a penny from him. It was bitter cold, and she had only told a single fortune that day. "I might see him later. I could give him a message."

The Scot glanced at her, his expression cautious, but strangely greedy. "I hear his monkey died," he said softly.

"I heard the same." The animal had died of a chill and the man was grief stricken, mourning the loss of the income from the monkey's dancing.

His voice dropped a little further. "I have a need for the animal's body," he said. "I will pay for it handsomely. Here." He fumbled in his pocket. "A penny to tell the man that John Hunter has an offer for him." He held out the coin.

John Hunter—she knew the name. Surgeon to the king, he was. And, from the stories that she had heard, an unnaturally curious man. When the tiger died at the Royal Zoo, he had anatomized the beast and mounted the skeleton. When the Siamese twins in the Covent Garden freak show died, rumor had it that the manager had sold the body to Hunter for a tidy sum. People said he was a body-snatcher and a resurrectionist.

"And what would you do with the body?" she asked him. "You'll anatomize it, won't you?" She hadn't cared much for the monkey, a dirty, noisy animal that spent more time scratching for fleas than it did dancing. But it seemed unnatural to want to poke and pry into its innards. "Why don't you let the poor beast rest in peace?"

"Would you bury the beast so its body can rot, benefiting no one?" he asked angrily. "Why is it that people have no trouble eating the meat of a cow—but they consider it wrong to examine the dead animal too closely? Yes, I'll anatomize the beast. I'll examine the organs and see what killed it. I'll study the muscles and mount the bones so that I can study them later. And when I'm done, I'll add a few humble observations to our knowledge of natural philosophy." His tone was bitter, and she had the feeling he was talking to himself, as much as to her. "A patient of mine, a young boy, died today of a coughing disease. When I wished to examine his lungs, to see how the disease had affected them, what influence my treatment had had, his father forbade it. The ignorant fool. What I learned from his son's body might have helped me heal another child. But instead his son's body must rot in peace and children must go on dying. How can I learn to cure what ails people, if I can't observe the action of disease on the body? Would you have doctors continue in ignorance, peddling salves and tonics that work indifferently well? Little better than butchers, most of them."

Kathleen stayed in the shadows, startled by his vehemence.

He held out the penny again, his face softening as if he repented his outburst. "Come on, lass, take the penny and tell the man if you see him." He glanced at the sign that a clerk had sketched for Kathleen in exchange for his fortune: an open hand with the palm exposed, the life line marked in black ink. "I'll give you another penny to tell my fortune."

For two pennies, she left her stool and stepped from her stall. In the light of the sun, he saw her clearly for the first time. "Ah," he said. His voice was that of a man discovering an unexpected treasure. He stared at her honestly, not troubling to hide his interest. "Your back—how long has it been like that?"

"Since I was a babe." She pulled the shawl more tightly around her shoulders—distressed both by the cold and by the way he studied her. She was used to people who stared, but his interest was more intense than that of the casual passerby.

"Does it pain you?" he asked.

She nodded cautiously. "When the weather's cold, it does." She took the two coins and held his hand in hers, turning the palm up to the light so that she could study the lines. She stared for a moment, and the patterns emerged from the crisscrossing lines. "You will meet someone very important, very powerful. He has something you want very much. Some secret you are lacking." She frowned at the lines. "You want something and you get it, but when you do, it will not be what you wanted." She shook her head, staring at the lines. "There is something that you do not understand, something important."

He laughed abruptly at this last. "That is not the future. That is now. There are many things I do not understand."

She shook her head and released his hand. "That is all I can tell you." She started to turn away, but he called her back.

"Wait," he said urgently. "I have a salve that might help your aches." He wet his lips and his expression was that of a greedy child. "If you come to my examination room, I will give you some. My house is on Jermyn Street. Anyone nearby can tell you the way there."

Kathleen studied his face. He did, in his own peculiar way, wish to give her relief from her pain. But he also had an unhealthy desire to know the twists of her bones. She did not trust him.

"I would like to examine you," he said. "Perhaps I can help."

"I'll give some thought to it," she said, and turned away from the eagerness in his eyes. She had lived in London long enough to be wary.

* * *

John Hunter was, without a doubt, a curious man. He started out as a curious boy, naturally enough.

When John was just eight, he found a burrow in the winter-blasted kitchen garden of his parents' Scottish farm. Curious about the animal inside, he dug beneath the frost into the cold soil, where he found a toad lying in a tunnel of its own making. The animal was cold and motionless—by all appearances, stone dead. But when he held it tightly, he thought he felt a stirring inside the cold body—the beating of its tiny heart. He slipped the animal into the pocket of his britches and smuggled it past his mother into the house.

He set the stiff creature just behind the coal scuttle, where it would be warmed by the heat of the fire and left it there during supper. When he checked on it just before bed, the creature had stirred to reluctant life. It blinked at him lazily and then slowly hopped across the hearth rug.

His mother caught him. "What have you there, Johnnie? Lord save me—where did you get that beast?"

Despite his protests, she cast the toad back into the garden. In the morning, he found the chilly corpse huddled beneath a clump of straw. He warmed it in his hands, but it did not move. He snuck it into the house and warmed it by the fire, but the beast did not return to life. He puzzled over it: why had the beast perished when it was returned to the cold?

In the back of the chicken run, where his mother wouldn't catch him, John anatomized the body with his pocketknife, delving into its innards to see if he could learn why the beast had died.

John Hunter grew up. As a boy of twelve, he loitered with his cousin by the churchyard. His parents were inside, christening his youngest sister. Bored with the proceedings and ignored by the adults, the boys had slipped from the church.

Late afternoon clouds hung low in the sky, as gray as the tombstones in the churchyard. John and his cousin leaned on the stone wall, idly chatting.

"The churchyard's haunted," John's cousin said. "At night, the ghost of old man MacDonald wanders among

the graves, looking for children who are out too late."
MacDonald, an old man who had died a month before,
had had a reputation for disliking small boys.

John looked doubtful.

"You don't believe in ghosts?" His cousin's tone was
challenging.

John considered the question carefully. He was a methodical boy. "I've never seen one. Have you?"

His cousin hesitated, and then decided to stick to the
truth. "No, but I've heard about them." He wet his lips,
studying John's face. "If you don't believe in ghosts, then I
dare you to run around the old man's grave. Three times.
Counterclockwise."

John thought about it. "If I run round it counterclockwise, that'll bring bad luck," he said. "I believe in bad
luck."

"Then just go out and touch the grave and come back. I
dare you."

John stared out into the graveyard. It seemed darker
now—the low-hanging clouds stole the light from the day.
The old man's grave was a long way off. He was afraid, but
he was also curious, and the second emotion was the more
powerful of the two. What would a ghost look like?

"Or else you have to say that you believe in ghosts," his
cousin went on.

In the end, it was John's own curiosity, not his cousin's
taunting, that drove him on. John climbed the churchyard wall, scuffing the knee of his best pants against the
damp stone. With a nonchalance he did not feel, he
strolled toward the grave. The graveyard was very quiet.
In the hush, he listened to the tiny skittering sounds of
birds in the trees, the whisper of his pantlegs brushing
against the wet grass. Suddenly brave, he reached out
and touched the wing of a stone angel. Cool stone,
nothing more. The air smelled of dampness and fresh-
turned soil, only that. He slowed his footsteps, waiting
for something to happen in the stillness. He glanced
back at his cousin and was startled by how far he had
come: his cousin's face was a spot of white against the
darkness of the churchyard wall.

When he reached the old man's grave, he laid his hand

on the stone and waited. Nothing happened. He stood
still, almost disappointed. He had, up to that moment,
been willing to believe in the ghost, if the ghost had
chosen to present himself. John lingered for a moment,
studying the new stone marker, chose a single flower
from the bouquet beside the grave, and then walked
back.

From a distance, he could see his cousin's pale face, his
wide eyes. John handed his cousin the flower from the old
man's grave. "I guess I don't believe in ghosts," he said
and realized it was true.

Years later, John climbed another graveyard wall—this
one in London. The stones were slippery beneath his
hands. It was a moonless night in early winter. John
Hunter and a fellow student, bent on acquiring essential
supplies for their anatomy classes, wore workmen's clothing that was stained with clay from past excursions.

John ghosted along the paths of the deserted graveyard,
sniffing the air for the scent of freshly dug earth. At the far
corner of the yard, he found what he was looking for: the
new grave of a young woman, dead of childbirth just one
day past.

Thomas, his colleague, lifted the flowers that decorated
the grave, setting them on a nearby grave. Working
quickly, John started digging, using a wooden shovel to
avoid the telltale rattle of metal on stones. Thomas spread
a canvas sheet over the grass, and John heaped the loose
soil on top of the cloth. The exertion of digging warmed
him pleasantly. When he tired of digging, Thomas took
over, digging silently while John kept watch.

"Is that a sound?" Thomas whispered, looking up from
the grave and cocking his head in the direction of the
church.

"Just the wind," John muttered. "Nothing more."

Thomas shivered, looking over his shoulder. "A nasty
business, this," he murmured. "I don't like it."

John glanced at his friend and shook his head. "Hush,"
he said. "Too much talk." John took another turn in the
grave, digging quickly down to the coffin lid. He neatly
slipped the broad iron hooks under the edges of the lid,

up near the head of the coffin. He climbed from the grave and then he and Thomas hauled up on the rope. The lid cracked with a dull splintering sound, and John lowered himself into the grave to lift the broken wood out.

After that, it was easy enough to slide a rope around the shoulders of the corpse and pull her through the opening. They stripped the body—stealing clothing carried a greater penalty than stealing a body alone—and slipped the naked cadaver into a canvas sack. They refilled the grave, leaving no evidence that they had passed that way.

John arranged the flowers tenderly on the grave, then slung the sack over his shoulder. The two men left the graveyard as silently as they had come.

After delivering their burden to their surgical school, they stopped in the tavern. John was cheerful, but he noticed that Thomas seemed morose. "What is it, Thomas, my lad? We did a fine job—the body's in the school, ready for tomorrow's lesson, and there's no harm done."

Thomas shook his head. "Doesn't it bother you?" he asked softly.

John looked up from his beer. "What should be bothering me?"

"Creeping about in the churchyard at night," Thomas murmured.

John took another swallow of beer. He did not understand Thomas's need to chatter on about the matter. John was not fond of the late-night escapades, but he accepted them as necessary to his training as a surgeon and took them as a matter of course. He could not learn about human anatomy without dissecting cadavers.

"If we do not get the bodies, we cannot learn anatomy," John said. "And if we do not learn anatomy, then how can we be surgeons?" It seemed obvious enough.

Thomas shrugged, staring into his beer. "It doesn't sit right," he said. "That's all."

John studied his friend's face, frowning. "What is it that bothers you, Thomas? The woman is dead and gone. We cannot hurt her by taking her body."

Thomas was watching him with a peculiar expression. John shook his head, bewildered by his friend's mood. It seemed to him sometimes that understanding human anatomy was simple compared to understanding the peculiarities of the human heart.

There was, perhaps, a bit of something missing in John Hunter, some bit of human sympathy, some bit of wonder, some bit of fear of the unknown. You might say he was a brave man, but it was not truly bravery, because he saw no reason to be afraid. You might say he was a devil, completely lacking in common human compassion, but you would be wrong there as well. He had compassion of a sort—he dearly desired to help those who were ailing and in pain. But he lacked a sympathy with those who would leave the dead untouched. When life had fled, a body—be it mother or wife or beloved child—was dead meat. He did not understand those who saw it differently.

And so John Hunter became a surgeon. But he did not limit his investigations to the human body. He was a man of boundless curiosity, eager to investigate everything that nature had to offer. He concerned himself with the habits of hedgehogs, the animal heat of growing vegetables, the behavior of cuckoo birds, and the natural history of the viviparous lizard. He collected information like a jackdaw gathering shiny bits of metal. He discovered, by experiment, that the heart of a frog continued beating for hours after the animal's spinal cord had been severed. He learned that eels could survive near-freezing temperatures. He developed a method for artificially stimulating the production of pearls by river mussels. In all his studies, he found human curiosities most interesting. By examining anomalies, he felt he could gain an understanding of the normal way of things.

Now of course Charlie Bryne and John Hunter must come together—you know that as well as I do. And so it was that on a sunny day, John Hunter went down to Covent Garden. He had stopped at the freak show to see if the showman had obtained any specimens for him. Every now and again, the man picked up something that John found of interest: the tattooed forearm of a South Sea Islander, for example, preserved in brine by a seaman with a liking for oddities; or the skull of a pig that was born with a single eye.

That afternoon, the showman had nothing to offer, and **John** strolled through the market. As he walked past an **aisle** of vegetable stalls, he heard the sweet song of a **greenfinch**, sounding over the calls of the melon seller. He followed the birdsong to the end of the aisle. There a man stood beside a cage filled with songbirds that chirped and fluttered their wings against the rough wooden slats. In his hand, the bird seller held a smaller cage, in which a gaudily colored bird sat on a perch.

"It's God's truth," the bird seller was saying to a young woman. "I bought this bird from a sailor who had just come from the West Indies. A bird like this—why it can be taught to talk just as clear as a person. Two shillings is an uncommonly low price for such a bird."

John stepped closer, peering at the bird. Without a doubt, the bird was a greenfinch; the gaudy colors were painted on.

"That's too dear for me," the young woman said, stepping back from the cage. "Though I'm sure it's a wonderful bird."

The bird seller cast John a glance and decided he was the more likely prospect. "You look like a discerning gentleman, sir, one who would appreciate a rare bird. Very rare, indeed."

John snorted. "You're a fool, man, or you take me for one. The bird is a greenfinch that you've painted up like a Drury Lane tart." John pursed his lips and whistled a credible imitation of the greenfinch's song. The bird in the cage stirred in response, then returned the song, staring about as if searching for its rival.

"What a pretty song," the bird seller exclaimed. "I've never heard a greenfinch sing like that in all my days."

"Then you've never heard a greenfinch sing," John said abruptly. The attempt at deception, however clumsy, annoyed him. "A greenfinch is worth three pence, but with a little paint, you've more than tripled the price. I've half a mind to—"

The bird seller's eyes widened as he looked past John. "You there," he cried. John looked around in time to see finches and sparrows explode through an opening in their cage and make for the open sky. Beside the cage stood an enormous man. In one hand he held the wooden slat that he had ripped from the cage; in the other, a wooden staff decorated with hawthorn blossoms.

"God save us!" shouted the bird seller, running to the broken cage. The last of the sparrows flicked its tail and took flight, leaving the cage empty save for loose feathers and bird droppings. The bird seller began to shriek. "You blasted noddy-headed fool!" He turned on the big man, raising his hand as if to strike.

The man straightened to his full height and glared down at the bird seller. "They wanted to go free," the big man said.

John stared at the giant, amazed at his dimensions. He had, on occasion, visited freak shows that advertised tall men or giants, but this man topped them all.

The bird seller lowered his hand, his fury tempered by a fearful respect. But he continued shouting. "Who's going to pay for my birds? They were my livelihood, and now they've flown. I'll call the constable on you, you great lout."

"Here, man," John said hastily. "I am sure that the constable would be interested in this foreign bird that you painted at home."

The bird seller glanced uneasily at his one remaining bird. "Now, sir, there's no need of that. This quarrel is none of yours."

John reached into his purse. "Stop your shouting," he said, handing the man a few coins. "Take this for your trouble, and leave well enough alone."

"Hours of collecting for nothing." The bird seller continued complaining bitterly as he pocketed the coins.

"What about that one?" the giant asked, waving a hand at the caged bird.

John dug two shillings from his pocket and took the cage. Then he glanced again at the giant and suggested, with a jerk of his head, that they leave the place before the grumbling bird seller changed his mind. The giant led the way down to the River Thames. At the river steps, he sat down and held out a hand for the cage. Heedless of the mud and fascinated by the big man, John sat on the stone beside him.

"Poor bird," the giant muttered, looking at the greenfinch.

"The color will wash off," John said. "I'm sure the bird seller used the cheapest paint he could find."

The giant opened the cage door and the bird hopped out onto the man's finger. He splashed the bird with river water. The runoff was scarlet, and the tail feathers lost a touch of color.

John marveled at the bird's passivity—no doubt it was stunned by the heat of the day. But more than that, he marveled at the giant. A magnificent specimen, John thought. He wondered, gazing at the man's oversize hands, what the bones looked like underneath. Ah, what he would give for a skeleton like this man's in his collection.

The man's face was broad and young looking. His blue eyes were a little wild—a hint of lunacy there.

"Why did you pay for the birds I let go?" the giant asked John.

"I wanted to make your acquaintance," John answered honestly. "I've never seen a man as big as you before." He was watching the giant closely. "Do your hands pain you? I noticed the knuckles seemed reddened."

"They ache, right enough."

"I thought so. Your knees and hips—they give you pain too?"

"My knees, and hips, and feet, and hands. They all ache, God save me. They have since I came to London."

John nodded thoughtfully. "I have a salve that might help a bit with that," he said slowly. "Worth a try. If you'd like to come to my office, I could give you some."

The giant looked down at John. He seemed to be grateful for the man's attention. "Perhaps I will."

Just a few days later, in the dissecting room of his Jermyn Street house, John Hunter instructed a group of would-be surgeons in human anatomy. The corpse of an old man lay face down on the dissecting table. Over the course of his instruction, Hunter had neatly laid back the layers of skin and fibrous tissue covering the muscles of the lower leg, lecturing his students on the treatment of injuries to the Achilles tendon. He stressed, as always, the need to experiment and observe.

Only after dissecting the leg to the hip did he complete his lecture and dismiss the students. He watched them go, wondering if any of the lot would ever amount to much. Or would they become like their learned teachers at St. George's, relying on historical hearsay, failing to test and experiment and observe.

Hunter removed his bloodstained smock and washed his hands in a basin of clear water. He was climbing the stairs that connected his basement dissecting room with the rest of the house, when Mrs. Shields, the housekeeper, appeared in the doorway.

"A tall man named Charlie Bryne is here to see you," she said, looking a little flustered. "A very tall man."

"Very good, Mrs. Shields," John exclaimed. "Very good indeed. Send him right in."

The giant stood uneasily by the fire in the small room that served as John Hunter's examination room. He was out of his element, John thought. By the river, he had seemed confident, powerful. In this confined space, he lacked that expansive vitality. His shoulders were hunched, as if the ceiling were pressing too close. His face was pale. His hands were clasped behind his back, like a schoolboy who had been told not to touch anything. John studied him, estimating how large a display case he would need for the skeleton.

"I've come for that salve you told me about," Charlie said. "I thought it might help warm me."

"I'm so glad you could come," John exclaimed. "Sit down. Mrs. Shields will bring us some tea—or perhaps a glass of sherry. That would help warm you."

"I've never tried sherry," Charlie said.

"Then you must try it now," John said. "Please sit down." He gestured to a chair. "How's the greenfinch? Did its feathers come clean?"

Charlie nodded. "It flew off. Back to the country."

Mrs. Shields brought the sherry, pouring the glasses and setting the tray down on the table by the fire. John lifted his glass and smiled at Charlie. "Here's to the birds. I'm glad they didn't die uselessly in the smokes of London."

"Aye," Charlie said, and sipped his sherry.

John hesitated for a moment, considering his words,

then spoke quickly, eager not to miss the opportunity. "Would you mind if I took a few measurements while you're here. Your body temperature, your heart rate—a few simple things, really."

Charlie frowned. "Why do you want all that?"

John chose his words carefully. "I study people like you," he said.

Charlie shook his head. "I do not think there are any other people like me."

John waved a hand to dismiss the objection. "Not precisely like you," he said. "Not giants. But people who are smaller than most, or bigger, or somehow different. The differences are where Nature's secrets lie. I have dedicated myself to the study of amazing things. By studying these things, I learn about the world. If I knew why some lambs grew two heads, I'd know why most grow only one."

Charlie finished his glass of sherry and John poured him another. "Why do you want to know that?"

John set his glass of sherry on the table and leaned forward. "Your body is a remarkable machine, Charlie. When you will it, your fingers move, your eyes blink, you stand, you sit." He reached out and tapped lightly on Charlie's chest. "Your heart beats in your chest, steady as a clock. Why?" John sat back. "You grow and keep on growing, so much larger than other men. Why?"

"Because the old blood runs in my veins," Charlie said, but John ignored the interruption.

"The answer's in there," John said. "In your body. Ticking like a clock."

Charlie glanced uneasily at his own chest.

"I want to understand these things," John murmured.

"Perhaps you cannot understand," Charlie said. He drained his second glass of sherry and held out his glass so that John could fill it again.

"I just don't know enough," John said. "Nature is keeping her secrets, but I will outsmart her." He sipped his own sherry. "If you will do me the great favor of letting me take a few measurements . . ."

Charlie shrugged. "As you like," he said.

John counted Charlie's pulse, took his temperature,

measured his height, his girth, the length of his hands, his feet, the reach of his outstretched hands, and the circumference of his head. As he worked, noting each measurement in the pages of a little book, John made conversation. "I have the bones of a great whale, strung together just as they were when the animal lived. Fascinating creature."

"I have never seen a whale," Charlie said. "Biggest fish there is, they say."

"I've never encountered a live one, but a student of mine supplied me with the pickled carcasses of two small-ish specimens. They're less like a fish, from the build of their skeleton, and more like a cow."

"A cow that spends all its life at sea?" Charlie commented. "Not bloody likely."

John shrugged. "They lack the gills of a fish, but have lungs of a sort. Most peculiar. I've preserved their skeletons in my museum. The skeleton betrays much about the working of the body." He settled back into his chair, done with measurements for just then. "We share an interest in natural history," John said. "Perhaps you would like to come to my country house sometime. See my gardens, my menagerie. A pleasant break from the streets of London." He watched Charlie's face for a sign of fear. Ah, the man was an innocent; he smiled at John.

"I'd like that," Charlie murmured. "That I would."

They became friends, of a sort. On many a fine afternoon, John went to meet Charlie at his rooms. Sometimes, he brought the giant a bottle of sherry and they sat by the fire and talked. John brought a salve that seemed to ease the pain in Charlie's hands, though he still complained of aching knees and hips. He seemed to feel most comfortable by the fire.

In his own way, John genuinely liked the giant. The man fascinated him. John had decided quite early in their acquaintance that Charlie was quite mad. He had a peculiar turn of mind—he told John quite seriously about the most amazing things: haunted meadows and ghostly kings and magic swords. John could tell, from Charlie's wild tale of his own conception, that the man was of illegitimate birth. Charlie told John about his quest—he had to bring the Irish back to Ireland—and John nodded politely, accepting this as just one more indication of the giant's madness.

John was struck by the giant's remarkable staff and its seemingly permanent crown of flowers, though he gave no credence to the miracles Charlie claimed it had performed. He examined it closely, verifying that the blossoms sprouted directly from the wood. He had heard that the branches of certain trees in the West Indies continued to bear leaves even after they had been cut from the parent tree, and he speculated that the staff might be of a similar plant, one that only resembled the common hawthorn. He wanted to cut the staff in half to see if the wood were green inside, but Charlie would not allow it, would not even allow the staff out of his sight.

As the weeks passed, it became obvious that London did not agree with Charlie. Clearly, the man was dying. His hands trembled as he raised a glass of sherry to his lips; he could never get warm. He developed a cough that made his frame shake like an oak tree in a gale. His skin grew pale and broken blood vessels in his nose and cheeks betrayed his affection for gin. He took to wearing shoes, trying desperately to keep his feet warm. John noted Charlie's decline with a mixture of regret and anticipation. He would miss the opportunity to study the living giant, of course, but he was eager to examine the body and bones.

He worried, sometimes, about Charlie's drinking habits. If the giant died in the gutter, who could know where his body might end up. Body snatchers abounded, and John feared that some other surgeon might obtain the body.

It was during this time, on a fine sunny afternoon, that John took Charlie to his country house at Earl's Court. They rode in John's coach, though the giant had to hunch his shoulders and bow his head to fit in the seat. The lethargy that had grown habitual seemed to drop away from the giant as soon as they left London. Charlie stared out the window, grinning at the trees and meadows.

"It's wonderful," he said. "Just wonderful to see green fields again."

At Earl's Court, John took Charlie around the grounds,

showing him the exotic beasts and fowl. Charlie gaped at the zebra and smooth-skinned Asian water buffalo that shared a paddock, shook his head in amazement at the two young leopards and the African lion. In the conservatory, he marveled at John's beehive, a box that had been built of plate glass. Beneath the glass, the worker bees hurried through the complex combs, going about their business. Through the glass and from the surrounding fields came the faint sound of buzzing.

"It reminds me of home," Charlie said, his voice a soft rumble. "I used to sleep in my mother's fields, listening to the sound of the bees in the clover. A beautiful sound."

"I've studied the pitch of their humming and compared it to the pianoforte," John said. "It's treble A above middle C."

Charlie did not seem to be listening. He was leaning close to the glass, watching the workers making their way through the combs. "So many of them, so busy."

"An average of approximately three thousand four hundred to a hive, by my count. And there's always a queen bee, you know. In every hive I've checked."

Charlie held out his hand, and a bee that was returning from the fields landed on a finger.

"Careful there," John said. "They've a nasty, irritable temper. I was stung four times last week."

"They'll not sting me," Charlie said. The insect crawled over the massive hand, its wings buzzing, but it never stung.

"Come," said John. "There's more to see."

John led the way to the fishpond, where he bred carp, tench, leeches, and eels for experiments. On the way, he noticed that larks, finches, and other small birds seemed to be particularly abundant in the fields that day—the grass was alive with them. They fluttered up from the grass before them, circling the giant's head before flying away. Once, to John's amazement, a lark landed on Charlie's shoulder, tipped back its head to release a torrent of song, then flew away. John was wondering at what had brought the birds to this place when Charlie fell behind. John looked back to see the man unfastening his shoes. One large foot was already bare.

"Feels good underfoot," Charlie said. "Warm. Not like the streets of London." He took off his other shoe and set the pair beside a fencepost. Straightening up, he lifted his arms over his head in a prodigious stretch. He looked healthier than he had for weeks.

"The sunshine agrees with you," John commented. He considered the giant for a moment. "You could stay here for a time, if you like." That would solve so many problems—Charlie might live longer, but John would no longer have to worry about losing the body. The situation would be under his control.

Charlie's face brightened momentarily, but then he frowned and shook his head. "I cannot do that."

"I could take you into London, now and again," John persisted. "But you could stay out here the rest of the time. The city air's unhealthy. It does you no good."

Charlie shook his head stubbornly. "Until I can return to Ireland, I must stay in London. That is where the Irish are and that is where I must stay."

"As you will," John said. He considered, as he walked, whether the right time had come to ask the giant about his bones. He tried to introduce the notion of scientific investigation gently. "You must see my other animals." He led the way back to the paddocks surrounding the house. He stopped by the pigpen and leaned on the fence. "I've found pigs to be the best for experimentation. They are easily managed and breed well in captivity." The old sow had pushed close to the fence and was staring up at Charlie. The tall man leaned over to scratch the top of her head, and she sighed in contentment.

"What has happened to her piglets?" Charlie asked. All three of the young animals bore scars on their right hind leg and limped a little.

"They are part of an experiment," John explained. "I am investigating the way bones grow. The French botanist Henri Duhmamel du Monceau claims that they increase by accretion throughout their length. I maintain that they grow from the extremities." He explained his experimental procedure to Charlie. He had operated on all the piglets. On each one, he had laid bare the bone of the right rear leg, drilled two holes precisely two inches apart, inserted lead shot in the holes, and then stitched up the incision again. In the weeks following the operation, John was butchering the piglets one by one, at weekly intervals, and checking the bone. Though the leg bone had lengthened overall, the distance between the deposits of lead was the same as it had been on the day that he inserted it. This supported his hypothesis that bones grew through accretion at the ends, not in midspan.

Charlie stared at the piglets in the pen. "Why is it you want to know how bones grow?" he asked at last. "Isn't it enough that they do. By God's grace, they grow quite well."

"Can't always trust in God's grace," John said briskly.

"What else is there?"

"Knowledge," John said. "Sometimes, they do not grow, or they grow improperly. I want to know why." He gazed at the piglets. "There is so much to know," he murmured. "Do you know, Charlie, if I could look at your bones, I might be able to tell why they pain you so. It would not help you, but it might help someone else whose bones ache."

"My bones?" Charlie stared at him, his eyes suddenly wide. "You want to see my bones?"

"When you die, Charlie, as we all must do," John said gently. "If I could take your body—"

Charlie was backing away from him, his expression shocked. "My bones, John? What would you do with my bones?"

"Examine them, Charlie." John spread his hand, the gesture of a reasonable man making a reasonable proposal. "You'll have no more use for them, once you're dead."

Charlie was shaking his head. His big hands formed fists at his sides. "My bones must return to Ireland," he said. "That's where they belong. I promised my father—"

"Superstition, Charlie," John said gently. "You must not take it so seriously."

Charlie turned and fled. Startled by Charlie's reaction, John called after him, but the giant did not look back. John ran after him, but did not have a chance of overtaking him. Finally, he let the man go, knowing that he would eventually return to his rooms in London.

John was sorry that Charlie had reacted so precipitously.

He reviewed the conversation in his mind, wondering how he might have made his suggestion more delicately. In the end, he decided that nothing he could say would have overcome the giant's superstition, and John made peace with himself. He spent that night at Earl's Court, dissecting a series of worker bees, an exacting task that soothed his nerves.

The next day, on his morning stroll, John noticed a new variety of flower growing in the meadow. The plants grew low to the ground and bore tiny golden blossoms. They grew only in discreet patches. John realized, on close examination, that the flowers had sprouted in the giant's footprints. He attributed this curious effect to the compression of the soil beneath Charlie's feet and drew up plans for a series of experiments to test the sprouting of seeds under pressure.

Charlie heard John's voice calling him back, but he did not stop. It was a cold afternoon, and the walk back to London was a long one. A farmer gave him a ride for a few miles in an ox-drawn cart filled with straw, but he walked the rest. His legs ached by the time he reached the outskirts of the city proper. He let his head hang, unwilling to look up and see the smoky sky overhead. The road was cold and hard beneath his bare feet.

When rain began to fall, he made no effort to take shelter. The cold drops soaked his coat, plastered his hair to his head, ran down his cheeks like dirty tears, leaving tracks of soot behind.

Back at the rooms, he fell ill and lay on the straw-tick mattress that served as his bed, unable and unwilling to move. "It's the gin," Vance said. "I told you it'd be the death of you." Charlie did not reply. He lay on the pallet of blankets that served as his bed, staring into the flames of the fire.

A few days later, Kathleen found him there. When he did not come to visit her stall in Covent Garden, she came looking for him. On the door beside the cane shop, a notice said: "No show today. Come back tomorrow." By the look of it, the notice was several days old. When

Kathleen banged on the door, Mary, the landlady, answered and regarded her with a sour look.

"I have come to see Charlie," Kathleen said. "I'm a friend."

"Visit him quick," Mary said in a scornful tone. "He may not have much time left." She let Kathleen in and the hunchback found her way through the dimly lit, stale-smelling rooms to Charlie's bedside.

He lay on a straw-tick mattress by a fire that burned low. Light from the glowing coals gave his face a ruddy color that did not match his feverish eyes and mournful expression. He was shivering despite the blankets that covered him. "Ah, Kathleen," he murmured. "Sit with me for a time. I am lonely now, very lonely."

Sometimes, he shivered and huddled closer to the fire; sometimes, he threw off all his blankets, suddenly drenched in sweat. He complained that his head ached constantly.

He was sick and delirious for three days, and she stayed with him, bringing him bread and cheese to eat, tucking the blankets close around his shoulders, holding his hand so that he would know he was not alone. On the seventh day, he came to himself again. Kathleen had fallen asleep on the floor beside his mattress, and she woke to see him watching her.

"Kathleen," he said. His eyes were sad, but the fever had left them. "What are you doing here?"

"Taking care of you, Charlie my lad."

"There's not much use to that now," he muttered. He shook his head weakly. "I've been foolish. I thought that the magic would be strong enough. But that's dead and gone. The world is changing."

"Don't say that, Charlie." Now that he was finally giving up his mad notions, it pained her to see it.

"I'll die here in London."

"No, Charlie," she said, "you'll get better soon." He just shook his head, recognizing the lie.

"Have you seen Joe Vance?" he asked.

Kathleen went out looking for Vance. After the darkened room, the courtyard seemed brilliantly lit. She found Vance lounging in the gray light that passed for sunshine in London, practicing a game involving three shells and a pea. When she told him that Charlie wanted to see him, he reluctantly followed her into the room.

"You're looking bad," Vance said. "That doctor—John Hunter—came to see you again. Says he might be able to give you something for the fever, if he could see you. A swell gentleman, by the look of him."

Charlie shook his head. "I told you I will not see him."

"Been a week since any money came in," Vance said slowly. "And Mary will be looking for her rent, come Monday."

Charlie said nothing. He was watching the flames, ignoring Vance's words. When Vance stood up, as if preparing to go, he roused himself. "You got to help me, Joe," he said. "Can you tell me where I'd find an honest undertaker?"

Mr. Fields, undertaker and friend of Joe Vance, studied Charlie with an expert eye and decided that he wouldn't last long. His face was pale and wet with sweat; his eyes were bloodshot.

"You're interested in a coffin?" said Fields. "I'll have to build it special. That'll be extra."

"You must make the arrangements for me," Charlie muttered weakly. He reached out and grasped Fields's hand. "Take my body back to Ireland. To my mother's farm. You must see to it. I'll pay."

"I've heard of Chinamen sending their bones home," the undertaker said, "but never an Irishman."

"Please," Charlie said hoarsely, squeezing the man's hand. "You must see to it." He fumbled in his bedclothes and pulled out a small pouch that clinked in his hand. Fields eyed it, assessing its contents. "You must take me home safe."

"For a price, anything can be arranged," Fields said heartily. "You can rest easy, Mr. Bryne."

Kathleen nursed Charlie as best she could. But when her money ran out, she had to return to her stall in the afternoons and evenings to earn the money she needed to bring him food. She brought him bread and cheese and mutton stew, though he did not eat half of what she brought.

It rained that week, a dark sooty rain that turned the streets to mud. The costermongers went out late and came in early, with little profit to show for their efforts. The mud clung to the wheels of coaches and to the horses' hooves, and the hackney drivers cursed the weather. The men who carried sedan chairs got chilblains.

Early in the morning on the seventh day of rain, all the dogs of St. Giles Rookery congregated at the door to the cane maker's shop. The cane maker tried to drive them away with kicks and curses, but as often as he scattered them, they returned. He gave up at last and tried to ignore them, glancing out only occasionally to see the filthy mongrels sitting beneath his sign. Surprisingly, the dogs did not fight.

The cats came later, slinking over the rooftops. Despite the rain, they crouched above the cane maker's shop, glowering at the people in the street below. Strangely, the dogs did not bark at the cats and the cats did not yowl at the dogs. They waited quietly.

Early in the afternoon, a sparrow came to perch on the wooden sign that marked the cane maker's shop. For a time, it sat alone in the rain, its feathers fluffed against the cold. Then it was joined by another sparrow and a pair of finches. A little later, four mourning doves came to perch on the sign, not far from the cats. But the cats made no move to stalk them.

The cane maker looked up when a sound that was at once familiar and strange penetrated his consciousness, making its way past the rattle of coach wheels and the cursing of drivers. He paused, brush in hand. Still holding the cane that he had been varnishing, he went to the doorway, following the sound that called up memories of his boyhood in the country. Sitting on his sign, above the filthy street, a meadowlark was singing its heart out.

From the eaves, the mourning doves watched him with their bright black eyes. From the gutter, the dogs regarded him sadly. The cane maker looked up at the small, gold-flecked bird, then retreated into his shop.

* * *

Twilight settled over London. The light had a peculiarly gray tone, as if the city had sucked all color and life from the air. The proprietor of a pie shop was lighting an oil lamp to hang in the door of his establishment. Here and there, the yellow glow of burning lamps marked the shops and taverns that remained open.

Joe Vance emerged from the hallway beside the cane maker's shop, kicked his way through the crowd of waiting dogs, and made his way to the nearest tavern. Just inside the door he surveyed the smoky interior, then made his way to the corner table, where the undertaker waited with John Hunter.

"How fares the patient?" the undertaker asked jovially. He had been drinking gin, by the smell of it, and he was smiling, an expression that sat uncomfortably on his long face.

"Won't be long now," Vance said. "I took him a bottle of gin to ease the pain."

"And hurry him along," said Fields, chuckling. He grinned at John Hunter, but John glared back, not sharing the joke.

"I'd help him if I could," John muttered defensively.

"Certainly you would, Dr. Hunter," Vance said expansively. "We all would. Why, I care about the lad as if he were my own son. Isn't that so, Fields?"

John scowled and shook his head, believing none of it. "Let's get on to business," he said.

The undertaker nodded and spoke softly. "Now, we were discussing the price. Dr. Hunter had offered twenty pounds for the body."

"Twenty pounds?" Vance scowled, forgetting his love for the giant at the mention of money. "Out of the question."

"It does seem inadequate for the unusual merchandise we have to offer," the undertaker murmured. "It seems to me that ten times that amount would be fair."

John Hunter looked up from his beer. "You'll find few takers for such merchandise."

"Ah, you would be surprised," said the undertaker. "My conversations with the head surgeon at St. George's Hospital suggest that there may be a number of takers."

"Thirty pounds," John said.

The bargaining was protracted. Vance spoke of his great affection for the giant so eloquently that his eyes became moist with tears. He was the giant's friend, perhaps his only friend, and he would never consider the doctor's offer were it not for his own need for capital. Persuaded by his own eloquence, he felt a brief pang of regret, but dismissed it as John raised the price.

Fields stressed the rarity of the commodity they offered. "Unique on the face of the earth," he said. "An opportunity like this comes along once in a lifetime—if you're lucky."

John was the least garrulous of the lot, protesting that the two of them had unrealistic notions of their merchandise's value. But clearly Vance and Fields had the advantage. Finally, after much gin and talk, John settled at one hundred pounds and would not budge. They drank to seal the bargain.

The clock was striking eleven when Vance went to check on the giant. The street seemed unnaturally quiet. In the dim light of the tavern's lantern, Vance could see that the dogs were still waiting. He heard a rustle of feathers above his head. Suddenly, the lark sang, a sweet burst of glory, like a sudden ray of sunshine in a dark place. The largest of the mongrels tilted back his head and began to howl, and the rest joined in, wailing like banshees.

A man in a nightshirt flung open the window above Vance's head and shouted at the dogs, but the howling continued. The shouting was followed by a pail of water and then the contents of a chamberpot. Vance quickly ducked for the protection of the tavern doorway. Retreating inside, he said to Fields and John Hunter, "I suppose he's dead."

In the dark of night, with the help of Vance and Fields, John Hunter stripped the corpse of the dead giant, slipped a sack over the body, and loaded the sack into his coach. In his haste to be off, he overlooked the giant's staff, which was propped in the corner by the fire.

The pack of mongrels that hung about the door followed the coach for half a mile or so, but he lost them after that. At Earl's Court, the coachman, who had grown used to nocturnal errands, helped him load the body into a barrow and transport it to the basement workshop.

Alone with the cadaver, John hesitated. "So Charlie," he muttered. "You came to me after all, whether you would or not. I feel half-sorry for you, but I suppose you died happy enough." He shook his head, thinking of the giant's superstition and ignorance. Then he wielded his sharp knife and prepared Charlie's bones for the boiling pot.

It was nearly dawn when he became aware that the caged lark in the next room was singing its heart out. He cocked his head to listen, wondering what had prompted the bird to sing. In the months that he had kept it in confinement beneath the earth, the lark had never to his knowledge sung a note.

Putting the last bone in the pot, John went to investigate, but the bird fell silent at his approach and never sang again.

Charlie was gone when Kathleen returned from Covent Garden that night. His room was dark and the fire had burned out. His clothing was scattered about the straw-tick mattress, and she guessed at what had happened.

When she found his staff by the fireside, its blossoms wilted and dry, she knew he was dead. He never would have left without it. She took the staff with her when she left. It had a nice feel in her hand and it reminded her of Charlie.

It was strange, but her hump never ached when she held the staff in her hand. Free of the pain, she drank less gin. After a time, it seemed to her that the hump was beginning to shrink. And then she was sure of it: the twist in her back grew straighter every day.

Her livelihood shrank with her hump—no one would pay for a fortune from a straight-backed Irishwoman. She lost business to the fortune-teller on the other side of the garden, a dark-skinned man who wore multicolored scarves and stared into a crystal to see the future. Finally, with the last of her earnings, Kathleen returned to Ireland. There was no reason to stay in London, and the staff in her hand gave her the urge to wander. She went to Ireland and wandered the winding roads, telling stories in return for a bit of food and a place to sleep. Sometimes, she told stories of London. Sometimes, she talked about a giant named Charlie, and in her tales he grew to nearly the size of Bran the Blessed. It was not a bad life.

A month of wandering and she found herself in County Derry. Enquiring here and there, she found her way to the wild pastureland known as the Giant's Boneyard. There she leaned the staff against the largest boulder and stood for a time, looking out over the valley and thinking of Charlie. At last, she decided to walk back to the village and look for a friendly home where she might sleep—but when she went to pick up the staff she found that it had taken root. White blossoms sprouted from the dry wood, and new green shoots reached for the gray sky. She left it there, where it belonged. She had had it long enough.

Eventually, Kathleen married a farmer. As a farmer's wife, she took care of the land. It was a hard life, but one for which she was well suited, with her strong back and willing ways.

John Hunter examined Charlie Bryne's skeleton carefully, but the doctor died without learning why Charlie had grown so large. More than one hundred years after Hunter's death, a surgeon named Harvey Williams Cushing examined Charlie's skull and noticed a deformity in the bone that had covered the pituitary gland. This observation ultimately led to Cushing's discovery that the pituitary plays a role in controlling human growth, one more small piece in the great puzzle that John Hunter was trying to solve.

Cushing did not explain why birds often congregated at the window of the room in which the giant's bones hung. The sill was thick with their droppings. Sometimes, they would rattle on the glass with their beaks and flap their wings impatiently, as if demanding to be let in.

Perhaps Cushing did not notice them. Like Hunter, he was preoccupied with understanding what made the human body tick. He had no time for the foolishness of birds, the poetry of cloud formations, the illegible scrawls left by snails crawling across the slate paving stones in the garden.

* * *

That's the truth, as near as I can tell it. Oh, historians may quibble with some events I have described. I can find no historical documentation detailing the flowers that grew on Charlie's staff or mentioning the staff at all, for that matter. And perhaps the birds did not really gather at the window to pay court to Charlie's bones. I can find no records that say they did—but then, I can find no denial of it either. Surely these are minor points. At its heart, the tale is true.

Charlie Bryne is dead and gone and his bones still hang in London's Royal College of Surgeons. In the Giant's Boneyard, songbirds nest in the hawthorn thicket that has grown up near the boulder that old people call the Giant's Skull. In this lonely spot, there lingers a sense of sadness and loss. Sometimes, a foolish traveler, heading home late at night, will feel a sudden chill as he passes the field. When the chill touches him, he'll clutch his coat around him, glance back over his shoulder like a man pursued by ghosts, and hurry home to the safety of electric lighting, content to live in a world where ghosts do not walk and bones rest easy.

Afterword—Why I Write

When I was a little girl, my mother read *The Lion, The Witch, and The Wardrobe*, by C. S. Lewis, aloud to me and my brothers. The story fascinated me: these kids walked through a perfectly ordinary wardrobe into a new world. After hearing that story I was convinced, beyond any doubt, that there were other worlds out there, just waiting for me to find them.

When I was old enough to read for myself, I read other stories about secret places and powerful magic: the Oz books; *Five Children and It*, by E. Nesbit; *The Borrowers*, by Mary Norton; and *The Time Garden, Half Magic*, and numerous other magical books by Edward Eager. When I was a little older, I branched out into science fiction and adventure fiction, reading all the Tarzan and Doc Savage books from my older brother's collection. These seemed to me to be extensions of the original impulse: They all dealt with worlds that were more dangerous, more beautiful, and more intriguing than the one in which I lived.

When I wasn't reading about secret places, I would look for secret places to call my own. I couldn't find a magic wardrobe, so I had to make do. I cleared a patch of ground in a secluded corner of the backyard (back behind the big pussy willow bush where no one ever went) and I planted crocuses and Johnny-jump-ups to make a secret garden. I couldn't go past a hole in a hedge or a cave or a culvert or a dark passageway without peering into the darkness and wondering if this were the one that led to a new world. In best junior scientist fashion, I learned to identify edible wild foods: young plantain leaves

313

and such. I was, I think, planning to live off the land when something happened. I didn't know what the event would be or when it would come along, but I knew that something momentous was going to happen. I might need to be able to recognize edible plants when I found the way through and ended up in Oz or Perelandra or Narnia or wherever it was I would finally end up.

In the course of growing up, I never really quit looking for the secret door, the hidden passage, the opening to another dimension or another time. But at some point I suppose I realized that the secret way out would not just appear to me. I had to create my own secret ways. And so I started to spin daydreams. Not daydreams like getting a pony or climbing to the top of the mulberry tree in the backyard. Daydreams that were even more improbable— like saving a princess from a dragon or sailing off with pirates to do piratical things that involved a great deal of swashbuckling swordplay.

Of course, I continued to read like a maniac, devouring the imaginary worlds of science fiction and fantasy writers and using them to fuel my own adventures. In my version of the great twister, Dorothy had a companion named Pat Murphy on her trip to Oz. And Pat Murphy—a scrawny fourth grader with harlequin glasses and a mighty left hook—was certainly along when Tarzan visited the City of Gold.

Unlike those amazing writers who started putting words on paper when they were barely old enough to clutch the pen, I kept these daydreams to myself. After all, part of the value of secret places is their privacy. If anyone could get on my pirate ship and sail off to adventure, then everyone would. And the secret would be out. So I kept my heroic fantasies to myself.

Along the way, the characters in my internal stories began to change. Sometimes I didn't save the day—I just watched as someone else got to be the hero. As the stories evolved, the plots changed too, continuing to entirely new conclusions, new adventures, new worlds. When an adventure took a wrong turn, I would go back and fix it, rethink my actions or the actions of my characters in a way that was just not possible in life.

It wasn't until I was in college that it occurred to me that I might actually write some stories down. Lois Natanson, a wonderful literature teacher, read one of my papers and told me I was an excellent writer. That was the first time that anyone had ever told me I could write and write well. And so I began to try to write stories.

Strangely enough, I didn't initially write about the secret people and places I knew. They were secret, remember? Instead, I tried to write what I now think of as other people's stories, stories that didn't give too much of my own stuff away. I tried to write like authors I admired—like Ursula Le Guin, like Kate Wilhelm, like Margaret Atwood. And then one day I wrote a story about a place that was my own, and it was like coming home, stepping into Narnia, touching down in Oz. And there was no turning back.

Looking back on the stories in this book, written over the last decade or so, I see traces of my childhood reading and daydreaming. Many of my stories deal with outsiders, people who are trapped in a world where they do not belong. Sam, the Neanderthal who has been yanked from his own time; the nameless alien woman who lingers in Mexico, unable to find her way home; Rachel, the chimp with the mind of a teenage girl—these are characters who have, in a sense, found that secret door I was always looking for. They've entered a new world filled with exotic things and strange people; it just happens to be the world in which we live every day.

Many of my stories take place in foreign countries. I travel as often as I can manage, and I come home with stories about the Bay Islands off the coast of Honduras, about Mexico's Yucatan penninsula, about Nepal, places that are strange and alien, as exotic as Oz, as mysterious as Perelandra.

When I was a kid, I knew that fantastic things were waiting just around the corner, lingering in the shadows, lurking behind the rhododendron bush. Some were nice and some were horrible—like the witches under the bed or the monsters that hid in storm drains. I imagined their lives and they became real. Now that I'm a grown-up, I am doing what I wanted to do then: I am opening the secret doorway and letting them into our world; I am walking through the secret passage and visiting theirs.

I still can't walk past a cave without peering inside, and on some level I still believe in the witches under the bed and the value of the magic penny that I hope someday to find in a crack in the sidewalk.

That's one of the reasons I write.

About the Author

Pat Murphy lives in San Francisco, where she edits the *Exploratorium Quarterly*, an idiosyncratic magazine of science, art, and human perception.

In 1987 she won Nebula Awards for both her novel *The Falling Woman* and her novelette "Rachel in Love." Her short fiction has appeared in many magazines and anthologies.

Her cat is named Potato and her favorite color is ultraviolet.

BANTAM SPECTRA SPECIAL EDITIONS

A program dedicated to masterful works of fantastic fiction by many of today's most visionary writers.

■

FULL SPECTRUM 2 edited by Lou Aronica, Shawna McCarthy, Amy Stout, and Patrick LoBrutto

NO ENEMY BUT TIME by Michael Bishop

UNICORN MOUNTAIN by Michael Bishop

STRANGE TOYS by Patricia Geary

RUMORS OF SPRING by Richard Grant

STRANGE INVASION by Michael Kandel

OUT ON BLUE SIX by Ian McDonald

THE NEXUS by Mike McQuay

THE CITY, NOT LONG AFTER by Pat Murphy

POINTS OF DEPARTURE by Pat Murphy

PHASES OF GRAVITY by Dan Simmons

GYPSIES by Robert Charles Wilson

A HIDDEN PLACE by Robert Charles Wilson

MEMORY WIRE by Robert Charles Wilson

■

On sale now wherever Bantam Spectra books are sold

DON'T MISS THEM!

FROM THE AUTHOR OF
The Gate to Women's Country

<u>GRASS</u>
by
Sheri S. Tepper

"**Grass** is so good you may want to lend it to friends who don't like science fiction. Tepper is a wide and subtle artist. She manages things in **Grass** with consummate skill that other writers are well advised not to attempt."

—*Washington Post Book World*

"A splendid achievement . . . fascinating . . . a rigorously constructed parable about necessary (and unnecessary) trade-offs between independence and interdependence. Richly imagined action scenes alternate with lively dialogue that wrestles with fundamental questions of good and evil. Ms. Tepper is as successful in bringing to life intelligent aliens as she is in creating believable human characters."

—*New York Times Book Review*

"Tepper's talent for creating evocative alien landscapes reinforces the depth of her insights into the complexities of human society and the human heart."

—*Library Journal*

**Now on sale in paperback
wherever Bantam Spectra Books are sold**

**The extraordinary novelization
of the landmark TBS series.**

VOICE OF THE PLANET
Michael Tobias

"This book is a cry in the fading light of Earth.
Michael Tobias has written a book that must be read
by every person interested in continuing to eat and to
breathe. Believe me, you will be excited to know that
there is a chance to save ourselves from the apoca-
lypse and astonishingly, Michael Tobias weaves his
story through the stark facts entertainingly and irre-
sistably. This book is a must read."

—William Shatner

♦

An ecology professor travels to Nepal to track down the
source of persistent and inexplicable messages urging him
to write a book about the fate of the Earth. What he discovers
is an ancient monastery is nothing less than the incarnate
spirit of the Earth herself—*Gaia*. Her message is urgent and
compelling. Humanity and all our world are at risk—through
pollution, overpopulation, extinction of species and other
critical concerns.

Voice of the Planet—now a major TBS miniseries starring
William Shatner and Faye Dunaway as the voice of Gaia,
scheduled to air in the Summer of 1990—takes the reader
on a spiralling odyssey to the farthest reaches of our world,
past, present and future, to explore what we've done—and
what we can do—to the only world humanity calls home.

**A Bantam Spectra Book
Coming in July, 1990**